Dear Jesse

Our God can
truly do
exceedingly —
abundantly —
above —

Love and God bless,

Joan Deneve
Eph. 3:20

JOAN DENEVE

SAVING ERIC

Saving Eric

© 2015 Joan Deneve

ISBN-13: 978-1-938092-76-3
ISBN-10: 1938092767

All Scriptures are taken from the King James Version.

Published by Write Integrity Press, 2631 Holly Springs Pkwy, Box 35, Holly Springs, GA 30142.

 www.WriteIntegrity.com

Printed in the United States of America.

Dedication

For Mama
Whose love gave me roots
And Rene'
Whose love gives me wings

*"For I, the Lord thy God, will hold thy right hand,
saying unto thee,
'Fear not, I will help thee.'"
Isaiah 41:13*

With Special Thanks

The list of people who helped make this book a reality is a long one. Each person brought his own unique and indispensable contribution for which I will be forever grateful. My feeble attempt to express my gratitude here pales in comparison to the huge part they played. Like the writer of Hebrews 11, I want to name each one and expound on each contribution. Bear with me. I will attempt the impossible to do them justice and still keep it short.

I must begin with Nancy Kimball. I'm convinced that God brought her into my life, for such a time as this. *Saving Eric* would not have been finished and certainly not published had she not taken me under her wing. This brilliant writer painstakingly taught me the rudiments of deep point of view and plot structure, and her influence and thumbprint can be seen on each page. Like me, Nancy is a hero-junkie, and she honored me and my main character by naming her beautiful stud of a dog, Eric T. I am forever grateful for her generosity and friendship that have changed my life in so many ways.

My family: Rene', my rock and the reason I'm still breathing. My children: Jeremiah, the best son in the world and the doctor who was never too busy to help his mother sort out the medical technicalities of the mission hospital. Jessie, my writer daughter and quite possibly the best human I know. She and her husband Michael were my "go-to" people for encouragement and computer expertise. My seven heartbeats: Auston, Ethan, Hannah, Lacey, Haley, Cloe, and Christian. My dear mother who has always believed in whatever I tried to do. Harvie and my "Pest," my best cheerleaders, who let me practically live at their house for months during the tedious process of hammering out my manuscript. My sisters Phalia and Sheila who spent hours reading every version and were always quick to offer praise, encouragement and genuine help. And my nephew Richard (Red) for his help in understanding what an amputee goes through. What a hero! Shonna Smith (my Becky) my phenomenal niece who has the computer skills of a genius and the patience of a saint. My nephew Shane

Smith who does whatever he can to make my life better, whether it means spending hours helping me develop my author web page or indulging my Mickey addiction by taking me to Disneyworld. All my family, my nieces and nephews, for your unfailing love and encouragement. It means so much.

My friends: Carol Parks, my spiritual mentor who loved me enough to be a beta reader. Her love, encouragement, insight, and prayers have kept me going. Michele Bradley, my Alabama best friend who is one of the most Christ-like people I know. She goes out of her way to bless, encourage and spoil me. Dianne Gaines, my soul sister who encouraged me to "write the vision" down. The "gym gang" my dear, dear teacher friends and co-workers whom I love so much. And my students, past and present, who have taught this teacher so much about genuine love and grace. How blessed I have been! All my dear sisters at church who love, laugh, and pray with me.

Beth Wasson, my forever friend, who has seen me go through many stages in my life and has loved me through them all. And her son, Eric.

Tyler Templeton, one of my heroes, who is the inspiration for the Templeton name.

My writer friends who trudged this journey with me: Carolyn Hill, the first person who took me under her wing. This sweet angel took the time to offer real help and praise to a very scared, insecure fledgling writer. My other writer friends whom I've met along the way. Diane Dean White, Gretchen, Kathleen, Lisa, Joy, Linden, Virginia Tenery, and my dear Nikki (AKA April Jatindranath) These scribe sisters became friends, mentors, and cheerleaders. I'm so blessed to know all of them. And my guy writer friends too: Scott, and Dickie, and Matthew. A host of others too numerous to name. Fay Lamb, who is never too busy to answer questions or offer help. And Tracy Ruckman, a talented woman of faith who has a great vision for what God can do through the printed word. My writer friends from Write Integrity Press and Pix-N-Pens, whom though I've never met, feel like family.

Jesus Christ, my hero, my champion, my redeemer, my Lord and my Savior. Without Him, I can do nothing.

Chapter One

The morning sun piercing through cloud cover did little to lighten Eric Templeton's mood. Only justice would. In his nine years as an agent, he had never failed to complete a mission—until now. Almost eight months to the day after he'd left, Eric approached CIA Headquarters with nothing but a fresh scar to show for his efforts. Unacceptable, especially for a Templeton. Today, he would face the traitor who'd orchestrated Stuart Harris's death. And almost caused Eric the same fate.

Eric entered the atrium and checked the time on his phone while switching it to vibrate. The third degree from his father would have to wait. He lengthened his stride to bypass General Robert Templeton's office, but a chance glimpse of the tiny woman hunched over her desk stopped him. Her hair was whiter, and her glasses bigger, but everything else remained the same. The engraved nameplate precisely positioned in front of her computer hadn't moved in twenty years and still read Mildred Ware. A spinster, married to her job. By all accounts a good marriage—a perfectionist, working for a man who demanded perfection.

He entered the outer office without making a sound. "How's my favorite girl?"

"Eric!" The spry little woman sprang from her chair and raced around her desk. Too late to shield his injured shoulder from her embrace, Eric hid the wince with a chuckle. She was shorter than he remembered. He leaned closer and kissed the top of her head, being careful not to muss the hairstyle she'd worn since the day he'd met her.

"Your father said you'd be coming in this morning. I'll let him know you're here."

"Not yet."

She paused, and he explained. "Tell Dad I'll stop by after the meeting with the director."

That seemed to satisfy her, but then she reached to give his cheek a gentle pat. "We thought we'd lost you. It's good to have you home."

His mouth went dry. Kindness. The one thing that could make him crumble. He captured one of her hands and squeezed. "See you later."

She returned to her desk as if she needed to regain her composure, and he turned back to the cold, gray hallway. The conference room, one of the few with no windows, loomed ahead on the right. Being the first to arrive might give him an edge.

Assistant Director Tom Reznik apparently had the same idea. Already seated at the oval table, he glanced up and muttered, "Eric."

Every hair on the back of Eric's neck stood at attention. He took the hot seat at the debriefing table and leveled his gaze at the man he held responsible for the bullet wound to his shoulder. "Sir."

Reznik tapped the page within the folder in his hand. "Says here some self-appointed vigilante killed two cartel operatives four miles from where you were stationed. I don't suppose you know anything about that."

Eric didn't blink or flinch, the same as when he opened fire on the pair of human traffickers. He'd led the terrified girls back to their home after cutting the ropes at their wrists. Not his mandate but not something he regretted. He shrugged instead. "I read the same report you did."

Reznik narrowed his gaze. "Right." He shut the folder. "We'll get to the bottom of it, as well as why your op failed."

They wanted answers.

So did he.

Eric raised his chin a notch. "I don't suppose you'd know anything about the ambush that killed my informant and blew my cover. Anything not mentioned in the report."

The second hand on the clock behind them ticked like the dry-fire of a weapon. The widened pupils, flared nostrils, and tight lips—everything Reznik was too weak to hide—told Eric all he needed to know. The opening door broke the standoff.

Director Harold McDowall assumed his place at the head of the table and folded his hands over his rotund stomach. He angled his chair toward Eric and gave one of his rare smiles. "Glad you made it in one piece. Already lost one of our best men down there. When you went dark, we thought we'd lost you too." The director glanced at Reznik as if seeking confirmation. "Good thing we were wrong, eh, Tom?"

The smile Reznik returned didn't reach his eyes.

Pleasantries over, McDowall swiveled back and reached for the file lying closed in front of the assistant director. "Tell us what you've got."

"Not much," Eric said. "Stuart Harris was getting close when his cover was blown. After they killed him, Ramirez tightened security."

McDowall opened the folder. The top photo of Stuart's body reached out and kicked Eric square in the gut. But Templetons never backed down or away, so he leaned forward for a closer look.

The director flipped the photo and gave Eric the famous deadpan stare. "You were down there a long time."

A statement, not a question.

"Yes, sir. Stuart discovered there are personnel in key countries accepting bribes. High-level connections with enough power to trump customs and security."

The director's steepled fingers tapped his mouth. "So if we can't stop the cartel, we aim for the people on the take."

"Exactly. I found an informant who knew Stuart. We struck a deal. Names of contacts in exchange for asylum in the States."

"Go on."

Eric eyed Reznik before he answered. "The meeting was sabotaged. Guerrillas opened up."

"The informant?"

"Killed before I could reach him."

"You went off radar for two months. What were you doing?" Tom Reznik spoke for the first time since the meeting began.

Need-to-know. Getting Diego's family out of the country wasn't information either of them needed. "I was shot during the ambush. A bartender dug the bullet out. I was laid up for a while. Did some snooping. Tried to track down answers about Stuart's death. Figured I owed him that."

"Find anything?"

Nothing he wanted Reznik to know right now. Eric kept his expression neutral and shook his head. "Dead ends."

Questions hovered in the air. Eric waited.

With a long exhale, McDowall closed the folder and pushed back from the table. He stood, signaling the end of the meeting. "I fly to Belgium this afternoon. I'll look over the report, and we'll talk more when I get back."

Eric nodded and once again made eye contact with Reznik before following the director out of the room. Not the kind of guy he wanted to turn his back on.

〰〰〰〰

Miss Mildred kept her fingers poised on the keyboard when he entered his father's office suite again. "That was fast." She smiled and nodded toward the closed door. "Go on in. The general's expecting you."

He was expecting him all right. The debriefing was a cakewalk compared with what lay ahead. Templetons don't fail.

His dad rose and met Eric halfway with a handshake and a surprisingly genuine smile. "Hello, Son."

"Good to see you, Dad." He meant it, but it'd be even better after they got the lecture behind them.

"Sit down." His dad gestured to the brown leather chair. "Would you like some coffee?"

"Sure." Eric fought the shock at seeing how much his dad had aged. Could eight months have made that big of a difference? His dad pressed the intercom button. Eric used the time to check out the room. Nothing had changed in this Spartan, well-organized space that smelled of wood, leather, and old books.

"So, you're finally home."

"Yes." His dad would have to work for it.

"Took you longer this time. We expected you back months ago."

"It was a tough go for a while."

"I heard." The smile, genuine or not, disappeared.

Eric shifted in his seat and glanced at the standard regulation clock. Its ticking hammered into the silence. His dad stood and looked out the window, his hands clasped behind his back.

"Two months off grid." His father's profile silhouetted against the window emphasized the uncharacteristic stoop of his shoulders. Eric dismissed the crazy urge to walk around the desk and hug the man who had always been like a rock to him.

"Son?"

Eric straightened as if he'd been caught sleeping in class. "Sir?"

"I asked what you were doing all that time."

Miss Mildred bustled into the room. Perfect timing. She handed him a cup with creamy brown liquid. Templetons drank their coffee black, and he'd been prepared to in front of his father. She gave him a knowing smirk before she left the room, and he took a quick sip to hide his own.

His father, now back in his seat, had the "I'm waiting" look.

"Guerillas ambushed the meeting. Took out my source." He should stop there. "I took a bullet to the shoulder."

Eric recognized the scowl. Had seen it many times. Disappointment.

"Sounds to me like you're losing your touch."

Losing his touch? The vein protruding on his dad's forehead warned Eric to let it go. But he couldn't—not this time. He placed the cup on the table beside him with a thump and met his father's glare head on. "I was set up."

"Set up? No, son. You've gotten cocky." He leaned forward, his face red. "And you're going to get yourself killed."

"Like Stuart?"

His dad stiffened. "What do you mean?"

Eric ignored the voice screaming for him to shut up. "Stuart was on to something that got him killed."

His dad jeered with the supreme look Eric hated. "So that's why you volunteered for this assignment. Now you listen to me. Stuart Harris was a paranoid renegade." He pointed his finger, each jab emphasizing his words. "You do the job you're sent to do and quit snooping into things that don't concern you. Keep your nose clean and your mouth shut. You hear me?"

Loud and clear. Eric regretted his words the instant he'd spoken. Why put his father's career and maybe even his life in jeopardy over something he couldn't prove? Yet. "Yes, sir."

His father stood. "Good."

That was it? Hardly a warmup to the "You're a Templeton" speech, but no need to push his luck.

Eric stood too.

His dad ushered him to the door, and with a wave to Miss Mildred, Eric left the office to face the third and most difficult challenge of the day.

He took the stairs to the fourth floor and transitioned to the Old Headquarters Building. His personal mandate drove him through a maze of hallways and back down some stairs to the main lobby.

A pedestal with a glass-encased *Book of Honor* stood like a sentinel in front of a stark white wall spangled with stars. Black stars, lined up like the crosses at Arlington. The caption above them read, "In honor of those members of the Central Intelligence Agency who gave their lives in service of their country."

He tried to swallow the lump in his throat as he moved around the pedestal and touched the last star. Stuart's star, newer and blacker than the rest. Anger and guilt welled up, smothering his grief. "Reznik's going down, Stu. I swear, I'll stop him," he whispered, his voice a quiet eulogy. "No more good men—"

Muffled sounds from the corridor interrupted his oath. He backed away from the wall, turned and left the building.

SAVING ERIC

CHAPTER TWO

Eric loosened his tie as he bolted down the steps. Meetings behind him, he put the top down on his black GT convertible and drove off. The brisk Virginia air washed over him, nothing like the hot mugginess of Honduras. Good day for a run.

Food first. He zipped into the grocery store parking lot and a walking skeleton with yellow fur rounded the corner of the dumpster. Eric's stomach clenched. Strays got him every time.

Simon DoRight, Eric's moral compass and voice of reason, said ignore it. Simon was right, as usual. Eric would be on the road soon, maybe for months. The kitten would be fatter but no better off than now. Eric offered a lame "Sorry" and shut the car door.

The smell of fresh-baked bread and fried chicken hit him the moment the automatic doors sprang open. It'd been a long time. His mouth watered as he threw more than he intended into the cart. He maneuvered to the shortest line and found himself sandwiched between an elderly woman with a handful of coupons and a young mother with twins. He backed away and nodded to the frazzled woman. "You go ahead. I forgot something."

More like changed his mind. Aisle seven. *Shut up, Simon.*

Eric left the store and put the bags, including the one with the litter and cat food, in the car before he turned toward the Dumpster. He crouched and held out his hand to the pathetic creature with eyes dominating its scrawny face. Starved for more than food, the kitten ran to him and pressed its nose against his fingers. "Today's your lucky day, little—" He turned it around, held up the pencil-thin tail, and took his best guess. "—girl?"

Back at the apartment, he ripped off a jagged piece of bread with his teeth before popping open the can of cat food. As he raked meaty flakes into the bowl, the kitten latched onto his leg and tried to climb up his khaki pants. He grinned and pried each claw free. "So you've got a nose as good as mine, do you?"

She wrangled from his grasp and lunged for his chest. Her claws penetrated his shirt barely missing the fresh scar on his shoulder. "Okay, okay." With the bowl in one hand and the kitten in the other, he set them both on the floor. She claimed the food with possessive growls, and her belly swelled before his eyes.

That should keep her occupied while he put up the groceries. He gulped some orange juice from the carton not caring that some trickled down his chin. One more bite of bread would have to hold him. He changed into running shorts, grabbed his iPod, prepared, and then introduced the kitten to the litter box before heading out the door.

The storm from the night before had left few spring blossoms on the trees. Most lay clustered on the sidewalks mingled with ribbons of wet pollen. Avoiding puddles, he picked up the pace.

You're losing your touch. He'd never admit it, but those words hit a nerve better than any bullet.

The increased blood flow made his shoulder wound throb. He rubbed it as he waited for traffic at an intersection. The light changed, and he sprinted across, waving to the car that yielded to him.

Reznik. The man sickened him. How long had he been on the take? How many missions had he sabotaged to keep the cartel money coming in? Worst of all, how many people died? Like Diego. And Stuart.

Reznik would try to eliminate him next. Unless he eliminated Reznik first. Tempting, but not smart. Not something he could stomach either.

Adrenaline kicked. He opted for the streets with hills, and then sprinted the final stretch to the apartment. Once inside, he headed to the fridge for a bottle of water. The phone rang before he could twist off the cap. Langley. Tom Reznik's office.

"Templeton here."

"Eric, Tom Reznik. We have a situation in Zambia. One of the rookies blew his cover and needs special ops to get him out. I know you've just returned, but McDowall and I agree you're the kid's best chance of getting out alive."

Truth or trap? Eric hesitated, and his fingers tightened around the bottle. There could be only one answer. "Yes, sir."

"Great. I'll send the instructions by courier. You mind arranging the flight?"

"I'll take care of it."

Eric opened the bottle and drained half. Then he secured the flight. Tonight at 2300. Six hours. He'd have to move fast. He spread his cache of weapons on the table and with methodical precision, inspected his tools, each bearing its own battle scars. He caressed the M4, savoring the cold metal in his hands. His knife, a favorite asset for speed and silence, was as sharp as his instincts. Into his tactical bag they went, along with the short-barrel automatic rifle and extra clips.

After the courier's arrival, Eric showered, dressed in black, and threw enough clothes into his duffle bag for a few days. The little furry head peeking from inside the bag gave him a wild idea. He chuckled and stuffed her into a makeshift carrier. Then he snatched up the food and litter and loaded the Mustang.

Eric whipped into his father's driveway, scrawled a hasty note, and then deposited the carrier with the supplies at the door. With a quick apology to the newly christened Lucky, he rang the doorbell and raced back to his car. He backed out but paused long enough to get a glimpse of his father's face. Oh yeah. Priceless. With a wave good-bye, he peeled off down the road to the airfield.

The loadmaster met Eric at the top of the ramp and took his bags. "Good evening, Mr. Templeton."

"Hi, Gabe. Looks like an all-nighter."

"Yes, sir."

Eric settled in his seat and buckled as Gabe stored his gear in the cargo bay. He retrieved the folder from his briefcase and read over the instructions again. The walled compound surrounded an open courtyard. Intel pinpointed the agent in a corner room on the second floor close to the stairs. Eric studied the layout for over an hour and scoped out his plan. No airfield for miles and no quick get-away, but one little detail swayed the odds in his favor.

Toby Williams, proud owner of a South African air transport service, and Eric's go-to secret weapon for under-the-radar special ops. Like a flying Houdini, he could maneuver his chopper in and out of a tight spot before anybody heard him coming.

"Gabe, tell the pilot to divert to the airfield in Harare, Zimbabwe."

"Copy."

The loud drone of the airplane lulled Eric into a fitful sleep until a pocket of turbulence jerked him awake. Too keyed up to relax again, he dug in his bag for some Big Red and his iPod. Music blasted through his ear buds as he stared out the window. Black nothingness surrounded him, and a sense of dread he couldn't shake constricted his chest. It would be a long night.

During the pit stop for fuel, Eric left the plane to enlist the help of his back-up man. With a wave to the flight crew, he tipped his hand as if holding a cup and mouthed "Coffee."

Eric waited to clear the corner of the building to reach for his phone. Then with backup secured, he entered the hangar from the rear and went straight for the coffee. He placed the stirrer in the middle of the cup half-expecting it to remain upright in the sludge he'd poured. Double cream barely tinted the liquid to a shade more like the motor oil in his Mustang. Shop coffee. Possibly the worst he'd ever had.

"You actually drink that stuff, sir?"

Eric swirled the liquid and then slung what was left onto the pavement.

"Not this time." He crushed the cup and preceded Gabe up the steps.

⌇⌇⌇⌇⌇

Eric left the airstrip and hiked due west. Shafts of gold streaked above the horizon, lighting purple clouds from behind. A breathtaking sight, but he kept his focus on uneven terrain hoping to cover the four kilometers to the rendezvous point before total darkness set in. The bag weighed heavy on his good arm, but his sensitive shoulder balked every time he tried to switch the gear.

He reached the open field cocooned by cragged rock formations. Thick underbrush lined the other side. Eric propped against a tree. He bent to pick up a stick and stood to mull over the time he'd been the rookie who'd blown his cover. Stu came for him, bailed him out, and returned him to the hot spot. "Get back on that horse and finish the job." That one kick in the pants kept his fledging career from tanking before it ever got off the ground. From then on, as far as he was concerned, everything out of Stu's mouth had been pure gold.

Chopper blades sliced through his reverie. Eric darted out of the undergrowth and threw his gear in the back.

"Like old times." Toby shouted above the noise of the engine. "Climb in." He held out his hand palm up, and Eric slapped his own on top.

"Hey, man. Thanks for showing up."

"No problem. Where to?"

Eric swiped his hand across his neck like a knife. "We need to talk."

Toby cut the engine and shook his head as Eric filled him in on the assault in Honduras and the breach in the agency.

"Stuart was on to him. Got him killed."

Toby whistled. "You need to take this guy out."

"I need proof. That's the problem. Resources are in his favor." Eric snapped the twig he held in his hand and threw it out the open door. "This may be a trap, and you might get hurt."

"No, you could get hurt." Toby's wide eyes illumined his dark face. "You need me, Bro."

"I was hoping you'd say that." He shifted in his seat. "But I'm serious. Reznik's playing hard ball."

"So, why go through with it if you think it's a setup?"

Eric flicked the mosquito on his arm. "Two reasons. If it's legit, there's a guy out there who needs our help. But if it's a trap, I plan to turn the tables on him and prove he sent me on a bogus mission." His father's words reached across the ocean. *You've gotten cocky.* "I need to be smarter than he is."

Toby rubbed his jaw and looked into the open field beyond the cockpit. "Let's do it."

A fist-bump sealed the deal, and Eric spread out the map. "We fly into Zambia. The agent is barricaded in a walled compound twenty kilometers outside Lusaka. They're watching him, but according to my information, he's not being guarded. He knows I'm coming. With speed and surprise, we should be able to get in and out with no problem."

Toby pursed his lips and leaned over the map. "I can fly outside the city. We have a hangar there. Good place to hide out if there's trouble."

"Drop me off a couple of kilometers away." Eric unraveled a wire and earplugs and handed them to Toby. "I'll wear this mike. If things go south, we'll have to get out fast."

Few words passed between them during the flight. As they neared the drop-off point, Eric leapt from the chopper before it touched down, and disappeared into the darkness. He reached the compound and waited in the underbrush, his night vision goggles focused into the darkness. Nothing stirred. "Okay, Tobe. Going in."

Hugging his M4 to his chest, Eric slipped through the arched opening to the courtyard. He crouched and ran to the stone stairway on the far wall of the compound. Midway up, he paused to scope out the landing to the agent's room. Flattened against the wall, he tightened his hold on his weapon. Sweat dripped down his face, his mind clicking through his options.

His gut still screamed trap.

Moving nothing but his eyes, Eric searched for an alternate route. Just in case.

Silencer in place, he shifted his weight, getting ready to spring in case a guard appeared. He reached the second level keeping his head low. With his back to the door, Eric moved to the side and reached back to twist the doorknob with all the finesse of a safecracker. Unlocked. Using the butt of his M4, he nudged the door open. It triggered a familiar click and sent his instincts into overdrive. He cursed, his one option a flying leap over the rail to the open court below. The blast pulverized the door and rained debris over him as he thudded to the ground. He staggered up, and a bullet hit him in the right shoulder. His one good shoulder.

Anger and adrenaline took over. His new mandate—survive the trap. Using his left hand, he fired his automatic weapon blindly into the open and then spun away, dodging return gunfire. Something bit into his right calf and sent him sprawling. His hand automatically went to his gear as he rolled with the fall. He ripped out the pin, counted to three and aimed toward the muzzle flashes into the darkness. Doubled over in agony, he clutched his leg. Still there but not working. He half-crawled, half-hopped to the arched opening. Toby's chopper swooped down and fired above Eric. Home free. One flying leap and they could high tail it out of there. A third bullet penetrated his back, and he collapsed in the swirling dust.

Toby landed and lit out of the chopper. He sent a barrage of gunfire into the compound and snatched Eric's vest with one hand. Walking backward and firing as he went, he dragged Eric to the cockpit and pushed him into the seat.

Toby let out a yell when a bullet ripped through his thigh. The gear pouch at Eric's side gaped open. Toby grabbed one of the grenades and jerked out the pin. He heaved it back and ducked under the rotating blades to the other side.

The blast gave them a reprieve, and Toby got airborne. "Hang on, Eric."

As soon as he could safely put the chopper down, he sought a pulse in Eric's neck. At Eric's low moan, Toby let out the breath he was holding. Still alive. Barely. It would take a lot more than his first aid kit to keep him that way. He stuffed some bandages on the shoulder and applied pressure. Then he caught a glimpse of Eric's leg. He took the rest of the gauze and wrapped it around the wound. Eric moaned again. "Stay with me, pal. We gotta get you some help."

With some effort, Toby repositioned Eric and buckled him in. His own leg gave way as he tried to run back around to the seat. He gripped the thigh and hobbled into place. No more gauze. A shop rag in the back would have to do.

"God. Help me."

He grabbed the map, and took off to the one place they could go for help.

CHAPTER THREE

Before closing the Bible, Brock Whitfield traced the familiar passage with his fingers. Exceedingly, abundantly above all he could ask or think. He rose from the recliner and stretched before returning the Bible to the bedside table. He dressed in a brightly-colored short sleeved shirt and khaki pants, his standard uniform since arriving in Africa twenty-five years before. His bedroom, the largest in the staff dormitory, carried with it the distinction of opening onto the covered terrace, his favorite spot on the compound.

Brock opened French doors to the terrace and surveyed the landscape still shrouded in morning mist. Grassy hills flanked the eastern horizon where pink clouds burnished with flecks of gold spangled the skyline. He smiled and whispered his daily greeting, "Thank you for this glorious day."

"Hey, Dad."

He turned at the sound of his daughter's voice. Ellie used her hip to push open the door from the hallway and shuffled toward him with two cups of coffee.

He rushed to help. "Thanks, sweetheart. You almost missed the best part."

"Yeah, I'm dragging today. I didn't have time to get out of my PJ's. Get dressed or get coffee." She grinned and handed him his cup.

"Good choice." He chuckled and guided her to the chairs. "He's outdone Himself this time."

Ellie glanced at the sun cresting the hills. "Wow, I think you're right." She cocked her head back to him. "You know you say that every day."

"And I mean it every day." He reached over to push the soon-to-be mother cat from Ellie's chair.

Ellie plopped down and nudged the cat's belly with her toes. "Poor Lucy. She's so pregnant."

He pulled his chair closer to Ellie. The cat waddled over to him and rubbed against his leg. "And persistent." He placed her on his lap and tucked his hand around her swollen girth to keep her from rolling off.

Ellie positioned her feet on the table in front of her chair and sipped the coffee. "So, what's on the agenda today?"

"I think it'll be slow." He took off his glasses to clear away a smudge with the edge of his shirt. "Two patients are well enough to go home. I thought about taking a trip to Luanda today or tomorrow," he said as casually as if it were only a trip across the compound.

"Really?" She put her feet back on the concrete and leaned forward. "Can I go too?"

The pulsating gyration of helicopter blades interrupted his reply. It swooped in, flying fast and low, scattering the birds from the adjacent field.

The chopper touched down in the clearing not far from the staff dormitory. Toby stumbled out amidst wind and dust. "Help! Dr. Brock."

Brock jumped up knocking the cat to the ground. "Wake up the team, Ellie." He started to run but turned back. "Bring a stretcher."

Toby collapsed a few feet from the helicopter. Brock reached him in seconds and crouched beside him. "What happened?"

Toby grabbed his hands and gasped, "Help my friend, Doc. He's hurt bad."

Brock ran to the helicopter and ducked under the still-rotating blades. His mouth tightened. A man's blood-soaked body lay slumped in the seat. He checked for a pulse and lifted one of the man's eyelids noting the dilated pupil.

Toby struggled back dragging his left leg and cut the engine.

Brock unbuckled the seatbelt and helped Will and Moses transfer the man to the stretcher. "Get him to surgery. Tell Rocco to get the blood units ready. Type him and get some blood into him right away."

He turned his attention back to Toby who leaned against the seat. "Can you walk, son, or do you need a stretcher?"

Toby waved him on. "Just save Eric, Doc. I'm okay."

Brock put his arm around Toby to give support.

"Walk with me. Maybe we should transport him to the hospital at Luanda."

"No." Toby stiffened. "I'll explain later. We gotta lay low for a while."

Lay low? He stopped short. "Tobias, have you done something illegal?"

"No, no, nothing like that." He raised his hand from his leg as if swearing to the truth. "Trust me. I'll explain. Just don't let him die."

"We'll do what we can."

"Please, Doc. He can't die yet."

Brock barreled into surgery fully aware they would need a miracle. He helped Moses and William lift the man from the stretcher to the table. The men worked together to cut off the bloody clothes.

"Let's see what we've got, boys."

Rocco probed the chest. "Two bullet wounds—no, three. I don't know. All this blood might be hiding another wound."

"Blood pressure?"

"Eighty-five over forty-eight."

Brock counted as his fingers pressed the man's wrist. Pulse 144.

At the large sink, Will and Rocco made room as he joined them to scrub.

Ellie raced into the room out of breath and dressed in scrubs. "I'm here." She pushed in beside him and stuck her hands in the stream of water. He moved closer to Rocco to give her more room but remained quiet as he scoured his nails and prayed.

A few minutes into surgery, Brock realized the full extent of the internal damage. He moved swiftly but methodically to obtain hemostasis and gain control of the bleeding. Rocco kept up with his pace and seemed to anticipate the next instrument he required. Moses stood by to offer whatever help he could, even if only to wipe sweat from a brow.

Brock's mouth twisted under his mask when he reached what was left of the injured leg. "Shattered tibia." He spoke more to himself than to the ones assisting him. "We'll do damage control now. Get the fragments out and deal with this when he's more stable."

Three hours and forty-eight minutes later, exhausted and drenched in sweat, he finished suturing. Despite the grim sight of blood spattered on the floor and all around them, their patient was still alive. He stepped away from the table and slid his mask from his face.

"Good work, everyone." He tore off his gloves. "We've done our part for now. Join me in prayer that God helps him pull through."

〜〜〜〜

Brock went looking for Toby and found him asleep in the adjacent room. He placed his hand on Toby's shoulder. Toby jerked awake and struggled to sit up.

"Is he gonna make it, Doc?"

"God willing. He made it through surgery." He pulled a stool closer. "Let's have a look at your leg."

"I think the bullet went clean through."

He cut the bloody material around the wound. "I think you're right." He pulled some antiseptic and gauze from a supply drawer. "This might sting a bit."

Toby's hands curled into fists as liquid fizzed around the hole the bullet had left.

"You feel like telling me what happened? I'd like to know what we're up against."

"Sure." Toby sucked in air and continued in a strained voice. "It was a trap."

"You were ambushed?"

"Yeah. Okay, it's like this. Eric works for the CIA. He was getting close to exposing a leak at the agency."

Brock nodded and poured more antiseptic on a cloth. "Let's get the back. One more little sting and the worst will be over."

Toby's knee jerked and almost clipped Brock in the face. "Whew." Toby continued through clenched teeth. "Anyway, the guy that set Eric up will keep trying to find him."

"I see." Offering sanctuary could place the entire team in danger. He wadded up the soiled cloth and met Toby's gaze. "Do you trust he's telling the truth?"

Toby wiped the sweat running down his face. "He's my best friend. I'd trust him with my life."

"You almost did. But at least your injuries aren't as extensive as his." He tossed the soiled cloth into the hamper and picked up the gauze. "What'd you say his name was?"

"Eric." Toby leaned closer to survey the wound. "Eric Templeton."

Brock's hands froze midway around the thigh, his entire body tightening. "What did you say?"

"Eric Templeton."

Eric Templeton. Dear God, was it possible?

"Doc?"

Brock tried to steady his hands and resume bandaging Toby's thigh. Thank God he found out after the surgery and not before. Not even his own daughter knew how he was connected to the young man struggling to live in the next room. "What can you tell me about him?"

"We've been friends since high school. Went to West Point together. To tell you the truth, he's the reason I made it through West Point. He's like my brother. His father's Robert Templeton, a retired general who works as a liaison between the military and the CIA. "

The same Eric Templeton, all right. "What about his father?" The one man he hoped to avoid for the rest of his life. "Wouldn't he send protection?"

Toby shook his head. "Eric doesn't want to get him involved—not without proof."

Brock released the breath he held and tried to grasp it was truly Eric.

"Eric's a good guy, Doc, but he needs the Lord. I've tried to talk to him some, but I lose my courage every time. Last night, I promised God if He'd please just let him live, I'd do better."

Brock's legs threatened to buckle as he stood. He gripped Toby's shoulder and gave it a gentle squeeze. "We'll pray you get another chance."

Another chance. Was that what God was giving him in all this? He walked to the window and rubbed the stubble of his beard.

Uncharted territory.

CHAPTER FOUR

With more questions than answers, Brock returned like a homing pigeon to the recovery area and joined Rocco at the bedside. "Still hanging on?"

Rocco nodded, not taking his eyes from the patient.

Ellie stood on the other side with her hands on the bedrail. "It's a miracle he's still breathing."

"A miracle," he whispered and took a long look at Eric, seeing him again as if it were the first time. Gratitude welled up like a geyser, and Brock found it almost impossible to stay in one spot. "Can you two hold the fort?"

"Sure thing." Rocco grabbed a stool from across the room and slid it closer to the bed. "We've got this."

"Let me know if anything changes." Only one other person on the compound could appreciate the magnitude of what God had done. He found him, still in OR cleaning. "Nice work. An hour ago, this place looked like a war zone."

"We had good help." Moses rinsed the mop and gestured to his wife.

"Good help, indeed. Thank you, Miriam."

She smiled, with perfectly-formed teeth made especially for smiling. "I am happy to help." She peeled off rubber gloves and with a regal wave, picked up the container of soiled cloths and left the room.

Brock walked over and placed his hand on Will's shoulder. "I'd like you to transfer one of the hospital beds to the staff quarters. Ask Al to give you a hand."

Will finished wiping down the sink. "Staff quarters?"

"Right. The room across from mine. I'll explain later."

"No problem, Doc."

He waited for Will to leave and then pulled over a couple of stools. "Sit down, my friend. I need a moment."

Moses sat and used a paper towel to wipe his neck and brow. "How is he?"

"Stable, thank God. Rocco and Ellie are with him."

"What about Toby?'

"Shaken and weak. His leg will be sore for a while." He took a deep breath and released it slowly. "You won't believe what Toby told me."

Moses raised his brows.

"That young man in there"—Brock cocked his head toward the recovery room—"is Eric Templeton."

Moses' eyes widened. "Eric? The one—" He covered his mouth and glanced at the door. "Are you sure it's the same person?"

Brock nodded. "Incredible, isn't it? I couldn't believe it myself."

"How can this be?" Moses pivoted back. "Does Toby know? Is that why he brought him here?"

"No, no. You and I are the only ones who know. I'd like to keep it that way for now."

"Yes, of course." Moses paused. "What do you need from me, my brother?"

"Pray." He raked his hand through his hair and didn't try to hide his pent-up emotion. "I've prayed for Eric Templeton for almost thirty years, but in all those years, in all those prayers, I never imagined I would see him again."

"Come with me." Moses stood and gestured for Brock to follow. "I'd like a second look now that I know who he is."

Neither spoke as they walked the short distance to recovery. As they neared the door, Brock grabbed his friend's arm to hold him back. "One more thing. Toby indicated he and Eric are still in some kind of danger."

"I see. That's why you want him in staff quarters?"

"For his safety." Mostly true and a lot easier to explain than his need to be near Eric.

CHAPTER FIVE

More to satisfy her curiosity than her father's hunger, Ellie balanced the tray in one hand and pushed open the door with the other. "Hungry?"

The two men standing by the bed turned, and Al rushed over. "Let me help you with that, little lady."

Before she could protest, he took the tray and set it on the table beside the bed.

"Thank you."

"Yes, Ma'am. I was just going."

Her dad gave her elbow a little tweak and then walked Al to the door. "Thanks for bringing the cot."

"Glad to."

She stole a quick look at the patient before her dad turned and bypassed her for the food. "Good timing. I was starving." He picked up a wedge of the sandwich and swiped melted cheese oozing from the middle. "Hmm." He took a bite and closed his eyes in what could only be ecstatic appreciation.

Dad loved grilled cheese. Who knew? Even after a year and a half, apparently she still had much to learn.

She grinned as he popped the last bite of sandwich into his mouth. "Nicci told me to make sure you eat."

He laughed and reached for the apple on the tray. "And you can bet she'll check to see if the tray is empty when you return it."

"You look like you could use a break. Why don't you let me stay with him tonight?" She followed his gaze to Eric's ashen face. "You took him off the ventilator. How is he?"

Almost as if on cue, Eric groaned, and they both moved to stand beside the bed. "Holding steady, but his fever's up a bit."

He showed her the stats. "Same as last night. Usually tapers off in the morning."

She scanned the entries. "You upped the antibiotics."

"Thought he could use the edge." Lines of fatigue etched his face.

"Dad, you're dead on your feet. Let me stay with him."

He shook his head. "Then you'll be the one dead on your feet."

"Not much going on at the clinic. I can take a nap tomorrow."

"Okay. You talked me into it."

Finally. A chance to do something for the man who went out of his way to do for everyone else. "Great." She handed him the tray before he could change his mind. "Take this back. Nicci will be proud."

"Can I get you anything?"

"No, thanks. I'm good."

"Yes. You are." He leaned closer and kissed her on the forehead. "I'll bring you some of Nicci's coffee in the morning."

"Deal."

Alone with this intriguing patient, Ellie studied his still form. She reached over the bedrail and probed for his pulse. Warmth emanated from his arm. She smoothed back thick dark hair from his forehead and sponged his face with a cool cloth. His almost imperceptible moan wrenched her heart. She took his hand as she often did with her patients, but this time it was her pulse that sped up. Who was this guy, and why did her dad devote so much of his time to him? For some reason she couldn't explain, she was drawn to him herself. She remained by his side for what seemed like hours.

Around one thirty, Eric stirred and seemed restless. Still too early for more pain medication, she stilled him with her hand on his chest. So many wounds and so many scars. Who did this to him? And why?

~~~~

The next morning, Ellie contorted her body to work out the kinks in her back as she jotted down Eric's stats. Her dad showed up and swapped the chart in her hand for a cup of coffee.

"You wonderful man." She sat in the chair by the bed and hugged the cup with both hands.

"I owed you some gesture of appreciation." He slid another chair closer to her and sat. "I don't think I moved all night."

The tapping at the door made them both turn around.

"Can I come in?"

"Of course." Her dad jumped up to grab another chair. "How's your leg?"

Toby limped over and eased himself down. "Coming along. A little sore, but it's coming along."

"Toby, my daughter, Ellie."

"Glad to meet you. You weren't here the last time I came."

"No." She reached in front of her dad and extended her hand. "I've only been here about a year and a half."

Toby nudged her dad with his elbow. "You know, I still think about that summer I came with my church group. Going on twenty years now. You remember that, Doc?"

"I sure do."

"You changed my life. I won't never forget that."

Her throat tightened. She'd turned fifteen that summer. If she'd come to her dad then instead of wasting twenty more years—

"God changed your life, son. It was my privilege to be a part of it. By the way, how is your grandmother?"

"Good. Real good. Big Mama lives with Mama and Dad now."

Eric moaned, and her dad opened a drawer and pulled out a syringe.

Toby moved aside as her dad injected morphine into Eric's arm. "Is he coming around?"

Ellie placed her hand on Toby's shoulder. "We're keeping him heavily sedated to give his body a chance to heal."

Her dad removed the needle and with a small piece of gauze, applied pressure to the spot. "He's not out of the woods yet."

Toby cracked his knuckles. "Man, I hate this waiting." He stood and walked stiff-legged to the window.

Ellie took the empty syringe from her dad and threw it away. "I'm curious. How did you become friends?"

Toby turned. "We went to the same high school." He walked back to his chair and sat with his leg extended. "Eric was a quiet kid. Always seemed a little lonely to me. Here I had all my brothers and sisters. Eric had his dad. That was it. So I invited him over. My mom loved cooking for him."

"What happened to his mother?" She shamelessly pumped for information.

"Up and left. His two older sisters went with her. Eric stayed with his dad. He was something like thirteen, I guess. He didn't talk much about it."

Her heart lurched. Her hand found the strand of hair she twisted when she needed to fidget.

Toby looked at the floor and shook his head. "His dad was a piece of work. Tough as nails." He nodded toward the bed. "Tough on Eric."

"What do you mean?" Her dad asked the question before she could.

"General Robert Templeton. Eric tried real hard to make his Dad proud, but no matter what he did, it was never enough."

Ellie met her father's gaze. She didn't need a crystal ball to know what he was thinking.

"Eric just tried harder. I remember one time back in high school, Eric limped off the football field after the first quarter and didn't go back in for the rest of the game. His dad lit into him as soon as he got home."

"Lit into him?"

"Mostly yelled. Told him to suck it up and quit being a sissy. No telling what else. Eric told me to get out of there."

The coffee in her stomach turned to acid.

"Turned out he had a broken ankle. My mom took him to the doctor when she noticed he could barely walk. Eric begged the doctor not to put it in a cast. When his dad saw it, he didn't speak to Eric for three days." Toby leaned closer. "Eric never said, but I think he'd take a beating any day over the silent treatment."

Her dad's jaw worked as he blinked. She fought her own tears as she imagined Eric as a teenager enduring an untreated break for days and far worse at the hands of his own father. She steered the conversation to a safer topic. "Dad said you attended West Point. How were things there?"

"West Point?" Toby leaned back and crossed his arms over his chest. "Eric was the best at everything. No matter what, hands down, he was the best. When we graduated, the agency snatched him up for special ops. I specialized in helicopters. I didn't see him again until Afghanistan. He was working undercover. I was assigned to transport this CIA operative on a covert mission across the Saudi border. Didn't know it was Eric 'til he was buckled in the seat. We found out we work real well together." Toby paused and lowered his voice as if his words were top secret. "Dr. Brock, I brought him here because I didn't know what else to do. This guy in the agency, he won't stop until he finds Eric. The fewer people who know Eric's here, the safer he'll be. "

"I see." Her dad rubbed his chin. "We can trust our staff to be discreet, but we'll keep him away from the nationals who come here to be treated."

Eric became restless.

"Go get some rest." Her dad gave Toby a reassuring smile. "We'll talk more later."

Toby joined them by the bed and whispered almost to himself. "I was scared out of my mind that night. I kept begging God to let him live."

"You did the right thing, son. Keep praying for him."

"I hope he makes it." Toby turned and limped out of the room.

The knot in Ellie's stomach traveled up and lay heavy in her chest. Her dad opened his arm and with a slight nod motioned for her to come to him.

"Stirred every sensitive bone in your little body, didn't it?"

"How'd you guess?"

"You and I are cut out of the same cloth, and it's killing me." With his arm holding her secure, he placed his other hand over Eric's heart.

"Dear Father, thank You for sparing their lives and letting Toby bring Eric here. We ask You, our Great Physician, to heal his battered body—"

She quit trying to hold back her own tears when her dad's prayer faltered.

"And Father, Eric's soul is in need of healing as much as his body. Restore him to wholeness and to You. Amen."

She reached for the box of tissues and handed one to her dad. "What's going to happen, Dad?

"I don't know, honey. We'll have to trust the One who does."

CHAPTER SIX

Tom Reznik faced the window above the kitchen sink and shouted into his phone. "What do you mean you aren't sure? Find him. Finish it." He flung the phone across the counter. Incompetent idiots.

He stalked out the back door to the patio and lit a cigarette, his hands shaking. Not the time to lose his head. If Eric Templeton wouldn't just die like the others, it was time for Plan B.

With another deep drag, he flicked the cigarette into the yard and returned to the kitchen. He retrieved the phone from the counter and hit the director's number.

"Harold? Tom."

A number of minutes later, he pulled his black Lexus into the designated parking space and rehearsed the bill of goods he was resolved to sell to McDowall.

"Let the director know I'm here, would you, Faye?" He strode into his office to grab the folder for the meeting. She buzzed him almost immediately.

"Director McDowall is ready to see you."

"Thanks." With a forced smile plastered across his face, he walked past her into the corridor. A familiar bitter twinge reared as he walked to the office that should have been his. Two men passed him as they left the conference room. He met Bob Templeton's gaze, and for one brief moment regretted what he was about to do.

He paused at the door and glanced back, hoping Templeton wouldn't see him entering McDowall's office.

"Go right in, Mr. Reznik."

"Thank you."

The important little man remained focused on some important little papers. McDowall stuffed them in the top left drawer and gestured to a chair. "What can I do for you?"

He unbuttoned his coat as he sat. "Bad news, I'm afraid," he spoke with an exaggerated tone of regret.

"Oh?"

Hit fast. Hit hard. "Templeton's gone rogue."

The director sucked in his breath as if he'd been punched in the chest. "What?"

Reznik plopped the folder on the desk and slid it to McDowall. "It's all there. Taking bribes. Selling secrets."

McDowall reached for the file without dropping his gaze. "I don't understand."

Their eyes locked. It reminded Reznik of his quarterback days. On the field, in the lineup staring down the opponent. "Come on, Harold. Spy 101. Trust no one. Suspect everyone. Stuart Harris was on to him. Called me shortly before he was killed."

"You think Eric had something to do with Stuart's death?"

He shrugged. "Didn't want to believe it myself." He stood and paced. "Templeton's playing us." He pointed his finger at McDowall, blending the right amount of remorse and disgust in his tone. "He's playing *you*."

The director slumped forward and thumbed through the papers in the folder.

He sat again and pounded harder. "I've been watching, waiting. I knew he'd eventually get sloppy. Careless."

"It doesn't add up." McDowall huffed out his breath as if it were too heavy and then closed the folder. "You heard him at the debriefing. He—"

"Yeah. Classic. Look, the guy is arrogant and cocky. Don't tell me you haven't noticed he disappears for weeks at a time. Breaks protocol. Doesn't check in."

The director flinched. Reznik hammered away like a prized fighter going for the knockout. "After the debriefing, I contacted one of my sources in Honduras. According to him, there was no guerrilla attack. He said Eric took out the informant himself."

McDowall pivoted his chair and stared out the window, his fingers steepled under his chin. Seconds that seemed like minutes passed before he swiveled back and heaved a sigh. "Bring him in, and we'll get to the bottom of this."

Phase one complete. "That's the problem. He's disappeared again."

"What do you mean?" McDowall's jaw tightened.

"Skipped town as soon as you left for Brussels. Crew said he arranged for a flight to Zambia but then switched to Zimbabwe. Hasn't been confirmed, but it seems Eric was ambushed by an unforgiving creditor when he failed to deliver the goods."

"He's dead?"

"Missing. Wounded. Possibly dead. Sources say someone helped him."

"I see." McDowall gave him the poker-faced stare. "You've got men checking hospitals?"

"Already on it." He shifted in his seat. McDowall was unreadable.

"Keep this on the down-low for a couple more days. I'm not ready to tell Bob his son's a traitor."

"Will do." He rose and reached for the folder.

"Leave it. I want to take a closer look."

"Sure." He dropped it back on the desk and left the office exulting in his superiority over McDowall.

He ducked into the restroom to avoid another encounter with Templeton. He smiled at his reflection as he washed his hands. *Good work, Reznik. We need more men like you.* He laughed a bitter laugh. *Men we can trust.* He crushed the wet paper towel and lobbed it into the trash.

CHAPTER SEVEN

Ellie didn't have to look far to find her dad. Morning sunlight streamed through dusty venetian blinds and formed a crisscross pattern on the floor. Eric's raspy breaths replaced the hum of the ventilator. Her dad had encased Eric's hand in both of his and appeared to be praying. She remained by the door and glanced down the hallway. Should she interrupt? Not like him to be late to a meeting, especially one he'd called. She padded over to him and touched his arm.

"Dad?"

He released Eric's hand and turned. "Ellie. I didn't hear you come in."

Moisture streaked his cheeks and disappeared into his beard. Her eyes flew to Eric's monitor. "Is he worse?"

He shook his head. "He's holding his own."

"Do I need to stay with him during the meeting?"

He gave her a blank look, and then his eyes widened. He checked his watch and winced. "Time got away from me. No. I want you there too."

Her dad's normal gait doubled as he turned to leave, and she raced to keep up. Laughter echoed down the hall. Probably Rocco entertaining the group. She followed her dad into the dining area where the aroma of Nicci's special blend of African coffee filled the room. The large oval table had been converted to a conference table with extra chairs to the side.

"I'm going to grab a cup of coffee. You want one too, Dad?"

He nodded and slid back the chair at the head of the table but remained standing. To his right, Moses sat with Miriam by his side. Rocco took the chair on the left. The shaggy cut of his sandy blond hair and his carefree, happy-go-lucky attitude made him seem more like a surfer from California than a doctor from Michigan. His brother-in-law, Will, sat beside him. Their three-month medical missions experience had kicked up a notch when Toby arrived with Eric. Mac and Al sat at the end of the table across from Toby. He must have asked about a problem on the helicopter. Al said he'd take a look after the meeting.

She placed her dad's coffee in front of him and then sat by Miriam.

Nicci backed through the double doors in the far right corner of the room carrying a large tray of muffins. The petite African national managed the kitchen and almost singlehandedly cooked all the meals for the staff and in-house patients. Nicci placed the muffins in the center of the table and turned to go.

"Nicci, you think of everything. Why don't you pull up a chair beside Ellie? I'd like you to stay."

Nicci pivoted back and nodded to her dad. Ellie scooted her chair closer to Miriam to make room. "Dad's right. You spoil us."

Nicci looped her arm through Ellie's. "I enjoy it."

"I apologize for being late to my own meeting." Her dad stood with clipboard in hand and reached in his top pocket for his glasses. "Let me begin by saying how much I appreciate you." He opened his mouth to continue but soon closed it and looked down. He removed his glasses and pinched the bridge of his nose.

Panic constricted her chest. Only three times in her life had she seen her dad cry. Two of them today. He must be sick. Maybe even dying, and he called this meeting to break the news. There'd be a service in the chapel across from the clinic. Hundreds of grateful nationals surrounding his flower-strewn casket singing "In the Sweet By and By" in rich African harmony.

"Sorry. I've been a little emotional lately."

Her dad's words snapped her back to the meeting.

"I wanted to thank you for the excellent work you do. These past four days, you've doubled up and kept the clinic right on schedule." He directed his gaze to the end of the table. "Mac, good job on those village vaccinations. You tackled them alone and somehow got them all done."

Mac raised his hand to acknowledge her dad's remarks and accidentally bumped his coffee. Toby jerked his chair back to avoid the splash. Nicci sprang into action for more napkins.

"Sorry, guys." Mac stood to help dab up the spill. "At least I'm not this clumsy with a needle."

Her dad continued, going down the list. "Al and Will, you made sure those supplies, not to mention the extra blood units, made it here on time. Good job."

Then he placed his hand on Moses' shoulder. "And Moses, Ellie, and Rocco—" Her dad again dropped his gaze and fingered the edge of the paper on his clipboard. "I, uh ... I want you to know I'm aware of all you do. I notice." His husky voice became a whisper. "God notices."

A hush fell over them. Silent respect for the man who outworked them all.

Not surprising, Rocco broke the silence. "Hey, we're just trying to keep up with you, Doc."

Everyone chuckled, including her dad.

"God has given us a unique challenge." Her dad sat but continued speaking. "I've asked Toby to share some things you might need to know."

Toby twisted the soiled napkin in his hand and cleared his throat. It didn't seem to help that every eye was trained on him. "As I told Doc here, Eric's been my friend since high school. I guess the main thing you need to know is Eric's in a lot of trouble." His voice shook when he spoke. "I don't know how much to tell them," Toby addressed her dad.

"Take your time. They can handle whatever you have to say."

He nodded, took a deep breath, and then blew it out. "Okay, here goes. Eric works for the CIA. He uncovered a leak in the agency. Bottom line, that leak wants him dead."

Toby's words hit Ellie harder this time than she thought they would. She didn't even know the man, but something in her wanted to rise up and fight for him. She met her dad's gaze. His expression was somber, unreadable.

"You saved that boy's life, son."

Toby nodded. "Well, I got him here. Seems to me that you all saved his life."

Her dad smiled. She'd put money on what he'd say next.

"To tell the truth, God spared his life. He used the team to do it."

Her money would've been safe. "He has a long road to recovery," her dad continued. "He'll be here quite some time."

"Yeah." Toby agreed. "That's why you need to know the risks. The mole back at the agency has connections with a lot of power. I knew I couldn't get him to a hospital. That's the first place those guys would look."

"Do you think they'll come here?" Her voice came out like a squeak.

He shrugged. "Not anytime soon. With luck, they'll assume he died. But from what I know about the agency, they won't give up 'til they have a body and DNA match."

Ellie pressed her hand against her throat. Her imagination ran wild, this time with commandos dressed in black storming the mission compound.

Toby seemed to be through talking. He'd told them the problem. What about the solution?

"We have our work cut out for us, don't we, Team? Eric needs more than physical healing. He'll be conscious soon, and our time with him is limited. Look for opportunities to show him God's love and God's truth."

He took a deep breath as he stood. "One last thing. I don't think we're in any danger, but just to be sure, refrain from talking about the American patient. Most of the visitors to the clinic are unaware of his presence here. I'd like to keep it that way."

Then her dad said the words she most needed to hear. "God never makes a mistake. He brought Eric here to us and has kept him alive. Pray with me for Eric's protection and, most importantly, for his salvation."

Of course. That's why her dad hovered over Eric. He was storming heaven over Eric's soul. Just like he did for her. It was clear to her now. Her daddy was going to bat for Eric Templeton, and it was just a matter of time.

CHAPTER EIGHT

He was on a bed or maybe a cot. Not the ground and not a filthy room above the tavern in Honduras. The air smelled clean, fresh, not like stale beer. Disjointed images and thoughts collided but disappeared when he tried to latch onto any of them. He wanted to rub his head and clear his mind, but he couldn't make either hand work.

His ears picked up the distant hum of a fan and the ticking of a clock. Langley? Conference room? Closer to him something clattered like a clipboard dropping on a table.

Vicious pain ripped through his gut when he struggled to rise.

"Lie still, Eric." A gentle hand on his chest pushed him back down.

His eyes finally cooperated and opened. The only light in the dim room shone behind a woman beside his bed. It cast an iridescent glow around golden hair that tumbled loose, framing her face. He blinked to focus. Even in the sludge of his mind, two things became clear. The woman was gorgeous, and she was no threat.

She smiled. He opened his mouth, but no words came out. Was she an angel? Did that mean he was dead?

Her touch was soft on his arm, the only part of him that didn't hurt.

"I'll be right back." She turned to go, and he scanned the room scoping out possible escape routes. His bed faced a window with shades drawn. No light peeked through. Must be night. To his left near the only door to the room, another door stood ajar revealing a white porcelain sink.

The sound of footsteps and muffled voices drifted closer with one voice louder than the rest.

"'Bout time you woke up." Toby cleared the doorway. "Took me three days to clean up all the blood you left in my chopper." He reached the bed and grabbed Eric's hand.

"What happened?" Eric managed a croaking whisper.

An older man edged in front of Toby. "Rest for now. We'll explain everything soon." He injected something into the IV and tapped the tube leading to his arm.

The searing pain extending from his gut down to his right leg eased. The man's mouth moved, and Eric strained to hear. Something about God …

The next time he awoke, the room was full of light. No way of knowing how much time had passed. He closed his eyes to concentrate. The horror of that night flooded back.

Reznik. He had to find Toby and get out of there. Now.

He clenched his teeth and raised his head to survey his injuries. Tight, white bandages encased his upper torso. Half of his body wasn't cooperating. His stomach tightened. What if he were paralyzed? His elevated right leg looked twice its normal size.

Urgency won out over pain. He brought his left arm up to his mouth and used his teeth to snatch out the IV and blood tubing. Sweat dripped down his face as he grabbed the rail to pull himself over. He grunted and cursed each time he had to stop and rest. The veins on his left arm protruded as he inched himself closer to the edge. With a deep breath, he swung his good leg over the side. He reached for his other leg to drag it across the bed. Each movement brought waves of nausea. He lay still, resting on his left side. Then with a heaving war cry, he pushed up and slid his left foot down until it touched the cold tile on the floor. The room swirled around him, and everything went black.

Brock found Eric in a heap by the bed. Blood trickled from a gash on his temple. He hurried to the door. "Rocco, I need your help!"

"Yeah, Doc? Whoa." Rocco raced to the other side of Eric. "What happened?"

"I don't know. I stepped out for a minute and then found him like this."

"I'd better get Toby."

"Good idea." He scanned Eric for more damage. Blood seeped through the bandage on his chest. Must have pulled some stitches loose.

Toby rushed in ahead of Rocco and knelt by Eric. "Crazy fool. What was he thinking?"

Brock ignored the rant and gestured. "Position yourself under his shoulders. I'll take this side. Rocco, hold his injured leg steady."

On three, the men hoisted Eric to the bed. Toby grimaced. "Good thing he's out cold."

They slid him to the center of the bed. Rocco tied off the left arm above the elbow and poked around for a vein.

Brock stepped around Toby to inspect the gash on Eric's head. Toby stepped back and almost knocked over the IV stand. He fumbled with his hands and raised anguished eyes. "Tell me what I can do, Doc."

Brock kept pressure on the gash. "You can find Ellie. Tell her to bring a butterfly bandage."

Toby nodded and took off as if Eric's life depended on him.

Rocco cocked his head toward the drawer beside the bed. "There's some in there."

"I know." He lifted the compress and checked the cut.

Rocco grinned as he secured the needle with adhesive. "You are one smart dude, Doc."

His mouth twisted. "If I were smart, I wouldn't have left Eric alone."

"Don't beat yourself up. Most patients in his condition don't move."

~~~~~

The room was darker when Eric came to. A man with a partially closed book in his lap sat beside his bed and appeared to be dozing. Same man he had seen with Toby. Well-trimmed beard. Thick gray hair. A stethoscope hung from his neck. A doctor. But where? No doctor in the States would wear a shirt so bright it almost glowed in the dark. Still in Africa? He gave the room the once over again. Not much about it looked like a hospital room.

His escape attempt must have earned him a babysitter. He raised the only arm that would work to finger the lump on his forehead. The tubes connected to his arm jangled.

The man jerked awake and grabbed the book before it slid off his lap. "Eric. Hello."

Out of habit, Eric went into red alert until kind brown eyes seemed to smile at him. The man posed no danger.

"I'm Brock Whitfield. Most people around here call me Doc."

The guy barking at him from the doorway interrupted his reply. "Man, what kind of fool stunt were you pulling? I didn't drag your bloody body out of that hellhole for you to go killing yourself here."

Eric mustered a weak grin. "Tobe." He strained to get out the words. His throat felt tight and dry. "Why are you limping?"

"You don't miss nothing, do you?" He slid a stool closer to the doctor. "I took a bullet to get you outta there."

"You were shot?"

"Yeah." Toby grinned at Doc. "I couldn't let you get all the glory."

"Not much glory." He rasped. Each deep breath stabbed his chest. "Whole thing backfired." His words sparked a more pressing need. "Need my clothes. Gotta get out of here."

"Not an option, pal. Maybe if you're buck naked, you'll stay in bed."

"Is he awake?" The soft voice he'd heard before filtered into the room.

Doc turned and held out his hand to the beautiful woman. "Yes."

"Eric, this is my daughter, Ellie."

So the angel was real.

She moved closer and placed her hands on the bedrail. "Hello. I'm so glad you're awake."

He tried to shake the fog in his brain and return her smile. Her hair was pulled back in a ponytail. Maybe younger than he first thought. Still beautiful. He hadn't dreamed that.

She looked at her dad with what seemed to be genuine affection. "He had us going for a while, didn't he?"

Doc moved to the foot of the bed. "She's right. You had us pretty worried." He patted Eric's left leg. "Try to tough it out a little longer in this old bed of yours. I don't want you undoing anymore of my handiwork."

"Yes sir." His hand rubbed the bandages on his abdomen. "Lesson learned."

Toby folded his arms across his chest and scoffed, "Yeah, you always did have to learn the hard way."

Even the grin was an effort. He closed his eyes and tried to breathe a full breath.

Cool fingers gave his hand a gentle squeeze. "Get some rest now." The angel. "One of us will be back soon."

A calloused hand replaced the soft one. "You came mighty close to dying." Toby's voice lost its gruffness and sounded far away. "I love you, brother."

CHAPTER NINE

A stabbing pain hit Eric that would have raised him off the bed if he could move. He wasn't sure which was worse, the pain or the helplessness. He closed his eyes and balled his hand into a fist. Okay. Pain wins. He inhaled slowly and tried to recall the mind over matter tricks he'd learned in training.

With a soft knock, a man peeked around the door. Ebony skin blended with the dimness of the room. "Hello, Eric." The man entered and flicked on the lamp. "My name is Moses."

Eric managed a nod.

"I didn't wake you, did I?" The man's lyrical African accent sounded apologetic.

"No."

Fingers that could have easily palmed a basketball encased Eric's hand. "I was eager to meet you. We praise God you're alive." His leathery face crinkled into a broad smile revealing a slight gap in otherwise perfect teeth. "You are truly a miracle."

Not exactly what he'd call it especially with every nerve in his body screaming at him. He met the man's open, friendly gaze. "Yeah, that's what I hear."

"Would you like for me to raise the top of your bed?"

He nodded. "That'd be great."

Moses cranked a lever at the foot of the bed. "How's that?"

Eric winced with the movement.

"Too much?" Moses poised his hand above the handle.

"No. It's okay."

Moses studied him. "Your pain is bad."

Eric didn't respond.

With a quick glance at the chart, Moses nodded. "Close enough."

Eric lay still, reassessing his earlier call. The helplessness was worse. Much worse.

"Here we are." Moses held a syringe. "Dr. Brock said to give you something stronger if you needed it."

Cool liquid traveled up his arm. He closed his eyes and gave in to the release. Good stuff.

The man beside his bed chuckled. "Yes. Very good stuff."

He must have said it out loud.

◢◥◢◥◢◥

Brock left his bathroom carrying his travel bag of toiletries. Moses stood at the door with Eric's chart.

"Come in, my friend. How was Eric?"

"In pain."

He nodded and gestured to the recliner in the corner. "Please sit. I'm almost through packing." He placed some socks in the overnight bag and zipped it. "He'll stay in pain until we can fix that leg." He sat on the edge of the bed.

Moses handed him the chart. "Will and I have the truck loaded with supplies. We should be ready to head out at first light."

He read over Eric's last vitals and looked up over his glasses. "Did the syringes we ordered arrive?"

Moses nodded. "This morning. We won't run out this time. Rocco organized it all. You'll be impressed."

"Rocco's a great blessing, isn't he? Too bad he's only here for three months."

Moses leaned forward, his hands clasped, elbows resting on his thighs. "Will and I can handle this trip if you want to stay."

He'd like nothing better, but he shook his head. "I feel God would have me keep to my plan to go."

He smiled at Moses and let the companionable silence of old friends linger.

"Are you going to tell him?"

"You know, you have an uncanny ability to read my thoughts." Brock released a sigh. "I want to, but so far, God hasn't given me the green light to say anything. Pray for me. I don't want to rush ahead of God's timing and mess up what God's doing here."

"I am praying. He will make it plain to you."

"Moses, I feel as I did a year and a half ago when Ellie came here in such bad shape."

"I remember it well."

He stared at the floor. "I'll never forget it. She was fragile and broken, and I didn't know how to reach her. I've never prayed so hard in my life."

"But look at Ellie now. What a difference."

"You can say that again. Our gracious God healed her broken heart." He walked over to the window. A full moon cast a silver sheen over the landscape he loved. "Now, it seems an even greater challenge faces me." He paused, shaking his head. "My heart is fairly bursting with the love I feel for that boy in there."

The chair creaked and then Moses joined him at the window.

"If God allows me to lead Eric to Jesus, to be a part of the answer to my own prayers—" His voice choked. "It will be too much." He turned, his unshed tears blurring the image of Moses. "There will be no greater moment for me. I'll feel like Elijah and will want to be taken up to heaven in a chariot of fire."

"Then leave me your mantle, brother." Moses slapped him on the back. "And grant me a double portion of your spirit."

He needed that laugh. When he finally confessed to Eric exactly who he was, no one would be laughing. Not for a long time.

CHAPTER TEN

Eric twisted toward the clock above the cabinet by his bed. 0400. Even without the searing pain down his leg, there would be no more sleep for a while.

The blast. The barrage of gunfire. Being trapped with no way of escape. The circle of regret trudged through his mind. It had happened so fast. What could he have done differently?

His name had probably moved to the top of Reznik's hit list. He needed a new plan of counterattack.

The man he wanted to see came in. "Good morning. I took a chance you'd be awake." Dr. Brock smiled as he walked over and encased Eric's hand in both of his. If bedside manner counted for anything, this guy was a pro. "Moses said he increased your pain medication. Did you sleep better?"

"Yeah." Pain ripped through him as he shifted his position. "Think it's worn off."

Doc nodded and released Eric's hand. He turned on the lamp beside the bed and picked up the chart. "You had extensive internal damage. We had to remove your spleen." His expression became more serious. "You nearly bled out."

Eric waited for the good news, the you'll-be-back-on-your-feet-in-no-time bit.

Doc put the chart down and propped his arms on the bed rail. "A bullet shattered your tibia. You'll need more surgery. We considered transporting you to the bigger hospital at Luanda, but Toby advised against it."

"Toby told you what happened?"

Doc's mouth tightened in a thin line, and he nodded. "But you'll be safe here." He reached over the rail and patted Eric's hand. "We've separated you from the rest of the patients." He gave a sweeping glance around the room. "You're actually in the staff living quarters. Only our staff knows you're here."

"I'll leave as soon as Toby can arrange it."

Doc met his gaze with an almost apologetic grin. "About that. Even with surgery, you won't be able to put any weight on your leg for two to three months."

Every stitch in his gut tightened.

"Your immobility increases the risk for blood clots. I can't risk giving you blood thinners until your internal injuries have a chance to heal. We'll let you get up some during the day. In a wheelchair first, and when you're stronger, we'll try you on crutches."

Forget the wheelchair. He'd start on crutches. "When can you fix my leg?"

Doc scooted a stool over and sat with his hands folded on his lap. "Not sure. It's beyond my confidence as a surgeon and will require a specialist."

Not the good news he'd hoped for.

"You're an exceptional young man, Eric."

His bitter chuckle stabbed his ribs. Shot up in a bogus mission and rendered helpless was nowhere close to exceptional.

"I mean it." Doc leaned closer. "It took courage for you to storm that compound. You're a fighter. And I have to tell you, I've never had a patient in your shape make it off the bed. You're made of some tough stuff. I'm proud of you."

His voice held no hint of deception. Only kindness. Compassion. The knot in Eric's throat sank to his chest. Words he'd craved all his life. From a man who barely knew anything about him. He swallowed hard and looked away, relieved when the doctor stood and eliminated the need to respond.

"I have to leave for a couple of weeks. Ellie'll be in charge while I'm away."

The pretty girl with the smile. The news sent an unexpected jolt to his pulse. "Did Toby bring my clothes?"

"Yes. I'm glad you mentioned it. Rocco can help you. He's a doctor visiting from the states. About your age. You'll like him. But you'll have to promise not to try to run away again."

Eric relaxed when Doc grinned. "Yes, sir. I'll behave."

Doc placed his hand on Eric's shoulder. "I know you will. Now, I'm going to take out the catheter." He moved to the end of the bed and lifted the sheet, talking as he worked. "I'll leave the tube in your side. It'll keep your lung from collapsing, and we hope, keep you from getting pneumonia." He straightened his stance and pointed to the bandage wrapped around Eric's chest. "The bullet that penetrated your back did quite a bit of damage. Ripped through your spleen, pierced your lung and nicked your liver before it exited your side over here."

Next, Doc took a syringe from the drawer. "Rocco will stay close to you for a few days and help get you to the bathroom. He's a funny guy. Will keep you in stitches." He chuckled and injected something into the IV. "The pain will ease up a little now, and you can get more rest." His tone changed. "It's pretty clear to me that God spared your life, son. Think about that while I'm gone."

The relief was almost immediate as was his descent into sleep. His last conscious thoughts were of Doc's words he hadn't known he'd needed as much as the morphine.

Proud. Of me.

SAVING ERIC

CHAPTER ELEVEN

Ellie pried loose the wet strand plastered across her cheek and combed through her hair. A hint of mousse, scrunched through the sleek curtain, created a wavy disarray around her shoulders. Her best look and almost as easy as her usual ponytail. She used the wet towel to clear a spot on the bathroom mirror and applied more than her usual swipe of mascara. Then her bare feet padded across the room to the closet, and she stood before it, tapping her lips with her forefinger. Definitely the baby blue scrubs, the ones she wore when she needed to have a good day. Or added confidence. Today she could use both.

She made the bed, stacked the pillow shams against the headboard and then plopped down on the edge to put on her shoes.

Right on time, her dad gave a soft knock at her door. "Ellie?"

"Just a minute." She tied the last double knot and bounced off the bed. He'd be surprised to find her up and dressed before sunrise. "Come in."

Her dad pushed open the door and stopped suddenly. He saw right through her, but he didn't comment. Bless him. He stood there, dressed as always in khaki shorts. The African shirt he wore today had red and black diamond squares laced together with what appeared to be emerald green vines. Still a very attractive man, with his head full of hair, more salt than pepper. No wonder her mother fell for him. But how her gentle-souled father fell for such an acid-tongued woman remained a mystery. "We're about to head out. Any last minute questions?"

She pulled the door closed and walked with him down the hall to the terrace. "I don't think so. You'll keep your cell phone handy, won't you?"

He nodded. "But the reception comes and goes."

Her heart froze. "What if I need you?"

Her dad pushed through the double doors leading to the terrace and held one open for her. "Tell you what. I'll check in every day when I have a good signal. How's that?"

"Better than nothing." She bent down to pet Lucy and tried to sound casual. "How is he today?"

"Improving. I took out the catheter, so he can get up some. I gave him pain medication. He'll probably sleep most of the day."

She straightened but couldn't keep the tremor out of her voice. "Just hurry back."

Her dad kissed her forehead. "I promise. You'll do fine, sweetheart. Look over there." He gestured with a nod of his head. "I was hoping the sun would make it up before I left. It's a good sign."

She followed his gaze and smiled. "I think the sun waits for you to reach the terrace to make its appearance."

They rounded the corner of the staff quarters and joined Rocco and the others at the all-terrain Land Rover that looked like a plus-sized jeep.

Her dad gave her a quick hug and climbed in behind the wheel. "Hold the fort."

Moses rode shotgun. He gave a sweeping wave with his long arm, and then he wrapped his fingers around the top of the cab.

Will sat in the back between some boxes.

Two weeks was a long time.

Rocco must have thought it too. "I hope the villagers don't have any serious outbreaks. Like cholera or something."

"And I hope nobody comes looking for Eric."

His eyes widened. "I never thought of that."

Ellie grinned. "I'll make you a deal. I'll handle the cholera, and you keep the bad guys away."

"Hmm. I think I'd rather take my chances with cholera."

Ellie scanned the area as if expecting guerrilla fighters to converge on their compound. "Me too."

SAVING ERIC

CHAPTER TWELVE

Eric awoke from his drug-induced sleep with a desperate need to get up.

"Eric?" A guy stumbled up from the cot in the corner and clicked on the lamp beside the bed. "I'm Rocco, your beck-and-call man."

"Good timing, Rocco." Eric squinted at the new doctor. "I'm in need of, uh, a little help."

"Help?" Rocco rubbed his tousled sandy-blond hair, and then his face relaxed into an easy smile. "I'll get the bed pan."

Eric shook his head and fastened his hand on the rail. "No, just help me up."

Rocco hesitated but then sprang into action. "Okay, pal. Roll over to your side." He moved toward the headboard. "When you push up, I'll support your back."

His gut felt like he'd been cut in two, but he managed to sit upright.

Rocco lowered the bed rail and swung Eric's left leg over the side. He took one look at Eric's face, and his mouth tightened. "Sit there for a couple of minutes to let your blood pressure equalize."

Even nodding brought a fresh onslaught of pain.

"You ready to tackle the next step?"

"Yeah." Eric mumbled through clenched teeth.

"I'm going to swing your bad leg over." Rocco scratched his head and gave Eric an apologetic look. "No way around it. This sucker's gonna hurt."

Eric braced himself and tried to picture what he'd do if his dad were in the room. The mind game worked until his leg cleared the bed. Blood pulsated down, sending shafts of pain searing through every nerve. He cried out, and his hand gripped the edge until his knuckles blended with the white of the sheet.

"Might be too soon, man."

"No." His chest strained against the bandages as his breaths came in short gasps. "I can do it."

"Hold on. I'll move the wheelchair closer."

Eric shook his head and nodded to the corner.

Rocco followed his gaze. "Crutches?"

To Eric's relief, Rocco didn't argue, but walked to the corner to get them. "This crutch under your bad shoulder will probably kill you." He seemed to be thinking out loud. "Tell you what. Put this crutch under your good shoulder, and I'll be the crutch on the other side."

His good shoulder? The one barely healed from Honduras? He conjured one of his father's disapproving looks and positioned the crutch under his left shoulder. Every muscle in his arm flexed and strained to support his body. Rocco steadied him, and for one brief moment he stood.

"Rocco, I—"

"Whoa there, buddy." Rocco caught him before he hit the floor. "Lie back down, and let's try something else."

Twenty minutes of agony, and he was back to square one. Eric cursed his weakness but didn't argue when Rocco returned with an oval-shaped bed pan. Toby called it right. Eric always had to learn the hard way. A cold sweat came over him. He turned his head, and hot liquid spewed out of his mouth.

Rocco ran to the bathroom and returned with a cool compress and a container he placed by Eric's mouth.

"Sorry." Eric moaned between gasps.

"No problem. It's what I'm here for. Hey, I'll be right back. Don't move, or you'll fall off the bed."

Eric lay in a miserable heap clutching the side of the bed as if his life depended on it. He didn't bother opening his eyes when Rocco returned.

"Relief's on the way, dude. This Phenergan works fast." He sponged Eric's face. "I'm going to move you away from the edge."

Eric was no help as Rocco inched him back to the middle of the bed. He must have dozed. The next time he opened his eyes, the angel stood beside his bed, her hair loose, free, and hugging her shoulders. So pretty.

She smiled at him. Did he say that out loud too?

Soft fingers applied pressure to the inside of his wrist. She whispered something to the guy standing next to her. What was his name? Rock?

Ellie was almost too tired to shed the baby blue scrubs. She swept her hair up in a ponytail and brushed her teeth. One day down, thirteen to go. Today had been so busy, she'd hardly had time to eat, but somehow Eric never left her mind. Rocco filled her in about how determined Eric was to walk on his own. A man in his condition. How crazy was that? No. More like amazing. A human dynamo. A real hero, according to Toby. And even in his weakened condition, ruggedly handsome enough to make her weak in the knees. That was crazy for sure. The guy worked in a whole different world and probably left a broken heart everywhere he went. She rinsed, wiped her mouth, and then stared at her reflection for a long time. Time to get a grip before this Rambo got a grip on her.

Her body craved sleep, but before she pulled back the covers, she dropped to her knees beside the bed. "Dear Lord, it took me so long to heal from Allen. I don't want that to happen again. Send me a man who loves You. Someone like my dad."

With a tug, she freed her hair and fluffed it before turning out the light. She let herself relax into the mattress with a sigh and whispered into the stillness. "And help Eric."

SAVING ERIC

CHAPTER THIRTEEN

A couple of days later, Rocco helped Eric shave and washed the remnants of matted blood from his hair. Eric brushed his teeth with his good hand, and Rocco helped him into his boxers and athletic shorts.

He sat in the chair so weak he could barely support his head. "Thanks. I feel human again."

Rocco lifted the end of the mattress and tucked the sheet under it. "That's what I like to hear. You're starting to get some color back. For a while there, you blended in with this sheet." He worked fast. "There you go. Ready to get back in bed?"

Eric shook his head. "Not yet."

Rocco piled up the laundry and rummaged in the drawer of the bedside table. He juggled gauze, tape, and scissors, and used his foot to push a stool closer to Eric. He straddled the seat and leaned over to inspect Eric's leg. "I'm going to move it out just a little."

Eric gripped the arm of the chair and tried to hide the wince as Rocco cut away the soiled bandage.

"I arrived only a few days before Toby brought you here. I'm part of a short-term medical missions team." Doctors must be trained to talk to their patients during procedures. Or maybe Rocco liked to talk. Not that he minded. Doc was right. Rocco was easy to like.

With the bandage removed, Eric had his first look at his leg. The skin above his knee was swollen and below it, a mutilated purple and red block of throbbing agony.

He shifted in his seat hoping for relief. "So you're a doctor?"

Rocco looked up with a lopsided grin. "Almost. Would have been done, but I took a year off to work in a research program. I'll finish my rotations next spring." He applied what must have been an antibiotic, wrapped some gauze around the knee, and worked his way down.

Eric almost came out of his chair.

"Sorry. I know this hurts." He stopped wrapping and looked up. "You want a stick to bite."

Eric laughed. "Doc said you'd have me in stitches."

"Stitches, huh?" He grinned. "Good one. Wish I'd thought of it first."

"You ... come here ... as ... humanitarians?"

"You could say that. Our church back home has partnered with Dr. Brock for over twenty years. There's actually a waiting list."

Rocco secured the tape at the bottom, and Eric released his death grip on the arm of the chair. "I don't get it. I've traveled all over the world, but I've never met anyone like the people around here."

This time Rocco laughed. "I guess that makes us even. I don't think any of us have met someone like you."

"Eric, my man."

No mistaking the voice. Eric shifted toward the door. "Toby, come in. My personal valet just finished cleaning me up."

Toby's eyes widened. "No way. You didn't make a joke. Tell me you didn't just make a joke." He looked at Rocco. "Whose blood did you pump into him?"

Eric gave them both a wry smile. "Very funny."

Rocco pivoted on his stool. "How's your leg today?"

"Oh, you know me. I don't complain." Toby exaggerated his limp.

Rocco rolled his eyes and shook his head. "Hobble over here and take my place. I've got to get busy, or Ellie'll come looking for me." He stood and placed his hand on Eric's shoulder. "Later, dude."

Toby eased down on the stool and propped his leg on the bedrail. "You're looking good. A lot better than you did."

Enough of the small talk. "How far are we? Any chance they could trace us back here?"

"Nah. No way. We're in central Angola."

Angola. One country over. "How far in?"

Toby scratched his head and looked around the room as if searching for the answer. "I don't think it has a name. Somewhere to the south of Luanda."

"Until they find a body, Reznik and his thugs will keep digging."

"Your dad will think you're dead."

"With luck, they'll all think I'm dead." He needed a clear head. And he needed a plan. "You'd better get back to your job. Stay away for a while. No calls."

His friend pursed his lips and nodded. "Yeah. I guess you're right. But I'll keep my ears open." Toby cracked his knuckles and rose to go. "You're in good hands. Take care.""

"Watch your back, Tobe." Eric braced for the parting slap on the back, but Toby's hand stopped in mid-air and in one smooth transition swung over to Eric's left shoulder to give it a gentle squeeze.

"I'll show up sometime and check on you."

Toby left after a quick fist bump, and Eric gauged the distance to the window. He could do it. Might be slow, but he had to try. He maneuvered off the chair and steadied himself with one crutch. Sweat covered his face by the time he crossed to the window to get his first glimpse of the outside. Grass and shrubs extended to a red dirt and gravel road, apparently the only access to the area. Across the road, a field covered with patches of shrubs and vegetation stretched to a line of trees. The rolling hills behind the trees surrounded the tan stucco buildings on the compound. One building almost directly across the road from his room stood apart from the rest and looked like a small house. Windows lined the side he could see and a raised cross hung over the double doors. Of course. A mission hospital would have a chapel.

He leaned closer to the window and craned his head to get a better view. The dirt road squeezed between the chapel and what seemed to be a warehouse with windows. Cement steps with a metal handrail led to double screen doors. Movement caught his eye. An African national flung open the door as a short blond woman shot out of the building. Even from this distance, he couldn't mistake the concern etched in her profile. The dark man followed. Too short to be Moses. They disappeared down the road beside the chapel. Within seconds, the man came back into view carrying a child. The little head fell limp from the man's arm.

Eric's gaze remained glued to the corner of the chapel. His fingers tightened on the handgrip of his crutch. Where was she? Two men he didn't recognize sprinted out and went down the same road carrying a gurney. Then Ellie reappeared. Blood and red dirt soiled the front of her scrubs. The men followed with an unconscious woman on the gurney.

Only after they re-entered the building did he relax his grip and take a full breath. Pain shot up his leg and reminded him he'd been up too long. By the time he made it back to the bed, his breathing came in heaves as if he were on the last stretch of a marathon. He sat on the edge, and the next thing he knew, Ellie was calling his name.

He opened his eyes. Ellie stood before him. No dirt or blood. Had he dreamed it?

"Let me help you." Her hand was gentle on his bandaged arm.

He tried but couldn't seem to move. Her face came in full view as she bent to eye level. "I'm going to raise you to a sitting position."

She moved into place before his mind registered her words. Cool fingers slid under his neck. "Don't turn on your back. It'll pull your stitches less if you roll up sideways."

He tightened his gut as much as he could without crying out. She did most of the work and somehow managed to get him upright. Her hand remained on his shoulder. "Catch your breath."

Good idea. He breathed deeply. A clean smell clung to her. Sweet. Like perfumed soap. Not overpowering. She stepped away and poured some water from a plastic container into a cup.

"Before we try to move you again, take this."

His pain pill. Must be close to six o'clock. Her hand held the cup, and she guided the straw to his mouth. He downed the pill and drank all the water. His body craved more.

"Thank you." His voice sounded weak even to his ears.

She smiled and placed the cup on the bedside table. "You were thirsty." As if reading his mind, she added, "I'll give you more when I get you settled back in bed."

She sat in the chair across from his bed and rubbed her eyes.

"I saw you this afternoon."

Her hand dropped, and her brow furrowed.

"Out there." He gestured with a nod of his head. "You and another man. I don't think it was Moses."

She looked at the window and back to him. "How did—" the confused look cleared and she gave a brief nod. "Oh. Rocco got you out of bed. Looks like he cleaned off the rest of the blood too."

The pill worked its magic. The pain lessened, and his tongue loosened. "Looks like you got the blood off you too."

She scanned the front of her t-shirt as if she expected the blood to still be there. She raised her head. Dark smudges he had missed before shadowed her eyes.

"Yeah. Off me at least. It might become a permanent part of my scrubs. They're in my room soaking."

"What happened?"

Her gaze dropped. Maybe he shouldn't have asked. Violation of patient/doctor privacy must be universal.

"A Mingazi woman fought a panther that had attacked her son." Ellie spoke before he could apologize. She swiped a tear halfway down her cheek. "Sorry. I can usually detach, but mothers fighting for their children get me every time."

He slammed down the memory of his own mother and focused on Ellie's words.

"That woman somehow found the strength to carry her son for miles." Her lower lip trembled. "She died before we could get her off the gurney. It's like she was holding on just to get him here."

"What about her son?"

Ellie shook her head. "Rocco tried for over ten minutes to resuscitate him." The raw emotion displayed across her face gave way to a tremulous smile. "At least she didn't live to see that."

The twinge wrenching his gut had nothing to do with his injuries. "Tough day." Lame, but it was all he could think of to say.

"Yeah." She rose and opened the drawer of his bedside table. "But we save more lives than we lose. That's what makes it bearable." She took out the blood pressure cuff and stethoscope. "I'll check your stats and then help you stretch out on the bed. You must be exhausted." The thermometer she stuck under his tongue prevented his reply. With the cuff in place on his left arm, she pumped it until every vein on his forearm protruded. He sat still and counted as blood pulsated past his ear. The cuff came off, and he almost bit through the thermometer when she slid the end piece of the stethoscope across strategic places on his chest. She leaned closer and part of her hair brushed across his face.

"Your heart rate is elevated."

No kidding.

She took the thermometer and held it at eye level. "A little over one hundred. Not unusual for nighttime." After jotting something down on his chart, she chunked the plastic sleeve from the thermometer into the trash and put the rest of the instruments back in the drawer. "Rocco will be here soon. You want me to help you get settled before he gets here?"

"No. That's okay. I'll wait for him."

She nodded. "I'll try to track him down and hurry him up."

"You don't have to. The pain pill kicked in."

Her face softened. "Thanks for asking about this afternoon. It helped to talk about it."

His mind clicked off possible replies. No problem. Anytime. My pleasure. In the end, he smiled and gave her a brief nod. Good call.

She took his hand. Her fingers were warmer. "Sleep well. I'll check on you tomorrow."

The sweet scent of her lingered long after she left the room. He replayed their conversation, surprised at his own reaction. Seen through Ellie's eyes, those innocent victims had pierced his death-hardened armor. And not just them. Miss Ellie Whitfield, the angel with a heart full of compassion, threatened to break past his self-imposed barrier to stay detached. What was he thinking? She saved lives. He took them. No way would he stand a chance with her.

"Hey, man, sorry it took me so long."

For once, he welcomed the chance to get back in bed. "No problem. Ellie mentioned you'd had a busy afternoon."

"For sure. We've been slammed since Doc left a couple days ago."

Rocco helped him to the bathroom and then settled him into bed.

"I'll check on you later."

"No need." The guy was a walking zombie. "Just leave a pain pill, and I'll be good 'til morning."

"You sure?"

Eric nodded.

Rocco checked the chart. "Will do, pal, but don't take it until at least two." He placed the pill and a bottle of water on the edge of the bedside table and then flipped off the light. "See you in the morning."

The movement stirred up his angry leg. It would be a long night.

~~~~~~

Ellie closed the door and leaned against it. Her cheeks expanded with the deep breath she slowly released. What a day. God must be testing her. Took every bit of her self-control not to lose it in the clinic. Bless Rocco. He must have known. Somehow she managed to keep it together until she made it back to her room.

And then Eric. Why was this guy getting to her? Probably because he was forbidden fruit. Yeah, the whole wanting-what you-can't-have syndrome. Or maybe it was the way he seemed to hang on every word she said as if he could see into her soul. Either he was a good actor or—

No. She wouldn't go there. The vertebrae popped as she twisted and stretched. She didn't bother undressing but fell across the bed kicking her shoes off and listening to the twin thumps hit the concrete floor. She was just exhausted. That was all. Nothing to do with Eric. Or that she was vulnerable. And lonely.

CHAPTER FOURTEEN

The next day, Eric opted to stay in the recliner by the bed when Rocco went back to the clinic. He'd have to ask if they had any books around here. Anything to take his mind off his dead-end thoughts.

A door closed and someone with a light tread walked down the hall. He glanced at the clock. Earlier than usual.

"Good morning." Ellie came closer and placed her hand on his shoulder. Seemed to be the standard greeting around here. Must be some kind of therapeutic touch. Not that he minded. She smiled. "You look better. Sleep well?"

"I did. Thanks."

"That's good. I was a little worried. Thought I'd check on you before going over to the clinic." She picked up his chart and sat on the edge of his bed. Her forefinger slid down the page, and then she glanced up at him. Her crooked smile revealed a very prominent dimple on her right cheek.

He tried not to stare. How had he missed it?

"When you're stronger, I'll take you for a little walk. There's something I want to show you."

"Let's go now." He pushed up from the chair and reached for the shirt Rocco had placed on the end of the bed.

"Oh." Her blue eyes grew larger. "I don't know. You don't need to rush it."

"I'm going crazy in here." Eric balanced on his good leg and fumbled with the shirt. He stopped and turned. "You probably don't have time." He started to ease back into the chair. "It can wait."

She bounced up. "I have time. Let me help you." She took his right hand. "Relax your fingers, and I'll slip your hand through this sleeve."

He closed his eyes and breathed in the clean scent of her hair.

"Eric?" She stood before him poised with his other sleeve. With her guiding him, he maneuvered his arm through the narrow tunnel of cloth. Her fingers lightly traced the scar on his good shoulder. "What happened there?"

He glanced down. The Honduras scar. Ugly and jagged. "Another skirmish I got myself into."

He raised his head and their eyes locked before she whipped around to hand him his crutch. He didn't bother with the buttons since most of his chest was still covered with gauze.

"Thanks." He wasn't sure what fascinated him more. Her blush or her attempt to hide it.

Simon DoRight perched on his shoulder. *Back off and stop flirting.*

"Toby told us you work for the CIA."

"Toby has a big mouth." So did Simon.

"He had to explain about all those bullet wounds. Dad asked if you had done something illegal." The dimple appeared again. "He said Toby stopped dead and almost fainted."

Eric gripped his side. "Don't make me laugh."

"Sorry. Feels like it's ripping your gut, doesn't it?" She went to the closet to get his shoes and gave him a sideways glance. "So, you're a spy? Like James Bond or something?"

"Not even close. His gadgets are way cooler."

She chuckled. "Why don't you sit down, and I'll help you with your shoes, uh, shoe." She knelt on one knee in front of him. "Okay. Hand me your foot."

Eric moved his foot toward her and stopped midair.

"What's wrong?"

"I hate being helpless."

"You're not helpless. You're injured." She took his foot gingerly into her hands. "I'll try not to hurt you." Ellie bit her lower lip as she placed the shoe on his foot and propped it up on her thigh to tie it. Her hair provided a wavy curtain around her face as she focused on her task. When she finished, she stood with hands on her hips and a satisfied grin on her face. "There."

He shifted to stand, but Ellie sat, apparently in no hurry for their walk. "So, what exactly does a spy do?"

"I could tell you but…" He gave her his best straight-faced stare.

Her eyes widened and she blurted out, "You'd have to kill me?" A lyrical laugh escaped from the enchanting pixie on the edge of his bed. She seemed to have no clue what she was doing to him. "I asked for that one." She hopped up and extended her hand. "You ready for that walk now?"

Ready and willing but not quite able. He couldn't hide the grimace as he struggled to stand. Ellie rushed to his side to steady him.

"Eric, you're not up to it today." She turned his body and pushed him onto the bed with a single nudge.

He held up a hand in protest. "I am. Let me try again."

Ellie hesitated holding the crutch. "Tell you what. It's almost time for more pain medication." She left, but quickly returned with an enormous pill and a glass of water. She smiled as she placed it in his hand. "Sit for a while and let it take effect." She took his glass and set it on the table beside the bed. Her eyes strayed to his chest. "I was a little worried when Toby brought your clothes."

"Worried?"

This time she met his gaze. "I was afraid you'd try to bolt again."

He tried not to laugh. It hurt too much. "No, ma'am." He rasped out the words. "I promised your dad I would behave and not give you a hard time."

Her face softened. "Dad spoils me."

He could see why. "Must have been great growing up with a dad like him."

She looked down and fidgeted with a fingernail. "I didn't actually grow up around him." She tucked a strand of hair behind her ear. "I've only recently reconnected with him."

Smooth, Templeton. He scrambled for words. "I'm sorry."

She raised her head, and her eyes narrowed as if she were in deep thought. "But don't form a bad opinion of my dad. My mother left him when I was three. He always supported us well though. Too well, really. I grew up very spoiled."

The medication kicked in and knocked Simon off his high horse. Barriers came down, and he plunged in. "No way. I've seen spoiled women. You aren't one of them."

She dropped her gaze and resumed work on the fingernail. "Thanks. I've changed a lot since I've been here."

"I don't want to pry, but I'm confused. How could a mission doctor make enough to support his family?"

"Dad wasn't always a missionary."

"He made money before he came here?"

"Millions."

His poker face deserted him.

"But he didn't make millions. He inherited them. I'll tell you the whole story sometime but—"

"You'll have to kill me?" He was fast becoming putty in her hands.

"Oh, you're good." Her eyes danced until his hand clutched his right side. "Sorry. I promise I won't make you laugh again. I couldn't resist."

"No. It's worth it. I haven't laughed in a very long time, and yes, I want to hear the whole story."

"It's a great story, one that would rival some of your spy tales."

He grinned. "He didn't do anything illegal, did he?"

Ellie's face fell. Not the response he expected. In fact, no response at all. He scrambled for some kind of damage control only he didn't know what damage he'd done.

"Um, no. His millions are legit." She stood, her face unreadable. "Ready for that walk now?"

Ready or not, he seized the chance to redeem himself. He nodded and took the crutch from her.

"Good, we'll take it slow. Rest your arm on my shoulder, and I'll help balance your bad side."

Ellie smiled up at him as she wrapped her arm around his waist. Eric for once was thankful for the gnawing pain as he breathed in the scent of her hair.

"Eric, you can lean on me more. You're not hurting me."

No, ma'am, he couldn't. "I'm okay. It feels good to be up."

"I'm glad to hear it because I really want to show you something."

"What?"

"You'll see."

That impish grin of hers taunted him and played havoc with his already irregular breaths. He licked his lips and swallowed hard. "Much farther?"

"No." She stopped short. "Are you okay? Do you need to rest?"

"No. I'm fine."

She stiffened and scanned his face.

"Come on." He leaned forward. "Show me your surprise."

Her hold relaxed as they cleared his doorway and entered the hall. "That's my dad's room there. You're actually right across the hall from him."

A quick glance was all he could spare. Each step produced a new sensation of pain that he refused to acknowledge, especially to her.

"Just through those doors." Her breathing sounded almost as labored as his. "We're an awkward pair. We wouldn't do too well in a three-legged race."

He grinned, but couldn't muster the breath to respond.

Once outside, the landscape gave him the perfect excuse to take a break. Wildflowers, shrubs and grasses surrounded the terrace. Wild, yet tamed as if each cluster had been put there on purpose. Beyond the field, trees stacked up against sloping hills and created a 3-D panorama.

"Wow. Is this what you wanted to show me?"

"Pretty spectacular, huh? But my surprise is over there, in that little shed." She nudged him over to the door, cracked it open, and whispered, "Meet Lucy and her babies!"

Three kittens that looked more like gerbils rooted at their mother's belly. He returned her amused gaze and admitted something he'd never told anyone. "Cats are my weakness."

She nodded as if they shared a secret. "Mine too. Lean on the door a minute." Ellie stooped to pick up a ball of white fur with yellow patches. "This one's the runt." She snuggled the kitten close to her cheek. "And my favorite."

He smiled at Ellie and reached to stroke the fur between the tiny ears. With no warning, the crutch slipped, and his shattered leg fielded the brunt of his weight. Ellie lunged for him with her free hand, and the excruciating pain found a way to double when she grabbed his arm. His vision dimmed as his good leg buckled. He hit the shed and slid to the concrete fighting back every expletive he knew.

Ellie knelt beside him, still clutching the squirming, frightened kitten. "I am so sorry." Her voice sounded far away. "Eric?"

He forced air into his tight chest and opened his eyes.

"I shouldn't have grabbed your arm."

He wanted to reassure her but couldn't unclench his jaw. He closed his eyes again.

"Oh, Eric. You're as white as this shed. Tell me what to do."

"Let me … rest … a minute." He breathed deeply and willed himself to recover. Ellie left and returned with a wet cloth. She knelt beside him and sponged his face.

He couldn't move or talk but managed to open his eyes in time to see a tear spill down her cheek.

"Hey." His voice was barely a whisper.

She shook her head. "I shouldn't have brought you out here. Your shoulder. I feel so bad."

"Put. Weight. On leg." He heaved a breath. "Shoulder's fine." A half-smile was all he could produce. "Worth it."

"Let me see." She planted her hand on the concrete and leaned over his body, using her other hand to push back his shirt. "Your wound's reopened."

He relaxed his head against the doorjamb of the shed. She moved closer seemingly unaware her face was almost touching his.

His good hand reached to smooth back the hair that had fallen across her face, and without thinking it through, he kissed the corner of her mouth right below the dimple. Her lips parted as if she only then realized how close she was. She didn't pull away. Open invitation. Why was he hesitating?

He leaned back, and caressed her cheek tracing the trail the tear had made. "Good thing I'm incapacitated right now, or you'd be in trouble."

To his surprise, she smiled but didn't pull away. "I may be small, but I think I can take you."

"I have no doubt." His admiration of her grew a notch. "Slide that chair over here. I'll try to get into it."

"Okay." She moved quickly and returned holding the chair steady for him. The muscles in his good arm flexed and grew taut as he struggled to push up onto the chair. He groaned and finally sank down into it.

"I should find Rocco."

"Don't go." His gaze flew to her face. "Please."

She hesitated and then pulled a chair beside him. "Take all the time you need."

He closed his eyes and tried to wait out the slowly retreating pain. After a while, he opened them again to find her focused on him. "Have you been staring at me this whole time?"

"Um-hmm. I'm plotting what I'll do if you pass out."

"CPR?"

She shook her head. "It would open every stitch on your chest."

"What then?"

"Just don't pass out."

He shifted and tried to stand.

Ellie jumped up. "Stay there. I'll get a wheelchair for you."

He shook his head. "I think I can make it."

She hesitated but gave him the crutch and then positioned herself on his other side.

No small talk this time. They moved slowly toward his room. Something was wrong. He could feel warm blood oozing through the bandage on his chest, and it hurt to breathe.

He leaned heavily on Ellie. "Hold up a minute."

"Sure." Her eyes were huge. She bit her lower lip. "We're almost there."

He looked toward his door. *Come on, Templeton, man up.* He eased forward and talked, not only to take his mind off his agony but also to set her mind at ease. "Found a stray kitten." Each stilted word stabbed his chest. "Half-starved. Took it home. Fed it. Knew I'd have to get rid of it." He paused to catch his breath. "Sucker for strays. Named it Lucky. Job came up. Left it with Dad. Probably took it out back and shot it."

Ellie stopped, her mouth gaping.

He appreciated the break. "My father hates cats. 'Real men don't own cats.' Determined to make a real man out of me."

"Looks like he did a pretty good job."

"Not really. I like cats."

Her smile warmed him as she tightened her hold around his waist and nudged him the rest of the way. "We made it."

He almost collapsed on the bed. Ellie stepped away and gasped, "Eric, you're hemorrhaging!"

She helped him relax against his pillow and hurried from the room. "Don't move."

Eric nodded but didn't try to respond.

"Guess what?" She returned and grazed an area with an alcohol wipe before sticking a needle into his bicep. "I'm giving you the good stuff."

The morphine worked almost immediately. As soon as he drifted off, Ellie cut away the bandage. The stitches on his side had pulled loose. Easy fix. She applied pressure and whispered a quick prayer that was the only damage done in the fall. After a few minutes, she added a couple of stitches. Not quite as neat as her dad's, but it would do. She secured the new bandage, oddly glad he was out cold. Those dark eyes had the power to penetrate her soul. He must have known she would have welcomed his kiss, yet he didn't try. Spoke volumes for the kind of man he was.

A quick glance at the clock jolted her back to reality. She cleared away the mess and washed her hands and then returned to his bed to raise the rail. Her fingers smoothed back the thick dark hair and lingered on his forehead. She reached for a thermometer and slipped it under his tongue holding it in place against his slack mouth. Concern and years of training kept her mind focused on the task. The mercury still teetered around one hundred. She pulled a stethoscope from a drawer and listened to the wheezing in his chest. They'd have to keep a close watch on him for the rest of the day.

She kneeled beside his bed, folding his limp hand between her own. "Lord." Her heart was full, but no words seemed adequate. "Help him." She put her forehead against his still hand. "And help me."

Ellie and Rocco stayed with him in shifts, but she checked on Eric throughout the day. That evening, she looked in one last time and joined Rocco by the bed. "Still asleep?"

"Yeah." He took the stethoscope from his neck and handed it to her. "Take a listen."

She guided the chest-piece to several places before glancing at Rocco. "Sounds garbled."

"I thought so too."

"I'll be right back." Ellie looked at her watch and grabbed her phone from her pocket. She punched her father's number with shaking hands and used her hip to push open the terrace doors. *Please, God. Let it go through.* With the sound of his mellow "Hello" she released the breath she held. "Sorry to wake you, Dad. It's Eric. He fell earlier today. He's been going downhill ever since."

"Is he running a fever?"

"Low grade. Hasn't dropped below 100. Tachycardic. Oxygen saturation 85% on room air."

"What about his blood pressure?"

"A little low but holding steady."

Her father's deep sigh echoed through the phone. "Okay. Draw blood cultures and check his hemoglobin and hematocrit. If it's dropping, we'll know he's bleeding. Start an IV fluid. A liter or two of bolus. Keep him still."

She straightened and pulled a note pad and pen from her other pocket. "You think he's bleeding internally?"

"Not sure. Oh, one more thing. Check arterial blood gas to find out if the oxygen level we're picking up is real or not. That could clue us in to why his heart rate is accelerated."

Ellie wedged her phone between her shoulder and her ear as she wrote down the instructions. "I'll keep you posted."

"You sound tired."

His sympathetic tone toppled her resolve. She reached for a chair and let out the tears she'd been holding back. She hunched over, one hand clutching her lifeline to her dad, the other covering her drenched face. "Sorry. I'm worried." More like terrified. What if he died? As bad as it was losing the Mingazi mother yesterday, this was worse. This was Eric. And suddenly she realized he was already more than a patient to her. "He'll be all right, won't he, Dad?"

His voice was soft, barely audible. "I don't know."

Not the reassuring words she craved. She pulled up her legs and wrapped her arms around them. "So you're worried too?"

"I'm concerned, yes." She waited for him to finish, hoping for anything to make her feel better. "But I know God is in control."

She should know that too. But God let the mother die yesterday. "I wish you were here." Someone who could do something.

"I know, honey. I'll come if I can. Eric's made it this far. I'm counting on God to pull him through."

Her heart sank. "I hope you're right. Thanks, Dad."

She slipped the phone back into her pocket. The jotted notes were almost illegible. One day, she'd have to ask her dad how to trust God when she was scared to death.

Chapter Fifteen

Ellie rejoined Rocco and showed him the list of instructions. His forehead wrinkled and he held the note sideways.

"Sorry." She took one edge and read through the scribbles.

"On it." Rocco left the room.

Ellie moved to the bed. Each raspy breath a guilty reminder she shouldn't have taken him to the terrace. She took his hand, and his fingers curled around hers.

She leaned closer and whispered, "You're awake."

"Hm." He opened his eyes for a brief moment and gave a weak smile.

Rocco wheeled in the cart containing IV tubing, tape, syringes and two liters of crystalloid for resuscitation.

"Guess what, old man. I'm bringing back your old friend." Rocco inserted the needle and taped it in place. "There. We're gonna get this super juice flowing through you again." He tapped the line to clear any bubbles and adjusted the flow rate. "You haven't been hanging around that Kryptonite again, have you?"

Eric didn't respond.

Ellie remained by his side as he dozed off and on. She sponged his fevered brow between his jerking awake with glazed eyes. By midnight, he started to hallucinate.

Rocco's mouth tightened. "Oxygen saturation getting lower."

Ellie nodded. "Face mask?"

"Yeah."

Ellie bit her lip as she helped Rocco secure it in place. Less than twelve hours ago, they walked the few steps to the terrace. Now, Eric was barely coherent. The next three hours seemed an eternity.

"I'll be back." Ellie cleared the terrace doors and pulled her phone from her pocket. The whirl of an approaching helicopter could mean only one thing. Her dad had come to her instead.

~~~~~

Fear turned to full-blown panic at the sight of Ellie running across the compound to the helicopter. She reached him before the blades stopped rotating, and he braced for the worst.

"Oh, Dad. I'm so glad you're here. His fever's spiking."

The whine of the rotating helicopter blades faded as they slowed to a stop. Toby waved them on. "Go on, Doc. I've got your bags. I'm right behind you."

He nodded and hurried off with Ellie.

Rocco looked up as he and Ellie sprinted into Eric's room. "Thank God. The cavalry's arrived. His fever's 104.2. Heart rate hasn't dropped below one hundred thirty. Pulled out his IV twice. He's in and out."

He registered Rocco's update, never taking his gaze off Eric. He took the chart and pored over Eric's vitals from the last twelve hours. "O2 below ninety percent."

"Yeah. I drew the ABG. His partial pressure of oxygen was fifty-five on six liters nasal cannula."

Brock reached over the bed rail and placed his hand on Eric's chest. "It's worse than I thought. Oxygen's getting to his lungs but not to his bloodstream."

Rocco's mouth thinned. "Blood clot?"

"That's my guess."

Eric jerked and tried to sit up. His hand flung up as he gripped the guardrail. For a brief moment, he opened his eyes.

"Eric, it's Dr. Brock. Can you hear me?"

Langley. Dark, empty. Must make it to Dad. Footsteps closing in. Hands grab. Can't break free.

Brock stood back as Rocco wrestled Eric's flailing arm. "Man, he's one strong dude. Toby, help me hold him down."

"Careful for the IV, men. Ellie get the flush." Brock grabbed her wrist as she turned toward the door. "And the code cart."

Ellie's eyes grew wide. "The code cart?"

"Just a precaution." One he prayed wouldn't be needed.

Hands at my throat. Can't breathe. Must fight harder. The floor crumbles under my feet—I fall—hard.

Ellie pressed her fingers tight against Eric's neck to check his pulse. His body spasmed and then collapsed back to the sweat-drenched mattress. Toby and Rocco released their hold. The racing pulse she felt frightened her more than his stillness. "Heart rate one fifty."

"Turn the oxygen on fifteen liters. Get the respiratory box out of the code cart." Her dad placed the ambu bag mask over Eric's nose and mouth. "Ellie, draw up versed, succinylcholine, and profofol. We have to intubate him."

Not a pit. A dungeon. Cold. A door opens. A familiar silhouette fills the doorway. "Dad?" Must get up. "Dad, you came."

Dad's face morphs into Tom Reznik. He comes closer, carrying an axe. He shoves me down, and I slide backward to get away. Reznik laughs as I back up to the wall with nowhere to escape. He swings the blade over his shoulder to strike. My eyes close, and I tense for the blow.

"Enough!"

A voice like a thunderclap penetrates the room. A stranger steps out of the shadows and takes the axe. Reznik's form melts into the floor. The stranger holds out his hand.

"Come."

～

"We're losing him."

A stabbing fear pierced Brock's heart. *Please, Jesus.* Not on his watch. He grasped the laryngoscope and slung the ventilating bag on the bed. He pried open Eric's mouth. "Ellie, tube."

No hesitation, her shaking hands placed the clear, curved endotracheal tube into his waiting palm. Brock took it and guided it deep into the back of Eric's throat.

"Pull the stylet," he ordered as he slipped it past the vocal cords into the trachea. "Rocco, hold the tube at his teeth. Don't let it move. Ellie, bag for me."

He glanced over at the wide-eyed black man huddled in a corner of the room. "Toby, mark the time."

～

I try to stand but my leg buckles under me.

The stranger scoops me into his arms.

He walks toward a door which shines with a brilliant light. Warmth courses over me as I meet the man's gaze.

The stranger smiles and gestures to someone beyond the doorway.

"Nicholas, this is Eric."

The man called Nicholas rushes over, and the stranger places me into his arms.

～

Brock reached for the stethoscope hanging from the IV pole. He couldn't bear the fear in his daughter's eyes any more than the silence emanating from the stethoscope on Eric's chest.

"Keep bagging Ellie." He spoke as he began chest compressions. Shoulders firm, elbows straight, hand clasped over hand. His upper body rocked rapidly with the rhythm.

Please God. Not now. Not Eric too.

A smiling woman and a young girl walk over to us. The woman is beautiful. I can't take my eyes off her. She releases the hand of the child to touch my face.

"Eric."

She speaks my name. Such a lovely voice. Love emanates from the man and woman. She raises my hand to her lips and then holds it against her cheek. The child slides between the man and the woman.

"Eric, you're here."

The stranger picks her up, and she wraps her arm around his neck. She touches the stranger's face and turns it to her. "Can he stay?"

His words were gentle. "No, sweet one. Not yet."

Brock held his chest compressions, giving the defibrillator time to detect any electrical activity originating from Eric's heart. "Hold the respirations."

Only a narrow green ribbon raced across the screen, a flat line. No shocks or defibrillator would help this rhythm. Only CPR and drugs could give him a chance.

"Rocco, epinephrine and atrophine."

A lifetime of regrets settled between Brock's shoulders as he resumed compressions with greater urgency. "Come on, son. Stay with us. And one, and two, and three ..."

"It's time to go back."

My hands clutch his garment. "No, I can't go back."

"You must." The stranger smiles and gently pries my fingers loose. "It's not your time."

"I'll be alone again. Please. Let me stay."

The stranger's hands cup my face, and he looks into my eyes. "I tell you the truth. You will not be alone. I will be with you. You will not see me, but you must trust me. I will be with you."

The stranger releases my hand.

"Rest now, Eric."

I fall from his arms and gasp for air.

∿∿∿∿

Sweat poured down his face as Brock pumped Eric's still form.

"Hold your compressions." Rocco held up a palm. "I think I feel a pulse."

Brock lifted his hands and waited, barely breathing.

Rocco nodded. "He's definitely got a pulse."

A rapid fury of peaks and valleys now replaced the once thin flat line on the monitor. Brock moved back from Eric's chest. "Thank you, Jesus."

"Check his blood pressure, Ellie, and get the ventilator. Put him on assist control. Rocco, secure the tube. He'll need sedation. Bolus him with IV fluid."

Brock grabbed the nearest chair and collapsed into it. Ellie connected the ventilator tubing to the endotracheal tube and met Brock's eyes over Eric's bed. No words were needed. She nodded, and he stood to position the stethoscope to the center of Eric's chest. Fast, strong. He moved over the lungs. Left lung coarse and garbled. Pneumonia?

"Rocco, keep him on antibiotics. And grab the heparin from the pharmacy. I'm worried he might have a pulmonary embolism."

Brock moved around the bed and put his arm around Ellie. She leaned into his embrace lifting her hand from the guardrail to his chest.

Rocco barreled back into the room. "Man, what a save."
He hung the fluids on the IV pole.

Brock glanced over to Toby, still hovering in the corner
and uncharacteristically quiet. "How long?"

"Two minutes, eighteen seconds."

SAVING ERIC

CHAPTER SIXTEEN

Sunlight filtered through the closed blinds. Eric squinted as he opened his eyes. Rocco stood beside his bed switching out IV fluids.

"Man, it's good to see you." Rocco felt for his pulse and then raised the earpiece of the stethoscope to listen to his chest. "Now, that's what I like to hear." He removed it from his neck and hung it on the IV pole. "Welcome back."

Eric's swollen throat made swallowing difficult. His jaw felt bruised as if he'd been hit a few times. He attempted to ask Rocco about it, but by the time he could form the words, Rocco spoke again. "I was given strict orders to find somebody the minute you woke up." With a pat to Eric's hand, he left the room.

Eric moved his hand over his chest. Maybe the same two-by-four that hit his jaw clipped him in the ribs too. He winced as his fingers found a tender spot. Light footsteps raced down the hallway, and his breath caught when Ellie cleared the doorway. She rushed to his bed and swooped up his hand with both of hers. "Eric—" Tears welled up and choked her words. She lifted a forefinger and gave him a sheepish grin. "Give me a minute."

There wasn't much else he could do, not knowing what happened or what to say. Except the obvious. "Being around me"—Could the hoarse, guttural voice be his?—"seems to make you cry."

"I know." She laughed as she wiped her cheek with the back of her hand and then reached for a tissue. "Crazy, isn't it?"

Crazy all right. "You remember what I did the last time you cried?"

Her smile told him she remembered very well.

"Come. Sit by me."

She turned to slide the chair closer.

"No." He patted the bed. "By me."

She released the chair but didn't move. "I'm afraid I'll hurt you."

He raised his elbow to make more room, and after a moment's hesitation, she eased by his side. The tears had stopped, but her wet eyelashes spiked against her deep blue eyes. Her sweet innocence caught him in a spell, and no voice, not even Simon's, could make him tear his gaze from her.

She took his hand and held it on her lap. "Your last setback scared me to death."

"What happened?"

"We think a blood clot broke loose and went to your lungs. You had pneumonia. Your fever went off the charts. You even hallucinated."

"Hallucinated?"

"Yeah. It took both Rocco and Toby to hold you down."

"Toby?" Eric narrowed his eyes, trying to remember. "I thought he left."

"He did. He flew Dad back."

Eric lifted his hand and rubbed his eyes. "Everything's jumbled up. I can't think straight." He moved his hand and met her gaze. "Could I have some water?"

The bed shifted as she rose to get it. She returned and guided the straw between his lips. "Here you go." Her fingers were cool on his cheeks as he drained the glass. She placed the empty cup on the table, reclaimed her spot beside him and found his hand again. "We shouldn't have gone to the terrace." She wouldn't look at him. "It's my fault you had that setback."

His effort to turn and look her full in the face proved futile. "You didn't exactly twist my arm."

She winced and gave him a crooked grin. "Actually, I did."

Stupid choice of words. At least she grinned. "Like I said before, worth it."

"Good try. But it was too soon. I went against my better judgment."

He knew exactly how she felt. He'd been kicking himself ever since the night of the ambush. He could at least steer the conversation away from her self-imposed guilt. "So are you a nurse or a doctor?"

"Technically, neither. Or both. Depends on your perspective. I'm a physician assistant. Back in the States, I was the person who did most of the work while the actual doctor got most of the money. But here, Dad works circles around me."

He wanted to hear more. Her words calmed him, made him breathe better. He asked her another question, one that would take a while to answer. "What keeps you in Africa?"

She shifted and slid her knee toward his chest and then crossed her other leg on top. "It might seem silly, but Africa gets in your soul almost."

"Not silly. I've thought the same thing."

She smiled, mostly with her eyes.

"What about it gets in your soul?" He'd keep asking questions. Anything to keep her from leaving.

Her gaze traveled from him to the wall behind his bed as if she were picturing what to say. "I'd have to say the children. Big trusting eyes. Smiles that seem to spread from one ear to the other."

Her soft voice and her fingers kneading his had an almost hypnotic effect on him. He fought to keep his eyes open.

"It's hard to lose one. Dad said when he first came here, many children died from a cholera outbreak. He waged a one-man campaign to get clean water to the villages surrounding our area."

She quit talking. He turned his head. His brows lifted, dragging with them his heavy lids.

"I need to quit rambling and let you rest."

He shook his head. "I like to hear you talk." He wouldn't care if she read a dictionary. "How long have you been working with your dad?" Proof he'd been paying attention.

"Um. About a year and a half."

He bypassed Simon's warning and barreled ahead. "You got a guy in the States waiting for you to come back home?"

Silence. Her gaze dropped to the hand holding his.

"Sorry. None of my business."

"No, it's okay. No guy." With a gentle squeeze, she released his hand and stood. "Well, I've got to get busy." She raised the bedrail. "Get some rest." At the door, she paused and grinned back at him. "Next time, you're doing the talking."

At least, he hadn't driven her away for good. Lesson learned. When the next time rolled around, he'd better listen to Simon.

CHAPTER SEVENTEEN

"Hey, man." Rocco's voice jolted Eric awake. "Somebody here wants to meet the compound celebrity."

A short, wiry man approached and placed his hands on the bedrail. "It's good to see what you look like without all that blood."

Rocco stood beside him, his arms crossed. "This is Will. One of the guys who brought you in."

Eric shifted and nodded his thanks.

"I've been with Moses in the villages. Heard we missed the excitement."

Rocco went to the foot of the bed. "Want me to raise your head?"

"Sure." The rasp hadn't disappeared.

"I won't miss these hand-cranked hospital beds when we go back home. How's that?"

"Good." The manual lever creaked as Rocco pushed it under the bed. He straightened and moved closer to Will. "You're finally getting some color back into your ghostly self. Feel like getting spruced up?"

"Yeah. That'd be great."

"Okay, pal. You're getting the works." Rocco stepped into the bathroom and grabbed the supplies from under the sink. "Will, get the gauze and tape. Hey, you should tell Eric some of the stuff you told me. You had some excitement of your own."

Will rummaged in the drawer as he talked. "This was my first experience with a mobile medical unit. Pretty primitive conditions."

The guys worked together as Will rattled off details.

"Our truck had a close call with a rhino. We stalled out in his territory. Moses didn't seem too worried, probably because the rhinos were on my side. We finally made it. Villagers came out of nowhere. We hardly had time to eat. Wiped all three of us out. Even the hard cots and the mosquitoes couldn't keep us awake."

"There you go." Rocco secured the last adhesive on the chest bandage. "Will, slide that chair over here while I get the sheets." He looked at Eric. "Can you handle sitting for a few minutes while Will and I change your bed?"

The room swirled as they helped him transition to the chair. The setback Ellie talked about must've been a doozy. Rocco put toothpaste on a toothbrush and handed it to Eric.

"Tackle this, and we'll tackle your bed."

His body felt like jelly. He propped his elbow on the arm of the chair and lowered his head to meet his hand. He closed his eyes. Toothpaste had never tasted so good.

Will grabbed the other end of a sheet. "There was a man with a big tumor growing out of his neck." He gestured with his hands. "It looked like he was growing another head or something. Good thing Doc was still there to tackle that one. Some of the villagers call him the miracle worker."

Will tucked in the top sheet and sat at the foot of the bed. Rocco retrieved the toothbrush and placed a glass of water in Eric's hand. Eric stared at the glass willing his hand to move.

"Hold it. I forgot something." Rocco grabbed a straw from a drawer and plopped it in the glass. He wrapped his hand around Eric's and helped lift the water to his mouth. "Sorry, man. I might be rushing things a bit. Here's your pain pill. Wash it down, and I'll take your glass." He used the wet towel to wipe Eric's mouth.

"Not many people know that Doc is rich," Will continued. "You'd never know it by looking at him."

Eric shook his head. Will would never make it as an agent. The guy was a goldmine of info and almost as loose-lipped as Toby.

"Only child and heir to what was once Whitfield Oil. All his inheritance is in a trust set up to sustain this clinic. Pretty nice by African standards." Will glanced at Rocco. "Wish we could come more often, don't you?"

Eric put two and two together. "You came here together?"

Rocco nodded. "We arrived three days before you. Man, you're one resilient dude. I'm telling you, when your heart stopped the other day, I wasn't sure we could get you back."

"My heart stopped?"

"Doc went to work. CPR on steroids." Rocco gave a visual demonstration mimicking the moves. "He was like a machine."

Eric's stomach clenched.

"It was crazy. Longest two minutes of my life. The whole room stopped breathing with you. I guess those villagers are right. Doc is a miracle worker."

"Yeah." His voice was barely a whisper. "I guess so."

"Ready to get back in bed?"

Eric pulled himself out of his stupor. "Not just yet."

"Okay, man, we're outta here then. We'll pop in later."

"Thanks, guys."

"You bet." Rocco gave his shoulder the requisite squeeze and left.

Two minutes. The hallucination. Bits of it flittered through his memory. The dark. The cold. The stranger. He closed his eyes and tried to recall the details. A man. A woman. No face materialized in his memory. But her voice. Almost … angelic. Must've been the drugs.

"Look at you. Out of bed."

How did he miss hearing her come down the hall?

"Looks like Rocco worked his magic on you again."

The only magic in the room came closer and sat on the freshly made bed. No scrubs today. White t-shirt and khaki shorts and hair pulled back in a ponytail. Her legs dangled over the side of the bed, not quite reaching the floor.

"How are you feeling?"

He lifted his head and hoped he looked stronger than he felt. "Happy to be out of bed. Will and Rocco just left. They entertained me with their stories."

"Lucky you. I could listen to them all day. And that reminds me." She grinned and pointed her finger. "It's your turn, mister."

"My turn?"

"To do the talking."

Not his strength. His face must have shown it.

"It doesn't have to be about your work." She bounced off the bed and opened the blinds talking as she went. "Tell me anything. Something safe. Like from your childhood."

"I don't think there'd be much to interest you."

"Let me decide that."

He'd never been with a woman who actually wanted to know something about him. He stalled while his OCD search engine went into overdrive. His childhood. Not much there worth talking about. Especially to a woman he'd like to impress.

Little Miss Determination plopped back on his bed and crossed her arms. "I'm not leaving 'til you tell me something.

He grabbed the first thing he could think of. "Okay. My dad loved old detective movies. So by the time I was fourteen, I had watched every one of the old Sherlock Holmes movies." He gave her a 'there now' grin.

Her face went blank.

"You know, the old black and white movies with Basil Rathbone."

She shook her head.

He'd have to explain before he crashed and burned. "Here's the point. That's when I realized I had this ability to notice things other people miss. It became my hobby. Well, obsession really. Like my superman alter-ego. I'd look for details. Try to get inside people's heads and figure out what made them tick."

"So what kind of details do you look for?"

"Take you for instance." He propped his elbow on the arm rest and shifted to look at her. "You rarely wear your hair the same way two days in a row. And you're right-handed, but when you wear your hair loose, you twirl one of the strands with your left hand especially when something bothers you. You love cats. That one was easy. You leave your room at five each morning and close your door. It sounds different from Rocco's. I have to strain to hear you walk because you're so light on your feet. There's a certain way you hold your mouth that produces a dimple on your right cheek. Sometimes it's a smile but sometimes it's when you're concentrating on something, like when you checked out my shoulder on the terrace. You're sensitive and caring, which makes the health care profession a good one for you. I've seen you cry three times. Each time, it was for someone other than you. You have a quick wit. Your blue eyes sparkle when you laugh and turn darker when you're troubled about something. You express your affection with touch, like your dad. Basically, you're a happy person." And whenever she entered his room, like magic, he was happy too. "So how'd I do?"

Her left hand strayed to her hair as if she'd forgotten it was in a ponytail. She placed her palm on her cheek instead. "Wow. You weren't kidding."

"Obvious things anyone could see." He was still working on the not so obvious. Like what brought her to Africa and why she stayed. And what man had broken her heart.

"I'll have to try it sometime." Her face brightened with her new inspiration. "I can try it today. I'm going with Miriam to a little village across the river in Huambro."

"Miriam?"

"Moses' wife. I don't think you've met her. You would like her."

He nodded, more concerned about another day without Ellie. "What will you be doing?"

"A little bit of everything. Lots of children. Nicci, the girl who does most of the cooking around here, makes cookies and muffins for us to take. We do some basic first aid. In the afternoon, we teach them Bible stories. Those little kids love hearing about Jesus."

Jesus rolled off her tongue as if it were the most natural thing in the world. Reality squeezed his heart. Two separate worlds.

"When will you be back?" He tried to sound curious and not desperate.

"Definitely tonight. We try not to stay overnight." She shuddered making her ponytail swish. "I'm too scared of snakes."

He catalogued her last tidbit of information as she stood and placed her hand on his shoulder.

"I'll come back tonight and tell you about it if you're still awake."

He'd be awake. No matter what.

CHAPTER EIGHTEEN

Eric glanced at the clock when Ellie left the room. Only 0900. An endless day stretched ahead of him. No way around it, he had to get away from this place. Eyes closed, he leaned back in the chair and assessed the situation. A bum leg. A man out to kill him. A woman from a different world. Not many options.

He jerked upright at the touch on his arm. Twice in one day. Definitely slipping.

"Sorry to wake you. I need to check your blood pressure." Doc secured the instruments from the drawer. "Nice to see you in a chair."

"I couldn't take one more hour in bed." Eric lifted his arm as Doc wrapped the cuff around it. "I heard today you saved my life again. You're making a habit of it."

The doctor smiled as he positioned the stethoscope on the crook of Eric's elbow. He listened and jotted something on the chart before meeting Eric's gaze. "You had us very worried. That last episode really tested my faith."

"What happened?"

Brock sat on the bed and faced him. "Your heart stopped. Technically, you died."

Died. The word slapped him in the face and hit him harder than Rocco's account of CPR. His gut tightened. "I think I had some kind of out-of-body experience. It was crazy."

Doc nodded. "Delirium does that. You want to talk about it?"

"No. I want to forget it, and I can't."

"You will. Give it time. Let's get you on the bed. I want to check your leg." Doc helped him stretch on the bed and loosened the flexible cast. "How does your leg feel? On a scale of one to ten, with ten being the worst, how painful is it?"

"Off the chart."

"I was afraid of that." Doc cut away the bandage where the bullet had penetrated the flesh and examined the torpedo-sized leg. "You hide your pain well."

"Not really." Eric ground out the words through his clenched jaw. He clutched the sheet in his hand to keep from coming off the bed and only breathed easier when Doc refastened the cast and reached for a nearby stool.

"Eric, when you first got here, our main objective was to keep you alive. We removed the bullets and pumped blood back into you. But your leg sustained the worst damage." He gestured without touching the area. "The bullet entered here and shattered your tibia. I couldn't patch it." Doc stood and moved closer, folding his hands over the rail. "Here's what we're up against." His expression sobered, and Eric braced. "You need more surgery. Surgery I'm not equipped to perform. Even with surgery, you most likely will have a limp. Worst case scenario, you could lose your leg."

Eric's insides twisted. He had known all along it might come to this, but Doc's words pierced whatever denial he had managed to build.

"I'd like to bring in an orthopedic specialist to take a look. An old colleague of mine. Think about it. I'll make the call as soon as you give me the go ahead."

"I can't lose my leg."

"I know, son. I don't want you to lose it. Your best bet is to let this guy work his magic on you. He's good. I trust him."

Eric scanned the ceiling. Doc's best bet wasn't the guarantee he needed. He turned back and met Doc's gaze. "Make the call."

"I'll call him later today. It's the middle of the night in Chicago."

Eric nodded but didn't respond. He winced when he tried to take a deep breath.

"I may have cracked a rib or two when I was performing CPR."

He blew out what little air he had taken in. He wanted to thank the doctor for saving his life, but he couldn't. Not without losing his grip on the last bit of composure he maintained.

"Is there anything I can get you?"

Eric closed his eyes and shook his head. Doc's hand covered his. Eric welcomed it and resisted the urge to cling to it like a sissy.

"I've seen God do some amazing things since I came to Africa. Try not to worry about your leg. You've already beaten the odds twice. God's not finished with you. Our God specializes in miracles, and I know in my heart, everything is going to work out for you."

For some crazy reason, Doc's words made him feel better. Maybe it was enough that Doc believed it. He managed to open his eyes and croak a weak "Thanks."

"Now, before I go, I'm going to give you something stronger for pain."

Relief, even if temporary, coursed up his arm. Doc held his hand and remained with him as he drifted off. A comfort he would never have requested, but one he wouldn't refuse, just like all the other gestures of affection from these good people. It was the drug talking. He knew it but didn't care. His fingers tightened around the hand that held his. Just for a little while, he'd let himself—

He slept hard and woke with a jolt, waking Rocco who dozed in the recliner by the bed.

"Hey, man. You been awake long?"

"No. Just woke up. Slept like a rock."

"Yeah. I didn't have the heart to wake you to check your vitals, so I squeezed in a quick nap myself." Rocco yawned and laced his hands, stretching them over his head.

Eric watched with envy and silently cursed his own disabled body.

"Roc, help me up."

"Sure thing, pal." He handed Eric a crutch and then positioned himself on Eric's right side. "I'll help you to the bathroom and then go get your supper tray."

Eric paused and gave Rocco a sideways glance. "Don't tell me. Broth and jello."

"You are one sharp dude. Chicken or beef?"

"Surprise me."

Rocco paused at the bathroom door. "Can you maneuver in here 'til I get back?"

"Yeah." His left leg shook from the strain of supporting his whole weight. He steadied himself at the sink and splashed water on his face. On impulse, he leaned over to wet his whole head hoping to wash away his surly mood. Using only his good hand, he towel-dried his hair and then brushed his teeth.

Rocco appeared with his tray. "Beef."

Eric eyed the broth. "You know. I'm still stuffed from lunch."

"Good try. I happen to know you slept right through lunch. Come on, man. I can't return this untouched. Nicci would have my hide."

"Give it to the cat."

Rocco put the tray on the bedside table and straddled the stool. "Tough day?"

Eric labored to the bed and turned. "It shows?"

"No. I'm a professional, trained to spot subtle changes."

Eric smiled. "Sorry. I'm not a good patient tonight."

"You kidding me? You're handling it better than I would."

Eric sat on the bed. "Doc told me the options for this leg. None of them appealing."

Rocco for once didn't crack a joke. "You can handle whatever happens." He took Eric's crutch and propped it against the wall.

"I can't lose my leg."

"You may not have to. But I'm telling you straight. If you lose your leg, you're man enough to deal with it."

Eric looked down. "I'm not dealing with it."

Rocco lowered the bedrail and sat next to Eric. "Things seem worse at night." He handed Eric some applesauce and a spoon. "Try to eat this. I need to give you a pain pill. Might offset your nausea if you have something on your stomach."

Eric took the applesauce and tore the plastic off the top. "Thanks."

"You bet." He left the pill and some water. "I have to do rounds at the clinic. I'll be back later."

The pain pill remained where Rocco had left it. He said too much when he was doped up, and tonight, he needed a clear head. Not once during his career had he ever let himself get close to a woman. Until now.

He couldn't control what happened to his leg. Reznik would have to wait until he was stronger. But he had to get a grip on his feelings for Ellie. Now. Before she got hurt.

〰〰〰〰

The sun had set by the time Ellie backed the jeep up to the clinic. The porch light came on, and Rocco propped open the double doors.

"Welcome back." He jumped over the last step sending a spray of gravel into the nearby grass. "We were starting to get worried."

Moses seemed to come from nowhere and took the box from her. "Rocco and I will unload, Missi. Go now. Nicci left two plates in the warmer for when you returned."

Other than cold water, there was only one thing Ellie wanted. "Great. Miriam and I will take you up on the offer."

She grabbed two bottles from the cooler and handed one to Miriam. As they approached the side door of the staff dormitory, Ellie's steps slowed. "You go ahead. I don't think I can eat right now."

Miriam scanned Ellie's face. "Are you unwell?"

"No. I'm fine. Just a little keyed up."

"Of course." Miriam squeezed Ellie's hand. "It was a good day."

"A very good day." Her gratitude spilled into the hug she gave Miriam. "Tell Nicci thank you for me."

The light from her dad's office made the hallway leading to it seem even darker. Her pace quickened, and by the time she reached his door she was out of breath. Her dad was seated at his desk. He glanced over his reading glasses and waved her in but continued to speak on the phone.

"Order whatever you think you might need and have it shipped to the mission." He jotted something on the notepad in front of him. "That's right. Let me know when you have a date."

Ellie sat and poured some water on her hand to spritz her face. Then she drained the rest of the bottle and tossed it into the trash can. Her dad finished his call and walked around the desk to greet her. "Everything go all right?"

"Perfect." She stood and returned his hug. "They didn't want us to leave."

"Is that why you got in late?"

She shook her head. "I missed one of the turns. We were talking and got distracted. I drove around in circles, terrified I'd run out of gas, and finally found the right road. Thanks to Miriam."

He took a deep breath and blew it out. "I'm glad you made it."

"Had you worried, huh?"

"Not at all." He raised his brows with mock innocence. "Unless you count the times I checked the clock and asked Rocco if you were back yet."

They leaned against his desk, and she looped her arm through his. "I knew you'd come looking for me. It's the only reason I didn't panic."

"Thank God I didn't have to. I was talking to my friend about Eric's leg when you came in."

"What'd he say?"

"He agreed to come take a look. He's going to order the X-ray equipment we'll need and ship it here."

"Good time to upgrade.

He grinned. "Exactly." He twisted slightly and lowered his head to make eye contact. "What's on your mind, Ellie?"

She had almost talked herself out of telling him. "Okay. Can you read everyone's mind or is it just mine?"

"Just the people I care about. But I can't take credit. I knew you wouldn't walk down a dark hallway just to say hello." His eyes softened as he held her gaze. "What's up, honey?"

Her throat tightened as it always did when she was about to cry. She swallowed hard and leaned forward aiming her words to the floor. "When I came here, I didn't think I'd ever love again." She raised her head. "And that was okay because I've never been happier." She dropped her gaze again. "But then Toby brought Eric here, and almost before I realized it, my heart started to feel again."

Ellie peeked to gauge his reaction. He gave her the understanding look she loved. He would hear her out without interrupting no matter how stupid or wrong she was. One of the many ways he differed from her mother.

Ellie propelled herself from the desk and paced. "I tell myself all the right things. But when I'm with him, I just fall deeper." She stopped suddenly and pivoted to face him. "I should stay away from him, shouldn't I?"

He merely smiled and handed her the box of tissues.

She took two, thankful to have something to twist. She dropped back into her chair. "Tell me what to do, Dad."

With one arm supporting the other, her dad clasped his chin and crooked a finger over his mouth as if he were deep in thought. He took his time before answering, as he always did when the answer involved lives. He went to the other chair in front of the desk and pulled it closer. "I don't need to remind you how complicated Eric's life is right now."

She nodded. "It's impossible." She said it to save him the trouble.

"Humanly speaking, yes." He dragged the last word out as if there were more. "But with God, all things are possible."

She scanned his face with a surge of hope. Was he seriously saying she and Eric might have a future together? "I don't understand."

"Honey, Eric needs God. Now more than ever. I think your feelings for him can be a good thing. Pray for him. Share your faith with him."

Panic shattered the fragile hope. Talk to Eric about God? Just thinking about it made her hyperventilate. "I wouldn't know how. What if it made him angry?"

"Then you wouldn't have lost anything, and it would solve the problem of your growing attraction."

Her dad could tell her the truth no matter how painful and somehow find a way to take the sting out of it. He reached across her lap and encased her icy fingers in his warm hand. "But I seriously doubt anything you have to say would make him angry."

"Does anything ever frighten you, Dad?"

He chuckled. "When you first came here, I was terrified."

"Really? You never showed it." Maybe he had, but she'd been too immersed in her own pain to notice. "Why?"

"I wanted so much to get to know you and somehow make up for all the years I missed. But more than that, I wanted to introduce you to the wonderful God I love and serve. I was afraid, just like you are now. In fact, the risk of alienating you even further kept me awake at night."

"I never knew."

"One night, God showed me a verse that turned my whole attitude around." He released her hand and partially rose to reach the Bible lying on a stack of folders on his desk. He flipped through the pages and used his index finger to scan down the columns. "Here it is." He read it aloud. "There is no fear in love, but perfect love casteth out fear."

Not quite the epiphany she hoped for.

"That night, I asked God to give me that kind of love. His love. And boy, did He." He covered his mouth with his hand and tilted his head to look at her. "I felt free. For the first time since your arrival in Africa, I cared more about what you needed and less about what you thought of me."

"I'm glad you never gave up even when I was so unlovable."

"Hurting." He slid his arm around her and nudged her closer. "Never unlovable. And now, Eric is hurting. He needs our love. He needs someone to fight for him."

"Like you fought for me." She kissed him on the cheek and rose to go. "Should I tell him—everything?"

"Only God can answer that. But if you think God can use your story to help Eric, don't hold back."

"Thanks, Dad. You always tell me just what I need to hear."

He rose too and walked with her to the door. "You would've figured it out without me."

"Maybe. But I'm glad I didn't have to. Love you."

Her steps were lighter as she walked down the hall to her room. She closed the door and then dropped to her knees with the same urgency that had driven her to her dad's office.

Perfect love casts out fear.

She knelt beside her bed, the crushing weight in her chest replaced by an overpowering love. "Open Eric's heart to Your truth." Her forehead rested on her folded hands. "And fill the emptiness in my heart when he leaves."

~~~~~~~~

The minute hand had barely moved when Eric checked the clock again. No closing doors. No footsteps. Only constant ticking like drips from a leaky faucet, crickets outside his window, and jaw-splitting pain.

She wasn't coming. The pill lay where Rocco had left it. Eric stood and gripped the edge of the bedside table to steady himself and then balanced so he could open the bottle of water. With one more glance at the clock, he washed down the pill. With any luck, it would knock him out. Fast.

He used the crutch to push open the bathroom door. Maybe she wasn't back yet. No. She wouldn't travel after dark. He rinsed and wiped his mouth. If the jeep had broken down, Doc would've found her and brought her back. He finished his nightly ritual like a mindless robot.

Giddy relief flooded over him at the sound of movement in his room. She was back. He ran his hand through his hair and then opened the door.

Rocco turned, clipboard in hand. "Looks like you beat me to it. I came to help you get ready for bed."

"Yeah. I'm ready to sink into oblivion." He sat and waited for the drill. Thermometer. Blood pressure. Pulse.

"Hey. Good news." He jotted down the numbers and glanced up. "Regular diet tomorrow. If I know Nicci, she'll make it special for you."

Eric nodded without smiling.

"You want another pill?"

"Just took one." And it started to kick in, replacing the raw edginess with a euphoric sense of well-being. It loosened his tongue and what was left of his usual restraint. "Do you know if Ellie made it back?"

"Yeah. Finally. We were getting a little worried. She rolled in about two hours ago."

Two hours. At least she was back. And safe. Rocco helped him position his leg on the raised pillow and then covered the rest of him with the sheet.

He went to sleep almost immediately and dreamed Ellie came to his room. Waves of golden hair framed her face, like the first time he saw her. She moved in closer and took his hand as she always did. Then the smile, that opened his ribcage and helped him breathe. His beautiful angel. She leaned down and kissed his cheek and then left the room. The dream shifted. Strength returned to his legs and he ran the hills by his apartment. A dark sedan tailed him, and he ducked into an alley. The car screeched but couldn't make the turn. His fingers closed around his gun as he flattened himself against the wall. One shot left. He'd have to make it count. Light footsteps echoed off the building. What was Ellie doing here? He raced toward her as Reznik rounded a corner. A shot rang out and he took a flying leap to push her out of the way. The bullet tore through his leg. He twisted as he fell and took his one shot. Ellie screamed, and he jolted awake trying to suck air into his lungs. No alley and no Reznik. Just his dark room. And the pain. Always the pain.

He ripped away the sheet and gripped the bedrail to pull himself up. This time he took both crutches and cursed as he placed one under his injured arm. He paused at the door to get his bearings and then hung a right toward the terrace doors. Cool air revived him enough to make it to a chair. His breaths came in quick jerks as if he'd actually run those hills by his apartment. He'd never been more desperate or more alone.

The doors creaked behind him, and Eric cut a quick glance back. Doc's unmistakable form moved closer and flailed an outstretched arm until it connected with the chair next to him. "I was walking down the hall when I saw you come out here. Everything all right?"

Eric's fingers tightened around the armrest of the chair. The concern in Doc's voice almost unraveled the last shred of control he held onto.

The guy was good at reading people. He hesitated only a moment and then continued with a detached, almost upbeat tone. "I spoke with my friend. If things go as planned, he'll be here by the end of next week. And that's good. It'll give your other injuries more time to heal."

Eric propped his leg on the table in front of him. "Tell me straight up. Am I going to lose my leg?"

Darkness kept Eric from reading Doc's face. "If there is any possible way to save it, Dr. Robinson will."

Doctor lingo. Meant he was probably going to lose it. Eric forced air into his tight chest. "Listen. My whole life is already mapped out, and there's no contingency for being a cripple. I'm backed into a corner, and I don't see a way out." He wanted a guarantee. Something not even Doc could give.

Doc stood and walked to the edge of the terrace, his silhouette barely distinguishable from the open field across the gravel road. He turned and the darkness seemed to muffle his words. "God specializes in impossible situations, son. He could give you a way out."

Eric figured they'd find a way to preach to him while he was here. He grappled to find a way to close the door he hadn't meant to open. "I appreciate your effort, but God's not something I believe in—and even if I did, I don't have time to wait for some kind of miracle."

He didn't get the debate he expected. Instead, Doc returned to his seat and responded in a pleasant voice as if he were discussing tomorrow's weather. "Fair enough. But if you don't mind, I'd like to leave a Bible in your room. You've got at least two weeks to kill. It might help take your mind off your troubles."

This would be where his dad would tell the good doctor where he could put his Bible. But this man had saved Eric's life. And he was Ellie's father. Two good reasons to play along. He nodded.

Doc came nearer and placed his hand on Eric's shoulder, the cue he was about to leave. "I'm going to bed. Would you like some help back to your room?"

"No, thanks. I think I'll stay out here for a while."

"All right then. I'll see you tomorrow."

As soon as Doc left, the mother cat pushed open the shed door and padded over to him. She rubbed against his left leg. He picked her up and settled her on his lap. A cat. And God. And a girl he was falling for.

If Reznik didn't kill him, his dad would.

CHAPTER NINETEEN

"Wake up, you lazy bum. We gotta talk."

Eric's left hand groped for the gun he usually wore strapped to his chest. The fog in his brain cleared as Toby came into focus. "What's up?"

Toby's face remained passive. His visit could mean only one thing.

"Plenty. Reznik's ratted you out to the director."

Eric flipped back the sheet and swung his leg over the side. He couldn't take this news lying down. "How'd you hear?"

Toby talked as he slid the stool closer to the bed. "Lisa called me to give me a heads up."

Lisa. If it had been anyone else, he'd suspect another trap. "What does she know?"

"Not much. Right now, you're MIA and presumed dead, but according to her, the director has issued the order to keep looking and bring you in. She said Reznik's out for your blood."

He expected as much from Reznik, but the director? The news hit him like a two by four to the gut. "Reznik's got all the blood he's going to get from me." His hand curled into a fist. "I've got to find a way to smoke that snake out."

"Now you're talking. Count me in." Toby reached over and picked up a black book from the bedside table. "What's this? You been reading the Bible?"

Eric glanced at the book and shrugged. "Doc must have left it there this morning."

With the director on board, it was just a matter of time. How could Eric go up against the resources of the agency and expect to win?

Toby paced by his bed rambling about something.

Eric repeated the only word he heard. "Promise?"

"I promised God if He'd let you live, I'd tell you about Jesus."

Eric stifled a groan. "Tobe, I—"

Toby held up his hand. "Let me get this out. Listen, I prayed the whole night I flew you here. And I stood in that corner over there when you up and died on us. Longest two minutes of my life. I know, 'cause I timed it. I don't think I took one breath that whole time." Toby's eyes reddened. "All I could think was, 'What if this was really it?'"

The same thought had crossed Eric's mind a few times too.

"This might sound silly, but I begged God to take me and not you 'cause I knew you weren't ready yet."

He dropped his gaze, unable to meet Toby's eyes. "I don't know what to say."

"Don't say nothing. Just let me talk before I chicken out." He cracked his knuckles and left the stool, carrying the Bible with him. "I'm not good at this. I just know what happened to me. Doc told me all about Jesus. How much Jesus loved me. How He came to this world to die for my sins. So I prayed. Told Jesus I was sorry and asked Him to be my Savior."

"I don't understand." His mind skipped over the Jesus part. "You did all this since you brought me here?"

Toby's brow furrowed. "Since I—no. I came here with my church youth group. It was the summer of my junior year."

Some of the puzzle fell into place. "That's how you knew to bring me here?"

Toby nodded. "I had to get you some help. I figured you'd be safe here, at least for a while. But when I thought you weren't going to make it, I begged God to keep you alive. Because you need Jesus, brother."

What he needed was a way to turn the tables on Reznik—
not another sermon. But he wouldn't blow Toby off. He owed
him more than that. "I appreciate your concern, Tobe."

"Promise me you'll think about what I said."

Toby had him over a barrel. Then the lyrical voice he'd
been waiting to hear spared him from having to reply.

"Toby?" Ellie seemed to bounce into the room looking
better than a person had a right to in pink hospital scrubs. "I
didn't hear the helicopter fly in. When'd you get here?"

"About a half hour ago. I left my chopper at the hangar in
Luanda and then drove a jeep here."

"It's good to see you. How's your leg?"

"Almost as good as new." He demonstrated with a step.

"That's great. Will you be staying a while?"

Toby cut his eyes over to Eric as if unsure what he could
say. "No. I'm off to our Tanzania base." He started to place the
Bible back on the bedside table, but she intercepted it.

"Wow. This looks just like the one Dad gave me when I
first came here." She flipped through the pages and gave a
nervous laugh. "Oh. It *is* my Bible." She hugged it close to her
chest as if it were a love letter from a boyfriend. "There's
something special about the first Bible you ever read. Did Dad
let you borrow it?"

Something territorial reared up. "Your dad left it for me. It
was there when I woke up."

Her gaze connected with his for the first time since she'd
entered the room. "How are you today?" She smiled as she
placed the Bible on the table. "I stopped by last night, but you
were pretty out of it."

"You came by last night?"

She nodded. "It was later than I intended."

So that part wasn't a dream. He must've said something.
Why else would her cheeks pick up the color of her scrubs?

She checked her watch. "I wish I could stay longer now."

What? She was leaving again?

"Toby, I hope you stop by the clinic to see Dad before you go."

"I'm heading that way now."

"Good. I'll walk with you."

Toby walked over to Eric. "Watch your back, bro." His bear-like grip on Eri's left hand almost made him wince.

"You too."

Ellie came behind Toby and put her feather touch on his arm. "I'll see you later."

He nodded and hoped he didn't look too eager. She paused at the door and glanced back. Their eyes met for one brief moment. She moved her hand from the door molding and gave him a quick wave, and then she was gone.

Eric scanned the empty room and tried to deny how much he depended on her presence. He reached for the Bible, the one she'd hugged to her heart, and did something he didn't think he'd ever do. He opened it and started reading.

∿∿∿∿

Ellie couldn't keep the grin off her face. She walked gingerly down the hallway carrying two cups of coffee, one with no sugar and extra cream.

Her prayer last night had freed her more than she thought possible. It didn't matter they had no future together. He was here now. He had feelings for her too even if he tried not to show it. A girl could tell. That look he gave her this morning. Coffee sloshed onto her hand, and she slowed her step.

And last night he called her his beautiful angel. He was probably too out to remember. But she would never forget.

He was up and dressed, his leg propped on a stool in front of the recliner. His hands steepled in front of him, he seemed lost in thought.

"I'm back. Toby told me how you like your coffee."

His expression changed from battle-ready to gratitude as he took the coffee from her. "Thanks. This is one time I appreciate Toby's big mouth."

She settled on the end of his bed across from him and nestled her cup between her hands. "I never drank coffee until I came here."

"Tell me again. How long have you been in Africa?"

"In October, it'll be two years." Her heart hammered at what he might ask next. She glanced out the window and steered the conversation in a different direction. "I've got a couple of hours to kill. Would you like to take a stroll out to the terrace?"

"You bet I would." He leaned forward and set down his cup. He pushed up and balanced on one leg to reach for the crutches wedged between the table and the bed.

She rose from the edge of the bed and waited, not knowing whether to offer her help or to let him manage alone. "Looks like you no longer need a human crutch."

His hand froze on the last crutch and then let it fall back against the wall before he pivoted to face her. "Yes, I do."

"Stay put. I'll take our coffee out to the terrace and come back for you."

He grinned. "Yes, ma'am."

She grabbed the two cups and rushed past him out the door. She returned, out of breath. He stood where she'd left him, his right leg bent and his foot suspended behind him. He moved away from the table to make room for her, and both of them fumbled in place like awkward kids at their first dance.

The tight bandages were gone with only a gray T-shirt between her hand and his rock-hard torso. His right arm wrapped around her shoulder this time instead of hanging loose between them. They took their first halting step together.

"It might be easier for you to use the other crutch."

His hand tightened his grip as if trying to prevent her from pulling away. "Not really. I used both crutches last night. It wasn't pretty."

She moved closer, filling in the space between them. He seemed stronger this time and could talk without getting winded. They reached the end of the hall much faster than before. She backed against the door and held it open. A faint hint of their soap hit her as he hobbled past. A musky scent she loved, especially on him. She swallowed hard and let the door close behind her.

Eric paused outside the door. He needed to catch his breath and not just from the exertion. It was a mistake to have her hold onto him. She molded perfectly to his side and left him hungering for more.

He settled into a chair and used both hands to manhandle his useless limb to rest on the patio table in front of him.

Ellie grabbed a cushion from a nearby chair and placed it under his swollen foot. "There."

"Thanks."

She was still bent over his leg trying to position it. "You're welcome."

His heart flip-flopped at her grin. "I mean for rescuing me for a couple of hours. It's good to be out of that room."

She pulled her chair closer and handed him his coffee. "I bet. I'm enjoying it too." She took a sip and looked out toward the trees at the end of the field. "It's so pretty here. Peaceful."

The cat appeared and bypassed him for Ellie. Traitor. Not that he blamed her. He'd do the same.

Ellie rubbed the furry head. "Hello, Lucy. How are those babies?"

Lucy. He knew it started with an L. "She came to me last night."

Her hand stilled, and she cocked her head. "Last night?"

"More like early this morning. Sometime around one thirty. Your dad was still up."

"My dad's amazing. He goes to bed after I do and gets up way before, especially if he's concerned about a patient."

That patient would be him. Eric moved him to the top of the list of people he respected and admired—even ahead of his dad, to the place Stuart had left vacant.

Ellie slouched, and her head rested on the back of her chair. With her elbows on the armrests, she cradled the coffee cup on her stomach. She closed her eyes and hummed. "I feel like a turtle on a rock." Her profile was upturned to the sun. Her lips relaxed and slightly parted.

He took another sip of his coffee and forced himself to look away before she opened her eyes and caught him staring.

Without warning, she sat upright. "Toby brought bad news, didn't he?"

He nodded and met her gaze. "Not anything I didn't already suspect."

"That's what had you up in the middle of the night?"

"You're practicing your Sherlock skills."

"I am. How am I doing?"

"Close. Actually a nightmare drove me out here." In that split-second, he went against protocol and his own gut warning him to stop. "The nightmare was about you."

Her eyebrows raised, but she said nothing.

"The guy at the agency who wants me out of the way was closing in. And then, out of nowhere you showed up. He aimed, and you froze. The only good thing about the dream was both my legs worked. I made a leap and shoved you out of the way."

Her eyes grew large, darker. "Did he shoot you?"

"Yeah, in the leg, but I twisted in midair and got off a single round. You screamed, and I woke up." He left out the part about the cold sweat and hands that shook so bad he needed both crutches to help steady himself. He'd said too much already.

She deposited her cup on the table beside his foot. "Being with you makes me feel safe."

He almost chuckled until he glanced up. She wasn't joking. Wasn't flirting or delivering a line. Just transparent. Vulnerable. For one crazy moment, he wanted to be the man who would always keep her safe. But even Doc's God wouldn't be able to pull that one off. Right now, he couldn't even keep himself safe.

"I'm sorry I didn't make it to your room before you went to sleep. I had some troubling thoughts of my own that I needed to talk over with my dad."

"Everything all right?"

"Not yet, but it will be."

He wouldn't pry. At least not about that. "You said you didn't grow up around your dad. What changed? What brought you to Africa?"

The cat beside Ellie's chair came alive. Gravel crunched, and then Doc rounded the corner by the shed. His face broke into a grin as soon as he saw them. "Hello, you two. Enjoying this lovely day?"

Eric straightened in his chair and repressed his compulsive need to stand every time Doc approached.

"Yes," Ellie answered before he could. "Thanks to you."

"You're welcome, honey."

Doc gave Eric's right arm a slight nudge as he moved behind the chair to stand beside Ellie. "You deserve some time off after yesterday." His hand rested on her shoulder, and she raised hers to caress it. One of the many demonstrations of affection he'd seen that made him think they belonged to some exclusive club he very much wanted to be a part of. Even Lucy was part of the group weaving between Doc's legs and Ellie's chair.

Then Doc moved behind his chair and placed both hands on his shoulders as if he were Doc's long lost son. Lucy jumped onto his lap and moved up his chest to get to Doc's hands.

Ellie chuckled. "See. I told you Lucy will do anything to claim someone's undivided attention."

Doc kept his left hand planted on Eric and freed his other one to push Lucy away from Eric's bandaged shoulder. "Get down, girl."

"She's all right." He wasn't much different from the cat. At that moment, he was part of the club, and he'd do just about anything to stay there.

SAVING ERIC

CHAPTER TWENTY

Eric figured he missed his chance to fill in the gaps from Ellie's life. Not that he minded Doc's interruption.

Ellie waited until her dad entered the building and then turned back to Eric. "When your leg gets better, I'll take you to see the chapel."

"Let's go now."

"Somehow I knew you'd say that." Ellie rubbed a spot on her forehead. "All right, but I'm getting your other crutch first."

Probably a good idea. She returned carrying the crutch in one hand and a bottle of water and a pill in the other.

"Take this."

He downed it and pushed up. "Lead the way."

"We'll take it slow. It's just around the corner."

Just around the corner felt more like a marathon, but he wasn't about to let her know it. Good thing he took the medication. Ellie scanned his face every few seconds. It was worth each gut-wrenching step to be out of his room doing something. To be with her.

Ellie scooted ahead to open one of the large wooden doors. She stood beside him and surveyed the room with a pleased expression as if she were welcoming him to her private sitting room. "I practically lived here when I first came to Africa."

He could see why. Simple, almost rustic with the smell of wood that reminded him of something, but he couldn't remember what. Rows of benches divided by a center aisle led to a platform and a podium. The atmosphere was cool and hushed and made him feel he ought to whisper. Maybe because she did. Ellie moved toward the front with her gaze focused on the stained glass window behind the podium. The light from the early afternoon sun cast a golden glow on the glass, making it seem backlit.

Impressive. So was Ellie's face, which glowed almost as much as the cut glass.

"If you look real close, His eyes seem to follow you. I used to sit right here and stare up at the risen Jesus and hope He'd talk to me right out of the glass."

He took his gaze off her long enough to get a glimpse of this Jesus. He stood dressed in a white robe with arms outstretched. The left side of the window showed a larger than life crucifix of a broken and bloody man with a drooping head. Much different from the welcoming and almost regal version on the right. A scene a person could stare at for a long time.

"Probably sounds silly."

Loose waves blocked her expression. He moved them back to meet her gaze. "No, it doesn't."

She smiled as if grateful he understood. "It's still my favorite place on the compound." She turned her attention back to him. "You mind if we sit a while?"

He shook his head more relieved than he would let on that he didn't have to walk back yet. She picked a bench, and he filed in after her. They had barely settled when she got up and sat backward on the opposite bench so she could face him.

"Would you like to prop up your leg?"

"Yeah."

She helped him lift it and grimaced when he winced. "Sorry."

"It's okay." The words came out more strained than he intended. "It'll be better when I keep it still." He dropped one of the crutches to the floor and kept the other one upright to lean on for leverage.

She crossed her ankles and wiped her hands on her scrubs. "If you still want to hear what brought me to Africa, I'm ready to tell you. I haven't before now because I really enjoy the friendship developing between us." She paused and then added, "I don't want anything to change it."

Her transparency blew him away, and for the first time in his life, he dropped his guard enough to be transparent too. "Nothing you say will change that. But you don't have to tell me anything if you don't want."

"I want to. It's kind of a long story so let me know if I start to bore you."

He played along. "Deal."

"I fell in love four years ago."

Bingo. He knew it was a broken heart.

"Allen was handsome and so much fun. A pharmaceutical rep who came by the doctor's office where I worked. I only saw him whenever he came through town. It started off slow until our first real date. From that night on, whenever he was in our area, he stayed at my place. And I was a goner. He'd come about every six weeks and stay for a week. And I. Lived. For. Those. Weeks."

His jaw grew tighter. The guy was a player. Probably married. He hoped he was wrong.

"After we'd been together about a year, I suspected he might propose. In December of that year, I came down with a horrible bout of the flu. The ring I'd hoped to get for Christmas didn't happen. But then we spent two wonderful weeks in January so I figured maybe he'd propose on Valentine's. And then something happened that would change my life forever."

His stomach knotted, but he kept his expression the same.

"I found out I was pregnant." She folded her lips in but not before he detected the slight quiver. "Allen didn't take the news well. Said I got pregnant on purpose so he'd feel obligated to marry me. And then he told me to get rid of it. Big fight. Before he left, he tried to get me to make an appointment to have the abortion. But I just couldn't." She got up and walked to the front and pulled some tissues from the box under the podium.

"You can stop if you want to."

She shook her head. "It helps to talk about it." She moved to her spot across from him. "When it became clear it was him or the baby…" She took a deep breath and swallowed. "I gave in." She hung her head and became still as a statue. "My baby wasn't the only one who died that day."

He squeezed the side of his crutch until his knuckles turned white. He wanted to hold her. Make her forget her pain. "I'm sorry."

Ellie raised her head and smiled. "Me too. I wish I could go back and change what happened. I was such a fool. I planned a special candlelit dinner at my place. That night, he showed up but never even came all the way into the apartment. Told me he'd made the decision to work things out with his wife." She twisted the wadded up tissues in her hand. "I didn't even know he was married. I begged him not to leave. Told him I wasn't pregnant anymore, and I'd do anything to make it work. He just stared at me and told me it was over. Then he left and never looked back. Not once."

Personal hits were forbidden, but maybe this one time he could make an exception.

"I couldn't eat, or sleep, or work. All I could do was sit on the sofa and cry. One day, I took an entire bottle of sleeping pills. I don't think I really wanted to die. I just didn't want to live anymore."

Suicide. The news broadsided him. He leaned forward and took one of her hands. "What happened?"

"My mother came to my apartment that afternoon. My socialite mother, can you believe that? We hadn't talked in months. She never just dropped by. Dad said God must have sent her."

If that were true, he'd have to rethink his opinion about God.

"She called 9-1-1 and then called my dad. Dad came for me himself, and when I was released from the hospital, he flew me back here. The change of location helped for sure, but I had a hard time climbing out of my depression. I tried. I really did try to snap out of it. Dad never once made me feel guilty. But one day, he told me something that changed my life."

"What was that?"

"He told me about how he came to know Jesus while he was in prison."

Prison? Doc? Years of practice kept the shock from showing on his face.

"He told me about his own struggle with guilt. That got my attention because I struggled with so much guilt myself."

Guilt. He'd shut that door a long time ago. Had to, or he'd never have made it through his rookie years. Compared to him, Doc and Ellie were saints.

"A prison chaplain told him that Jesus died for all his sins and was willing to wipe his slate clean. I listened politely, and I was happy for Dad, but I didn't understand it. Or want to."

Now that he could relate to.

"But he gave me a Bible to read. And I don't know." She shrugged her shoulders as if trying to nail down the experience. "I guess since he was so sweet and understanding, I kind of owed it to him to at least try. So I did." She straightened and gazed around the chapel. "I read a lot in here. And I'd stare at the stained glass a lot. And sometimes, I'd ask Dad questions." She leaned closer. "You know what he did that meant more than anything to me?"

His eyes widened automatically, mirroring hers. He shook his head and tried to keep the grin from his face. She apparently had no idea how irresistibly cute she was.

"He didn't push. He answered my questions and that was it. No pressure. After about four months, I was ready to commit my life to Jesus. Dad prayed with me on that bench right up there." She turned and pointed to a bench three rows from the front.

The tears were gone from the puffy eyes. The radiant smile returned and with it, the Ellie he'd come to know. And love.

"It didn't happen overnight, but little by little, I healed and experienced a joy I never thought possible. But I didn't think I could ever learn to care for another man." She lifted her chin. "Then you came along. Before I knew what was happening, the shell I had built around my heart started to crack. Maybe I felt safe because I knew there was no possible way we could have a relationship. So I relaxed around you. Enjoyed getting to know you. Little by little, I realized there must be men out there I could trust. Men like you, who do the right thing no matter what it costs. I'm so grateful." She squeezed his hand that still held hers. "Being around you helped me live again. Love again."

The meaning between her words sliced through him. She loved him.

"So I told you my story because I care so much for you." She continued before he could grasp the fact she'd said she loved him. "I told you because I want you to know my Jesus. I want you to know the peace and forgiveness only He can give."

He'd never had any trouble saying what was expected, especially to a woman. Until now. Words tossed around in his brain but formed no coherent reply. He took his first deep breath since they'd entered the chapel. What could he say? That he loved her more than he thought possible for a man to love a woman? That he needed her to breathe? She'd pulled the pin from his heart without meaning to. If he let go—

No. She'd known enough pain. She'd said *men like him,* but she didn't know him, not really. Or that he'd been planning Allen's execution even while she cried. He wasn't good enough for Ellie. Or Ellie's God.

"You don't have to say anything." She stood and with her hands on his shoulders, leaned over and kissed his forehead. "Thank you for listening."

What was left of his confidence forced him to meet her gaze. "Thank you for trusting me enough to tell me." He reached up and cupped her face. "Ellie, I—"

Her finger on his lips stopped him. "Promise me you'll give God a try."

His hand captured hers again. He kissed the finger still held close to his mouth and nodded. He could deny her nothing.

CHAPTER TWENTY-ONE

Eric could have sworn he hadn't closed his eyes all night but he must have dozed sometime before dawn. He threw back the sheet and slid the purple foot he could no longer feel to the edge of the bed. With his hand fastened on the bedrail, he swung his leg over. Feeling came back full force as the useless foot made contact with the floor.

He white-knuckled his way to the wall and snatched down the clock. Instead of smashing it on the floor, he flipped it over and removed the battery before stuffing them both in the table beside his bed. There. No more constant ticking to mock him. He grabbed some clothes from the closet and hopped to the bathroom.

He was feeling reckless enough to tackle a shower on one leg. Possibly the world's fastest shower. He somehow finished and dressed without passing out. Cool air hit his face when he opened the bathroom door and revived him enough to make it to the recliner.

Rocco came in and shook his head. "You are one determined dude, you know that?"

"Sorry, Roc. I'm going stir crazy."

"Yeah. I would be too." He bent to reattach the cast and then straightened and placed his hand on Eric's shoulder. "I'll get you some coffee."

Rocco left, and almost immediately, Doc came in and gave him the affectionate pat he'd come to expect. "Good morning. I heard you were up early."

"I didn't sleep."

He opened the drawer to get the stethoscope and gave a quick glance to the now bare wall. "Clock keep you awake?"

Eric gave a mirthless chuckle. "I had a lot on my mind."

Doc nodded as he placed the end piece on Eric's chest. "Take a deep breath." He listened, then slipped the cord back around his neck and sat on the bed facing him. "Ellie told me about the talk she had with you yesterday. Can I help?"

No matter how awkward or uncomfortable this conversation was going to go, he was not a man who broke his promises. "I told Ellie I'd try to learn about God."

"I can help you with that." Doc reached for the Bible he'd placed on the table the day before. "Everything God wants us to know about Himself is found in this book."

"I actually read a little yesterday."

"What'd you think?"

"I didn't understand it."

"Most people don't the first time. If you'd like to tell me what exactly you know about God, we can start there."

Drill him on any political hotspot in the world, survival techniques in any climate, or the strategies for withstanding interrogation and torture, and he could stand and deliver. So for West Point's golden boy to know next to nothing about such a vastly important topic was difficult to admit.

"Eric?"

"Sorry." He met Doc's friendly stare. "Not much."

Doc's expression didn't change. "Okay. How about the Bible? Have you ever owned one?"

"No." Eric's eyes narrowed as a faint memory pushed to the surface. "Wait. I think I did. Some men gave out pocket-sized Bibles at school one year. Pretty sure I was in the fifth grade."

"Good. Did you read any of it?"

"No. Dad made sure of that. Saw it on my stack of books and asked me where I'd gotten it." The long-buried memory flooded back with clarity. He could've said more but stopped, whether out of respect for his father or for Doc he couldn't tell.

No need to reveal his dad's ballistic fit that ended with a shredded book in the garbage can. Then the hour-long tirade about how Templetons stood on their own two feet. "He made it clear there was no room for God or a Bible at our house. I never looked at another Bible again." Until he came here.

"Hey, guys." Rocco came in with two coffees. "Doc, Nicci wants you to stop by and eat something on your way to the clinic."

Doc took his coffee and grinned. "Nicci's our kitchen powerhouse and makes it her mission to spoil us."

Rocco came out of the bathroom with the wet towels. "Yeah. If she finds out you like something, she'll cook it every day for a week."

"You must have told her I liked broth and Jello."

Rocco howled. Doc laughed too. "Actually, we had to fight to keep her from sending something more substantial."

"I think I like this woman."

Rocco reached around Eric to switch out the trash bag in the can. "Wait 'til you meet her." He twisted the top of the bag to make a knot.

"Tell Ellie she can prep Somie for surgery. I'll be there within the hour."

"Will do."

Ellie at work. An image of her trailing behind the stretcher of a bloody woman popped into his mind.

"My friend from Chicago will be here in ten days." Doc's words jolted him back. "You can use that time to learn about God and then make up your own mind."

Eric nodded and sipped the coffee from the Styrofoam cup. Ten days. Not bad. Time enough to appease Doc and Ellie and maybe even satisfy his own latent curiosity about God. Defying his father's command in the process was its own adrenaline-filled reward. He set the coffee aside and shifted in his chair.

"Try reading this part." Doc opened the book and held it closer. "The book of John. It was the first part of the Bible I ever read, and to this day is still one of my favorites."

Eric took the Bible Doc handed him and held it as gingerly as if it were nitro glycerin. He hadn't felt this green since the first year at the agency.

"Ten days, Eric." Doc smiled as he rose and moved to Eric's side. "You're sharp. You'll figure it all out."

As soon as Doc left the room, Eric swapped the closed Bible for the coffee he'd placed on the bedside table. Still hot. He took a long sip and then balanced the cup on the armrest of his chair. His eyes went to the now-vacant spot where the clock had been and without missing a beat, studied the slant of the sun streaming through his window. Still midmorning. Ellie wouldn't show up for hours.

The antsy rawness he always felt with a new assignment revved his gut, only this time he couldn't run to clear his head. Before he could change his mind, he bolted from his chair and reached for both crutches. With the Bible tucked under his left arm, he moved like a man on a mission ready to knock this one out. Doc was right. He was a quick study. The chapel Ellie loved would be the new command center, and by the end of the day, he'd have the God thing figured out.

CHAPTER TWENTY-TWO

After a crazy busy day with barely time for a bathroom break, Ellie bypassed dinner with the team. Halfway down the hall, she pulled her ponytail loose and tousled her hair, taking time to massage her temples.

Who was she kidding? It wasn't the crazy day that had her barricaded in her room. It was Eric. She wasn't sure what mortified her more: the revelation of her dark past or her declaration that she had feelings for him. Either way, she wasn't sure she could face him again.

A long, hot shower. No. A bubble bath. Maybe it'd help her sleep better. She soaked a good while, sculpting the airy bubbles into shapes. She wasn't sorry she'd told him. Not really. Embarrassed maybe, but not sorry. It didn't matter that Eric knew the worst about her. God knew the worst too and loved her anyway. And like Miriam told her, "God takes our messes and gives us a message to share with others."

With a lighter attitude than when she entered the tub, she reached over to open the drain. The water chugged and gurgled as she toweled off and put on the flowing African sarong Nicci had made for her.

Someone knocked on her door. Probably Rocco. Her dad would've called her name as he knocked.

She opened the door and gasped, "Eric."

The stubble on his chin added to his raw masculine appeal and left her groping for just one of the things she'd rehearsed for this moment. She needed to say something. "Um. How are you?"

He stared at her for a long moment.

"Eric, is everything all right?"

His tortured eyes told her more than words. "Could we go somewhere and talk?"

"Of course. Let me get my shoes." She slipped them on and rushed back to the door. "Ready."

He had moved from the door and stood staring out the hall window at the dark compound beyond. His arm flexed on the crutch as he swung back to face her. "This can wait if it's not a good time."

"Now's a great time." She tried to reassure him with a smile. "In fact, I was about to come see you."

She closed the door, and he fell in step beside her.

"How'd the surgery go?"

Her pace slowed as she met his gaze. "The surgery?"

"Your dad told Rocco for you to prep someone for surgery."

"Oh, right. This morning. That one went great. And we did three other emergency surgeries since then."

"You've been busy."

"Yeah. It was crazy for a while." She paused when they reached his room. "Here or the terrace?"

"Terrace."

She whipped around him and opened one of the double doors. "The wind's blowing in from the west." She closed her eyes and took a deep breath. "You can almost smell the ocean."

He stayed by the door. "I didn't realize how dark it would be. Would you rather stay inside?"

How on earth did he find out she was afraid of the dark? "No. This is okay." Especially with every vestige of makeup scrubbed from her face. "Our eyes will adjust in no time."

They sat in their usual spot. Had this been any other time, she would have entertained him with her chit-chat. But something checked her compulsive need to fill every silence.

Before long, he cleared his throat. "I didn't sleep much last night."

That would make two of them.

"I couldn't get what you said out of my mind."

Even in the dark, she couldn't bring herself to meet his gaze. "You don't know how many times I regretted all I told you. I said too much."

His hand reached for hers. "You said exactly what I needed to hear. And I set out today to do what you asked. I even went to the chapel because that's where you went when you first came here. I had one mission. To find out all there was to know about God and then report back to you."

She was still learning herself, but knew enough to realize something big was happening. "What'd you find out?"

His hand tightened around hers. "I spent all day reading the Bible. Your dad told me to read the book of John. So I did. Twice. And now after all of that, I'm more confused than ever."

"It's all new to you." The desperation in his voice reminded her how hopeless her own search for God had seemed. "Dad can help you understand it."

"I want you to help me. Tell me again. What made you believe in God?"

Butterflies filled the empty space in her stomach. She needed to answer him well but wasn't sure she could. What made her believe in God? Had she ever figured it out? "It wasn't any one thing. It was lots of things."

He leaned closer. "Tell me. Please."

"It's like a thousand piece puzzle. You know. One of those hard ones, with little pieces that all look alike. Every day I listened to my dad talk. Or Miriam—she's Moses's wife. Sometimes I spent the day in the chapel reading the Bible on my own. Like you did today. Some of the pieces started to fall into place—pieces about God's love, or about Jesus; how God feels about sin in our lives; and about His forgiveness. It's weird but the more I learned, the more I wanted to learn, like the obsession to get the puzzle finished."

She would've stood and paced but she didn't want to let go of his hand. "Finally, I thought every piece was in place, but my dad helped me see a very important part was missing." She leaned back in her chair and shook her head. "I swear the man's a mind-reader. He found me in the chapel. Dad came in and sat beside me and practically handed me the missing piece. The risen Christ almost glowed from the sun streaming through it. Dad nodded to the image and said, 'His arms are open wide, and He's waiting for you. He won't force Himself into your life; you have to come to Him of your own free will and receive His gift of forgiveness.' And he asked me if I was ready to do that. I was, but I told Dad I didn't even know how to pray. He said it was no different from talking to him. I let him know there was a big difference. At least he was real and could talk back to me." She cocked her head back to Eric. "You know what Dad did?"

Even in the shadows, she could make out Eric's grin. "No. What?"

"He hugged me and said, 'Honey, Jesus is as real as I am. You just can't see Him. It takes a leap of faith.' And then he said, if I took that leap of faith, Jesus would be there to catch me. I can't remember the exact words I prayed. Something like I was ready to quit running. That I wanted His forgiveness even though I didn't deserve it. I've been a changed person ever since, and I know Jesus is real. Not because Dad says it. He's real to me." She paused not knowing what else to add. "I don't know if any of that made sense."

He leaned back in the chair but didn't release her hand. For the first time, his gaze left hers and he looked out toward the field. "It makes perfect sense." His fingers tightened around hers. "For someone like you."

"But not someone like you?"

"Your biggest crime was loving someone so much you were willing to do whatever it took to make him happy. Ellie, I—" He lowered his head, and she had to strain to hear. "I can't tell you some of the things I've done. If I did, you wouldn't want to be in the same room with me."

"God knows everything about you. He can forgive anything. He wants to forgive you."

"I'm not like you. I can't just take a leap of faith and expect everything to magically go away."

He released her hand and reached for the crutches by the chair. She stood when he did and moved in front of him to block his exit. "Give it time. God loves you." After a split second's hesitation, she placed her hand on his chest. "I love you."

The catch of his breath preceded the thud of the crutches that dropped to the concrete. He enveloped her in a crushing embrace. "I love you." Words that seemed more like a desperate cry than a declaration. "Ellie—"

"Don't talk. Just hold me."

His heart beat against her chest. Or was it hers? She nestled her face in the crook of his neck. His hand caressed her back. She could almost feel Jesus standing beside them with His arms around them both.

Eric was the first to pull away enough to look down at her. His finger traced the tip of her nose and tapped her lips. "At least we settled one thing tonight."

"That we love each other?"

"Um-Hmm. We've danced around it for weeks."

"You must have known. I'm not good at hiding my feelings."

"I am. Or I used to be." He bent down to get his crutches and turned back to face her. "I think I fell in love the moment I opened my eyes and saw the angel by my bed."

"Oh, Eric." She shook her head. "I'm no angel."

He moved closer, his lips warm against her forehead. "Come on. It's been a long day, and you need to rest."

Against her protests, he walked her all the way back to her room. She opened her door and turned back to face him, half-hoping he'd kiss her. He didn't. But his eyes softened as he held her gaze. With a light caress to her cheek, he turned to go.

She leaned against the door not trusting her legs to hold her and watched him maneuver down the hall. He stopped midway and turned. "I'm not leaving 'til you close that door."

She returned his grin and backed into the doorway. Her heart could have stayed there all night. But not her body. Or his either. With a sigh, she closed the door and dropped to her knees beside her bed.

CHAPTER TWENTY-THREE

A fresh influx of patients left Brock with no time to even check on Eric. He surveyed his newly-trimmed beard and then rinsed bits of hair down the drain. Eight days until Eric's surgery. No time to waste. He smoothed out a wrinkle in the bedspread and checked his watch. Five in the morning. Worth a try. He peeked into the room across the hall. Eric sat on the edge of the bed, the open Bible balanced on his lap.

"Good morning. I took a chance you might be up." The clock, still absent from the wall, couldn't be the culprit this time. Brock bypassed the recliner and sat next to Eric on the bed.

Eric glanced up and gave a half-smile that didn't quite reach his eyes. Eyes that held the same haunted look he'd seen many times. In prison, whenever he'd faced himself in the mirror.

"How are you doing?"

Eric dropped his gaze. "I thought I'd knock this God thing out in one afternoon. Didn't go as I planned."

If there was one thing Brock had learned from experience, it was not to rush what God was doing. He bit back any number of responses. Instead, he took a pen and notepad from his pocket and jotted down some Bible verse references. "Here. Sometime today look up these verses." He reached for the Bible and flipped to one of the front flaps. "This is the index of all the books in the Bible and their page numbers. This number," he pointed to the first one on the list, "indicates the chapter number. The next one, the number of the verse." He turned to the book of John. "Like this one. John, chapter 3 and verse 16, one of my favorites. The red print identifies the actual words Jesus spoke." He put the Bible back on Eric's lap. "And later today, if you'd like, we can talk."

Eric took the list and stared at it like a teenager who had just received a police citation.

"Would you be willing to do that?" He didn't usually push, but too much was at stake and time was short.

Eric met his gaze and nodded.

Brock wrapped his arm around Eric's shoulders and pulled him closer. "Great." Eric didn't stiffen. Good sign. "I'm sorry I have to leave you now, but I'll touch base with you later."

"Okay."

He stood and with a parting pat to Eric's shoulder, turned to leave the room. He wanted more than anything to stop by the chapel and spend the rest of the day in prayer. But duty called. So he headed to the clinic with his characteristic fast pace but kept a prayer constantly alive in his heart.

The hollow ache in Eric's chest had been there for years. Ever since he could remember. It'd hit him hard the day his mom left his dad, but he figured he'd outgrow it. Sometimes he thought it was gone for good, but it always seemed to pop up after a completed mission. Night flights on the way home were the worst. That empty space—a suffocating mixture of loneliness and guilt.

A good run usually lifted his mood and cleared his mind. He leaned over to survey what was left of his leg. There wouldn't be any running any time soon. Maybe never again.

Tears stung his eyes for the second time that morning. He'd almost lost it when Doc hugged him. He closed the Bible and reached for the crutches propped up by his bed. He could at least pace, even if it was slow. He went to the window and glanced at the sky. Was there really a God out there? What if Doc and Ellie and Toby were wrong? What if after this life was over, you just ceased to exist? Fell asleep.

Sleep. The idea appealed to him. Something he'd had trouble doing lately. He was tired. To the bone tired. Of the pain. Of the loneliness. Of the guilt he tried to deny.

What if he was wrong? And his dad? What if there really was a God? The thought sliced through his heart like one of Doc's scalpels. How many people could you kill before you crossed the line with God?

His heart sped up as if he'd already been running. Adrenaline kicked in. He zipped through his cleaning ritual with no dizzy spells. Even shaved. His khaki shorts had been cleaned and folded neatly at the bottom of a drawer. He bit back a curse when he moved his foot the wrong way. Then he found his white button up shirt, the one nice shirt he'd packed. He slipped it on and rolled up the sleeves.

He was getting out of this room. And going to church.

CHAPTER TWENTY-FOUR

His father's workshop. The smell Eric couldn't place before. Musky wood and varnish. A smell he always loved. The workshop was one of the few places he and his dad could work together in harmony. A good memory that made entering the chapel a little less intimidating.

He paused at the bench where he and Ellie had previously sat and then moved up three rows. The one where she had found God.

The list Doc gave him was a good idea. He worked better when given a task to complete.

He thumbed through the pages until he found the first verse, read it, and then moved on to the next, ready to knock the assignment out. When all ten had been checked off, he closed the Bible with a satisfied grin. Done.

He shifted and tried to stretch some of his cramped muscles. The right side of the stained glass caught his attention as he rubbed the back of his neck. Ellie was right. It did seem as if Jesus was looking right at him. The verses he'd just read. They all said something about Jesus. But what? The pressure was off now. He picked up the closed Bible lying beside him on the bench and flipped it open again. "For God so loved the world that He gave His only begotten Son, that whosoever believeth in Him, should not perish, but have everlasting life. For God sent not His son into the world to condemn the world, but that the world through Him might be saved."

The heel of his palm failed to massage away the sudden tightness in his chest. He closed the Bible, this time without the satisfied sense of accomplishment. He focused on the left side of the image. The one of Jesus hanging on a cross. Tears that seemed to stay close to the surface filled Eric's eyes. His gaze switched to the other side. Jesus, dressed in white, beckoned to him with outstretched arms.

"God, I've never prayed before.*" It's like talking to a real person.* "God. I'm in left field. Help me out. If you're real—"

His hand tightened into a fist. He wanted to believe. He just couldn't.

He stood and positioned his crutches, but before he turned to leave, he nodded to the image of Jesus.

Eric bolted upright at the scraping noise to his left and almost knocked the kitten off his lap.

Ellie stood a few feet from him with a chair in her hands as if she'd been caught shoplifting. "Sorry. I thought I was being quiet."

He stretched and smiled. She'd never make it as a thief. "I hoped you'd find me."

Ellie slid the chair the rest of the way and sat next to him. "I practiced my Sherlock skills. Which, by the way, just how did you figure out I'm afraid of the dark?"

He opened his mouth, but she cut him off. "And I know. You'll have to kill me. But it's worth it. So spill, Sherlock."

"Just a lucky guess." He wished it were more impressive, but he wouldn't lie.

"Really?"

"I detect a slight tinge of disbelief. Okay. And the fact you usually have a pocket flashlight. And before you turn off the lamp by my bed, you turn on the bathroom light because it's closer to the door. And then you switch on the flashlight before you turn off the bathroom light."

She stared at him. "A lucky guess, hmm?"

"Elementary, my dear."

"Oh, you're good."

Her laughter and praise worked better than the good stuff they pumped into his veins.

"What about you? What are you afraid of?"

His mouth went dry. No one had ever knocked on that door. Not even him. He steeled his face not to show she'd hit a nerve. Maybe he would have to give in and lie after all. Or maybe just bluff. "I don't know. Seems like a perfect opportunity to practice your skills."

She smiled and reached for his hand. "You're on. But it'll be harder for me."

"Oh yeah? Why is that?"

"Because your spy armor's tough to pierce."

Checkmate. Was she joking? Or skirting way too close to the truth?

Before he could respond, she leaned closer to pet the kitten on his lap. "I see you're trying to steal my kitten's affection."

A complete one-eighty, but he'd take it.

The sleeping kitten came to life and nibbled Ellie's knuckle. Eric nudged it aside. "I missed you." A pain seared through his calf like a red-hot poker that almost knocked him off his chair.

"I don't have to be Sherlock to know your leg's hurting."

"A bit." He tried but failed to keep the strain from his voice.

Ellie stood and walked behind. She wound her arms around his neck and rested her chin on top of his head.

He clasped one of her hands. The powdery smooth back of her hand smelled faintly of fruit, and like the kitten, he wanted to nibble it. From the looks of it, someone else had beaten him to it. "What happened here?"

"Oh that." She held it out and examined it more closely. "One of our little patients had a seizure. I forced his mouth open with my fingers instead of grabbing the proper instrument, so it was kind of my own fault. He was only five, but I knew better. I thought he was going to bite through before Rocco pried the little guy's mouth loose."

"Looks like it hurt."

"Occupational hazard. So, what have you been up to?"

So like her to deflect attention from herself. He rubbed over the broken skin and kissed it. "I spent the morning in the chapel. Your dad gave me a list of verses to read."

She laughed and her arms tightened around his neck. "It's probably the same list he gave me when I came here. Wore you out, huh? I'm sorry I woke you."

"Light sleeper. Occupational hazard."

Her hummed response was more like a chuckle. "You're sitting where I sit every morning, and Dad sits there." She gestured to the chair she'd slid by him. "We watch the sun rise almost every morning."

Ellie straightened, and her head left the top of his. Eric tightened his grasp on her hand unwilling to break the connection. She must have felt the same. She moved closer to the back of his chair, and this time he leaned his head against her midriff.

The kitten scaled Eric's chest and rooted herself under their clasped hands. Ellie laughed. "Looks like Bitsy is an attention junkie, just like her mama."

"Bitsy?"

"Yeah. She's the runt and such a little bitty thing. It started out as Little Bit, but then changed to Bitsy."

If he were a normal man with a normal job, he could share his life with the woman he loved. And have a cat and maybe even kids. He tried to keep the emotion from his voice. "Good name."

His hand left hers and gripped the armrest of his chair.

"Let's get you back to your room and get some pain meds in you."

Right then, if he had a machete, he'd take the leg off himself. He took the crutches she handed him and tried to suck it up and not wince while she helped him back to his room.

"Rest a while. Then if your leg feels better, I'll help you make it to the dining hall for supper tonight. Nicci's dying to meet you."

He sat on the edge of his bed and downed the pills she'd handed him. "I'd like that."

"Only if you feel up to it."

He'd feel up to it. No matter what.

SAVING ERIC

CHAPTER TWENTY-FIVE

Strong hands gripped Brock's upper arms and kept him from face planting the hall floor. His phone slipped from his grasp and went skidding across the smooth tiles.

"Forgive me." Moses steadied him and then rushed to retrieve the phone.

"Thank you." He took it from the long, leathery fingers and gave it a quick once-over. "But it was my fault. Was texting Ellie when I rounded the corner. It seems the Chicago team will arrive three days ahead of schedule."

Moses' eyes widened. "That doesn't leave much time."

"No, it doesn't." They reached the dining hall door, and Moses gestured for him to go first, a battle his self-effacing friend would not let him win. He nodded his appreciation and entered. Most of the team was already seated. "Hello, everyone. Ellie should be here any minute. I think she might bring Eric."

By the time he unfolded his napkin, Ellie came in, followed by Eric. Talking stopped, and all eyes went to the door.

"Sorry we're late."

He stood. "You're just in time. I was late too. Eric, you picked a good night to eat with us. The gang's all here."

Rocco scrambled to add another seat beside Ellie. "Here you go."

"No, sit here, Eric." Brock moved aside and gestured to his own chair. "Please. It'll give your leg more room."

Eric hesitated just as he himself would have if someone had offered him the head of the table. But to his credit, Eric nodded and sat where he was directed.

Ellie claimed the chair Rocco had brought and with an almost imperceptible nod gestured for him to take the coveted place by Eric. Now it was his turn to hesitate. He gave her hand a little tweak and then took the seat. The kitchen door swung open, and Nicci brought in a large tray of food.

"Curried rice." Ellie leaned forward and flashed her dimple at Eric. "You're in for a treat." As soon as the food had been placed on the center of the table, Ellie scooted from her chair and grabbed Nicci's hand. She guided her around the chairs and nudged her toward Eric who had already risen. "This is Nicci, the one we've told you so much about."

"Nicci." Eric balanced without his crutches and enveloped the hand she extended in both of his. "I'm happy to finally meet you."

For once, Nicci seemed at a loss. Eric covered without missing a beat. "Your coffee is what gets me out of bed every morning."

"I'm glad it pleases you."

"Dude, now you'll get it all day."

Eric grinned at Rocco. "That's the plan."

Nicci laughed and thumped Rocco on the back as she went to the kitchen for another tray. "He'll be getting your portion if you don't watch out."

Ellie continued her introductions. "I think you know Moses. This is Miriam, his wife and the woman who's been like a second mother to me."

Eric reached for the hand Miriam extended in front of Moses. "It's a pleasure, ma'am."

"And I think you've met everyone else." Eric smiled to the group, and Ellie moved back to her chair as Nicci brought in more food. "Oh, Nicci. Beef tips and mushrooms! I'm in heaven."

"Everything seems good when you're hungry, Missi."

He and Moses waited with palms face up for Eric to join their hands. The rest of the group sat with heads bowed. Brock whispered to Eric, "We pray before we eat."

Eric's expression cleared as he caught on and followed everyone's example. After the prayer, Ellie picked up the large bowl of rice and handed it to Eric.

"You're the honored guest tonight."

Again, Eric hesitated but took the bowl with his left hand and put very little food on his plate.

"I heard good news today." Brock spooned beef on top of his rice and handed the bowl to Ellie. "My friend from Chicago will arrive ahead of schedule."

Rocco took the bowl from Ellie and asked, "When will the new X-ray equipment get here?"

"In three days. The company's sending some techs to help set it up."

"Excellent. One of my best rotations was in orthopedic surgery. I may specialize in that area when I return to the States."

The chattering continued, but Eric remained quiet and moved his food around with his fork. "Doc, could I talk to you after dinner?"

"Of course." All day, Brock had a sense of anticipation, like something good was coming. The thought took what little appetite he had, and by the time everyone finished, his plate looked as untouched as Eric's.

They stood, and he turned to Ellie. "Eric and I are going to the terrace for a chat. Would you like to join us?"

"Not this time. I've got some reports to type, and then I'll help Rocco and Al get the room ready for the tech team."

He saw through her and loved her all the more for it. She went over to Eric and must have told him what she planned to do. She found a way to hug him around the crutches, and then Eric's gaze followed her out of the room.

Eric broke the silence as they walked toward the terrace. "You've made a wonderful compound here, Doc. I noticed the layout when I went to the chapel today."

"Thank you. God has blessed our ministry. In fact, we're getting ready to expand a little."

"You mean the equipment Rocco mentioned?"

He held open the terrace door. "Should arrive sometime on Thursday morning. Toby's company is flying it here."

Eric sat in the chair Ellie usually claimed.

"My goal is to add an orthopedic wing to the hospital." He slid his chair over to face Eric. "Did you read any of the verses I left for you?"

Eric nodded. "I spent most of the morning in the chapel."

"One of my favorite places on the property." He glanced up and scanned the area. "This terrace is the other one. I call it my sanctuary."

"I can see why. The landscape is beautiful."

"Look over there above that cluster of trees." He pointed across the field and slightly to the left. "The sun rises above the crest of that little hill. You should join us to watch the sun rise. It's a little ritual Ellie and I share with Lucy and her babies."

He got the smile he was going for, but then Eric's gaze dropped. It looked as if he'd have to get the ball rolling. "Do you have any questions?"

Eric cleared his throat but didn't raise his head. "Is it true?"

"Yes, Eric. Every word."

"How do you know? How can anyone know Jesus even existed?"

A legit question with no hint of sarcasm. Brock leaned back and rubbed his chin. "Well. It's an historical fact Jesus existed. It was also documented that Jesus died on a Roman cross. And then over five hundred witnesses saw Him after the resurrection. Either Jesus was telling the truth about Himself or He was the biggest charlatan who ever lived."

Eric met his gaze. "I never thought of that."

"Let me narrow it down. Something you can relate to. Picture a soldier in a battle who sees a grenade and throws himself on top to spare his buddies."

Eric's nod gave him the green light.

"That's what Jesus did but on a much grander scale. The holiness of God demanded judgment for sin. The love of God took the judgment on Himself. Eric, Jesus took the judgment for your sins on Himself. One of the verses you read today sums it up, 'The blood of Jesus Christ, God's Son, cleanseth us from all sin.' God loves you. He wants you to come to Him for forgiveness." He paused, but Eric didn't glance up. "You must have felt that today in the chapel."

Eric shifted in his seat and curled his fingers around the armrest. "I felt something." He gave a humorless laugh. "I even prayed for the first time."

"That's great."

Eric shrugged. "Nothing happened. I felt like I was talking to thin air."

"Give it time. He answers prayer in His own good time."

"I don't know. Blind faith goes against everything I've been trained to do. If God were real, why couldn't He show up? Just once?"

"He could. He could show up any time or anywhere. He chooses not to. He asks that we believe based on His word. Tell me. Didn't you know in your heart the words you read today were true?" He hoped the slight nod he saw wasn't imagined. "That was God, speaking to your heart, nudging you to come to Christ. Don't walk away from Him."

Eric raised his head and met his gaze. "Was it hard for you to take that step?"

The moment of truth. The one he'd rehearsed a million times. Eric had to know. Of course he had to know. But now?

"It's okay. You don't have to tell me."

"No. I very much want to tell you. Stay here. I'll be right back." His chair scraped on the concrete and almost overturned as he left.

Brock didn't bother to turn on the lamp when he entered his room. He went to the closet and fumbled for the brown leather satchel he kept tucked away in the corner. The folder, stashed behind other files of clippings and testimonials, was the only one with frayed edges. He pulled it out and held it close to his chest as he'd done every New Year's Eve for the past thirty years.

God, You've brought him this far. Don't let what I have to say drive him farther from You.

CHAPTER TWENTY-SIX

The little bit of food Eric had eaten seemed lodged in his throat. Talking to Doc was supposed to make him feel better. God loved him? So why the crushing weight in his chest? Doc returned with a manila file folder and placed a kerosene lantern beside his propped foot.

"There. That should give us enough light."

Eric leaned forward to move his leg. "Doc, I shouldn't have asked."

"Please. I want you to know. How much did Ellie tell you?"

No graceful way to back out, he settled in his chair with his hands folded in front of him. "Not much. She said you learned about God in prison. That's what blew me away. I can't imagine a guy like you in prison."

Doc gave a depreciating chuckle and sat across from him. "Believe me, it's not where I thought I would be. Thirty-three years ago, I went to a New Year's Eve party. Got rip-roaring drunk. After midnight, I got in my car confident I could drive. An old Chevy seemed to come out of nowhere. The police report said I was going sixty when I T-boned it. I was badly injured, but the man and woman in the car were killed on impact."

Doc? A drunk driver who'd taken the lives of two innocent people? The person he described bore no resemblance to the kind and selfless person before him.

"I learned about it when I awoke in the hospital. The man was a preacher. He, his wife, and child were going home after a church's New Year's Eve service." He raised his head as if jolted back to the present. "So you see, Eric. A guy like me really did belong in prison."

"That was a long time ago. You've paid your dues."

Doc held up his hand as if he needed to get out the full disclosure. "I was tried and convicted of vehicular homicide and sentenced to ten years. Profound guilt ate at me every second I was awake and tormented me every night in my dreams."

Another proof of the caliber of the man. Doc's revelation did nothing to shake Eric's respect.

He opened his mouth to speak, but Doc beat him to it. "You asked if it was hard to take the step to believe in God."

Eric nodded.

"One night, at one of my lowest moments, I gave up trying to sleep and turned on the clock radio next to my bed. The only station without static had the booming voice of a preacher." Doc's voice rose and mimicked. "'God can forgive your sins and take away your guilt no matter what you've done.' I pulled that radio close to my ear and held onto it like a drowning man clutching a life preserver. I asked one of the guards for a Bible. It's the same one I put in your room to read."

"And the one you gave Ellie when she came here." Eric wasn't sure why that meant so much to him.

"That's right. I looked up for myself the verses the guy on the radio had mentioned, but I couldn't make myself believe. It seemed too easy." Doc curled his hand into a fist and pounded the armrest. "If there was a hell, I figured I belonged there. One day I told the prison chaplain the whole story and about my struggle with guilt. He said something that changed my whole perspective."

"What?"

"That whether I came to Jesus or not, I could never restore the parents to that child. 'But if the Bible is true,' he said, 'that preacher you killed wouldn't want you to go to hell.'"

Eric couldn't have replied even if he found the right words.

"I began to believe there might be hope, that Jesus might actually love me and want me to choose His forgiveness. I knelt by my cot. I told God I was sor—" He paused until he could go on. "I was so sorry for the mess I'd made of my life. I begged God to forgive me even though I'd never deserve it."

The wet sheen on Doc's cheeks glowed in the lantern's soft light. "At that moment, my guilt disappeared. Gone. And I would've been content to stay in prison forever." He thumped his chest. "Because in here, I was free."

A twinge hit Eric again. Not once had he ever felt free. Doc stood and walked to the edge of the terrace. Eric remained still. Anything he could think to say would seem insignificant.

With a heavy sigh, Doc turned back and said, "There's more."

Eric shook his head. "I don't need to hear any more."

"But I *need* to tell you."

Doc's tone kept him from protesting further.

"With the help of the prison librarian, I located articles about the accident. I found a picture of the couple who'd died. Found their obituary." His head dropped and Eric strained to hear. "I guess I wanted to pay homage. Make amends somehow. It took me a while, but I found out their child had been adopted by the pastor's brother. Since the day I became a believer, I've prayed for that child. That God would make up to him for his parents' deaths and keep him safe. And most of all, that someone, somewhere would tell him about Jesus."

He paused, and without warning, Eric's radar went into full alert.

"I lost track for a few years, but a little over a month ago, a friend rescued him from the brink of death and brought him here. God graciously spared his life."

All the blood drained from Eric's face. He closed his eyes and tried to swallow the knot that threatened to choke him. "What are you saying?"

"Eric, you're the child from the accident."

He recoiled as if he'd been punched in the stomach. He brought his foot off the table and almost welcomed the pain when he tried to stand. Doc made a sudden move toward him but backed off when Eric raised his hand to stop him. His heart hammered, and he tried to suck in more air to keep from passing out. His body collapsed back into the support of the chair, but he couldn't bring himself to meet Doc's eyes. "I don't understand. My mother and father aren't really my parents?"

"I'm so sorry." He paused and then added, "You'll never know how sorry. I always assumed you knew."

Eric swiped away a tear before it reached his cheek and dared any more to fall. He bit the inside of his mouth until he tasted blood.

Doc returned to his chair and after a long moment, spoke, "Eric, you have a choice. You can choose the God of your real father, or you can choose the path of the man who raised you. But if you choose God and His forgiveness, you'll see your parents again. They're not dead. They're very much alive in heaven."

Eric reached for his crutches and stood, the pain in his chest canceling the one in his leg. "How can you be so sure? For all I know, they ceased to exist that night."

"There *is* life after death. I'm certain of it."

Eric had heard enough. "Sure. If God would magically let me see him. Or them. Just once. I'd believe. But we both know that isn't going to happen, don't we?" At that moment, he sounded just like his father. No. The man he thought was his father. His hand tightened around his crutch to keep from smashing something.

"I believe God loves you and will do whatever it takes to help you trust Him."

"Really? God loves me?" Every muscle tensed. He turned and glared at Doc. "So this God of yours put me in a home with a man who hated God."

Doc gripped Eric's arm but he jerked away. "No, Doc. Stay away from me. I don't want your sympathy."

Doc placed a folder on the table beside the lamp. "This contains information about your parents. Their names, their picture."

Eric glanced at the folder but only when Doc left the terrace did he let himself pick it up. His hands shook as if he were defusing a bomb. Who was he kidding? It *was* a bomb that just blew to bits everything he'd believed about his life, his identity, his whole existence. With a quick look to make sure he was still alone, he opened the folder.

The newspaper clipping on top showed a man and woman. He held it closer to examine every grainy detail. The woman in the picture was young and attractive, even with little makeup. She looked happy. Nothing like the cold and distant woman who raised him. The man had the kind of smile that could put you at ease. Warm and open. He stared at them for a long time until tears blurred the image. It was almost like he remembered them. Almost. The caption under the picture read, "Local pastor and wife die in tragic crash." He blinked to clear his vision and then read more. "Nicholas and Rebecca Templeton were pronounced dead on the scene ..."

Nicholas. The picture dropped from his hand. He heaved in deep breaths and then reached beside the chair for his crutches. He kept walking when he reached the edge of the terrace. It didn't matter where. The crutches slipped and almost sent him sprawling on the uneven ground, and by the time he reached the lone tree in the middle of the grassy field, he had to stop. With his back against the trunk, he slid down, pulled up his good leg, and propped his arm across his knee. The flexible cast around his mangled leg did little to provide comfort, but for once he didn't mind. At least the pain was real.

His entire life had been a lie. His father. Not his father, but the man he'd busted his gut trying to please. His mother, the woman who walked away and never looked back. Unwelcomed tears wet his face. A beetle crawled beside his leg and with one angry flick of his finger, it disappeared in the grass. Like all the men he'd killed, with one click of the trigger.

Maybe it's too late. Maybe there's no soul left in me.

Eric picked up a twig, snapped it in two, and then looked up at the sky. "God." That one word unleashed a lifetime of dammed-up tears with sobs that refused to be stifled. His heaving shoulders shook him from the tree, and he slid into an almost fetal position on his left side. He covered his eyes with his hand and wished the ground would swallow him up.

He must have slept. A night owl jolted him awake. Its screech, eerily similar to the scream of a child, made him grope for the gun he no longer wore. He pushed his cold, stiff body back against the tree and wiped away the dirt that seemed pasted to his cheek. The fog in his brain started to lift, and the whole sordid mess hit him again. Faint streaks of pink on the horizon got him moving. He couldn't face them. Not yet. Using his crutch as leverage, he forced himself to stand and then traveled with clumsy speed toward the buildings. He could use some of Nicci's coffee but not at the risk of seeing Doc or Ellie. He bypassed the terrace and went toward the chapel.

The hushed atmosphere there soothed him. Eric moved to the front until he stood before the image of the risen Christ, barely visible in the predawn light.

"It was you." His muffled voice broke the stillness of the chapel. He slid his fingers along the etched glass. "That night. You carried me and handed me to my father." His tears fell as did his crutches. His left leg supported his weight as he leaned into the image. "I believe. Jesus, I know you're real." Again, wracking sobs shook him with so much force, he feared he'd break the window. "Oh God. Help me."

You have a choice. You can choose the God of your real father.

His breathing slowed. He wiped his cheeks and hopped closer to the image on the left. Jesus on the cross with blood dripping from his head, his hands, his side.

That's what Jesus did, but on a grander scale. Jesus took the judgment for your sin on Himself."

He stooped to retrieve his crutches and backed away from the image. *You have a choice. You can choose the God of your real father.* His heart pounded against his chest. He wanted to fall to his knees. Instead, he gripped his crutches with the sides of his arms and raised his hands, palms up in front of him. Ellie's words came back to him, and it all seemed to make sense. "I choose you. The God of my father. I want you in my life." Tears came again, quiet ones he didn't bother to wipe away.

A sense of love so powerful it almost made him lose his balance filled up the empty place in his heart. And he took a deep breath, the first one in a very long time.

SAVING ERIC

CHAPTER TWENTY-SEVEN

Ellie walked past her father's room and did a double take at her dad in the recliner, an open Bible on his lap. She tapped the side of the open door. "Wake up, sleepyhead. The sun'll be up soon."

No response. For one heart stopping moment, she scanned his chest to see if it rose and fell and then rushed over to shake him. "Dad? Are you okay?"

He roused and seemed surprised to see her. "Oh. I dozed and lost track of time."

He looked as if he'd hardly slept. And Eric wasn't in his room when she peeked in to check on him. Something wasn't right. "How'd your talk go last night?"

"I left him on the terrace. He wanted to be alone for a while."

Wanted to be alone? "Dad, what's going on?"

"Sit down, sweetheart. I need to explain a few things. Things I told Eric last night that you need to hear as well."

She kept her focus on her dad's face and backed up to sit on his bed. "What things?"

"The man and woman who died in the accident—were Eric's parents."

"Parents?" She repeated the words as if he'd made some kind of mistake.

He didn't try to explain. He didn't speak, but his eyes held more sadness than she'd ever seen in them.

"And last night, you told him you caused the accident?" She had to talk it out. Piece by piece. "How'd he take it?"

Her dad dropped his gaze and closed the Bible on his lap.

"It was a great shock, as you can imagine. He needs time to process it all."

Eric's parents. Somehow this changed everything. "Dad, have you known the whole time?"

"Almost. After Toby said his full name, I started putting two and two together."

It all made sense now. Her dad's uncharacteristic emotion. His dogged determination to bring Eric back after he flat lined. "So that's why you took such an interest in him."

He nodded. "Honey, I owe him a great debt, but I must confess, I never thought God would bring him here or that I could somehow be a part of his coming to know God."

She jerked upright. "He knows God now?"

"Not yet. Like I said, he needs time."

Her shoulders sagged as the magnitude of the revelation hit her again. "What if he's angry and decides to walk out of our lives forever?"

"I had to take the risk. He deserves to know the truth." He rose from the chair and sat beside her on the bed. "About himself. About God too. I have to believe that's why God brought him here."

"Dad, I'm scared."

"We need to pray now more than ever. You can bet there's a spiritual battle being waged for his soul."

"We need to find him. He shouldn't be alone."

"He's not alone, honey." He checked his watch. "But why don't you get dressed and try to find him?" He smiled and hugged her close. "I have a feeling you're the one person he might want to see right now."

Ellie chewed the tip of her finger and scanned the trees across the field. Eric might've done something desperate like wander off into the wilderness. Or the chapel? Seemed too easy, but it wouldn't hurt to rule it out and maybe offer a quick prayer while she was there. She opened the heavy wooden door, and there he stood, near the podium, his focus on the glass image of the risen Christ. Relief was only half-lived. She still had to face him.

"Do you want to be alone?" Her whispered words seemed to fall flat on the wooden floors, but he must have heard. He turned and his gaze told her more than anything he could say.

He looked good with his rumpled shirt, tousled hair and unshaven jaw. He smiled, more with his eyes than his mouth. She closed the chapel door and leaned against it to keep from melting into a puddle on the floor.

He swung his crutches around to leave the platform, and she met him at the front bench. His shoulders tightened against his crutches and he opened his arms. Without hesitation, she moved into his embrace, and they held each other. No words. Just the gentle swell of his breathing and the steady beat of his heart.

His gravelly voice broke the silence. "Your dad and I talked last night."

She nodded against him. "He told me." She leaned back to gauge his reaction. "I can only imagine what it must have felt like to you."

"Yeah, it was a shock all right." He took a ragged breath and tried to shift his weight.

Poor guy. His body was probably screaming for relief. She could at least do something about that.

"Mind if we sit a little?" She led the way.

He settled on the bench beside her and blew out what seemed a grateful sigh. "So you didn't know?"

She shook her head. "Not until this morning. When I found out, all I wanted to do was find you. Make sure you were all right."

He reached for her hand but seemed so lost in his thoughts, he probably didn't realize it. "All my life, I felt like something was missing. There was this hole inside of me, but I never knew what it was or how to fill it." He stroked her wrist with his thumb. "My dad never touched me. Hardly even looked at me. And when he talked to me, it was usually to point out what I did wrong."

She gave his hand a gentle squeeze. A pitiful effort to let him know how much her heart hurt for him. "What about your mom?"

"My mom—" Eric's grip on her hand tightened, and he looked away. "She left when I was thirteen. I was in my room. Overheard them arguing." Eric stared straight ahead as if the whole scene were on display. "Watched from my upstairs window when she took off with my sisters. Never said good-bye. I found Dad and asked if she was coming back. I was crying. He slapped me so hard, it knocked me down. Told me to dry up." Eric's jaw tightened. "I dried up all right. Never cried again." He turned and gave her a lopsided smile. "Until I came here. Now, I can't seem to stop."

Compassion for the love-starved boy overpowered her. "You're nothing like them, you know." Her words must have hit home. Some of the tenseness left him. She leaned into him and nudged him with her shoulder.

"Last night, I was angry, confused. You name it. I couldn't go back to my room so I went to the field and sat under that big tree. I thought about my life. A lie. All of it. I was so desperate, I even tried praying. I got out one word and then fell apart."

Eric's voice deepened as if he were fighting tears. "I slept for a while, and when I woke, I wanted to run, hide. Somehow I ended up in here."

He stopped talking, and she scanned his face for any hint of what he might be thinking. What could she possibly say to make things right? "Eric, I'm so sorry. Dad's so sorry. He loves you so much. Please don't hate him."

His eyes softened as he smiled. He released her hand, wrapped his arm around her, then pulled her closer and kissed the side of her face above the temple. "How could I hate the father of the woman I love?"

Relief made her collapse into his embrace. "You're not angry?"

"Not anymore. I'm more stunned by what happened a few minutes ago."

She raised her head and looked at him.

"I prayed. For the first time in my life. To a God I believe in. I told Him I wanted Him, needed Him in my life."

It was her turn to be stunned. "Oh, Eric."

"And I know He heard me 'cause right after I prayed it's like—" He shook his head. "I can't describe it. Like a feeling of love invaded my whole body."

Invaded hers too. And joy. So much that only his injured leg kept her from jumping into his arms.

He gave her a sheepish grin. "You're the only woman I've ever seen laugh and cry at the same time."

"Happy tears." She rubbed her face against his shoulder and wiped her tears on his shirt. "Tell me more."

"This morning, I gave up. There was no more fight left in me. I chose Jesus." He shifted and turned to face her. "I don't have all the answers yet, but for the first time in my life, that's okay." He caressed her cheek with his left hand, his eyes dark and serious. "I don't deserve you."

His finger touched her lips and cut off her protest.

"I don't. Just like I don't deserve God's forgiveness. But something happened when I prayed. It's like the vice grip on my chest loosened. I felt free. And alive. I'm not willing to give that up." His hand reclaimed hers. "Or you either."

He stood and reached for his crutches before she could respond, which was a good thing. Her insides had turned to mush.

He looked back at her. "Walk me to my room?"

She nodded even though she wanted the moment to go on forever. They walked slowly to the terrace and started down the hallway. At his door, Eric turned. "Listen, I need to sort out a few things. Mind if we talk a little later? I have something to tell you and Doc that you won't believe."

CHAPTER TWENTY-EIGHT

Brock pushed his plate away. What little food he ate sat like concrete. Beside him, Moses seemed to have no trouble finishing his lunch. Out of the corner of his eye, he felt the curious glance, but Moses didn't question his lack of appetite. No word yet from Ellie or Eric. Neither showed for lunch. He retrieved the clipboard he'd propped beside his chair. Anything to keep him from seeking them out. The next move had to be Eric's, not his.

"After lunch, I'd like to check out the new room. Al said it's ready for the X-ray equipment."

Moses pushed back his chair.

"No. I didn't mean to rush you."

"I was finished." Moses picked up his own empty plate and reached for his as well.

"Thanks." He collected their glasses and put them beside the dirty plates stacked on the counter. Then he grabbed the clipboard he'd left on the table. "If all goes well, the equipment should be delivered sometime day after tomorrow."

Moses followed him out into the hallway. "When will the doctor arrive?"

"The next day. His tech team will help us set up and teach us how to use everything." The empty room smelled of fresh paint and wood. Brock stood in the middle and tried to envision where everything should go. "Al put in more electrical outlets and cabinets. Tell me what you think of this." He showed Moses the rough sketches he'd drawn.

"Yes. This will work nicely." Moses handed back the clipboard.

"At least until we build the new hospital wing."

A soft knock made them both turn. Eric hesitated at the door.

Brock smiled wider than usual. "Please. Come in."

Eric moved a couple of steps closer and nodded to Moses.

"It's good to see you, Eric." Moses closed the distance between them and patted Eric on the back. "But now, if you'll excuse me, I'll find Will and help him rearrange the supply room for the new equipment."

Eric moved aside to let Moses pass and raised his brows. "I can talk to you later if you're busy."

"No, not at all. Wait here, and I'll grab a couple of chairs." He rushed across the hall, afraid Eric would bolt. "Here we are." He folded one down and then positioned his to face Eric's. "Moses and I have been inspecting this room. It's for the new X-ray equipment."

Eric glanced around the room and then met his gaze. "Rocco told me I could probably find you here."

"Are you all right?" He scooted his chair closer and braced for whatever Eric came to say. The pause seemed like an eternity.

"I had to find you." Eric's jaw worked with emotion, and he dropped his gaze to his hands. "And thank you."

Thank him? He thought he'd prepared himself for anything. But thanks? He clenched his mouth shut to keep from blurting out again how sorry he was.

"I—uh—" Eric leaned back and raked his hand through his hair. "I wanted to thank you for telling me what you told me last night."

Relief washed over him. And pride for the young man who seemed more like a son every day. There were many things he wanted to say. But they could wait. This was about Eric.

"When you left, I walked out to the tree in the field."

The mahogany tree. The one he refused to have cut when they cleared the area for the buildings. His own refuge through many sleepless nights.

"I stayed the rest of the night. Thinking. Remembering." Eric rubbed his forehead and then he pinched his closed eyes with his thumb and forefinger.

It took every ounce of restraint not to bail him out. Whatever was pent up in there needed to come out.

"I prayed to Jesus." Eric's words were so quiet, Brock wasn't sure he heard right. "You helped me put the pieces together." He tapped the tips of his fingers. "This morning. In the chapel. I did what you said. I chose the God of my father— my real father."

It was almost too much. The answer to prayer he had longed to hear. He wanted to jump and kick up his heels but was afraid to move and break the spell.

Eric's grin dissolved his restraint.

Brock clapped his hands together and raised grateful eyes to heaven. "Thank you, sweet Jesus!" He bounded from his chair and engulfed Eric in his arms.

Eric rose and clung to him.

Brock tightened his hold. Here they stood, two damaged men made whole by the love of Christ. It was almost more than he could stand. "Does Ellie know?"

Eric broke his hold and wiped his eyes. "Yeah. I told her this morning. That's why I had to find you. I wanted to tell you in person before she did."

Brock sat once more and rode the high. Unshed tears blurred his vision. He pressed his fingers to his smiling lips and then placed his hand over his racing heart. "This is wonderful news. Wonderful news indeed. Tell me. How do you feel?"

"I can't explain it, but I feel like I've found something I've been looking for my whole life."

"I think you explained it very well."

Eric looked at him, his expression serious. "Thank you. For everything. I have more I want to tell you, but I'd like to wait until Ellie can hear it too."

"And I want to hear it all, but my heart is almost bursting now. Whenever you're ready. Maybe after dinner if you're up to it."

"That'll be great. I think I'll lie down for a while. I'm bushed."

"You do that." He stood and handed Eric the crutches. "We'll see you later."

Brock and Ellie ate their food with frequent glances at the door. Eric never arrived. After dinner, they both turned down the hallway toward Eric's room as if it'd been prearranged. They found him sprawled across the bed, his injured leg propped on a pillow and the other one slightly dangling off the side. He didn't stir as he usually did when someone entered his room.

They tiptoed closer.

"Looks like he's out," Ellie whispered. "I'm dying to hear the big news he has for us."

He nodded and patted the hand she'd hooked under his arm. How could anything top what had already happened in Eric's heart?

CHAPTER TWENTY-NINE

The sunrise couldn't be anything but glorious. Brock sat in his usual seat. Ellie stood behind him, her hands on his shoulders. At the familiar creaking, both turned toward the double doors.

"I hoped I'd find you two out here."

Ellie rushed over to Eric with Bitsy trailing behind her. "Dad and I came to your room last night, but we didn't have the heart to wake you."

Eric opened his arms to hug Ellie and smiled over her shoulder. "Morning, Doc."

"Good morning. So glad you joined us." He pulled over another chair.

"Thanks." Eric waited for Ellie to sit at his right and then sat between them. He propped his leg on the patio table, and then Bitsy jumped on his lap.

"You look better today. When Ellie and I peeked in, you were out cold."

"I slept better than I have in months." Eric reached for Ellie's hand but looked back to Brock. "I'd like your take on something that happened to me."

"Sure."

"When you left the terrace that night, I picked up the folder." Eric paused and stroked the kitten. "The picture of my parents was on top."

A familiar tightness squeezed Brock's chest. Every detail of that picture was etched in his memory. *Eric needs this.* He bolstered himself against the pain. "How'd that make you feel?"

"It blew me away." Eric took a deep breath and slowly expelled it. "I recognized them."

Was it possible for a child so young to remember? "You've seen their picture before?"

Eric shook his head. "Not their picture. The hallucination I had. You remember that weird dream I told you I had the night my heart stopped?"

Ellie gasped. So did Brock, but he kept his focus on Eric.

"There was a man who carried me to the doorway of a bright room. He told me there was someone he wanted me to meet. A man he called Nicholas met us at the door and took me into his arms. A woman joined us. She spoke my name, and then she kissed my cheek." Eric's left hand tightened to a fist, and his voice broke. "I'll never forget the feeling I had."

The predawn terrace held a holy silence, and not even the kitten moved.

"Tell us about it," Brock prodded.

Eric's eyes narrowed as he looked off into the distance. "I felt complete. Loved. Like I was where I belonged. Then a little girl ran up and hugged me and asked if I was going to stay. The first man told her no." He looked down and shook his head. "The man took me from Nicholas and said it was time to go back, but I didn't want to leave. I begged him to let me stay, but he released me, and it felt like lightning struck my body." He lifted his hand, palm up. "That's all I remember."

Brock's heart raced. He'd seen God do some incredible things since becoming a believer but this one topped them all.

"It was Jesus, wasn't it?"

"Yes, son. I believe it was. I told you once God would do whatever it took to convince you He is real."

Eric glanced back to Ellie. "You think I'm crazy?"

Her eyes widened. "Crazy? Oh no. I think you're a miracle."

~~~~~~

From where Eric sat, it looked as if the sun rose above Ellie's head. Made her almost glow. "Look." He nodded toward the horizon, and they followed his gaze. "I can't go back." Only when they both looked at him did he realize he'd said the words aloud. "I've changed. I can't go back to a loveless, meaningless existence."

Doc nodded as if he understood. "You have some unfinished business."

"I don't have any answers." He reached for the crutches and stood. "I don't want to lose my leg. I don't want to stand trial for treason." He moved behind Ellie and placed his hand on her shoulder like a man claiming his territory. "And I really don't want to lose Ellie."

The sun rose higher and the magic moment ended almost as fast as it had come. All that remained were the two people he loved more than anything and problems with no easy answers.

"You have God in your life now. He'll help you fight your battles."

Easy for Doc to say but not exactly something he could count on.

"God gave you a little glimpse of heaven. And you have become a child of God. Two miracles. Do you realize that?"

He had him there. "When you put it that way, yeah, I do."

"God finishes what He starts. Never forget God loves you. He loves you even more than Ellie or I love you." Doc smiled at Ellie and then back at him. "And we both love you very much."

His grip tightened on Ellie's shoulder. "I guess that makes three miracles. I've never felt so much love. I love you too."

Doc stood and rubbed his hands together. "Now, the first hurdle to overcome is the problem about your leg. The equipment arrives tomorrow, and my friend the day after. Let's see what else God has in store for you."

Eric dropped his gaze to his busted leg and swallowed. He didn't want to seem greedy, especially to God, but he needed one more miracle.

CHAPTER THIRTY

Eric propped the cumbersome leg on the stool in front of him and for the first time really looked at it. With methodical precision, he scanned every inch of his leg as if it were a topography map of his next assignment. There had to be something to give him hope that his leg might be saved. His finger poked the distended purple flesh of his foot. Still numb. The same experiment to his calf almost propelled him off his chair.

He had barely resumed normal breathing when Ellie breezed into his room. He straightened as if he had been caught snooping where he didn't belong.

"Good morning, handsome."

He swooped up the hand she extended to him and brought it to his lips. "Morning."

"You feel up to helping me this morning?"

"Yes ma'am. Hand me my crutch."

"You haven't heard what I need help with."

"Will you be there?"

"Just me. But it's boring and tedious."

"Hand me my crutch."

Ellie bent closer and grasped his face with her hands. "I love you, Eric Templeton, and I'm so happy about your newfound faith, I think I could fly." This time, she rewarded him with a kiss, and then straightened way too soon. "I'll fasten your cast." She connected the Velcro to the side and handed him the crutch. "Won't be long before you can shed this old thing and walk on your own."

"Can't come soon enough."

They left his room and walked down the hall.

"We're going to the pharmacy." Her eyes widened, and he tried to keep from grinning. Only Ellie could make a pharmacy sound like a place with buried treasure. "I have to inventory the latest shipment and restock the cabinets before the new equipment arrives later this morning."

She unlocked the door, and moved him toward a stool near the counter. "You can sit here and inventory the contents of these boxes. Then I'll put them in the cabinets."

She handed him a box and turned back toward the other counter. Before delving into another carton, she pulled something out of her pocket. Eric's hand stopped in mid-count. What was she doing? With one fluid movement, she flipped her hair over and put it into a ponytail. He swallowed hard as she bent to open a box on the floor. She stood and stretched to her full height to place some bottles on the top shelf then turned just enough for him to see her profile. She put her finger on her mouth as if pondering a problem. His heart beat in tune to the tapping on her lips. He wanted to kiss her again. Really kiss her. And then push away the tendrils of hair to kiss her neck just below her ears. And become intoxicated with the sweet, fresh scent of her hair.

Stop it.

Simon?

Eric shook himself out of his trance. "Ellie?"

She looked at him without straightening. "You need something?"

"Yeah. You mind? It'll just take a minute."

"Sure." She moved closer and waited for him to continue.

But he couldn't. His mouth suddenly went dry, and he feared his voice would crack like some teenager going through puberty.

"What is it?"

He stood so she wouldn't tower over him. "Ellie, I, uh—I'm thinking some pretty unholy thoughts about you right now."

Somehow her eyes grew even larger and her face turned the color of her t-shirt. His probably did too. The grin she gave him became a full-blown laugh. "I've had a few of those myself."

She had? He groaned and moved closer, ignoring Simon. "I've joked that if I weren't crippled, you'd be in trouble. Ellie, it's not a joke."

The enchanting creature before him took his hand and morphed into a serious woman. "I know. And if you weren't injured, *you'd* be the one in trouble. After your surgery, we'll have to deal with this."

She wanted him as much as he wanted her. The relief almost made his one good leg buckle. "I don't know the protocol here. You're the only woman I've ever truly loved. I don't know a whole lot about God yet, but I'm pretty sure He wouldn't sanction some of the things I've been thinking about."

She grinned again, clearly amused. "Oh, He'd sanction them. But at the right time. He makes that pretty plain."

He swallowed and tried to focus on her eyes and not her mouth. "God talks about sex in the Bible?"

"Who do you think created sex?"

She had him there.

"Next time you're reading the Bible, look up a book called the Song of Solomon. It's about the love between a man and a woman."

The grin disappeared, and she nibbled her lower lip. This time he had to force the issue. "What's wrong?"

"Nothing."

Was she really going to leave him hanging? His finger raised her chin. "Tell me."

Her fingers tied themselves into knots. "I was just thinking that I haven't had a—um, partner since I've become a follower of Christ. In the past, I was—way too open and trusting and well—" She looked down and then raised watery eyes that seemed even bluer. "I've changed. It's hard to put this into words because I love you with every ounce of my being. I just don't want you to think I'm easy."

He didn't need Simon this time. In that moment, the protector in him took over, and he made a solemn vow to love her and respect her. And protect her from him. So he leaned over and cupped her face and fought back his own tears. He kissed her tenderly, and she melted into him as he knew she would. And then he pulled himself away.

Even Simon would be proud.

Eric skipped lunch and took his Bible out to the terrace. Song of Solomon. He had just flipped to the page when Bitsy jumped on his lap. "Scoot over, Bits." He pushed her aside, and held her firmly on his left thigh and balanced the Bible on his right.

"Man, I wish I had a camera. A cat and a Bible. The guys at the agency would never let you live this down."

He couldn't weasel out of this one. "Hey, Tobe. Yeah, I'm a versatile guy all right." From out of nowhere, the new Eric took over. "It's good to see you, Toby. I can't thank you enough for saving my life." He looked down and focused on the kitten. The new Eric cried way too easily. "You've been a good friend to me."

"Aw, man, you trying to say you love me?"

Eric laughed. "Yeah, I guess so. Blame it on the pain meds. They make me emotional. Either that, or they've pumped a lot of female blood into me."

This time Toby laughed. "You ain't got nothing to worry about. But while we're getting all sentimental, let me tell you, brother, that I've seen you almost die and then actually die. All within the last month. I don't want to see no more of that." Toby gave him a lesser version of his usual shove to the shoulder. "No more of that. You hear me?"

"I hear you. Trust me. I don't want no more of that either."

"Well, I wasn't sure, seeing that Bible on your lap and all."

Eric flipped through some of the pages and then closed it. "Doc's been giving me a little God 101."

Toby's eyes widened. "So he gave you the 'Come to Jesus talk'?"

"Yeah, in fact, we've had a few 'Come to Jesus talks.'" Eric's voice grew low and serious. "Two days ago, I guess you could say I came to Jesus."

"You?" Toby lowered his chin and gave the I-don't-believe-it look. "Came to Jesus?"

Eric nodded.

"You asked Jesus into your heart?"

"Something like that."

Toby's eyes reddened. He stood and turned away.

"I should've died that night. You could've died too, but you risked it all to get me here. I owe you, man. It's a debt I'll never be able to pay." Eric put Bitsy down, struggled to get up and then hopped a few steps over to Toby who was still facing away. He embraced his friend with his good arm. "Thank you."

Toby wiped his face. "Now see what you've done? Made me go blubbering all over the place."

"It's okay, Tobe. I do it all the time."

"Yeah, well, I ain't got no drugs for my excuse."

SAVING ERIC

CHAPTER THIRTY-ONE

Eric sat in the recliner by his bed and tackled the Bible with the same gusto he put into his training manuals. The slight touch on his arm sent him into battle mode.

"Sorry. I didn't mean to startle you."

Eric eased back against the chair. Doc would make a great agent.

"Ah. I see you're reading the Bible. What part?"

Good thing he'd finished the Song of Solomon. "Gospel of John. Makes more sense this time."

"Believe it or not, you'll find new things no matter how many times you read it." He smiled and sat across from him on the bed. "We're installing the new equipment today, and tomorrow my friend from Chicago will be flying in. He'll check out your leg and decide what needs to be done. We'll do some tests tomorrow—whatever Dr. Robinson orders."

"Am I going to lose my leg?"

Doc shifted and rubbed the back of his neck.

"I know I've asked before, but I'm going into this blind. I'd like your opinion. No matter what it is."

"From the way your leg looked during the initial surgery, and from the way it's not healing, I'd say yes."

Other than his fingers pressing hard into the armrest, Eric fought hard to show nothing of the panic rising in him.

"But I didn't think you'd live through your first surgery. God miraculously saved your life then. He can save your leg now if He wants to."

"What if He doesn't want to?"

"Then God knows there's good that will come from losing your leg."

"Don't say that. How can losing my leg be good?"

"Losing your leg is not good."

"But you just said—"

"No. I meant God can bring good out of something bad. He does it all the time. The death of your parents was bad. Devastating in fact, but it was the catalyst that brought me to God."

"I know, Doc. I know. But I don't want to live with just one leg. I realize there are lots of people missing a limb or even two, but I don't want to be one of them."

"Eric, if I could take your place and do this for you, I would, but this is an assignment God's placing on you. You'll have to come to grips with it. God is using this challenge to help you learn to trust Him. No matter what—if He lets you keep your leg, or if He doesn't."

No guarantees. Zero control over the outcome. He could hardly breathe.

Doc's tone softened. "Son, you know I love you, don't you?"

Eric dropped his gaze and nodded slightly.

"Do you think I would do anything that would hurt you or bring you pain if it weren't for your ultimate good?"

Eric shook his head.

"God loves you more than I do."

"I know you believe that, but I don't feel it."

"You don't yet, but you will. I didn't either at first, but now, His love overwhelms me at times."

"So if I lose my leg, it's because God loves me?" He stood, every fiber of him struggling against what seemed to be inevitable.

"If God allows your leg to be taken, I assure you, it will be for your good. God's more concerned about your knowing Him and learning His ways than He is about your having two good legs. God wants you to give up control of your life and trust

Him. Your Commander-in-Chief. He wants to orchestrate your life according to His plan—not your plan."

If Doc was trying to cheer him up, it wasn't working.

"Sometime before surgery, talk it over with God. Keep praying until God gives you peace. Will you do that?"

Doc was the only guy on the planet who could back him into a corner. "Okay."

"Great. Now I need to check on a few things." He rose and placed his hand on Eric's shoulder. "No matter what happens, remember this: God is always good and always right."

Eric nodded but couldn't return the smile. His life had been turned upside down, and nothing about it seemed good. Or right.

Except Ellie. Hours went by before she came into his room with the smile that loosened the vice gripping his chest. She looked worn out. He stood and opened his arms, and without a word, she moved into them and wrapped her own around his waist.

"Long day?"

She nuzzled closer and gave a soft sigh. "Hm. But getting better by the second."

He turned her around and massaged her tense neck muscles.

Her head went limp and flopped forward. "Oh my goodness. That feels wonderful."

"I missed you today."

"Believe me. I wanted to come see you. Everyone else was tied up with the new equipment. I couldn't break away from the clinic even for a minute."

His fingers stilled. It hadn't hit him until that moment. He turned her around to face him and then held onto her shoulders to steady her. "You are killing yourselves to pull this off for me."

She took his hands and held them close to her heart. "Doing this for you brings us joy. *You* bring us joy."

He forced himself to meet her gaze. "I don't deserve it."

"Yes. You do. But it's not about deserving. It's about love."

Love. Like the love displayed all over her face as she raised his hands to her lips. She smiled at him, her expression sweet and tender and her once tired eyes now alive with adoration. He opened his mouth, but nothing came out. He stood rooted to the spot and offered her the only thing he had to give. A smile. Meant to reveal the depth of his own love. His hands cupped her face, and his thumb caressed her cheek. He held her gaze. "I love you," he whispered with the soft voice reserved only for her.

Her hands slid up his chest and came to rest behind his neck. "A little over a month ago, I didn't even know you existed. Now I don't know how I'll live without you. What's going to happen to us?"

He had no guarantees to give her, just like Doc had none for him. He kissed her forehead and gave the only answer he could. "I don't know, baby. God and I are working on it."

Her eyes remained on his for a moment. Then she nodded and settled her head against him. "Good. I've got a lot of faith in both of you."

It was up to him. And God. His heart almost thumped out of his chest. If she noticed, she didn't comment. He felt like he'd been thrown out of an airplane. With no parachute. And no safety net.

CHAPTER THIRTY-TWO

Eric stood at the sink brushing his teeth when Rocco cracked open the bathroom door.

"How's the pain on the pain-o-meter today?"

Eric rinsed and wiped his mouth. "About an eight. But my dread of this surgery is off the chart."

Rocco handed him the crutch. "Come on. I'm here to escort you to X-ray. We're dying to try out the new machines."

"Okay. Let me get my shoe."

"Hand it to me. I'll help you."

"The help I need is for you to talk me down from the ledge if I lose my leg on Monday."

"Sit a minute. Let's talk." Rocco pulled the chair closer to the bed. "Hey, man. I happen to know something about this guy Doc is flying in. He's the best there is, and if anybody can save your leg, he's the guy to do it." Rocco cleared his throat. "And we're all in your corner, pulling for you. You're at the top of our prayer list at every staff meeting. What you really need to dread is that guy over there."

Will waved from the doorway. "Will's controlling the X-ray equipment. Practiced on me. Can you believe that? I'm telling you. The power's gone to his head. I just hope he doesn't nuke you."

~~~~~~

After X-ray, Eric bypassed his room to sit on the shaded terrace.

Doc joined him a few minutes later. "Toby radioed. They're fifteen minutes out."

"Doc, you're spending a fortune on me."

Doc stared out at the field across the gravel road. "Not long after I became a Christian, I decided to give up all my money."

Eric gave him a disbelieving look. "You gave away your money? To whom?"

"God. I told God that from then on He could decide how to spend the money. God paid for all of this, not me."

"Nope. Not buying it. You're the one who ordered the X-ray machines. You're bringing the doctor here."

"I'm just obeying God. He told me to do it."

Eric heaved a sigh. "I don't care how you explain it."

Doc's face sobered as he leaned closer. "I'll let you in on a little secret. Every time I spend a lot of money like this, the strangest thing happens. Investments skyrocket, and the money increases. I've seen it time after time. There is more money now than when I began thirty years ago." He reached over to pat Eric's hand. "Don't give the money any more thought. It gives great joy. And besides, I owe you a great debt I'll never be able to repay."

Eric's throat tightened at Doc's pained expression. "You saved my life. Twice." He fought to keep his voice from breaking. "You taught me about Jesus. I'd say I'm the one who owes you."

Doc dropped his gaze as Eric knew he would.

Eric stood and put his hand on Doc's shoulder as Doc had done so many times to him. The dynamic little man with the big heart seemed to crumble, and for one brief moment, leaned into the embrace. Just as quickly, Doc straightened and raised tear-filled eyes. "Well, let me love you, and spoil you a little."

An approaching helicopter kept Eric from having to reply.

"Right on time. I'll help Carl get settled and then bring him by to meet you." With a quick squeeze to Eric's arm, Doc left.

Brock waited for the blades to slow to a stop before striding across the compound to the helicopter.

"Welcome, Carl."

"Brock. Long time." He pushed his hat back and glanced around. "I think you've added more buildings." Carl turned to the man and woman who had accompanied him. "You might remember Randall. And this is Amanda Cooper. I find I can't do surgery without them."

"Pleasure. Yes, hello." He reached behind Carl and shook their hands. "I understand. I have my own right hand people I can't do without."

"Moses still here?"

"Still here. Still working circles around me." He motioned for them to follow him to the hospital. "Right in here, everyone. Carl, this is Rocco and Will, two of my favorite short-term mission doctors. Guys, Dr. Carl Robinson, my good friend from Chicago."

"Your reputation precedes you, sir. It's a pleasure to meet you." Rocco handed him a large brown envelope.

"Thank you." He slid out the negatives and propped one on the screen. "Hmm." He took a pen from his pocket and pointed to the broken bone. "Look." Carl clasped his chin and crooked his finger against his tight lips. "I see why you called."

Brock's hopes sank as he looked over his friend's shoulder. The image on the screen sickened him. It would take a miracle.

Dr. Robinson placed the X-rays back in the envelope. "I'd like to talk to him."

No matter what had to be done. His new mantra. No matter what had to be done, he'd survive. And then he'd go after Reznik.

Eric sat on the edge of the bed, his heart thumping in time with the clock. An eternity went by before he heard footsteps in the hall. Doc entered the room with a tall man and what seemed to be his entourage.

"Eric, this is Dr. Robinson, my good friend, and arguably the best orthopedic surgeon in the States."

The doctor approached Eric with ease and looked him directly in the eye.

"Pleasure to meet you, Eric." His handshake was firm, confident. "I've heard good things about you."

"Thank you, sir."

"All right. Stretch out and let's see what we're up against." The doctor walked around the bed and removed the flexible cast, his face unreadable. He moved aside and gripped Eric's other calf to compare the two. Then he reattached the cast and returned to the other side. He grasped Eric's hand and helped him up then turned to the woman beside him. "Hand me the X-rays, please."

A hush fell over the room as the he took a negative from the envelope and held it up to the light. Eric didn't need to be a doctor to see the mangled mess in the image. Dr. Robinson leaned closer. "Your tibia. Right here." He pointed with the pen from his pocket. "These fragmented pieces might cause a problem."

Eric steeled his face from showing the disappointment he felt.

The doctor put the negative back into the envelope. "Here are our options. Once we go in, I can determine if I can patch you up. From the X-ray, I can tell you there's not enough bone to knit back together, but with some luck, we can attach the bone to a titanium rod. Lengthy convalescence, physical therapy, but you'll walk on it again."

An option he could live with.

"If there's not enough bone for the rod, we'll take off the leg just below the knee."

All eyes bore into him. He lifted his shoulders and raised his chin as if he were staring down a firing squad. *No matter what had to be done.*

Dr. Robinson turned to Doc. "I'd like to do the surgery first thing in the morning."

"We'll be ready."

The doctor focused again on Eric. "Any questions?"

"So, I won't know until after surgery if I have my leg or not?"

"No, but I'll make you this promise. I'll do all in my power to keep this leg attached to you. Fair enough?"

"Yes, sir. Thank you."

"Okay, young man. We're going to get settled. We'll see you bright and early tomorrow morning."

The room cleared but felt smaller than ever. If this were his last day with two legs, he wasn't going to waste it lying in bed. The tree or the chapel. He chose the chapel.

The late afternoon sun hit the stained glass at an angle that cast a warm glow over the room. Eric sat on a bench and picked up one of the Bibles near it. Too overwhelmed to read or to pray, he propped his elbows on the Bible and buried his face in his hands.

After a long while, he lifted his head and stared at the image of Jesus on the wall. If only he could say the right words. "Doc says You love me. If that's true, then please, I'm begging You, let me keep my leg."

He waited for the peace Doc said he'd feel. Nothing. But something Doc said popped into his mind. *God wants you to trust Him. Your Commander-in-Chief.*

Eric took a deep breath and slowly blew it out. Trust God? Even if it meant losing his leg? Was that even possible? His stomach knotted just thinking about it. He looked again at the image of Jesus. Zero control over the outcome. Zero experience with trusting a God he couldn't see or hear. He couldn't do it.

The door of the chapel opened. Doc and Ellie came in followed by the rest of the team. One by one they entered the building like a parade. Each met his eyes and smiled. Rocco brought up the rear and closed the door.

"Hey, man, you can run, but you can't hide."

"Believe me, Rocco, I wish I could run."

Ellie sat beside him. Rocco straddled the bench on his other side, and Doc positioned himself directly in front of Eric. The rest of the group filled in the empty spaces and formed a circle around him. No one spoke.

He wasn't sure he could. He cleared his throat. "Thanks for coming to my rescue." He looked down at his hands. "Means a lot."

Doc spoke. "All of us love you. We're here to show our support and pray with you."

Eric smiled his thanks. How had he survived this far without love in his life? "In case you haven't heard, I've become a follower of God."

"Welcome to the family." The unmistakable African accent could come from only one person. "You're truly our brother now." Moses' long arm had no trouble reaching around Ellie to pat him on the shoulder.

"I'm not very good at understanding it yet. I've been in here for most of the afternoon, praying God will heal my leg. Maybe you could pray for me. I don't have much faith."

Doc extended his hand across the aisle to Moses and also to Will on his left. "Let's pray now." Each one prayed, many with tears. Doc ended their prayer and then spoke once more to Eric. "We'll all be with you tomorrow. Some of us will be assisting Dr. Robinson. The rest will be in the next room. Remember, son, God will be with you. He'll never leave you."

He nodded and only then realized he felt better. Was this the peace Doc talked about? Everyone rose and connected in some way as they moved past him, beginning with Doc who embraced him. Others gave a touch to his arm or a pat on the back. Miriam and Nicci hugged him as well, and then there was just Ellie who moved to his side carrying one of his crutches. "You want to walk me home?"

"Yes, ma'am." He wrapped his arm around her. Out in the night air, the moon lit the landscape, and the gravel crunched under their feet.

"That meant a lot to me." Much more than he could put into words.

"It was Dad's idea. Everyone jumped at the chance."

A night owl screeched, and Ellie shuddered. "Sorry. I never get used to it. Freaks me out."

He squeezed her tighter. "Talk to me, Ellie."

"So are you all right about the surgery?"

"I'm trying to be. Talk to me. Take my mind off it."

She led him to one of the benches in front of the chapel. "Okay. You asked for it. But if one of those owls come swooping out of the sky, you're on your own, mister." She grinned, and he made a mental note to always sit to her right to keep a perfect view of the dimple.

He grinned back, feeling better already. "I'll take my chances."

She turned slightly toward him. "Help me out. I can't think of anything."

"Hm. How about a pet story? Or something about you and your dad?"

She stared at the ground, her finger tapping her mouth. Then with a quick intake of breath, she raised her head, her eyes wide and excited. "I've got it. And it's about a pet and Dad." Almost as quickly, her face clouded. "Maybe not. This one's kind of sad."

"You can't leave me hanging."

"Good, because it's the only thing I can come up with. So we had this dog."

He nodded, not caring what came out of her mouth. Her animated face was entertainment enough. "What kind?"

"Golden Retriever. Her name was Lady. I don't really have any memories of Dad and me when I was younger because, well you know. They split up when I was three. But there's a connection with the dog. Lady was like my best friend. I loved that dog. But when Mom left Dad, she got rid of the dog because she hated animals. Any kind of animal. And the only thing she hated more than animals was Dad. Okay, brace yourself for the sad part."

He nodded and took one of her hands and held on tight. "Ready."

"When Mom took us away from Dad, I cried 'til I threw up. Cried most of the night. But it was for Lady. Not Dad. In fact, I have one or two vague memories of the dog. None of Dad. Pathetic, isn't it?"

She was making light of it, but all he could think about was the little girl crying herself to sleep. "Your mother sounds a lot like my father."

She almost laughed. "She does, doesn't she? The next part is a little better. A couple of years later, I found some pictures in my sister's closet. We sat on the floor and looked through them. She told me all about Lady, how one of Dad's patients gave her to him because she loved her new nose. Now bear in mind I was only five at the time, but I couldn't figure out how the puppy got a new nose or how the woman knew the puppy loved it."

He burst out laughing. "That's a great story. I'll never be able to top it."

"You liked it?"

He wrapped his arm around her and pulled her close. "I loved it. It actually took my mind off the surgery. At least for a little while."

"Great. And tonight, instead of thinking about the surgery, you can think up your next story for me. It's your turn next time."

"Yes, ma'am. Come on. I'll walk you back to your room."

"You don't have to."

"Yes, I do." His smile softened his tone. "I want to."

They lingered at her door, and then he turned her around. "Off to bed now." She looked back at him, and their eyes met and locked. Neither moved, or spoke, or needed to.

SAVING ERIC

CHAPTER THIRTY-THREE

Eric hopped to the window and peeked through the blinds. Pitch black. Balancing on one leg, he scanned the dark compound. At least, the waiting would end today.

He headed to the bathroom. Rocco arrived as he finished brushing his teeth. "Dude, I'm glad you're in here. Doc ordered an enema for you."

Eric dug his fingers into the side of the sink. "You're kidding."

Rocco burst out laughing. "Yeah, but the look on your face was priceless."

Eric relaxed his death grip on the porcelain. "It's a good thing I'm a changed man. I've killed men for less."

Rocco held up both hands. "No tubes. Scouts honor. Just this stylish hospital gown." He swung wide the bathroom door to reveal the gurney he'd brought into the room. "Then your chariot awaits."

Eric hobbled over and hoisted himself up while Rocco held it steady. "Are you always this cheerful in the morning?"

"I'll let you in on a little secret. I'm sweating bullets for you. Making jokes is my way of coping." Rocco positioned the sheet over him. "You ought to hear me at funerals."

Eric laughed. Something he didn't think was possible, especially today. Ellie's smiling face greeted them as soon as they cleared the doorway. Then the whole team seemed to appear out of nowhere. The terrace doors gave a familiar creak, and Toby came running from behind. He clutched the safety rail and bent over to try to catch his breath. "Hey, bro, I was scared I wouldn't make it in time." Eric raised his hand, and Toby grasped it. "Got your back, man."

The room was starkly bright. Rocco inserted the IV into Eric's arm while he was still on the gurney. The crowd around him dispersed, and the small area became a beehive of activity. Doc took his hand and smiled. "Okay, son. Ready?"

"Yeah."

Doc nodded to someone behind Eric. Something cool slid up the vein in his arm, and the drug kicked in. No worries. Just love. If he could, he'd get off the gurney and hug everybody in the room.

Every beat of Brock's heart was a silent prayer as he scoured his hands. He raised the mask over his face and joined the man who would call the shots for this surgery. Rocco prepped Eric's leg with betadine and applied sterile drapes. Carl made the incision over the area where the tibia was fractured on the X-ray.

"Randall, let's clean up those bone fragments. Suction. There."

Brock stayed out of the way. The Chicago team moved with little direction as if the surgery had already been choreographed. His friend made quiet comments almost to himself. "Significant amount of soft tissue damage. Look, Brock. The trajectory of the bullet ripped through this area."

Brock nodded and helped clear the dead muscle and osseous debris so they could identify any remnant of healthy tissue.

"Hmmm. Not much left." Carl sighed as he surveyed the damage. "Well, we won't know if we don't at least try." He took the titanium rod and hammered it into place through a separate incision just below the knee. Under fluoroscopy, he pounded, twisted, and manipulated the rigid titanium prosthesis against the flaccid leg. He worked steadily to the point of perspiring through his cap and mask. Finally, he muttered under his breath and threw the blood-soaked sponge he held onto the floor.

Brock's chest tightened. He would gladly give all he had to spare Eric this pain. He panned the room searching for Ellie. She raised her chin and their eyes met.

Carl once again reached for the scalpel and completed the incision for the amputation. His team identified the artery and vein and doubly tied them and ligated the nerve. The bullet had done most of the work already, and it was over quickly.

Brock dropped his surgical mask. "Nice work, Carl."

"I wish I could've saved it."

"That leg was beyond saving."

Rocco wheeled Eric to post-op. No more words, only the clink of the instruments. Brock stayed close to the gurney. "I'll stay with him until he wakes up. I'd like to be the one to tell him. Rocco, you stay too."

Ellie joined them, her cheeks as white as Eric's sheet.

He needed Solomon's wisdom to know how to protect them both. "Ellie, it might be better for you to wait a little before he sees you."

"Really, Dad?" Tears had left a streak down her face and wet the mask draping her neck. "I want to be near him."

"I know, sweetheart, but let him hear the news first. I'll call you as soon as I can. I think he'd want it this way."

Her mouth tightened, and she reached up to rub the back of her neck. "You're probably right, but call me as soon as he asks for me."

"You know I will. Go wait with Toby. This will be tough on him too."

Both men sat quietly beside Eric's sleeping body. At the first indication that he was coming to, Brock leaned closer.

"Eric."

Eric opened his eyes slowly. "Over?"

"Yes, son. It's over."

Eric's face relaxed. "Thank God. Still there."

He started to tell him but couldn't. Eric mumbled something and drifted off again.

Brock rubbed his chin. This wasn't going to be easy.

∧∧∧∧∧

Eric took a deep breath and opened his eyes. Rocco stood beside him.

"Where's Ellie?"

Doc stepped in beside Rocco. "She's with Toby. Eric, Dr. Robinson couldn't save your leg."

His heart stopped and then sped up. He couldn't have heard right. He lifted his head. "Raise the sheet, Doc." He struggled to rise and forced words from his tight throat. "I feel it. It's still there."

"It's phantom pain. It's your body's way—"

"Let me see." He clutched Doc's scrubs.

"All right, son. I'll show you." Doc held up the sheet and carefully raised his head.

He stared at the bandaged stump that used to be his leg. It was gone. His leg was actually gone. He fell back onto the pillow and closed his eyes, his heaving chest the only sign of his inner panic. He swallowed hard and forced down the bile churning in his stomach. He would not throw up. A lone tear escaped and slid from his eye and past his ear. He fought hard for control, and his body reverted back to what it knew best, what it had been trained to do. The barrier raised, and his tears dried.

"Eric, do you want Ellie?"

"Eric." Doc spoke again, louder this time. "Ellie's worried. Do you want me to call her in here?"

Eric shook his head. Doc's hand grasped his. "Do you want me to leave you alone?"

Doc's gentle tone threatened his resolve. Eric squeezed his eyes tighter. The hand left his, and Eric's eyes flew open.

"No. Stay." He waited for Doc to return and take his hand before he closed his eyes again.

"Come on, Toby. We're going in." Ellie grabbed Toby's hand and pulled him with her. She led the way and didn't knock. Tension like a brick wall filled the room. Eric lay still, his eyes closed. The chalk-white pallor reminded her of his first days here. Her dad stood beside the bed with his hand on Eric's. Rocco stood at the foot of the bed. The tight line of his lips replaced the usual grin.

Her dad's initial smile disappeared as he shook his head. Ellie strained to hear his whispered words. "I don't think he's ready yet."

She couldn't have heard right. She barreled over to the bed and covered Eric's other hand.

"Has he come to yet?"

Eric turned. His face a lifeless mask revealing no emotion. His eyes, hollow sockets that looked right through her.

He pulled his hand from her grasp and placed his arm across his face.

Her dad rushed around the bed. "Come with me, sweetheart." He took her by the shoulders and turned her toward the door. With a side glance, he spoke to Toby. "Stay with him."

In the hall, Ellie leaned into her father's embrace wishing it were Eric's.

"He needs time." Her dad kept his arm around her and navigated her away from the recovery room and down the hall. "Come with me. I need to change, and we need to talk."

Her dad's room, with the comfortable smell of his things. She planted herself in the recliner while he rummaged through his dresser. She stared at the floor but could only see Eric's face. "Eric looked right through me, like he was dead."

"It's his body's way of shutting down until he's strong

enough to handle it."

She relaxed her head against the back of the chair. "Seeing him like this is killing me."

"It's killing me too. But he's got to go through it. And he will. He probably won't even remember these first few hours." Her dad walked over to her and leaned over to kiss her cheek. "I need to take a quick shower and get out of these scrubs. Why don't you find Nicci and ask her to make some coffee?"

She nodded and rose to go, but first she had to ask. "Dad, God could've healed Eric. Why didn't He?"

Her dad stopped in the doorway of his bathroom and turned to her. "I don't know, honey. We may never know. Sometimes God says no, and when He does, we have to trust Him."

⌁⌁⌁⌁

Ellie breathed easier as she peeked around her dad. Asleep. They joined Rocco and Toby by the bed.

"Ellie and I will stay with him." Her dad smiled and nodded. "You can get some rest."

"Doc, I need to get back, but call me if anything changes."

"Will do, Toby. Glad you could make it for the surgery."

"Me too. I wish I could stay."

Her dad wrapped his arm around Toby's shoulders and walked him and Rocco to the door. "You were here when he needed you. Don't worry. He'll be all right. Rocco, take your time. I'll call you if I need you."

"Okay. I'll get cleaned up and check on the clinic." Rocco looked back at Ellie and smiled. "See you later."

Ellie sat on one side and her dad on the other. She had planned to slip out if he stirred, but he woke suddenly. His eyes fixed on hers, never leaving her face. He moved his hand toward her, and she met it. He gave a gentle squeeze and closed his eyes again. Relief washed over her. Her fingers caressed his hand. She wanted to sit but couldn't risk pulling the chair closer. She wouldn't let go.

They stayed through the night, catching small naps when they could. The next morning, Eric's restless sleep calmed down.

"Go grab some breakfast and get freshened up. It'll make you feel better. Eric will need you more this afternoon."

She left and Brock prayed Eric would wake before Ellie returned. Eric's eyes fluttered open almost immediately. He glanced over at Ellie's empty chair. "Where is she?"

"Just left to take a shower and get some coffee."

Eric nodded.

Brock took a fortifying breath. "How are you doing?"

"You really want to know?"

"I really want to know."

Eric heaved a sigh. "I prayed. I thought God was going to let me keep it. He didn't." He shook his head. "Maybe He's punishing me for all I've done."

Brock's heart twisted at Eric's pained expression. "God's not punishing you, son. That's not how God operates."

"Then why? Why did I have to lose my leg?"

"I don't know. But here's the truth. God is good. He allows things in our lives for a purpose. He's God. He gets to call the shots."

Eric's chalky white face emphasized the dark shadows under his eyes. Eric stared at him for a long time and then looked away.

Brock dug his fingers into his palms. "Look at me."

Eric's mouth tightened, but he turned his head and met his gaze.

"Your leg is gone. Do you hear me? Gone. You'll never get it back. And now you have two choices. You can give up, or you can ask God to help you overcome this challenge." He softened his tone. "Let God help you. Let all of us who love you, help you. Lean on us. Lean on God until you're strong enough to bear it."

Gone. He'd never get it back. Eric didn't look away. Not once. Somehow the words got through. His hand inched toward Doc. "I need help."

Doc snatched it up and enclosed it in both of his. "We're here, son. You're not alone."

He was right. It was time he faced it, dealt with it, and moved on. "Would you help me up?"

"Of course." Doc lowered the rail and flipped back the sheet. "I'll get behind and help push you up."

Eric kept his eyes closed until he started to swing his legs over. Then he took his first up close look at the bandaged stump. "Oh God. Why?" The walls closed in and pushed the air out of his body. He needed to get out, but he was stuck. Trapped. Crippled. Forever. "Doc, I can't do this."

Doc tightened his hold as waves of grief crashed over Eric. Loud, wracking sobs rose from his deepest core, and only Doc's strong grip kept him from collapsing on the floor. More than once he lost his breath. His fingers dug deep as he clung to Doc's embrace. He wasn't manning up, but he didn't care. His fight was gone.

Just like his leg.

Only when his breathing slowed, did Doc loosen his hold. He shifted his position on the bed, his quiet voice like a salve on Eric's torn heart. "The healing will begin now. The worst is over."

Eric gave a half-hearted nod, too spent to speak in more than a whisper. "I hope you're right." Never before had he broken down and cried like a baby in front of someone else. He forced himself to meet Doc's gaze. Doc's face seemed as wet as his own, and in that moment he knew.

Real men can cry.

CHAPTER THIRTY-FOUR

Eric set his face and lifted his chin as Rocco and Doc moved him from the gurney to his bed. "Thank you." He meant it mostly for the lack of pity he saw in their faces. He forced a cheerfulness he couldn't feel and hung onto what shred of self-respect he still possessed. One meltdown was enough.

Rocco gave a matter-of-fact nod. "I'll be back a little later to check on you." He left, not waiting for a response.

"I'll be back later too. Dr. Robinson will be in shortly to talk with you."

Eric met Doc's gaze but didn't trust himself to reply. Doc squeezed his hand and left. Time alone. Just what he thought he wanted. Until he got it. He looked around the room. Blinds opened and raised. The clock back in place on the wall, ticking away. Nothing had changed.

Everything had changed.

Heavy footsteps approached his room and interrupted his brooding. Eric resisted the tension forming in his chest. The threat no longer existed. "Hello, Eric. You look much better today. More alert." Dr. Robinson came alone. He seemed larger than Eric remembered, and his commanding presence filled the room. He gave a relaxed smile as he pulled the stool closer to the bed. "I'll be leaving this afternoon, and I wanted to go over some things with you. First, let me tell you I'm sorry I couldn't save your leg."

"Me too. Thanks for doing all you could."

"Believe it or not, removing your leg will give you more options than had we tried to piece together those fragments."

Removing your leg. The one option he didn't want.

"Here's what you can expect. I don't have to tell you that the first few weeks are painful. No way around it. All those nerve ends we severed are screaming at you. We want to make you as comfortable as possible. Don't hesitate to ask for pain medication."

"It still feels like my leg's there."

"That's common and will lessen in time. Almost all amputees experience the sensation the limb is still there."

Eric heard amputee and little else. Another word for cripple.

"We can put a temporary plastic cast on while your leg is healing. It will help protect the incision and also help give you balance. Whenever we remove the sutures and staples, we need to fit you with a prosthesis."

"When will that be?"

"Anywhere from eight to twelve weeks. You can get two different prosthetic limbs. One is the Flex Rotate limb, good for everyday wear. The other is called the Flex Run. I hear you're a runner."

"I used to be."

Dr. Robinson's eyes softened. "You will be again. You'll be able to do anything you did before. It'll just take time."

Eric gave a deep sigh. "I hope so." He glanced at his leg propped up on a pillow. Blood seeped through the bandage.

The doctor leaned back and crossed his arms. "If there's any good news, you lost it at the best possible place. I was able to leave your knee cap intact. Your own knee bends and gives. It'll aid your adjustment time. The bad news is that it'll be a painful recovery, physically and emotionally. You'll need to come to the States to get the right fit as well as the help and support you'll need. Brock has my direct number. He or you can call my private line at any time.

"I appreciate that."

Dr. Robinson stood and walked around the bed. "Okay, let's take a look." He unwrapped the bandage. "Still a good bit of bleeding and drainage." He said almost to himself. "That'll slow down." The doctor removed the blood-soaked cloths, pursed his lips, and nodded. "Looks good."

Eric stole a quick glance. Nothing about that swollen purple stump looked good. Didn't feel good either. He kept his back side glued to the bed and refused to flinch as the doctor poked and prodded. He slid his hand beneath the blanket and gripped the sheet with his fist. By the time the new gauze was securely in place, he tasted blood on the inside of his mouth.

"There. Sorry, I know that hurt." He removed his disposable gloves and threw them away with the other soiled bandages. He stepped into the bathroom to wash his hands and spoke over his shoulder. "How are you coping?"

Dr. Robinson returned and sat as if he had all the time in the world.

Eric decided to tell the truth. "Not great but better than yesterday. I wanted a different option, but I'll be all right. I'll learn to adapt. Helps to know one day I can resume running. That was one of my questions."

"Absolutely. You'll enjoy a full and normal lifestyle. Any other questions?"

"I'd like to get up and move around. Any restrictions?"

"No, the only restriction is the amount of pain you'll be experiencing."

"It hurts whether I'm in bed or walking around. I'd rather be walking around."

Dr. Robinson smiled as he stood. "I can tell you're going to make the transition just fine." He shook Eric's hand. "I need to see you in eight weeks. But be sure to call if you have any problems."

"Thank you."

The doctor gave Eric a friendly pat and left the room.

Alone, Eric forced himself to look again. The possibility of
being killed on assignment had always loomed in the back of
his mind, but not once did he ever think he'd be maimed. His
throat closed and his chest heaved to get enough air. He
couldn't live like this. He didn't want to live like this. Oh God.

Eric stared at the window and tried to slow his breathing.
A white cloud floated across his view. He aimed at it and spoke
the only thing he could think to say. "God, help me."

Rocco came into the room. "Hey, pal. I saw Dr. Robinson
leave your room." He sat on the stool the doctor had left by the
bed. "What'd he say?"

Eric's mind went blank. He stared at his hands and tried to
clear the fog. "He, uh, said everything looks good."

Rocco stuck his feet on the bed rail and leaned forward.
"Doesn't feel so good, does it?"

Eric's lips tightened. Couldn't risk breaking down again.
Not in front of Rocco.

"Dude, do I need to get you a ladder?"

Eric cocked his head. Was this a sick joke? "A ladder?"

"Yeah. You said you might need me to talk you down
from the ledge."

Eric almost grinned. Almost. "No ladder. Seems I'm
minus one leg. Might need a safety net instead."

The witty comeback he expected didn't come. Instead, an
understanding look. No judgment.

"Dr. Robinson said I'd be able to do everything I used to
do. Everything but stand on my own two feet." Eric waited for
some kind of platitude but then barreled on. "I'm not the man I
used to be. I won't ever be that man again." There. He said it.
Now Rocco would tell him how that wasn't true.

"Yeah. I see what you mean."

Eric waited for more. The clock ticked on. If he had his
gun, he'd at least take care of the clock. He looked at Rocco, a

challenge in his eyes. He was done talking. There was nothing left to say.

After a long while, Rocco spoke. "I bet you've had a lot of close calls in your spy travels."

The knife in his gut twisted. No more lightning fast escapes. No more Houdini. So much for talking him off the ledge.

"When I did one of my rotations at a veteran's hospital, I learned something."

Here it comes. The platitude that would supposedly turn him around. "What?"

"Two legs don't make a man. The man who faces the fear and takes on the challenge in spite of it. Now that's a real man."

Two legs don't make a man. The help he asked for. The blasted tears threatened.

Rocco must have known. "Besides, think of all the cool one-legged man jokes you can tell now."

He chuckled in spite of himself and could breathe again.

"Can I get you anything before I head over to the clinic?"

"Yeah. My toothbrush and my razor."

"Dude. Are you back?"

"Not quite, but I'm getting there."

"That's what I like to hear."

Rocco helped him clean up. "There you go. I'll be back later to help you get out of this bed if you think you're up to it."

"That'd be great. Thanks for the ladder, Roc."

The smile was genuine. So was the nod.

"You mind finding Ellie for me?"

The lopsided grin was back. "You bet."

Rocco left, but his words stayed. Two legs don't make a man. He'd tackle this challenge the way he tackled every other challenge in his life. He'd be the best. He'd recover the fastest.

He'd walk without a limp. He'd run again. He'd show the world.

He'd show himself.

The light footsteps he'd been waiting for got louder as she approached. His heart raced, but his stomach tensed. Maybe he should sit, so he'd seem less helpless. No. Didn't want the first thing she saw to be the stump.

Ellie appeared almost immediately but hovered at the door as if waiting for permission. She held Bitsy close to her chest. His heart melted. She wore no false bravado, no fake smile to patronize him.

"My two favorite girls." His smile might have been a little forced, but she didn't seem to notice. She almost ran to his side. The kitten jumped from her grasp onto his chest. "Bits. You miss me?" The kitten climbed up his chest and found her spot close to his neck. Eric stroked the fur and glanced up at Ellie. "Hey, you." He let go of the kitten and reached for her. "I'm glad to see you."

She used both hands to grasp his and started to sit on what seemed to be the community stool.

"No. Wait. I'll sit up."

She moved quickly to put down the rail. He struggled to maneuver so he could swing his legs over and sit on the edge. Cold sweat broke out above his lip. He grimaced, determined to work through the excruciating pain. He squeezed Bitsy a little too hard, and she wiggled away from his grasp. Okay, maybe a dumb idea. Thank goodness Ellie didn't offer to help. When he could catch his breath, he rasped out, "Come sit by me."

"That's a lot of work to have me sit by you."

"Worth it." Words he'd said before, the first time she took him to the terrace.

She rewarded him with the dimple. She scooped up Bitsy and moved in closer.

He ignored his screaming leg and wrapped his arm around her. "I got a little lost, but I'm working my way back now."

She nudged him with her body. "Seeing you in so much pain ripped me apart."

"It's a little fuzzy to me, but I remember I woke up, and you put your hand on mine." His throat tightened. He paused until he could get it out. "Gave me something to hang on to."

Her head rested on his shoulder. "Are you all right now?"

"Not there yet. I'm still reeling from the shock. Your dad helped. He seems to know just what to say and when to say it. He let me sink into my hole and then gave me a little fatherly kick in the pants. Told me to snap out of it but with a lot more patience and understanding than my father would have." He kissed the top of her head. "You won't believe this, but today I had just prayed for God to help me, and Rocco showed up. Something he said clicked. So, I've made up my mind. I'm going to make you and your dad and the whole team proud of me. I'm going to beat this."

"There's no way I could be prouder of you."

The look she gave left him in no doubt. Made him want to fight harder and be worthy of her pride. And never lose it.

SAVING ERIC

CHAPTER THIRTY-FIVE

Waves of agonizing pain shot through his entire right side every time the swollen stump swung forward. He needed answers, and he was going to the one place he might find them. The chapel. He would be alone. Talk out loud to God.

He reached the terrace, spent and out of breath, and tried to calculate the remaining distance. He could call if off for today or keep going. The hesitation lasted only seconds before he sucked in a deep breath and went forward.

Memories of the last time he visited this place popped up as he entered the sanctuary. Could it have been only three days? He found his spot, sank down on the bench, and closed his eyes. He'd made it, and he settled in for a long stay. It'd take a while to work up the gumption to white-knuckle it back.

Moving prisms of color danced on the wall from the stained glass. His eyes zeroed in on Jesus. Tears fell, but he didn't try to stop them. He was done bargaining. And he was done with self-pity. "What's left of me is Yours, and I'm showing up for duty."

His throbbing leg drove him to change positions. He stretched it out on the bench and lay on his back staring up at the ceiling. "Right now, I could use Your help with Reznik. I can't outmaneuver this guy. He has all the resources of the agency leveled at me. God, I can't fight this and win."

Surrender.

He wasn't sure where the thought came from, but he toyed with it as he lay there. And then the fog lifted. So simple, he wondered why he hadn't thought of it before. The door at the back creaked open. Had to be Ellie or Doc.

"I never get tired of looking at that stained glass window."

Eric struggled to sit up. "Doc. Yeah, I like to sit here and look at it and talk to God. Feels like I'm not just talking into space."

"Would you rather be alone?" Doc waited before taking a seat.

Eric shook his head. "I'm glad you're here."

He smiled and sat. "Rocco told me you're very eager to get back to normal."

"I'm ready to accept this and move on."

"I knew you would."

"Your pep talk helped set me straight."

"I helped guide you to a conclusion you would eventually make on your own." Doc gave him the fatherly embrace Eric had come to rely on. "But now I need to talk with you again."

Eric tensed. Need to talk from his dad usually meant something unpleasant. "Sir?"

"I'm worried about you. This kind of recovery is extremely painful for the first few weeks. I'm afraid you're overdoing it. Rocco mentioned you're refusing your pain medication. Why, son?"

His stiff shoulders relaxed. "I don't know. I guess I need to prove to myself this isn't going to get me down."

Sounded lame even to him. He waited for Doc's rebuttal.

"Push yourself if you must. You've got good judgment. You'll know if you need medication."

Eric inhaled, the first really deep breath he'd taken in days.

"I've got to clear my name with the agency."

"Any ideas?"

He nodded. "A plan came to me as I was sitting here. It's crazy, but crazy enough to work. I can't believe I didn't think of it sooner. But I'll need your help."

"I'd love to help you. What'd you need?"

"I'd like you to go to Washington. Talk to someone who can help me set up a sting operation. Someone I can trust."

"Do you have someone in mind?"

"My father."

~~~~~

"You want me to go talk to your father?" Brock could feel the blood leaving his face. "And this needs to be done in person?"

"Yes. Tom Reznik is uncertain if I'm dead or alive, and he's desperate to find me and finish the job. Any phone communication to my father will jeopardize the success of the plan."

"Why don't you resurface? Go to your father and ask him to help you?"

"I thought of that."

For one brief moment, Brock started to relax.

"But Reznik has incriminating evidence on me. Trumped up but believable. And if they find me at Dad's, he could be implicated too. I really don't like those odds."

"Of course not. I see your point." He rubbed his chin and fought the sick feeling in the pit of his stomach. Eric needed him, and Doc would deliver even if it killed him. And it just might. "Tell me the plan."

"Something that's a little risky, but I think guaranteed to work."

"Risky?"

"I want Reznik to find out I'm here and get him to come for me. If my father is in on it first, he can convince the director to help us set up a sting operation."

"What if the director doesn't buy it?"

"I'll give myself up and take my chances. The director isn't the one I'm worried about. It's my dad. That's why I need you. A total stranger would carry no credibility. You have a connection with me and my dad. That's the one thing that might make it believable."

The lump in his throat became a fully mature knot in his stomach. Eric was right. He had to go.

"How exactly will this sting operation work?"

"That's the tricky part. Dad needs to explain everything to the director. With the director on board, he'll make sure Reznik is the one coming for me. Dad will get here ahead of him and help me bug my room. When Reznik comes, I'll have to trick him into confessing before he takes me out of here. If he gets me away, I'll never make it back to Langley alive."

"Do you think you can pull this off?"

A spark of life Brock hadn't seen in a long time lit Eric's eyes.

"It's the only option I've got. What do you think, Doc?"

"I don't know, son. It sounds dangerous. I don't want to pull you back from the brink of eternity again."

Eric smiled but said nothing.

Brock teetered, feeling he faced his own execution. "All right." Time to swallow his pride, and if he perished …"When do you want me to go?"

"As soon as possible. It'll take a few days for you and Dad to make the plans. In the meantime, I need to get stronger and clearer-headed. That's another reason I'm trying to handle the pain cold turkey."

Brock glanced at the image of Jesus in front of them. "I find it much easier to trust God with my own life than trust Him to take care of the people I love, especially when there's danger involved. We'll work out all the details later. Right now, I need to talk to God about it."

"Yes, sir. I'm counting on it."

Not long after Eric made it back to his room, the muscle spasms hit. Not just a Charlie horse. A whole stampede. Pacing and stretching used to be the answer, but how could he stretch something no longer there? He sat on the edge of his bed and propped his leg on the stool. A little relief came when he gripped his thigh and rocked it back and forth. Relief didn't last. His fingers clutched the side of his bed until they turned white. Maybe he'd pass out.

For once, the clock on the wall was his friend. Rocco would be coming soon. He could tough it out.

No. He couldn't. He had to find Rocco. Or anybody. Now. His crutches helped him reach Ellie's room with surprising speed. With no response to his knock, Eric hunched against the wall and slid down before his good leg gave way altogether. A door closed down the hall, and then the footsteps his ear had been trained to single out.

"Eric? Oh my goodness. Let's get you into my room."

Good plan, but he couldn't do it. Eyes closed, he held up a hand and shook his head. "Can't." So much for proving he was man enough to handle the pain.

Her hand was cool on his arm, but her voice sounded as desperate as he felt. "Dad, come to my room. It's Eric."

She smoothed the hair back from his forehead. "They're on the way."

Another spasm bent him over. Heavier footsteps and then Doc huffed out, "Ellie, get morphine and a muscle relaxer. Rocco, grab a wheelchair."

Eric didn't protest. He wouldn't care if they knocked him out. What little discipline he had left kept him from screaming out. The entire leg now shook from the spasms and sent a rippling effect across his whole body

Doc squatted beside him and tried to still his shakes. "Hang on, Eric."

He didn't respond. He couldn't. Rocco came back skidding the wheelchair to a stop, and they heaved him into it.

They wheeled him back to the room, and Ellie returned with two syringes. Doc took hold of his thigh while Ellie pushed the needle in above his knee. "There," she whispered. "It'll start to relax."

The next one went in his arm, and then they helped get him into bed.

"Lean into it, son. Try not to tense up."

The clock ticked off six minutes before Eric was able to talk. "Lesson learned, Doc. Might have overdone it a little today."

"Pain is always worse at night. Maybe you could give yourself permission to take some medication in the evening. Just 'til you're over the hump."

Eric barely nodded. If he moved, the pain might come back. He dragged his eyes open long enough to find Ellie. He'd tell them thanks later. Right now, the relief felt too good to disturb.

CHAPTER THIRTY-SIX

The morphine-induced sleep worked its magic. He awoke rested. Pain bearable. He folded his arm beneath his head and stared at the ceiling ready to work on strategy. Rocco's voice broke through his deep thoughts.

"Dude, you're up. Sleep okay?"

"Better than I have in days."

Rocco walked around the bed to get a look at his leg. "And you look better than you have in days. Maybe the worst is over."

He hoped so. It was time to put on his game face.

"If you'll help me get dressed, I'll eat breakfast in the dining hall with the team."

"That'll make one member of the team particularly happy."

"That's the plan."

Eric and Ellie lingered at the table after everyone else left.

"I have to inventory again. You want to help?"

"You bet."

Different room this time. Looked more like general supplies. Gloves, syringes, gauze, tape. He sat in a chair near the end of a counter. She put her hair in a ponytail and stooped to open a box. Deja vu. She stood on her toes and stretched to place containers on a top shelf.

Yeah. Just like last time.

What about your pledge to protect her. From yourself.

Simon, give me a break.

He reached for a knife and sliced through the top of the box. Nineteen, twenty. He set the containers on the counter and ripped into another box. "I worked out a plan to expose Reznik."

She put the last container on a shelf and turned. "Expose Reznik?"

"The traitor back at the agency. An idea came to me out of the blue. Can't believe I didn't think of it sooner."

He handed her the containers he had counted. She took them and opened the next cabinet. "What exactly does exposing Reznik involve?"

"I'll let him find me."

Her hand stopped midway to the shelf. He continued before she could ask questions.

"With inside help, of course. We'll set up a sting. His over-confidence will be his downfall."

The more he talked, the faster she stacked containers. She placed the last one and turned to face him, her lips tight and her eyes a darker blue than he remembered. She didn't speak, but the pulse in her neck fluttered like a bird beating its wing against its cage.

Awkward. He handed her more containers. She took them and set them aside without taking her eyes off him. "Can't you find some other way? Something safer?"

"Maybe. But this way's much more fun." Humor. Works for Rocco every time.

She sighed and pressed her palm to her forehead. "This isn't a joke, Eric. This is your life you're playing with."

"I'm not playing." Humor didn't work. He lowered his voice. "I'm dead serious." Probably should have chosen a better word. "The snake sold out one of the best agents in the field and got him killed. Not to mention, almost got me killed. Twice. Ellie, he's ruthless. And I'm going to stop him."

"Then go to the director. Tell him the truth. He'll believe you. He trusts you."

"I can't do that."

"You can't? Or you won't?"

Their eyes locked in a showdown. She looked away first.

"Come here, Ellie."

Her face remained turned from him. Her chin rose slightly. He had the insane impulse to kiss those pouty little lips. They charmed him almost as much as the dimple, which was clearly missing at the moment.

Using just one crutch, he stood and took a step toward her. He placed his hand on her arm, hoping she wouldn't pull away. "I won't leave anything to chance. I'm covering every detail."

Her mouth softened, her shoulders relaxed. He nudged her around to face him. For a brief moment, she met his gaze but then looked down. He took her trembling hand and tried to rub some warmth into the icy fingers.

She pulled out of his grasp and walked away. "I can't think when you're holding me."

He raked his hand through his hair. "What do you want from me, Ellie? What about this is bothering you so much? Don't you trust me?"

"Yes, Eric. I trust *you.*" She whirled back around. "But I saw the shape you were in when Toby brought you here. You said yourself this guy's ruthless. He wants you dead."

Reasoning with her wasn't working. Throbbing spasms pulsated up his leg. He needed to sit, but he'd keel over before he sat with her towering over him.

"What do you recommend I do? Wait for him to find me and drag me back to Washington to stand trial for treason?"

Ellie faced him with fire in her eyes. "You know that can't happen. You're not guilty."

"Yes it can, sweetheart." He regretted the sharp tone the minute the words left his mouth. He took a step toward her and lowered his voice. "That's if I ever make it back to Washington. It's more likely he'll arrange to have me ambushed and put in the report I died trying to escape."

She bit her lip and stared at him. "You've made up your mind, and nothing I say will make any difference. I think you like putting yourself in danger. Eric, you're clever. You could think of a safer way, but you don't want to. And I'm scared. I'm scared you'll get yourself killed. And if you survive this mess, it's just a matter of time before you'll miss the missions and the danger. You'll go back to it. I know you will." The conviction in her voice gave way to uncertainty. "Maybe we've been kidding ourselves."

His heart froze. How did it go from confronting Reznik to 'we're kidding ourselves'? "What are you saying?"

"I'm saying I love you too much to stand by and watch you get killed."

He could track down terrorists. He could kill without batting an eye, but he could not reason with an irrational woman.

"Ellie, I love you. God help me, I love you more than I've ever loved any other human on earth, but you're asking too much. I will not change what I have to do just to keep you from walking out on me. Either you can trust that I know what I'm doing, or you can walk away and figure I'm not worth the risk. I'm not going to force you to stay."

His hands tightened on his crutches. *Back down, Ellie. Don't walk away.*

Raw pain etched her face. "Eric. How can you say that? How can you tell me to walk away from you? Don't you love me enough to try to find another way?"

His brow came together. "I didn't—Ellie, I didn't tell you to walk away. I'm not the one who wants you to leave." He rubbed the back of his neck and cocked his head back toward her. "You're the one who said we've been kidding ourselves."

She looked like a scared animal about to bolt. "I don't know what to think. You aren't going to change your mind no matter how much danger it will be." Her shoulders squared.

"And I can't, I won't, stand by wringing my hands hoping it will somehow turn out all right."

He almost caved. All he had to do was back down, but he wouldn't do that, even for Ellie. A Templeton didn't back down.

"We both need some time to think this through. Let's talk about it tomorrow."

Her hands went limp. Her shoulders sagged, and her eyes closed.

Now what? He needed a manual. "Come on, honey. I'll walk you back."

"No. I need to be alone for a while." She turned and walked out creating a vortex that sucked the air out of the little room. He stayed where he was while his heart followed her right out the door. Too numb to move, he sat in the chair. Her footsteps became fainter, and then a door closed. He kept hoping she'd come back.

She didn't.

〰〰〰

Cutting his leg off was supposed to solve the problem. Eric sat on the edge of his bed, praying the spasms would subside.

Rocco came in. "Hey, man. You didn't show for dinner. You want me to bring—whoa. You okay?"

Rocco left before he could respond and returned with a syringe.

Eric straightened his arm. "If it's the good stuff, shoot me up."

Rocco swabbed his inner elbow with alcohol before the needle disappeared beneath his skin. "Rough day?"

"You have no idea."

"What happened?"

"I don't know. One minute everything was great, and then, out of nowhere, everything went haywire."

"You aren't talking about your leg, are you?"

"No."

"Want to talk about it?" Rocco pulled the stool closer.

"I've lost her."

Eric saw the grin before Rocco covered his mouth. "Your first fight?"

"And probably our last." He glanced up, daring Rocco to crack a joke.

"Not your last, dude. You won't be so lucky. First of many, I'm afraid. But making up is a whole lot of fun. You know the relief you feel when the morphine kicks in? Ain't nothing compared to making up after a fight."

"Rocco, this isn't funny. I'm dying inside."

"Yeah, I know. She probably is too. Everyone noticed neither of you showed for dinner."

"She didn't come to dinner?"

"No. We haven't seen her since early afternoon."

The knife in his gut twisted a little more.

"So why do you think you've lost her?"

He didn't have the energy to rehash it. "In a nutshell, we disagreed about something, and neither one of us is willing to budge."

"Classic. Happens to my wife and me all the time."

"And you're still together?"

"You bet. Together and happy. Hey, man, fighting doesn't mean you quit loving each other. You're just working out the wrinkles. Your love is strong enough to handle this little skirmish."

"It didn't feel little." Eric told him some of the details about his plan. "Ellie basically backed me into a corner. Told me to find some other way."

"Let me guess. She said, 'If you love me, you'll do it my way.'"

Eric jerked his gaze upward.

Rocco gave him a knowing look. "I live with a woman. They think on a whole different level. Don't try to figure them out. You can't. Just when you think you have, they'll do something off the wall."

Eric wondered if Rocco was trying to help or make him feel hopeless.

"You want some brotherly advice?"

Eric wasn't sure. Rocco didn't seem to know any more than he did. But he was running on empty. "Sure."

"Ellie's scared. She's afraid she's going to lose you."

Eric scratched his temple. "Let me get this straight. She's afraid she'll lose me, so she walks away from me?"

"Crazy, isn't it? So you need to reassure her. Make her believe you love her more than life itself."

"Roc, I won't back away from a confrontation with Reznik just to keep Ellie happy."

"If you play your cards right, you won't have to. You convince her you love her, and before you know it, she'll be telling you she wants you to do whatever you have to do."

Eric stared at him. "That doesn't make any sense."

Rocco grinned. "I know. But having a woman in your life sure is wonderful. Think about it. Do you want a nice, safe, sensible life, or a life full of love and obstacles?"

At the moment, he'd go with safe and sensible. "What if I go to her and she acts like she doesn't want me?"

"Dude, that's exactly what she'll do. Hey, man. This is your specialty. Find the crack in her armor and break through to her heart."

"I'd rather face a terrorist than an angry woman."

Rocco laughed. "Women have no idea how much power they have over us poor men."

When Rocco left, Eric stretched out on his bed and stared at the ceiling. The pain in his leg was easing up.

But the morphine didn't touch the pain in his heart.

Ellie closed the door and locked it before sprawling across the bed to sob out her misery. Thunder rumbled outside and echoed the storm raging inside. She flipped over and punched her pillow a couple of times and then curled herself around it.

Men.

She could pick them all right. An African hospital was supposed to be safe. No more jerks like Allen.

Just a wounded hero with a death wish. And this time she wouldn't lose him to a wife. No. This time he'd get himself killed—and kill what was left of her heart.

The next morning she woke with a blinding headache and swollen eyes. She couldn't face people, especially Eric. She went back to the supply room to finish the inventory. The dead-weight in her heart seemed to spread to her limbs. Like a robot, she counted out the boxes and put them on the shelf. She lost count more than once and finally gave up.

It couldn't work. What was she thinking? Suppose Eric did outsmart this guy? He wouldn't leave the agency. Not for long. It'd be just a matter of time before some international crisis popped up, and then he'd rush off to save the world.

She wouldn't survive it. She rubbed her forehead and tried to erase the headache.

"I'm sorry, God. My attitude stinks right now. And I can't change it. Give me something—to hang onto."

"Ah, there you are."

She jumped and placed her hand over her racing heart. "Dad. If I were Bitsy, I'd be hanging from the ceiling."

"Sorry. Missed you at breakfast. You okay, honey?"

Excuses paraded through her thoughts, but who was she kidding? Her dad could see right through her.

"Dad, you know how much I hate conflict. Most of the time, when there's a problem with somebody, I just give in to keep the peace."

He folded his hands over his chest and nodded for her to continue.

"But I can't give in this time. I can't stand by and watch Eric get himself killed. That's not okay with me. And he won't listen. He's so stubborn."

"I gather Eric told you what he planned to do."

"He's even excited about it." She raised her eyes to him. "Can't you talk to him? He listens to you. You can convince him to go back and tell them the truth."

"Ellie."

No one spoke her name like her dad. Gentle. Full of love. And his eyes. One look from those gray piercing eyes showed everything in his heart.

And saw everything in hers. She knew by the now familiar tone, he was about to tell her something she needed to hear.

"I had misgivings at first, too. But I've prayed about it. I think Eric's plan is a good one."

"How can you say that? This guy's not going to confess to Eric. He's going to kill him and take his dead body back to Langley as a trophy."

"Sit down. Let me explain." He sat across from her and took her hand. "Sweetheart, you think Eric is seeking out this guy as some sort of game because he likes the danger."

She nodded. "He can clear his reputation in a much safer way, but he won't even try."

"What you don't know is that Eric doesn't stand a chance if he goes back voluntarily. This guy at the agency has manufactured some incriminating evidence that puts Eric at the wrong place at the wrong time. If he goes back, it'll be his word against the other guy's. Honey, Eric's being set up, and time's running out. By his acting now, he takes back control of the situation. I trust him. I think he's doing the right thing. In fact, I'm going to Washington myself to try to get Eric's dad in on the plan."

"You're going to Washington?" Her one ally bailed on her. She chewed her lip, the turmoil inside tearing her apart. "I wish you could guarantee he won't be killed."

"No guarantee. But I don't think God would have brought him through two near-death experiences to let him be killed now."

"So tell me. How do you trust God when you're scared to death?"

He gave her a sympathetic smile. "It's never easy, especially when it's about someone you love." He released her hand and rubbed his chin as if pondering his answer. "God blesses even weak faith. And each time God answers, your faith grows a little more. God's giving you a golden opportunity to exercise your faith with this impossible situation." He released her hand and leaned back in his chair. "If it makes you feel any better, I'm not looking forward—"

His gaze left hers and focused on something behind her. She turned to see what claimed his attention.

Eric stood in the doorway. His pinched expression told her more than his leg was hurting. A mixture of guilt and relief fused through her.

Her dad rose and went to the door. "Eric. I'm glad to see you. I need to go over some things with Moses. Can we talk after dinner and finalize what I should tell your dad?"

Without taking his eyes off her, Eric nodded and shifted to let her dad squeeze past.

"Ellie, we need to talk."

CHAPTER THIRTY-SEVEN

"Is that an order or a request?"

Eric scanned every detail of Ellie's face. Dark circles. Swollen eyes. Looked like her night had been as rough as his. "A request." He'd beg if he had to. "But some place other than this room." He considered dropping the crutches and opening his arms, but he didn't have the guts. He was walking blind through a mine field. Her rejection would blow him to bits.

But she smiled and moved past him out the door. "On that, we agree. Pick the place."

They stood in the hall staring at each other, waiting for the other to make the first move.

Eric broke the silence. "Could we go get a cup of coffee?"

She nodded. "I'd like that."

Neither spoke on the way to the dining area. The breakfast crowd had cleared out.

Ellie moved past him. "You sit. I'll bring you a cup."

"Okay." He pulled out a chair for her and then went to the other side of the table. She brought their coffees, and he waited for her to sit before taking a seat himself. She wrapped her hands around her cup but kept her head down. He'd have to be the one to get the ball rolling.

"Last night was one of the longest nights of my life. I did a lot of thinking and praying. You win, darling. I'll find another way. I can't have anything between us. It's torture."

She raised her head at last, and he zoned in on every detail, not knowing how this would go down. One tear spilled over, and then another, but she managed a crooked little smile as if she were embarrassed. Her right hand clutched her coffee cup while she wiped her eyes with the back of her left hand.

Like a little child who was hurting.

It slayed him. His walls crumbled. She could ask for anything. He'd do it. Or die trying.

She took a shaky breath. "I did a lot of thinking and praying too. When you told me your plan yesterday, I panicked. I couldn't stand the thought of losing you. Which is crazy because I've known all along you'd have to go back—to a life I can't be a part of."

He didn't stop her or interrupt. But the knot in his chest loosened considerably.

"But Dad talked me through some of my fears. He explained things to me." She smiled up at him. "You don't have a choice. I see that now."

He reached across the table. Her hand released the death-grip on her cup and met his halfway.

"Ellie, I still have some details to work out, but I want you to know, I'm planning to spend the rest of my life with you."

He committed. The man who never committed just signed her name on his heart. He stood, no longer afraid of her rejection. "Come here. I need to hold you."

She laughed through her tears. "Is that an order or a request?"

"An order." He turned and braced with the table at his back and wrapped his arms around her.

Her face burrowed against his chest. "I've been afraid to hope."

Afraid to hope, but loved anyway. What kind of woman did that? He hugged her close and whispered against her ear. "Leaving you is not an option. I'll find a way to make it work."

"I trust you, Eric. But please don't be reckless and get yourself killed."

The lead weight lifted, and his heart soared. Ellie trusted him. At that moment, he was invincible.

He lifted her chin and traced the shadow under her eyes. "I won't be reckless. For the first time in my life, I have someone worth living for."

SAVING ERIC

CHAPTER THIRTY-EIGHT

Trees and houses blurred as the swarthy man with a thick accent maneuvered the taxi through the Virginia suburb. Brock considered telling the driver he was in no hurry. He gripped the handrail on the door as the taxi skidded around a tight corner. But then, dying in route wouldn't be such a bad thing.

Robert Templeton's house resembled many of the homes built during the early seventies. Two-story brick with a sloping manicured lawn. Brock asked the driver to wait for him. He envisioned racing back to the taxi with bullets whizzing past his head as he dove into the backseat yelling for the driver to step on it.

All of his prayers didn't make ringing the doorbell any easier. He waited a few seconds, but as he turned to leave, the door opened. Thirty-three years had not diminished the imposing stature of the man. Brock quelled the panic rising within him as he faced the general's stern expression.

"Yes?"

"Hello, General Templeton." He planned to blurt out his message and leave. "I have important information about your son."

Templeton's wide stance and folded arms seemed as rigid and formidable as the prison guards on Cell Block C. "Who are you? How do you know my son?"

"I'm Brock Whitfield, the—"

"I thought so." The general did little to hide the contempt in his tone. "You've got some nerve showing up at my house. I swore to myself if I ever saw you again, I'd kill you."

Brock expected this response. He supposed he should be thankful the man didn't reach for a gun.

"You're wasting your time. My son's dead."

"Wait." Brock's hand reached out to block the closing door. "Eric told me to ask about the cat he dropped off at your door."

Templeton froze and then turned.

Brock seized the opportunity. "Eric sent me to ask for your help."

The door opened to a barrage of questions that rattled off like gunfire. "Sent you? Where is he? Why didn't he come himself?"

"Sir, I'll be glad to answer all your questions, but we need to be someplace secure."

The general stared him down and then with a flick of his hand, gestured for him to follow. He led him to the back patio and motioned to a chair. "What's this about?"

Brock took a deep breath and began. "About eight weeks ago, Eric's friend Toby flew him into our mission compound."

"Where?"

"Just outside of Huambro, Angola."

"Go on."

"Eric had been badly wounded. Toby indicated to us that Eric had been set up and ambushed. He's been recovering at our mission hospital, but his wounds were extensive. He came very close to dying."

The general's eyes widened as if he were assessing the new information. "I was told Eric had been taking bribes and was killed in a deal gone sour."

"Do you believe that?"

With pursed lips, he sighed. "I don't know what to believe. They never recovered the body. Eric's disappeared before, but the evidence against him was convincing." He raised his eyebrows. "Where is he now? Why didn't he come himself?"

"As you said, the evidence points to him. He wants better odds before he returns to the States. But he's still recuperating." After a second's hesitation, Brock went for full disclosure. "We had to amputate his leg two weeks ago."

The man before him became a statue, his working jaw the only indication he had heard. He cursed under his breath and closed his eyes.

Brock continued in a quiet tone. "Are you aware of the person who sent Eric on his last assignment?"

The general's gaze narrowed. "His Honduras mission?"

Brock shook his head. "His assignment to Africa."

"There was no assignment. The flight crew told the director Eric requested the flight at the last minute. It looked like he was pulling another one of his stunts." He stood and walked to the edge of the patio. "I'd given up hope of ever seeing him again, but I never believed Eric was the traitor." He whipped around, his lifeless eyes now glinting with fire. "Why you, Whitfield? How are you involved in my son's life? They should have left you to rot in jail."

"You're right. They should have."

The general returned to his chair. "So explain how Eric ends up with you?"

"I became a Christian when I was in prison. Upon my release, I went to Africa to establish a mission hospital. I've prayed for Eric since the day I gave my life to Christ that I would one day be able to try to make it up to him."

"Wait a minute. Did you have something to do with him showing up at your place?"

"I didn't seek him out if that's what you mean. I only realized it was Eric when I talked to Toby after the initial surgery. I—"

"So you patch him up and take one of his legs while you're at it, and now your conscience feels better. Is that what this is all about? You—"

Brock flung up his hand. "I'm here to enlist your help. I can't undo the things I've done, but I'm committed, sir, to make amends to all the people who were involved in the tragedy. And from my heart, I will tell you how deeply sorry I am for causing your brother's and sister-in-law's deaths."

"Save your breath. Your apology doesn't cut it with me."

"I understand. But I'm here to help Eric. I'd like to tell you what Eric plans to do."

The general shrugged. "Go ahead. I'm listening, but I'd rather hear it from Eric."

Brock would like nothing better himself. "With the director on board, he'll send this guy to bring Eric in. Eric plans to set up a sting to secretly tape the man's confession. In that way, he'll be able to exonerate himself and expose the real mole."

The general gave a derisive snort. "Sounds like one of Eric's harebrained schemes."

Brock smiled. "Timing will be crucial. Eric believes this rogue agent plans to kill him before he ever reaches the States again."

"So who is this agent we're dealing with?"

"A man named Tom Reznik."

"Tom Reznik? Impossible." He shook his head, speaking more to himself. "Eric's got it wrong. It can't be Reznik."

"Well, I don't know this Tom Reznik, but I do know your son, and I trust his judgment. Eric's in trouble, and he's asking for your help." Brock forced himself to return the general's intimidating stare.

"All right. What does he need me to do?"

Brock took his first full breath since his arrival. "Secrecy is of the utmost importance. Eric thinks no one but the director should be in on the plan."

The slight nod encouraged Brock to go on. "The director will inform Reznik of Eric's whereabouts and ask him to go personally to insure Eric is brought back. Eric wants you to come first, secretly, of course, and bring the necessary taping equipment. He plans to trick Reznik into confessing. Then you show up and take him into custody."

"Where and when?"

"As soon as possible, inform the director of the plan. I have a private jet ready to take you to our compound. It'd be better for you not to use military transport. Reznik mustn't suspect any of this is a setup."

"What if Eric's wrong? What if it isn't Reznik?"

"He's willing to bet his life on his being right."

The pause seemed forever. "All right. First thing tomorrow morning, I'll let them know I'm taking a leave."

Brock's relief at that moment topped his relief when he first left the prison. He stood and reached in his pocket. "I'll return to the compound tomorrow. Here are the numbers to call when you're ready to board the jet."

Templeton took the paper with a grim twist to his mouth.

"Eric's looking forward to seeing you again." He didn't know why he said that. Maybe to cover the awkwardness of his departure. He hoped there was at least some truth to it.

～～～～

Bob Templeton navigated his visitor around the side of the house and returned to the patio. His knees almost buckled before he reached his chair. Eric was alive. And not the traitor they were making him out to be.

Tom Reznik. It all made sense. He wrapped his hand around his fist as he recalled the day McDowall and Reznik came together to his office to break the news. The folder in Reznik's hand had names, dates, and evidence connecting Eric to failed ops. Eric was on the take, they said, and now was missing and presumed dead.

His jaw tightened at the memory. Now, his boy needed his help. He walked back into the house with a spring in his step and a renewed sense of purpose. "What'd you know, Lucky? Eric's alive." She rubbed against his leg, and he stooped, glad no one could see Bob Templeton petting a cat.

The next day, he informed Harold McDowall of the plan. "I realize I'm asking you to go out on a limb and trust Eric over Reznik."

The director listened with a grave expression. "I found it hard to believe Eric had gone rogue. I've had some hunches. Been keeping my eyes and ears open. It was tough losing Eric on the heels of losing Stuart." He pressed his lips together and gave a quick nod as he stood. "I'm willing to gamble on Eric. I'll wait until you make it out there to put Reznik on Eric's scent."

The next day, he applied for an extended leave. Tom came to his office the day before his scheduled departure. "I hear you're off for a few weeks. Glad to hear it. It'll do you good."

"Yeah." He kept his focus on the papers he was putting into a briefcase. "I need to get away for a while. I've given up hope Eric's alive. And with all the evidence pointing in his direction, it's probably for the best. It's been two months. I have a gut feeling he's gone for good." He forced his fists to remain unclenched when Reznik gave him a sympathetic pat on the back.

That afternoon, adrenaline surged through him as he packed the taping equipment. At the last moment, he remembered to arrange to board Lucky. "Come on, girl. I'm bringing Eric home."

CHAPTER THIRTY-NINE

Ellie turned over, fluffed her pillow for the fifteenth time, and peeked at the alarm clock. Wide awake with two hours to go. Her full head and empty stomach made sleep impossible.

She lay on her back and folded her arms under her head. "Thank you, God, for bringing me to this wonderful place and letting me get to know my father. And for letting me know You too." She let her mind drift back to those first weeks in Africa. Something she didn't do often. "I was such a mess when I came here. Thank You for forgiving me and helping me forgive myself."

Eric. Thinking about him made her as giddy as a teenager. "I love him. So much. How could we ever be together? God, I don't even know how to pray. Work it out somehow. And take care of him. Protect him when he comes face to face with Tom Reznik. And help him today when he sees his dad."

General Templeton.

Panic got her moving. Her alarm went off as she finished applying mascara. She went looking for Eric and found him poised at the window staring out like a caged animal.

"I was hoping you'd be up."

He turned and smiled, and then his eyes widened. "Wow."

Busted. Sherlock saw right through her. Still, it was nice he noticed. "I have to make a good impression."

"I'm impressed." He opened his arm for her to come nearer.

"I mean your dad, silly." She ran her fingers through his still damp hair. "Looks like we had the same idea."

"Nothing I do impresses Dad." His head motioned to the bed. "Come sit by me."

She sat beside him and slid her arm through his. "I'm scared to death."

"I don't blame you. He's sent tougher people than you running for cover."

"Not exactly the reassurance I was going for. When he gets here, I'm making myself scarce."

"You're going to bail? What happened to the little woman who stands by her man?"

"He's on his own. You need to break the ice before I get the courage to meet him."

He kissed the side of her head. "Have you looked in a mirror lately? He'll think his son has great taste. What he won't like is this." His arm flexed as he gestured to his leg.

"This first meeting with him will be awkward, won't it?"

His nod was almost imperceptible. His edginess returned.

She moved her hand down his arm to clasp his and said the first thing that popped into her mind. "If he's anything like me, he'll be very thankful you're alive."

"Trust me, honey. My dad is nothing like you."

Her mind blanked for anything encouraging to say. "Hey. Want to walk me to breakfast?"

His eyes softened as he held her gaze. "You know what drives me wild?"

Some things crossed her mind as possibilities.

He leaned closer and kissed the side of her mouth. "Your dimple."

"My dimple?"

"I know. Go figure. I'm a slave to it. There's a certain way you curve your mouth that makes your dimple stand out. I try to make you grin just to see it. Gets me every time."

She knew the grin. Had practiced it many times in front of a mirror. She smiled innocently and produced it.

"You little vixen. You're flirting with me." He kissed it again and stood. "Let's go to breakfast while I can still pull myself away."

After breakfast, Eric went back to his room while Ellie went to the clinic. He sat in the chair and propped up his leg. The bandaged stump still sent a stab to his chest. He wondered if it always would. He reached for the Bible and found the pages about David's mighty men and his battles. Good distraction.

At the sound of the helicopter, his stomach tightened. He hid the Bible inside a drawer. A revelation for another day. His window provided a good view of the landing where he could watch his father's arrival unobserved. Moses and Doc walked out to greet him. The blades slowed, and his dad stepped out stiff and unsmiling. He nodded to Moses when Doc gestured to the tall man by his side but made no attempt to shake hands. No big surprise.

An insane impulse to hide came out of nowhere. Should he stand or sit or lie down and cover his leg with a sheet? Definitely stand. Like a man. The familiar creak of the terrace door meant they were seconds away.

God, You've got to help me with this one.

Doc ushered his dad into the room and left just as quickly. His dad seemed frozen to the spot. With a show of confidence Eric didn't feel, he propelled forward with his crutches. "Thank you for coming, Dad." Eric extended his hand and waited.

His dad hesitated as if in a daze and then shook it.

Eric backed up and gestured to the chair and then he sat on the bed. Too late, he realized his missing leg was eye level with his dad who seemed to be going out of his way to avoid looking at it.

"It was hard at first, but I've made peace with it."

His dad dropped his gaze.

"Look at it, Dad. It's all right. I'll get fitted with—"

"Stop it, Eric." He sprung from his chair and turned his back. "It's not all right." He cursed. "You're half a man."

Eric flinched, surprised his dad's words could still hurt. He managed a quiet response. "You're right. I'm not at all what I used to be."

His dad sighed but didn't turn. "I didn't mean that."

Eric eyed his father's stiff back more stooped than he remembered. He seemed older. Weaker. Like half the man he used to be.

Pity tempered Eric's voice to sound kind. "It's a shock at first. I'm still adjusting myself, and I've had more time than you to adapt."

His dad nodded but didn't speak. Eric let it drop.

"Tell me what the director said."

His dad came to life and pivoted back to face him. "Not sure he buys that it was Reznik, but he's willing to play along. This had better work, or you'll go down. Reznik has the goods. Papers, signatures, photos—you name it. McDowall's giving you a huge show of faith."

Eric chewed the inside of his mouth and nodded.

"Why Reznik? What put you on to him?"

"Stuart." He held up his hand. "I know you don't put much stock in his suspicions, but his contact, Diego, had a photo. It was Reznik. He used a different name, but Diego told Stuart this man had been paid off to make sure the CIA didn't interfere with the cartel's terrorist activities. The agency pulled Stuart from the mission, but he went off grid to do some snooping. Apparently got too close. Contacted me the night before he was killed and told me what I just told you. But I've got nothing concrete. I have the orders for this African assignment, but Reznik didn't sign them."

"If things go as planned, the director will let us know when Reznik boards the plane." His dad stared him down. "You'd better hope your bluff works. A lot's at stake."

"Right. If he gets me away from here, I won't make it to the airfield. And I've got a good reason to want to live. I've met a girl."

His dad smirked. "You usually meet women on assignments."

Eric shook his head. "This one's special. As soon as I tie up these loose ends, I'm going to marry her."

"Marry her? What'd you do? Get her pregnant? Pay her off. You can't have a wife. You know that."

His hands clenched. He would not fight with the man barely ten minutes after his arrival. But he wouldn't let it go either. His tone, when he had enough control to speak, did little to hide his fury. "I haven't slept with her."

His dad lost the smirk, and after a few tense seconds, Eric stood down. "But it's not because I haven't wanted to."

His father looked away and seemed at a loss for words. A first for him.

"Dinner's at 1700. I'll walk you to your room. You can unpack and rest a little. I'll find you before dinner and take you down to the dining hall. How's that?"

"Just point me in the right direction. You don't have to, uh, walk with me."

"No problem. Come with me. It's just down this hall." Awkward silence followed them. "Here it is. If you need anything, find anyone on the compound. They all know you're here, and they're good people."

Eric didn't wait for his dad to respond. He'd passed the first hurdle. Maybe not with flying colors, but at least the first meeting was over. No doubt his dad was as relieved as he.

He found Ellie between the clinic and the hospital. "There you are. I've been looking for you."

"I've been hiding out. So tell me."

"Tell you what?"

"How'd it go?"

"How'd what go?"

She punched his good shoulder. "Quit messing with me."

He laughed. "Okay, okay. Dad was his typical self."

"Did he give you a hard time? About anything?"

"You mean, did I tell him about you?"

"Not just about me." Ellie bit her lower lip and twirled a strand of her hair. "How'd he handle seeing you without your leg?"

"Like I said, typical Dad. But the worst is over." Her big blue eyes kept him from telling all his dad had said. "Dad'll be at dinner tonight."

"I won't be able to eat a bite."

"Good. Can I have your food, too? I've been starving lately."

"No, you most certainly cannot. You're tormenting me on purpose."

"Guilty. You're adorable when you're mad."

"Oh yeah?" She flung her arms around his neck. "And you're adorable when you're happy. I could listen to you laugh all day."

"If I ever get rid of these crutches, I'll laugh more often. Okay, baby, I have to find your dad. Save two places at dinner." He touched her arm as she turned to leave. "I'll make sure you get to sit between Dad and me."

Good thing his dad couldn't see his goofy grin when she rolled her eyes and strutted away from him. Things had changed in the last two months. His dad would have to adapt. Not something his dad was good at.

Eric approached Doc who was unloading the back of the Land Rover.

"Eric." Doc stopped and leaned against the side of the truck. "Everything go all right with your father?"

"Better than I thought it would. Want some help?"

"Carry this knapsack and walk with me. I'm leaving the rest of the supplies."

Eric took the knapsack but checked to see if it was empty. Two rolls of gauze didn't weigh much. Once inside the clinic, they went to the same supply room where he and Ellie had their disagreement. Eric emptied the boxes while Doc restocked the shelves.

"I don't think my dad knows what to do with the change in me. It's crazy, but I almost feel free around him. He said some pretty insulting things, but I mostly let them roll off my back. In fact, I'm having fun watching his reaction."

Doc placed the last container on the shelf and rubbed his hands together. "That's wonderful. Your father's a formidable man. I'm glad you threw him off balance a little."

"He doesn't know that I know about my parents, does he?"

"I didn't tell him. I wanted that to be your decision. I also didn't tell him about your newfound faith. But stop by my room later. I have something that might help you with your dad."

"Thanks, Doc. I'm walking blind here, and I need all the help I can get."

"You've had some rough days, but I think you've weathered the crisis. How's your pain these days?"

"Manageable. Worse at night. I'll survive it, and it'll get better."

"Attitude always helps. Tell me, when do you think Reznik will show up?"

"Could be soon. The director will call us when Reznik's on the plane. But I have something I need to talk over with you first."

"I'm done. Have a seat." Doc pulled up another chair and sat across from Eric. "What's on your mind?"

"Ellie. I guess you know we had a disagreement about Reznik coming here."

"She told me. She's resigned to it, but I don't think she likes it. Do you want me to talk to her?"

"No. She's been a sweetheart about the whole thing. What I need from you is some help keeping her safe."

Doc's eyes widened. "Safe? Do I need to send her away?"

"I'd actually like that, but knowing her, she'd pitch a fit and refuse to go. Ellie won't be in any danger as long as she stays out of sight. Reznik's sharp. I can't risk his using her as leverage to get me. I'm covering all my bases. Just help me keep her out of sight until it all goes down."

"I understand."

"Something else. I need to return to the States with my dad. To be debriefed about what I know, and possibly testify against Reznik. And then I'll be resigning from the agency. In person."

Doc seemed surprised. "Is this about your leg?"

"Partly. My ability to get in and out of a situation has been compromised. But it's more than that. I don't want it anymore. Lies, deception, stealing, killing, never trusting anyone, always being alone. I'm done. When I return to Africa—and I plan to return—I'd like to work for you. I can't patch anyone up, but I'll do whatever you need me to do."

"I can't think of anything I'd like better."

"There's one more thing." Momentary panic made him freeze. What man in his right mind would hand his daughter over to someone whose main occupation involved killing people? Someone who was about to be unemployed? Doc's head slanted toward him, and Eric opened his mouth to speak, hoping his voice wouldn't betray him. "With your permission, I want to marry Ellie."

The news, when it registered, lit Doc's face and energized him into action. He bounced from his chair and placed his arm around Eric's shoulders. "This is almost too good to be true. You're like a son to me whether you marry Ellie or not, but having you legally in my family makes it even more special."

Eric stood and let the relief wash over him. "Thank you. That means a lot to me." He leaned into Doc's embrace and then took a deep breath. "I need to get my composure. A missing leg is bad enough. If my dad caught a glimpse of tears, he'd save Reznik the trouble of hunting me down."

"I agree." Doc grinned as he wiped his own wet cheeks. "Need-to-know basis."

Bob Templeton slept a good part of the afternoon. Probably jet lag. And the shock of seeing Eric's missing leg. He thought he'd prepared himself to deal with it. He hadn't. Seeing Eric's bandaged stump made him want to vomit. Nothing would ever be the same. Eric's life might as well be over.

His fool son told him to look at it. That he'd made peace with it. What was wrong with the boy? He must be on some kind of happy juice. And the idiot thinks he wants to marry. After this Reznik thing, he'd have to set Eric straight.

The knock he'd been dreading came all too soon.

"Time for dinner."

He could say he wasn't hungry, but Templetons didn't run from a challenge. Maybe Whitfield wouldn't show. Eric seemed to like him. Could only mean Eric still didn't know. With any luck, it'd stay that way.

He opened the door and stepped out into the hall.

"This way, Dad. The staff here are great. You'll like them."

He bit back what he wanted to say. The dining hall was a big room with a large oval table in the center. Brock Whitfield and the man he met at the helicopter were already seated. After a brief nod, he chose a seat as far as possible from them.

"Dad, this is Ellie, the girl I told you about."

Not Eric's usual type. Beautiful all right, but lacking the polished sophistication of her predecessors. Nothing cold about this one. "Nice to meet you."

"It's nice to meet you too, General."

Eric pulled a chair out for her.

"You sit there, Dad."

He sat next to Eric and leaned forward to speak again to Ellie. "Do you work here at the hospital?"

"Yes. I help Dad with the patients. I've been here a little over a year and a half."

Dad? He followed her gaze to the man at the head of the table. Whitfield's daughter. The last nail in the coffin of their relationship.

He lost what little appetite he had. Others came in. A lively group Eric seemed very much at home with. He refused to bow his head and pretend to pray before the meal. But Eric joined right in and even tried to hold his hand before the prayer. His son had lost more than his leg, and if he weren't careful, he'd blow this meeting with Reznik.

The call came as dinner was concluding. He excused himself, relieved to have a reason to leave the room. Everything was going according to plan. Reznik was on the plane with an ETA of 0900.

He stayed at the door and announced to the group. "We got the call. If you'll excuse us, Eric and I need to go over some details."

It was going down faster than he thought, but it couldn't come fast enough. He had to get Eric away from this place, the sooner the better.

Ellie stood in the doorway as Eric approached with Rocco. He moved with confidence and even with crutches, looked like a predator. He talked in a low voice. Even Rocco looked serious. This couldn't be good.

Eric glanced at her and smiled. Rocco turned and waved before heading the other way.

"What were you two talking about?"

"Tomorrow. Rocco's going to help us catch Reznik."

"I don't think I want to know the details."

"I'll tell you whatever you want to know, but right now, come with me to the terrace."

The kittens swarmed around them as soon as they stepped outside.

"It's dark out here. I'll get some matches from Dad's room."

Ellie returned in less than a minute and found Eric harassing the kittens. She lit the candle in front of their chairs. "You're stirring them up."

"Ouch, Bits. Let go." He pried open the tiny mouth.

She reached for his hand and examined the damage. "You asked for it, you know."

"I can't resist. When she's feisty, I have to mess with her."

"Then no sympathy, mister." She wagged her finger at him.

He grabbed the hand she waved and held onto it. "Now look who's being feisty. I may have to mess with you."

"You'd better not. I can bite too."

"I'm not afraid of you, Ellie Whitfield."

"You ought to be, Eric Templeton."

"Okay, Miss Spitfire, I have good news and bad news. Which one first?"

"Bad."

"Reznik will get here around nine tomorrow morning. I need to get my game face on."

"I understand."

"I think it'd be better if I don't see you tomorrow until this is over."

The knot tightened in her stomach, but she didn't argue.

"I can't afford to worry about you. I don't want Reznik to see you at all."

The long talk she had with herself and with God paid off. She wouldn't add to his problems. Even if it killed her. "All right. I'll stay out of sight. But I'll be glad when this is over. So that was the bad news?"

"There's one more thing."

"You only get one piece of bad news. I'm ready for the good part."

"The good's coming, and you'll like it."

"Let's have it then."

"I have to go back to the States with Dad."

"With your dad? Not a week or two later?"

He shook his head. "The sooner I get this over with, the sooner I can come back."

He shifted in his chair and held both her hands. The candlelight gave an iridescent glow to the terrace. His gaze held hers, and the warmth and love she saw there made her forget her dread of what tomorrow might bring.

"You taught me what it feels like to love and be loved. And everything I learned left me hungering for more. I don't ever want to be without you." He leaned closer and caressed her cheek. "I love you, Ellie. I can't get on my knees right now, and I don't have a ring to put on your finger." He gripped her hand and brought it close to his chest. His voice broke, and he struggled to get out the rest. "But my heart is yours. All that's left of me and my life, is yours. Marry me. Marry me and be with me forever."

She'd dreamed of this moment, so many times as she lay in her bed. How she'd feel and how she'd respond if by some miracle he asked her. But never could she have imagined something as wonderful as this.

Simultaneously, he pushed up from his chair, and she rose to embrace him, becoming his sole support. They clung to each other for a long time until he pulled back enough to cup her face in his hands. "So is this a yes?"

"Yes." She flung her arms around his neck. "Yes. Yes. Yes."

He smiled, mostly with his eyes, and leaned in closer, barely an inch from her lips. "I love you."

He kissed her. Finally. And demonstrated better than with words the depth of his love and commitment. She kissed him back, loving the strength beneath his gentle caress.

Her legs became rubber, and she hoped she wouldn't lose her balance and make him lose his. "I love you so much. I didn't know it could be this wonderful."

His finger traced down her nose and tapped her mouth. "Your dimple sealed it for me. Gotta marry the girl to get the dimple." He paused as if he were trying to hang on to his composure. "And when I return, I'll bring the rings, if you trust me to pick them out."

"Are you kidding? You're the king of noticing details. You'll pick something I'll love."

"Now the pressure's on." He tightened his hold and whispered in her ear. "I love you, sweet angel. I'll come back as soon as I possibly can."

Fear made her tighten her hold on his broad shoulders. "Promise me you won't get killed."

He pulled back to study her a long moment. His eyes softened. She wanted to ask what he was thinking but the moment was too fragile. He gripped her shoulders and pressed his lips firmly against her forehead. He shifted to whisper in her ear. "Google floor plans and pick out a spot with a great view of the sunrise because I'm coming home to you, baby."

CHAPTER FORTY

Eric gripped the edges of the sink and wished again he could shift his weight. Adapting to life with a missing leg was one thing. Liking it was another.

In four hours, the man responsible for his missing leg and Stuart's death would walk into his room. Reznik would see him crippled and helpless, on display, like an animal with its leg in a trap, exposed and humiliated.

Appearing weak might work in his favor. The dark circles under his eyes might help too. He didn't sleep much. Only dozed enough for a nightmare to jerk him awake. Reznik dragged Ellie to a helicopter and took off before he could reach them. He awoke with sweat pooled on his heaving chest. Thank God, Doc would keep her out of sight.

"Dude, you're up and dressed already. You don't sleep much, do you?"

Eric used his crutch to push the bathroom door out of his way. "Morning, Rocco. Nightmares and leg cramps."

"Truth be told, I didn't sleep much either." Rocco slid the tray with gauze and tape closer to Eric's bed.

"Roc, if you're having second thoughts, say the word. We'll figure something else out."

"No way. I'm psyched. I just hope we can pull it off."

"You and me both."

"Okay, man. Lose the shirt. I'll get your dad, and we'll do the mummy thing."

By the time Eric unbuttoned his shirt and folded it beside him, Rocco returned with his dad who looked as if he hadn't slept either.

Eric stood like a statue and balanced with a hand propped on his dad's shoulder. His dad taped the mike close to the scar on his ribcage, and Rocco wrapped the bandages over it.

"There you are."

"Rocco, play the bad guy and let Dad get the volume adjusted."

"I was hoping you'd ask. Where'd you want me to stand?"

"Anywhere. These mikes have a fifteen-foot range."

Taking a wide stance, Rocco squinted and pointed his finger like a gun. "Stick'em up, wise guy. We got you covered, see."

Eric shook his head. "Don't tell me. Jimmy Cagney, right?"

"Pretty good, huh?"

"Don't quit your day job."

His dad came back to the room. "Picking up great."

Rocco cleared the trash off the tray. "Outta here for now." He headed out the door but looked back. "We're praying for you, pal."

Dad stayed behind and walked over to the window. "You have a lot of scars." He turned to face Eric. "How many times were you shot?"

"Three." Eric pointed to the one on his left shoulder. "The Honduras bullet. Ugliest scar thanks to the bartender who dug it out. This one," he pointed to the right shoulder with the fresh bandage wrapped over it, "happened that night. And these from the magic bullet that entered my back and ripped through a few vital organs before exiting here." His hand covered the area below his rib cage on the right. "I guess the one to my leg is pretty obvious."

"You've been through the wringer, son."

Eric stood rooted to the spot unaccustomed to receiving anything close to sympathy from his father.

His dad stared at the floor as if weighing his words, and then he met Eric's gaze. "Tom Reznik has to be stopped. And you're the man to do it."

You're the man to do it. Did he hear right? Inside, Eric stood tall on two legs. He wanted to tell his dad what his vote of confidence did for him, but he couldn't risk ruining the moment.

"Thanks, Dad."

The dismissive nod. "I'll leave you now and wait for word the chopper's on the way."

"I'm going to get some coffee from the dining area. You want to join me?"

He shook his head. "I'll go to my room and wait for the call."

Go to his room and avoid Doc. Eric played along. "Sure. I'll see you later."

Eric lived through each agonizing tick of the next two hours. The Bible in hand, he prayed for God to talk to him through His word and give him something he could hold onto.

Psalm 31:13-16 brought peace. "For I have heard the slander of many: fear was on every side: while they took counsel together against me, they devised to take away my life. But I trusted in Thee, O Lord: I said, Thou art my God. My times are in Thy hand: deliver me from the hand of mine enemies, and from them that persecute me. Make Thy face to shine upon Thy servant: save me for Thy mercies' sake."

Rocco popped his head in the doorway. "Chopper's on the way. Should be landing in the next few minutes." He left, and Eric put the Bible inside the drawer.

"Showtime. God, make this work."

His mind blanked like a dead computer screen when the terrace doors opened, but perfect peace took over the moment Rocco stepped into view.

"Eric, you have a visitor all the way from Washington." Rocco turned to Reznik. "I'll get his records and dismissal papers for you."

Eric's stare was wasted on the man whose eyes were glued to the missing leg.

"Well, well, well. The mighty Eric Templeton."

"Come to finish the job you started?"

"I've come to escort a traitor back to Washington." Reznik pulled out his gun. "This will be easier than I thought. Hands on your head."

Eric didn't move.

"Now."

Eric slowly raised his hands, the effort straining his right shoulder.

"On second thought, get up. Here, allow me." Reznik handed him the crutches as he leveled the gun at Eric's temple. "Don't try anything stupid." Reznik ran his hand over the bandages and located the microphone under the gauze. His eyes glinted as he spoke a little louder. "Whoever's in on this little charade has thirty seconds to get in here." Reznik snapped the microphone from the wire.

Eric's eyes never left Reznik as his dad came through the door.

"I'm disappointed, Eric. Did you really think I wouldn't check to see if you were wired? Come on. I knew you wouldn't let yourself be found if you didn't have some desperate trick up your sleeve. Over there, Bob. Keep your hands on that table where I can see them."

"Sorry, Dad."

Reznik backhanded Eric, knocking him back onto the bed.

"I've wanted to do that for a long time."

Eric wiped the blood trickling from his mouth but said nothing. At the sound of footsteps, Reznik pocketed the gun.

Rocco came in with a folder and clipboard. "Here you are, Eric. Hello, General. I guess you'll be going back with them." He turned back to Eric. "Be sure to sign the back." He stood with his arms folded and smiled at Reznik. "I bet this guy was glad to see you. Finally well enough to travel." He took back the clipboard and pen. "Great. May take a few minutes to get your prescriptions. Then you can be on your way."

Rocco left. Eric's cue to step up and be the man who'd bring Reznik down.

"Now what? How do you plan to explain Dad?"

Reznik retrieved the gun and stationed himself at the door. "Bleeding heart father came to rescue his son. McDowall will buy it."

Eric's hands tightened into fists as he cut his eyes to his dad.

"You two are breaking my heart. Pathetic. Both of you. I'll probably get a promotion out of this."

"I won't go down without a fight."

"Go for it. I've got enough on you to put you away for life."

"Not after what I have to tell them."

"Shut up, son."

"You ought to listen to your old man."

"Before you kill him too? You're going to have to kill both of us, and not even you will be able to explain that at Langley. "

"The chopper's taking us to an isolated airstrip. Unfortunately, the high and mighty Templetons thought they'd gang up on me. I had no choice but to defend myself."

"Someone will figure it out. Sometime, somewhere. You'll pay for all the evil you've done."

"The evil I've done?" Reznik's exaggerated laugh ended with a sneer. "Don't kid yourself. Everyone has a price. Even a Templeton."

"You've got nothing I want." Eric didn't try to hide his contempt.

"Your father's life for a signed confession."

"No, son. It's not worth it."

Eric stared a long time at his father, and then shook his head. "No deal. We're dead anyway."

Reznik shrugged. "It's your funeral."

Footsteps in the hall signaled Rocco's return. Reznik hid the gun again.

"Here you are, Eric."

"Thanks."

"Take it easy, man. Good meeting you, General. Hope you have a safe trip back."

As soon as Rocco cleared the doorway, Reznik took out handcuffs. "These might work better for you, Bob." He flipped one side around Dad's wrist and jerked it behind his back. "Now the other one." He locked them in place and then handed Eric the crutches. "Let's move. You first."

They left the terrace and moved slowly through the empty compound toward the helicopter. With thirty feet left to go, the underbrush in the nearby field came to life as camouflaged soldiers materialized.

"Stand down. Drop your weapon."

Eric pivoted to face his dad and prayed Reznik wouldn't do something stupid.

"We repeat. Drop your weapon."

Reznik darted his eyes over to the armed men. With a set jaw, he tightened his hold on his gun and aimed the barrel at his own temple. Eric flipped up his crutch and caught Reznik's elbow as the gun fired, grazing the top of Reznik's head. His dad whirled around and body slammed Reznik to the ground. Two men rushed over and pulled Reznik's arms tight behind his back. Eric secured the key to the handcuffs before they hauled him up and half-led, half-dragged the whimpering man away.

Eric balanced on one crutch and freed his dad's hands. "Great tackle."

Eric turned and met Reznik's gaze before they shoved him into the cargo bay of the helicopter. Blood streamed down his face, and hate flashed from his eyes.

His dad stood beside Eric and brushed dirt and gravel from his side. "I hope the second mike picked it up."

"Doesn't matter." Eric stared Reznik down as the chopper rose, leaving a swirl of dust in its wake. "His gun on your back is incrimination enough."

They walked back to the building, and Rocco met them at the terrace doors. Eric gave him a fist bump as he walked past. "You're good, Rocco. I didn't even see you do it."

"Can't take credit. I slipped it to your dad."

They entered Eric's room, and his dad detached the mike from the back of the table. "But you blocked his view long enough for me to hide it. Nice work."

"Thanks. By the way, smooth move by the dynamic duo. I watched you take him down." He opened the closet and pulled out Eric's duffle bag. "That was the real release form you signed. Looks like you're good to go."

Good to go. The words sucked the adrenaline out of him.

Rocco left, and his dad stood near the door.

"Go ahead, Dad. I'll catch up."

"No need. Toby's going to wait for you. I arranged for the special ops helicopter to take me to the airfield. You can meet me there later."

It took a second for the words to sink in. He nodded, grateful his dad wouldn't be there when he had to say his good-byes.

He waited for his dad to leave and then sank to his bed. A hollow victory. Sadness like a black curtain going down on a play smothered him. The evil man was caught and would face judgment.

But he still had only one leg. And Stuart and Diego were still dead.

CHAPTER FORTY-ONE

Thank You, God. Ellie's heart thumped against her hand on her chest. Only when Reznik was on board the chopper did she stir from her hiding place in the chapel. She found Eric seated on the edge of his bed. The predator look vanished the moment they made eye contact. She crossed the room before he could stand and surrounded him with her arms. He clung to her as fiercely as she clung to him, and only then did she realize she was still shaking.

She released her hold and touched the side of his mouth. "He hit you, didn't he?"

"Little man trying to look big." He grasped her hand and kissed it. "Hand me some scissors. Time to lose these fake bandages."

She pulled scissors out of the drawer and brushed his hand aside. "I've got this."

He placed his hands beside him on the bed while she concentrated on snipping through the gauze.

"There." She pulled it free from his chest and threw away the wadded up cloth. "You're good to go."

He gave a small nod. "Rocco said the same thing earlier. I'm not looking forward to leaving."

She tried to keep the tremor from her voice. "How long do you think you'll be gone?"

"I can tie up the agency loose ends in a week. Two at the most. Would've taken longer if we hadn't gotten him on tape."

"Having that back-up plan was brilliant."

"Yeah. A guy named Stuart taught me that little trick. I'll have to tell you about him sometime. Kind of poetic Stu had a part in bringing Reznik down. Anyway, I have to go to Chicago for a follow-up with Dr. Robinson. If all goes well, I hope to get back here in six weeks. With a fake leg and a real diamond."

He got the dimple for that one. "Size six, in case you're wondering."

He took her hand to examine it. He swallowed hard as he kneaded each finger. "I've said a lot of good-byes. Has never been hard until now." He stood without crutches. "Come here, you. Help me balance while I kiss you good-bye."

Every pep talk she'd had with herself didn't keep her lips from quivering as she moved to support him. His fingers grazed her chin, and the gentle look in his eyes told her he knew exactly how bad she felt. "Eric, if you don't kiss me soon, you'll be the one holding me up."

He kissed her with an intensity that left no doubt about his feelings. His hands moved to her neck, and he pulled her tighter against him. Then he pulled away, reached for his crutches, and stepped over to the window. "The whole team's out there." It looked as if every part of him had tensed to keep from breaking down. He cleared his throat before he continued. "I'll grab my bag. Walk with me."

She held back one of his crutches. "Let me carry this one." Her arm went around his waist. "I'm your crutch, remember?"

He looked away, and his voice broke. "Ellie, you're killing me."

She quit trying to be brave. Her voice barely rose above a whisper. "Come on, Rambo."

Eric synchronized his steps to Ellie's smaller ones as they walked to the group assembled at the helicopter. He ditched his pride as he embraced each member of the team who had become more of a family than he'd ever known.

Tears didn't matter. They were mirrored on the face of every person who hugged him and wished him well. Especially

Rocco, who handed him a bottle of pills. "Here you go, dude. Don't try to be too macho to use these when you need them. And you gotta come to Michigan. My family back home would love to meet an honest-to-goodness spy."

"Soon to be ex-spy." Eric moved to the man who had changed his life and tried to deliver the speech he'd prepared.

Doc wrapped his arms around him. "I'm so proud of you, son," he choked out.

Eric could only nod. One day he'd say more.

Eric hugged Ellie again, and then with a kiss to her forehead, he turned and boarded the helicopter. Toby took off, making the crowd drop back to avoid the spray of dust and gravel. Eric waved one last time and then dug around in the duffle bag for his sunglasses.

"You all right?" Toby shouted over the noise of the engine.

"I'm ready to get this over." Eric looked out over the African landscape. It gets in your soul, Ellie had said. The scrub brush, the winding rivers, the marshy water holes with wildebeests scattered on the fields. "I have a feeling the next two months will be almost as rough as the last two have been."

Toby leaned forward. "There's the airstrip. Looks like the plane's ready to go."

"Before we land, Tobe, I need one more favor."

"The last time I did you a favor, I got shot."

"You'll like this one. I want you to be my best man."

Toby's eyes widened. "You got engaged?"

Eric grinned. "Last night."

Toby's smile spread across his face. "Man, you don't waste no time."

"I've wasted too much time. That's the problem."

"Name the time and place, bro. I'll be there."

On the ground, Toby grabbed Eric's bag and loaded it. Then he gave Eric a bear hug. "'Til next time, man."

"Next time. Thanks, Tobe."

Eric slung his crutches into the open doorway and hopped the steps into Doc's private jet. He retrieved the crutches and nodded to the pilots before choosing the seat across the aisle from his dad. He considered taking off his sunglasses, but his red eyes kept them in place. He buckled his seat belt. "You see the look on Reznik's face when the armed soldiers appeared out of nowhere?"

"Yeah. But I still can't figure out why you stopped him from blowing his brains out."

"Reflex. And part of me wanted him to face up for what he'd done." Eric left it at that. His dad didn't need to know the real reason, but before Simon could stop him, he blurted out something equally as controversial. "I asked Ellie to marry me." He couldn't help it. He wanted to tell the world. Eric ignored the frown. It had to be said sooner or later. He wouldn't back down, not even to his father. "I plan to settle the unfinished business and then leave the agency for good."

His dad swore and shifted as if he were gearing up to do battle. "You're a fool. No woman's worth giving up a career."

Eric let him rant, but at the pause he jumped in. "I've changed. I don't want that life anymore."

His dad shook his head and muttered as he turned away. "Yeah, and I know why too."

"It's not just about Ellie."

"I am aware." His dad whipped back to him. "You had to listen to that religious mumbo jumbo, didn't you?" He threw his hands up as if mocking a desperate man. "And in your hour of weakness, you turned to God. Just look what God did for you." He flung his hand toward Eric's missing leg.

Eric stared at his dad and took some deep breaths, not trusting himself to talk. He turned away and gazed out the window. His voice when he spoke was low and controlled. "I will not argue with you. I'm a grown man, and I've chosen to have God in my life. No one forced me into it."

His dad cursed again and angled his body away from Eric. "You sound just like—"

"My father?"

His dad sucked in breath. Eric waited for the backlash.

"So Whitfield told you? Did he happen to mention he was the cause of your mother's and father's deaths?" He looked hard at Eric, his face lined with bitterness.

"He told me. God's forgiven him."

"Well, I haven't. And neither should you."

"He's not the same man."

"That doesn't change what he's done. He ought to pay, just like Reznik has to pay."

Eric wanted to say Doc has paid. He wanted to say a lot, but arguing was getting nowhere. He'd learned the hard way no amount of arguing could change Bob Templeton's mind.

His dad must have come to the same conclusion. Their conversation took a one hundred eighty. "I got some of your things out of the apartment, but the owner rented it to someone else. We thought you were dead, son. I kept your clothes and some other things, but you'll have to get another place to live."

"I was hoping I could live with you." *Where did that come from?*

"With me?" His dad rubbed the back of his neck.

"It'd be impractical to rent for two or three months."

His dad's lower lip jutted out as he shrugged. "Just don't try to shove God on me."

Eric grinned. "Do you really think I could shove anything on you?"

His dad opened his mouth as if to speak but nothing came out. After a moment, his jaw hardened. "Make sure you don't try."

"I tell you what. I won't try to tell you about God, if you won't try to discourage my belief about God. Fair enough?"

"Fair enough. But one word from you, and the deal's off."

"You're on." He reclined his seat and tried to move his leg to a more comfortable position. "Wake me when we're close." After a few minutes, he peeked at his dad's stern profile. It was going to be a long two months.

CHAPTER FORTY-TWO

Five hours after the last speck of the helicopter disappeared, Ellie wandered aimlessly down the hall to Eric's room. What better place to give in to her blue funk?

It was a long shot. Maybe his pillow had the imprint of his head or a slight remnant of his own masculine scent.

The blinds were open. Miriam had been there and removed every trace of Eric's presence. Ellie stared listlessly at the bed and then sat in the recliner where he usually sat.

"Dear Jesus, how can my heart be full of gratitude and sadness at the same time? I can never thank You enough for letting Eric live and letting him love me. And most of all for keeping him safe from that evil man. Help him while he's with his dad and bring him back soon." She stood and ran her fingers over the bedspread. "God, You're amazing."

The shadows deepened as the sun sank. The clock on the wall signaled it was time for dinner and the hurdle of eating beside Eric's empty chair.

The somber group in the dining area hardly resembled the lively group from the night before. Ellie sat next to her dad and from the looks of him, he'd struggled all afternoon too. She rearranged the food on her plate with no attempt to get anything past the lump in her throat.

After dinner, Ellie walked with her dad to the terrace. She picked up Bitsy and plopped down in her chair next to him. "I guess you can tell how sad I am. I've never been good at hiding how I feel."

"One of the things I love the most about you."

"I shouldn't be whining right now. I'm the luckiest girl in the world, but I'm lonely. Every time I go by Eric's room, I feel lost inside. And on top of that, Rocco and Will and their group will be leaving next week. It won't be the same around here."

He reached over and patted her hand. "We're all sad tonight. We wouldn't be human if we weren't."

She placed her other hand on top of his. How different her life would have been had she grown up around this wonderful man.

"Stay here. I have something I want to show you."

Bitsy jumped off her lap and followed her dad to the door. Ellie rested her head against the back of her chair. The night sky seemed identical to the one Eric and she had shared. Was it just last night? Now, he'd be somewhere over the Atlantic.

Her dad returned with a brown leather binder and pulled his chair closer.

He sat and spread the opened book on his knees. "My prayer journal. I showed this to Eric the night before his father arrived. You might want to see it too." He pointed to the top of the page. "Operation Eric Templeton. This whole section is dedicated to Eric. I began it shortly after I became a follower of Christ. I added some things the night after his arrival. On the left are my requests."

She reached for the book. "Eric's physical healing." Her finger traced to the right side of the page. "Check. Salvation. Revelation of parents. Injured leg. All checked off." Ellie raised her head. "You checked off the injured leg."

He nodded, "God answered. His will was done."

Her finger moved down the page. "Emotional healing. This one's not checked off."

"Not yet. Eric has scars buried so deep he may not even be aware they're there. The man who reared Eric was a tough and demanding man. God can use the next two months to help Eric deal with emotional baggage he's carried around for a long time."

"What did Eric say when you showed him?"

"Not much. In fact, he was very quiet. His biggest challenge will be to try to live out his new faith in front of a man who swears there's no God. He asked me to pray for them both."

Her dad's words poured cold water on her pity party. "Oh, Dad. I'm so ashamed. This separation will be a lot harder for Eric than for me."

"Missing the man you love when he's gone is nothing to be ashamed of. Your love and prayers will give him strength. Look, I've started a new page called Operation Bob Templeton. Eric's already signed up. You want to sign up too?"

"I don't know how you do it."

"Do what?"

"Always say what I need to put things into perspective."

He reached over and squeezed her hand. "Feel better?"

"Not a whole lot, but I will. I have a wedding to plan and a house-building project to supervise."

"He asked you, did he?"

"Mm-hmm. In fact, I was sitting in this very chair."

"First time I've seen your dimple since he left."

She slanted her head and wagged her finger at him. "You knew about this, didn't you?"

He chuckled. "He asked for my blessing yesterday. Your boyfriend moves fast when he makes up his mind."

"I hope he moves fast to get back to me."

"I'm sure he will. I couldn't be happier or prouder, honey."

"Me too. Eric wants me to pick out a spot and choose a floor plan from some he'll send me. We want to be married when he returns." She put her knees together and splayed out her feet as she bent down to pet Bitsy. "I hope it's soon."

He shifted in his chair to face her. "Whenever I start to feel lonely inside, I take all those feelings to Jesus. He's good at making me feel loved. Jesus wants our fellowship, Ellie, and while you and Eric must be apart, let Christ's love fill up that void. He's never let me down. He'll comfort you during this lonely time."

Ellie picked up Bitsy and nuzzled the fur on the top of her head. How blind and selfish she'd been. Probably no one in the world knew more about loneliness than her dad. She gave Bitsy one last nudge and set her down. "Thanks, Dad. I've already been praying. I think I'll take your advice." She arose and kissed him on the top of his head. "I love you so much."

He reached up and patted the hand on his shoulder. "I love you too, sweetheart."

Brock entered his room from the terrace and walked over to close the door to the hallway. Eric's empty room mocked him from across the hall. He grabbed his Bible and placed it before him as he knelt by the bed. Verses he'd marked through the years rose up like old friends. "Why art thou cast down, O my soul? Hope thou in God, for I shall yet praise Him, who is the health of my countenance, and my God."

He pushed himself up, grabbed a pen and his prayer journal, and sat in his recliner. He thumbed through the pages until he found the one dedicated solely to Ellie.

Godly husband for Ellie.

Check.

CHAPTER FORTY-THREE

Eric relaxed against the back of the seat, grateful his dad didn't try to engage him in conversation. To open his mouth would take too much effort. The street lights masked the darkness of the night as the taxi shot around another eighteen wheeler. The rain had stopped but the spray from the wet pavement splattered the windshield like water from a bucket. Not long after leaving the interstate, the taxi stopped, and Eric eyed his father's house with a mixture of dread and relief.

Eric opened his door and slung his duffle bag over his shoulder before sliding the crutches onto the pavement. His dad paid the driver and grabbed the bags from the trunk. He passed Eric as if he were trying to beat him to the door to unlock it.

The house looked and smelled the same as it had when he was a teenager. His gut twisted as he stood poised before the stairs to the bedrooms. He used to bound up those stairs three at a time. He gripped the handle of his crutch, and considered crashing on the sofa for the night. But Templetons didn't take the easy way out. Crutches under his left arm, Eric latched onto the bannister and soldiered his way up the mountain.

Sweat covered his face as he tackled the final step. His dad had dropped off his bag and then retreated behind his own closed bedroom door. Avoiding him or giving him privacy? Too tired to care, Eric hobbled across the hall anyway and leaned close to the crevice in the doorway. "'Night, Dad."

The door flew open before Eric could turn away. His dad, toothbrush in hand, stood before Eric with a t-shirt and boxers and a towel wrapped around his shoulders. "Good night. I put your bag in your old room. The clothes from your apartment are in there too."

"Thanks. I appreciate that."

His dad nodded and started to close the door, but Eric held up his hand to block it. "What time do you leave? I'd like to ride in with you."

"You're going in tomorrow?"

"I'm ready to put this behind me."

"0730."

"Okay. 'Night."

The door closed, and Eric went across the hall to his room. He found his phone and sat on the bed. Midnight here. A new day in Africa. Ellie would be up and probably at the clinic. He texted her. "Hi, Beautiful. Just got home. I'm beat, lonely, sad. Call you later. Love you."

The room had a musty, cooped up smell, and the memories it evoked did nothing to lift his spirit. He grabbed some things and headed to the bathroom down the hall. With luck, he could make it to bed in fifteen minutes. He checked the time again on his phone. No text. She must be busy.

The shooting pains up his leg had gotten more intense over the last couple of hours. Where were those pills Rocco had handed him? His duffle bag. On the floor in the foyer. Nice going, Templeton.

He muddled his way through the shower and wiped the steam off the mirror before he brushed his teeth. Escalating spasms doubled him over twice. He dressed as quickly as he could and tried not to make too much noise in the hallway. He hovered at his door. Should he tough it out or try to make it down the stairs for a pain pill? A spasm ripped through the tissue in his leg. He lost his balance and angled his crutches as leverage. When his good leg buckled, he fell against the wall and slid down. At least, he hadn't tumbled down the stairs. His breath caught as another spasmodic pain seared up his leg. None of this made sense. He hadn't had one of these episodes in over a week.

Please God. Don't let Dad see me like this. He gripped the stump of his leg and shook it, willing the cramp to ease.

～～～～

A crash outside his door jerked Bob Templeton awake from an already restless sleep. Eric sat on the floor, his face as white as his shirt. His mouth tightly clenched, he seemed to be shaking all over.

"Eric?"

No response.

"Son." He spoke sharper than he meant to.

"Bottle of pills. Bag." Eric lifted one hand from his leg to point downstairs.

He stepped over Eric and jumped two stairs at a time. He rifled through the black bag lying on the floor and grabbed the bottle and a glass of water from the kitchen before clipping back. "How many?"

Eric held up two fingers and then gripped his leg again. The shaking seemed to be worse.

"Here you go."

Eric didn't reach for the pills or open his eyes. "Son, are you having a convulsion or something? Do I need to call 9-1-1?"

Eric shook his head and spoke with his jaw clenched. "Spasms. Overstressed."

"What'd those butchers do to you? That quack had no business—I ought to sue him for all he's worth."

"Dad."

His son's desperate plea broke through his anger. "Here." He nudged the pills against Eric's tight mouth and held the water for him to drink. Most of it dribbled down his chin. Eric nodded and leaned his head back against the wall.

"Help me. Bed."

His hesitation lasted only a moment before he steadied his stance and grasped Eric under his arms. "Ready?"

When Eric nodded, he pulled him upright. "I'll get your crutches."

Eric shook his head. "Let me lean on you."

Adrenaline took over, and somehow they made it to Eric's bed. He pulled down the covers and helped Eric fall back.

"You want the sheet over you?"

Eric shook his head and pointed to the pillow. "Helps to prop it up."

He froze at his first up close look at Eric's leg. He'd rather crawl through a sewer than touch it.

"Grab the pillow, Dad. I'll raise my leg."

Bile rose in his throat as he stuffed the pillow under Eric's stump.

"There." He straightened and clutched his hands in front of him. "You need anything else?"

Eric opened his eyes and gave a weak smile. "No, thanks. It's starting to ease up."

"Well, then. I'll leave you now."

Eric nodded. "'Night."

He left Eric and went down to the kitchen. His hands shook as he reached for a glass and his bottle of Scotch.

CHAPTER FORTY-FOUR

Eric slid his hand across the bedside table and groped for his phone. Six thirty already? He peeked through one eye to make sure and then turned off the alarm. His jet-lagged body had succumbed to the sleep of the dead with the help of his double pain fix. Every part of him had leaden weights pushing him into his mattress. Get out of bed or explain to Dad why he decided not to go in after all. He flipped back the cover and swung his leg over the side.

Good thing field agents didn't have to adhere to Langley dress code. Khaki shorts would be his uniform until he had two legs to fill his long pants. He scripted his morning routine to avoid having to struggle back to his bedroom. He glanced at his dad's closed door and prayed it stayed that way until he made it down the stairs. Living with his dad would take some adjustments—and patience. Like no coffee creamer. A battle he'd have to fight, before tomorrow.

He took his coffee to the back patio and waited for his dad. The lawn had few frills but was well-manicured with some shrubs close to the house. No leaves moved on the maple tree beside the awning. It would be a hot one today. He wished he had his Bible, but it was still in his duffle bag in the foyer. Another battle he'd have to fight. And win.

"Ready?" His dad carried a travel-mug, and from the looks of him needed his morning coffee more than Eric did. If the truth were known, his dad probably would've stayed home. But there was no way he'd let his one-legged son outdo him on the first day back.

He followed his dad into the garage and stopped short. "My Mustang." Eric looked up in time to see his dad's self-satisfied smile.

"I hung onto it for a while hoping you'd show up."

Eric slid his hand along the side and then peered in the window and whistled. "You even had it detailed."

His dad stood poised at his open door. "Would you get in the car already? I don't want to be late."

"Yes, sir." Eric whirled around and flung the crutches in first. He kept his eyes on the Mustang as the garage doors closed. He would drive again. And run again. One day. "Do they know I lost my leg?"

"I informed the director. I'm sure he relayed the news to the department." His dad flicked on talk radio and accelerated around the truck in the right lane. "Do you want me to drop you off closer to the entrance?"

Eric bit the inside of his mouth and looked out his window. He'd take open hostility any day over patronizing. "I'm good."

They walked together into the building, with Eric determined to keep up with his dad's stride. The familiar two-toned gray walls triggered an unexpected catch in his chest. A lot had changed since he'd last walked these halls.

His dad paused at the door of his office. "I'll see you after the meeting."

Eric nodded and stuck his head inside. "Hello, Miss Mildred."

He'd never seen her move so fast. He braced against the door and hoped she wouldn't knock him off balance. Not today. Not in front of his dad. She barreled down on him with tears filling her eyes. "Oh, Eric. I didn't think I'd ever see you again." She wrapped her arms around him and seemed not to care that her hair smashed up against his chest. Eric grinned over her to his dad, who shook his head and went into his office.

"No, ma'am. They tried, but God had other plans."

She relaxed her grip enough to smile up at him. "I think you're right." She swiped her wet cheeks and stepped back. "I won't keep you. They're waiting for you in the conference room."

He would tell her one day how much he'd changed. She of all people would understand and even be happy. For now all he could manage was a quick "Thank you."

Eric gave a silent prayer of thanks for the deserted hall leading to the conference room. He had played this first meeting many times in his mind and dreaded the looks of sympathy he would inevitably have to face. At least, Reznik wouldn't be there with his condescending smile.

He'd prepared himself for every possible scenario except the one that greeted him. Thunderous applause exploded through the room as he entered to a standing ovation. The whole department crowded around him, slapping him on the back or on his arms. No sympathy. No awkwardness.

The real miracle of the day was that his eyes stayed dry. "Thank you so much." He smiled at the group as the noise died down. "You know, there was a time I would've given my right leg for a standing ovation like that." His first one-legged man joke. Rocco would be proud.

Laughter rippled through the room as the stout man who wielded the power in the agency, broke through the crowd. Director McDowall moved closer and placed his hand on Eric's shoulder. "The agency owes you a great debt. You paid a high price to stop Reznik."

"Thank you, sir. Not as high a price as Stuart. Reznik's no longer a threat to our men or our security. That's the most important thing."

More applause ushered in back slapping and hand shaking as the crowd dispersed and cleared the room. Left alone, the director motioned for Eric to sit at the conference table. The same chair Reznik had occupied a lifetime ago. Eric placed his crutches on the floor as Director McDowall took the seat at the head of the table.

"Good to have you back, Eric. The guards who brought in Tom delivered the tape." The director sighed with an ugly twist to his mouth, "You nailed him all right. I wish I'd picked up on it sooner."

An opinion he shared. He spoke in a quiet voice. "A clever man with resources in his favor." And no conscience. Eric filled him in on the details he couldn't have shared at the last meeting with Reznik seated across from him.

McDowall's eyes never left Eric's face. "Why didn't you tell me your suspicions?"

He raised his hands and let them drop. "I needed something concrete and was fool enough to think I could expose him on my own. My cocky attitude cost me my leg and almost my life."

The director pursed his lips. "Life in prison may look good by the time we're through. Some cartel members want his blood, and I'm tempted to hand him over."

The director swiveled as if to stand.

"One more thing, sir."

He turned back and raised his brows. "Sure. What's on your mind?"

"I'll be turning in my resignation this week."

The news seemed to knock the wind out of him. "Is this about your leg? Whatever you need to get back to normal, you've got. We're even providing a full-time driver for you." He placed his hand on top of Eric's arm. "We're going to take care of you."

That seemed to settle it for the man with the set jaw of a bulldog.

"I appreciate your support, but I've made up my mind."

"Nonsense. Give it time. Six months. You'll be back on your regular assignments. Don't do something you'll regret. You'd miss it if you left."

He would miss the job, no doubt about it. Just like he missed his leg, but things had changed. "It's more than that. Coming close to death gave me a new perspective on my life." Eric leveled his gaze and spoke with confidence. "My priorities have changed. I've become a Christian. And I've met the woman I plan to marry."

McDowall leaned forward. His folded hands tapping against his mouth hid his expression. "No hope of changing your mind?"

Like his dad, the director didn't take *no* well. "No, sir."

"I have two favors to ask."

Eric raised his eyes and waited.

"The experience you bring to the table can't be taught in a manual. While you're here, you could help train the new recruits."

Like Stuart had done for him. "I'd like that."

"And keep an open mind. I hate to lose you. An international crisis might develop, and we could use you even if it's just as a consultant. How about it?"

The offer caught him off guard. He needed advice, and the man he trusted the most was thousands of miles away. "I'll keep an open mind, but I can't commit to anything."

"Fair enough." McDowall stood, and the tightness in Eric's chest loosened considerably. "Come with me. I'll introduce you to the young man who'll be your chauffeur until you're driving again."

He easily kept up with the short man's steps as they walked down the gray corridor to his office. A young man in standard military uniform stood as they entered.

"Private Benton Kluchman will be your driver for the next few weeks."

Eric shook the cold but sweaty hand offered by the statue with stiff shoulders and a face that would crack if he smiled. Another by-the-book rookie from the looks of him. Brought back memories of himself before Stuart gave him a dose of reality. "Nice to meet you."

"Happy to be at your disposal, sir."

The guy reeked military precision. Simon cut off the grin that threatened to escape. *Behave yourself.*

The director shook Eric's hand. "I'll be in touch."

"Thank you, sir."

The private went to the door and held it open. "This way, sir."

"Go ahead. I'll pop in and say good-bye to my dad and meet you outside."

"Yes, sir. I'll drive around to the front and wait for you."

He'd let that one go. The rookie needed something to do. "Sure. That'd be great."

His muscles tightened with every step toward his dad's office. His leg throbbed, and he'd had enough questions for the day. "Miss Mildred, tell Dad I have a driver, and I'll see him this afternoon."

She glanced his way with the hint of a smile. "Of course." She gave a short wave and resumed typing.

Eric bypassed the ramp and descended the steps to the waiting car. He threw the crutches in the back and started a conversation he hoped would thaw some of the military ice. "This is great. I have to tell you, I dreaded having to depend on my dad to take me places. Believe me. You're one of my favorite people right now."

"Glad to be of assistance, sir."

"People call you Benton?"

The kid actually blushed. Must be the red hair.

"My family calls me Ben."

"Mind if I call you that?"

"No, sir."

"Good. And you can call me Eric."

The mask went up with the shoulders. "I'd prefer to show more respect if you don't mind, sir."

He did mind. Considered making it an order, something he would understand. "You know, I'm not technically your superior."

"Yes, sir."

Eric sighed. He'd tackle G.I. Joe another day. "Okay, Ben. First stop, a little jewelry store I've heard about."

Eric put away the rest of the groceries Ben had helped him bring in. He grabbed his cell and shot Ellie a quick text. "Can u talk?" The phone rang immediately.

"That was fast." His crooked shoulder cradled the phone as he repositioned containers in the fridge.

"Oh, Eric. I'm lost without you."

He grinned as he backed up to the stool at the kitchen counter and propped up against his crutch. "That makes two of us. Where are you right now?"

"In my room. I've been living for your call. What time is it there?"

"Two. You're five hours ahead until Daylight Savings ends. Then it'll be four."

"I hope you're here when Daylight Savings ends."

"Me too. I told the director I'd be resigning."

"How'd he take it?"

"About like my dad, but with a little more tact."

Her lilting chuckle sent a pang through him. He missed the dimple. "I bought you something today."

"Really? What? Tell me."

"It's a surprise. I'll mail it tomorrow."

"Give me a hint. Will I like it?"

"I hope so. It turns out I am a very wealthy man, my dear. I think the director is trying to buy me back. My plan is to spoil you rotten."

"Good plan. You know, I'm only marrying you for your money."

"Is that so? I'll take you any way I can get you. It's yours—every dime I own."

"You're so sweet."

"You ain't seen nothing yet. Hey, guess what? I have my own personal chauffeur. From the looks of him, he's scared to death of me."

"He ought to be, considering you're the best assassin the CIA has."

"Had. But in the meantime, the director wants me to help train the recruits."

She gave a little gasp. "Just what our country needs: more assassins running around."

"More good guys stopping the bad guys."

"You have a point. Maybe it'll help the time go by faster."

Eric was done talking about himself. "You know, you could hop on a plane, and we could elope by Friday."

"Don't tempt me. When you left yesterday, I thought I'd die. Seems longer than one day."

The stump of his leg throbbed. He propped it on the stool beside him. "Google house floor plans. We need a big house. Lots of room for children, and pets, and even your dad if he wants to live with us. You know, I'm only marrying you to get your dad."

"Too bad. I'm his favorite. Everybody knows it."

"You're everybody's favorite, especially mine. Have you picked a spot for us to build?"

"I was thinking in the field by the tree."

"Sweet. I'll find a contractor and scout out floor plans."

They talked over an hour. He squeezed in a pain pill to ward off the spasm he felt coming on while she rattled off mundane chitchat. He didn't want it to end. It almost made him miss her worse to hear her voice.

"Dad and I'll watch the sunrise tomorrow morning and send it on its way to you with all our love. You're the most wonderful man in the world, Eric Templeton."

His throat tightened. "Baby, I have to be. I'm marrying an angel. Tell Doc I said hello. I'll call you in the morning."

SAVING ERIC

CHAPTER FORTY-FIVE

After work, Bob stopped by the kennel. He entered the house with the cat carrier and litter box.

"That you, Dad?"

He opened the carrier and propelled her toward the kitchen. She would've stayed to rub against his legs had Eric not yelled out, "Hope you're in the mood for chicken and a salad."

Either she smelled the food or recognized Eric's voice. With her tail in the perpendicular radar position, she pranced off.

"Lucky? No way. Come here, girl. Look at you. Where's that yellow bag of bones I left here?"

Bob poked his head around the door. Eric, with the cat close to his chest, looked up and smiled. "You kept her."

He shrugged. The gratitude on Eric's face pleased him more than he was willing to admit.

"I didn't think you would."

"Figured if I kept her long enough, maybe you'd resurface and claim her. Good thing you're back. She almost drove me crazy."

The cat jumped out of Eric's hold and ran back to him. "See what I mean. You should've named her nuisance."

Eric laughed. "Looks like she's chosen a new owner."

"Don't get any bright ideas. That darn cat leaves when you do."

〰〰〰〰

The next few weeks made it clear to Bob Templeton his son had changed. Eric smiled more—even laughed and seemed to stand taller on one leg than he had on two. He stood erect, looked him in the eye, and initiated many of their conversations. The ever-present tension in their relationship disappeared. Things that used to get a rise out of Eric now seemed to roll off his back. Sometimes the unthinkable happened. Eric actually agreed with something he had said.

The real kicker happened the second night after his arrival. Eric began what became a nightly ritual of hugging him good night. After the third night, he realized his son intended to make a habit of these displays of affection. Going to bed early didn't provide the out he hoped for. Eric barged into his bedroom and literally kissed him on the forehead. After about a week, he grew accustomed to the gestures. By week three, he not only welcomed the embraces, he returned them.

True to his word, Eric didn't speak about God. Maybe his son would abandon that nonsense. At least, Eric kept the Bible in his bedroom and didn't parade it in front of him.

Life settled into a routine that, were the truth known, he didn't want to end. He found himself looking forward to coming home, knowing Eric would be there. Eric usually cooked supper for him. As they ate, Eric often asked questions, such as what his grandparents were like, or what kind of girls Bob had dated when he was a teenager. Sometimes, Eric surprised him by telling little tidbits about his own life. He was getting to know his son as never before.

Muscle spasms hit with less frequency. One night, Eric appeared at his bedroom door. Pain had him doubled over.

"Dad, you mind staying with me a bit?"

There was a time he would've belittled his son for such a request. What a fool he'd been. He dropped the book he'd been reading and helped Eric back to his bedroom.

"Sit with me. Talk to me a while."

Bob's mind drew a blank, but Eric's tightly clenched jaw made him scramble to say something. Anything. He pulled a chair over and started with tales of his boot camp days and then of his tour of duty in Germany. Eric almost smiled when he confessed how he'd puked his guts out when he drank his first beer. He talked until the crease in Eric's brow disappeared, and his breathing became deep and steady. He stayed for a long time, gazing at his boy, the boy who had been lost to him and had come home. Then he eased out of the chair and kissed the top of Eric's head.

Eric asked God to show him how to love this man who seemed to be wrapped in barbed wire.

At least he could try to fatten him up. His dad had lost so much weight, he looked like someone from Auschwitz. With recipes found on his phone, he and Ben stopped at the market almost every day to pick up something to make for dinner. The chicken fettuccini was a disaster. The noodles stuck together and the sauce had the consistency of paste. Then the perfectionist in him kicked in, and he became a pretty decent cook. Omelets became his specialty.

His dad was softening, but one wrong word could send them back to square one.

"I'm keeping my mouth shut until You make it plain it's time to talk. I can't afford to mess this up," he prayed.

At dinner one night, Eric passed the roasted chicken and asked a question that almost sent the platter to the floor.

"What was my father like?"

The hesitation stretched out. Eric's fork hovered in mid-air until his dad spoke in a low voice.

"Nick was a good kid. Three years younger than I was. I always felt like I had to protect him." He shrugged as he bit into his roll. "I guess I took after my father. Career military man. Tough as nails." His voice grew husky. "Nick was more like Mom. Kind, good sense of humor—always laughing. Nick and I were close." He spoke between bites and stared straight ahead as if Eric had disappeared from the room. "Dad was away a good bit so Nick counted on me for advice. Made me feel good. When Dad was killed in Nam, everything changed. I was seventeen. Tough time." He looked down at his plate and shook his head. "Not long after that, Mom found out she had cancer. She died less than a year later. I was man of the house so I sucked it up and took care of my kid brother the best way I knew how. Joined the military as soon as I turned eighteen. Nicky was fifteen. Went to stay with our aunt's family while I was stationed in Germany." His face turned bitter. "He started going to church. Found God he said. Claimed he was happier than he'd ever been."

Eric didn't move, afraid he'd break the spell. His dad shoved the plate away as if trying to push away the pain.

"I returned to the States just as Nick headed to some Bible-thumping seminary. Tried to talk him out of it. Was afraid he'd get brainwashed or something. We fell out. Didn't talk too much after that."

The room went silent. Eric prayed for wisdom and placed his hand on top of his father's. "You're the only father I've ever known. You took me in. Made sure I had a good education. You taught me respect, integrity. Pride in a job well done."

His dad tried to pull his hand away, but Eric wouldn't let it go.

"I didn't always like or understand how you did it, but you helped me become the man I am today. I'm grateful." He paused, and then decided to go for it. "And Dad, I love you."

His dad opened his mouth as if to respond but suddenly jerked his hand free and stumbled from the table.

Eric didn't regret what he'd said. He'd found the crack in his dad's armor just like Doc had found his.

It's okay, Dad. Templetons can cry.

CHAPTER FORTY-SIX

Ellie sat beside the eight-year-old who could pass for five. The half bed swallowed the tiny figure whose ebony body lay in stark contrast to the brilliant white sheets. The hand that had clutched with a death-tight grip now lay open and relaxed on hers, but she wouldn't leave him and risk his waking, alone and frightened. The soft touch on her arm almost made her fall off her chair.

"Toby flew in a few minutes ago and is looking for you."

The child stirred, and she lowered her voice. "Thanks, but I can't leave Mobezi yet."

Miriam gave a sympathetic nod. "Poor little chap. Doc said his appendix would have burst had they waited any longer. We could hear his moans across the compound."

Ellie stood and smoothed her hand over his forehead. "His mother must have been up for days. I don't think she's moved."

Miriam glanced at the crumpled form on the cot and then took Ellie's shoulders and moved her away from the bed. "You go. I'll stay with him."

Ellie lingered.

"Go. I promise I'll stay until his mother is awake."

"Don't you need to help Nicci?"

Miriam shook her head. "Nicci sent me to help you."

Ellie wrapped her arm around the lithe figure with not one spare ounce of fat. "Thank you, both."

She found Toby in the clinic talking to her dad. He sat on the edge of a cot, his legs swinging off the side. He jumped up as she approached.

"There you are. I have a special delivery from guess who. You're gonna like this one."

"I've liked them all. I think he tries to outdo himself every week. So where is it?"

"Too big to bring in here. You'll have to come out to the chopper with me."

"Too big?" She raised her eyebrows and gave her dad a sideways look. "Do you know about this one?"

He shrugged, but the twinkle in his eyes gave him away. "You'll just have to go see."

She followed Toby out to the helicopter and walked around to the cargo door.

"Not there. She rode up front."

"She?" Ellie moved to the side. A large crate with holes was strapped into the passenger seat. "Oh my goodness. What is it?"

"Here you go." Toby opened the crate and pulled out a golden retriever puppy.

"Awww. Come here, you sweet thing." The puppy squirmed and rooted up to lick her cheek. One whiff of puppy breath, and Ellie fell in love.

Toby's grin filled his face. "That little girl's come a long way to be with you." He handed her an envelope. "He sent this card. Something about a nose. Said you'd understand."

She supported her new baby in the crook of her elbow and read the note. "To my beautiful blond lady (#loveyournose #lovedimple2) ☺"

Her heart turned to liquid that found its way out of her eyes. Ellie gave the puppy an extra squeeze. "He won't be able to top this one." She stood on her toes and kissed Toby's cheek. "Thank you so much."

"Hey, I'm just the delivery man."

"Next time, deliver Eric back to me."

"I hear ya. Tell Doc I said bye."

Ellie nodded and caressed the puppy's ears as Toby loaded up to head back. She gave him a wave and went in search of her dad.

～～～～

Eric had spent a small fortune to find the right golden retriever, another one to get her pet passport indicating she'd had her required shots so that she could enter the country without quarantine, and even more money to airfreight her across the ocean. He would've paid anything, and he'd gladly spend another fortune to be there when Toby handed her his latest prize. He checked his phone throughout the day and tried to imagine when the puppy would arrive and how Ellie would react.

Eric had thrown pork chops on the grill when his dad opened the French doors and joined him on the patio.

"Hey, Dad. You're home early."

His dad dragged a chair out of the cloud of smoke and sank into it. "Mildred had an appointment this afternoon. I decided to call it a day, too."

"Great. Shouldn't take these long to cook."

"Take your time. I'm not very hungry."

Eric leaned against a column that supported the patio awning and swatted the mosquito on his arm. "I have to fly to Chicago to get fitted for my new leg. I'll be gone a few days. Why don't you take some time off and come along?"

"You want me to come along?" The cynical edge to his dad's voice would probably never disappear.

Eric turned the chops and basted them. "Sure. But if you don't want to—"

"No. I'll go. When do you leave?"

"As soon as you get work squared away, I'll make the reservations."

"Okay."

"Great." He sidestepped the smoke and basted the meat one last time. "Just a couple more minutes."

"I'll feed Lucky so maybe she'll let us eat in peace."

Eric grinned. "Fat chance."

His dad returned with the food bowl and Lucky close behind. "She can eat out here tonight."

"Good idea. And good timing. They're done."

His dad took the platter from Eric's hand as he moved into the kitchen. "Let me help you."

The old Eric would've bristled. The old dad wouldn't have offered. They'd come a long way. And now the Chicago trip. He actually wanted his dad to go. Small miracles.

He also wanted to tell his dad about the retriever. He wanted to talk about Ellie, and show him the pictures of the site of their house, and the foundation that had just been poured. And more than anything he wanted to talk to his dad about God. But there was no way. That would take a big miracle.

◢◣◢◣◢◣

Eric received Ellie's call as he was finishing dinner.

"Excuse me, Dad." He pushed back from the table and went to the patio. He answered as he closed the doors and hoped his dad wouldn't be able to hear him. As soon as he said hello she squealed into the phone.

"I love her!"

Eric kept his back to the patio door. No need for his dad to see his silly grin. "Cute, isn't she? She make the trip all right?"

"She whimpered a little when Toby got her out of the crate and wee-weed a long time when I put her down."

Eric smiled so much his jaw started to ache. He stared into the backyard but saw only the compound and the helicopter and the little puppy peeing on the grass. "What'd you name her?"

"Lady."

Of course. He knew before he asked.

"She's so adorable."

His heart melted when she hummed a wistful sigh into the phone. "You're spoiling me, you know. And you're spending a fortune on me. I feel bad. I'm not sending you anything."

"Your love's all I want." His foot kicked up a clod of dirt. "All I'll ever want."

"You're so good to me. You know I'd love you without the blue sapphire necklace, and the iPod with all my favorite music, and the adorable puppy who's curled up on the foot of my bed. And the framed picture of my dad and me and Lady. I must've been two. Priceless. How on earth did you dig that up?"

He chuckled. "I could tell you—"

Her laugh was exquisite torture. "I did it again. I'll never learn."

"I fly to Chicago this week to get my fake leg. You know what that means."

"You're coming back to me soon, I hope."

"That's the plan. You won't believe this, but my dad's going with me."

"To Chicago? I'm impressed. You want him to go?"

"I asked him. Little by little I'm wearing him down."

"You have that effect on people."

They talked until darkness settled over the yard. He glanced at the clock in the kitchen. His dad had cleared away the dishes and loaded the dishwasher.

"Almost midnight for you. You need to go to bed."

"I need to take Lady outside to go potty, and then I'll go to bed. I love you so, so much, you wonderful hunk of man."

"I'll call you in the morning."

"Eric, if you call me in the morning, it'll be the middle of the night for you."

"You don't want me to call you?"

"I don't want you to lose sleep to do it."

"I'll call you in the morning. Good night, honey. I love you."

CHAPTER FORTY-SEVEN

Three days later, Eric and his dad boarded the military charter to Chicago. The flight was shorter and more pleasant than their trip across the ocean. A prearranged driver met them at the airfield and chauffeured them to the hotel. Red carpet treatment. Losing a limb had its privileges.

He'd rather have his leg.

Their two-bedroom hotel suite opened into a plush living area. Nothing like the hole-in-the-wall rooms he took on assignment. Sixth floor with a balcony facing Lake Shore Drive. He slid open the glass doors and maneuvered to the railing. Perfect weather and a view that sent a stab to his chest. Runners sprinted along the trail adjacent to Lake Michigan. The same one he'd run himself many times on his stopovers in Chicago. The Lakeside breeze, the water sloshing up against the sailboats, the winding path through the trees all made this one of his favorite running courses.

His dad joined him on the balcony. "Good view."

Eric nodded. "The next time I come to Chicago, I'm going to be one of those runners down there."

"Hmm. Something to work toward."

"Concierge has a driver to take me to the doctor's office. We'll grab some lunch when I get back."

"Sounds good."

Eric didn't have to wait long in the examination room before Dr. Robinson bustled in.

"Great to see you again, Eric." The doctor shook his hand and clasped his right shoulder. "How've you been? You seem to handle yourself pretty well on these crutches."

"I'm ready to lose them."

"I bet." He gestured for Eric to sit on the exam table. "Let's have a look."

Eric propped up his leg, and Dr. Robinson went into professional mode. "Looks good. Ready to get these staples out?"

Eric nodded. The doctor opened the door and motioned for his assistant. A portly nurse entered with some instruments that looked like giant tweezers. Eric paid attention to the whole process as the two worked together. This would be the kind of thing Ellie would do. Good thing it wasn't Ellie. They hit a sensitive spot, but he didn't flinch.

"Sorry. I know it's still tender."

He must've flinched.

"Have you had much pain?"

Eric spoke to the head bent over his leg. "Yeah. Worse at night. Sometimes the spasms take me down. I try to ward them off before they get full-blown."

The doctor glanced up and nodded. "I've heard those spasms are the devil."

"They're getting farther apart."

Dr. Robinson pulled the last suture free. "There." Then he dragged over his stool as the assistant blotted the area and threw away the soiled gauze. She left the room, but the doctor stayed. Eric filled him in about his plans to move back to Africa and marry Ellie.

"Congratulations. I'm sure Brock's happy." The doctor stood and gave him a card with the name of the prosthetic group he'd see that afternoon. Then he handed him the crutches. "You won't need these much longer."

The doctor left the room, but Eric stayed behind and gave his leg the once over. Pink and swollen but free from the constricting staples. Not a pretty sight. He pushed and prodded the sensitive flesh and tried to imagine what it would feel like to put weight on it once more. He looked at the card Dr. Robinson had given him. He'd take fake leg over crutches any day.

〜〜〜〜

Eric went back to the hotel and found his dad on the balcony reading a book. He pushed aside the glass doors, and his dad glanced up.

"How'd it go?"

"Phase one over. Phase two this afternoon." Eric closed the distance and placed his hand on his dad's shoulder. "Enjoying this great weather?"

"And the sounds of the marina below. I'm glad I came. I've needed a little vacation."

Eric pulled over a chair and propped his crutch against the balcony rail. "You've lost some weight. You feel all right?"

"Feeling my age. That's all."

"You're not old, Dad."

"What'd the doctor say?"

Classic change of subject. "Everything looks good."

"You tell him about those episodes you have?"

"Yeah. Said they'll go away. I'm starving. Let's grab some lunch before my appointment this afternoon. Got a taste for anything?"

"No. You pick."

"There's a little bistro next door to the hotel. Great view of the lake."

They left the room and walked to the restaurant. Good thing it was nearby. The doctor's tweezers had stirred up all the angry nerve endings. The hostess seated them right away, probably thanks to the crutches.

Eric ordered a Cuban sandwich and Caesar salad. His dad chose a BLT. Eric lined up the salt and pepper shakers and tried to think of something to say.

"I love this place. I ate here three years ago on my stopover in Chicago. Food's good, but look at the place. It's like an alcove in a fisherman's wharf."

"I don't care what it looks like if the food's good."

The server returned with their sandwiches. Eric hoped the food was as good as he remembered. He bit into his sandwich and closed his eyes in appreciation. "Hmmm."

His dad picked at his BLT.

Eric nodded toward the plate. "Not good?"

"It's fine."

"Want a bite of mine? It's delicious."

"No."

Eric took another bite and wiped his mouth while his dad set the BLT on his plate and pushed it away.

"Sorry. Next time you can pick the place."

"The place is fine. I don't have much of an appetite lately."

Eric started to lose his own. "Have you thought about retiring?"

"Me?" His lower lip jutted out. "I plan to work 'til they kick me out."

"It's not about money, is it?"

"Nah. I'd go crazy after two days. My career's been my life. It's been your life too. You're going to miss it. You mark my words."

His dad's gaunt face, tired eyes, and increasingly stooped posture seemed more prominent in the new surroundings. Maybe he was depressed. Made sense. His only son, and for all intents and purposes, the only family member who gave a hoot about him, would be moving away soon. Eric stuffed down the guilt and changed the subject.

"I get fitted for my leg this afternoon. Want to tag along?"

"Sure."

Eric wiped his mouth and placed the wadded up napkin on the plate. "I'm done. They could wrap up your sandwich for later."

"No. I'm done too."

They left, and Eric hailed a taxi. Twenty minutes later, they entered the building and sat in the waiting area crowded with amputees of all ages. His father picked up a magazine, but Eric leaned back in his chair and observed the people with whom he now shared a bond.

They called his name, and Eric glanced at his dad. "Come with me. I need some moral support."

His dad closed the magazine and rose. "Just don't ask me to hold your hand."

The attendant led them through double doors and down a hallway to the consultation room.

As they neared the door, Eric kept a straight face but repositioned his crutch and reached for his dad's hand.

His dad slapped Eric's hand away. "Cut that out."

The next hour, the staff measured Eric's leg from every possible angle and showed him different prosthetic models. Eric slipped a notecard from his shirt pocket and fired off his questions. The most disappointing answer was that he'd have to ease into the device. Somehow, he'd envisioned getting the new leg and running along Lake Michigan at sunrise tomorrow morning.

"You'll have to wear this elastic bandage for the next few days. It's called the shrinker. Looks a lot like panty hose."

Eric wanted to skip this part. Maybe he inherited his lack of patience from the man seated beside him.

"We'll send the measurements and records to Walter Reed, and by Friday, you can get your new leg. You'll have to work up tolerance to wear it all the time. My best advice is for you to take it slowly and not overdo it."

Eric nodded but gave his dad a that-ain't-happening look. His dad almost grinned. A true grin emerged when the attendant slipped the elastic over Eric's stump.

"You tell anyone I have to wear panty hose on this leg, and Lucky stays with you for life."

Dad threw up his hands. "Your secret's safe with me."

They left the building and caught a taxi back to the hotel. Not the progress he'd hoped for, but underneath the disappointment, Eric pondered his latest revelation. Thirty-six years old, and he was only now discovering his dad almost had a sense of humor.

CHAPTER FORTY-EIGHT

Five days later, Eric entered Walter Reed to make friends with his new leg. He went alone to this appointment. He'd dealt with the loss of his leg as well as he could, but deep within, it was as sensitive an issue as the pink flesh throbbing below his right knee. Would he ever feel whole again?

It resembled a leg. It would support him and get him where he needed to go. He would wear it and be thankful. But it was fake. And ugly.

The prosthetist attached it with a warning. "Brace yourself. It'll hurt at first."

She spoke the truth. His fingers gripped the handhold of his crutches, and his teeth clamped down in a tight grimace. The only thing greater than the grinding pain was the determination to adapt, move on, and get back to Ellie. Sweat broke out on his brow and upper lip. He took a deep, heaving breath and pushed the crutches toward the attendant. Every muscle tensed as he took the first steps he had taken without a crutch in over four months.

Physical therapy would be every other day, and with hard work, he'd board a plane back to Africa in three weeks.

After dinner, the computer image of Ellie with Bitsy parading in front of the screen re-enforced his resolve to get back as soon as possible.

"How does Bits like Lady?"

"She arched her little back when I first introduced them, but now they're inseparable. I wish you could see them. They wrestle and chase each other, and sometimes they curl up together and take naps. Too cute. So tell me. Did you get your leg today?

"Yes ma'am. Turns out they have a series of artificial limbs made especially for spies. I'm getting the Super X model I can detach and use as a weapon. It's great. It even has a rocket booster so I can fly myself out of a dangerous situation."

"Oh, you. I almost believed you. You're just pulling my leg."

Eric laughed. "Good one. Was the pun intended?

"Yes. Thanks for noticing."

He detached it and held it up for her to see. "Here it is. Won't win any beauty contests, but as soon as I get the hang of walking on it, I'm coming home to you."

"That makes it beautiful to me." Her voice was as soft as the velvet box cradled in his hand.

He held it up to the screen. "I'll bring this when I come."

Her eyes widened. "Oh, let me see."

"I stood in the store forever trying to decide which one to get."

"If you're the one putting it on my finger, I wouldn't care if it came out of a Cracker Jack box."

"That's a relief."

"You're not going to show me, are you?"

He fingered it and almost opened it. "You really want me to?"

"No, I'll wait. But I'm so excited. And the house is looking like a real house, at least on the outside. I'll send a picture to your phone tomorrow."

"Send me a picture of you too. Baby, you need to get to bed. I'll call you in the morning."

Their hands met on the screen as they said good-bye. Eric remained in his seat long after the screen went dark. He opened the box and looked again at the ring he would soon put on Ellie's finger.

A month had gone by, and soon he would leave for a whole new life. Leaving his dad was his one and only regret. He reached for his Bible.

"God, I need a miracle."

SAVING ERIC

CHAPTER FORTY-NINE

Bob lathered his face and leaned closer to the mirror. He grabbed his razor and went to work. The future had never seemed bleaker. He shouldn't have agreed to let Eric stay with him.

He slid the razor under the stream of water and shook off a clump of shaving cream. Eric was Nicky all over. His tongue pushed his cheek out as he made a new streak down his face. Nicky. Everything changed when Nick turned to God. The razor nicked his chin, and he cursed. First Nicky. Now Eric. He used a warm washcloth to wipe his face. It was plain to him now. Whitfield had brainwashed Eric. Time to stop Eric from throwing away his career.

Bob walked into the kitchen geared for attack but stopped short when he saw his son standing on two feet without crutches.

"How's it feel?"

Eric gave him a quick glance as he turned down the heat under the skillet. "Like freedom, but it's going to take some getting used to."

"What's next?"

"Physical therapy Monday, Wednesday, and Friday. I have to learn how to walk again." Eric raked an omelet onto a plate. "Here you go."

He picked up his fork with no intention of waiting for Eric to get through with his token prayer.

"If things go as planned, I'll leave for Africa in about three weeks."

He nodded and took another bite.

"Ellie and I will get married soon after that. I'd like for you to come."

Sooner than he thought. He put down his fork and went on the offensive. "I'm curious. What made you turn to God?"

Eric's eyes widened as if he were about to choke.

Bob held up his hand. "Don't give me all the reasons you think I need God. But why you? Why now?"

Eric took a deep breath and looked down.

Seconds dragged by.

"Never mind. It's not important."

"No. I'd like to tell you."

"Some other time." He resumed eating and hoped Eric would let it drop.

Eric began with a voice so low he seemed to be talking to himself. "I blew the Honduras assignment. Big time." His head came up. "You remember that day in your office when you told me I was losing my touch? You were right."

He shook his head. "I shouldn't have said that. You were set up, like you said. Wasn't your fault."

"It was my fault. I underestimated Reznik, and my contact paid the price. When I got back, I was determined to stop him."

"Go on."

"When he sent me to Africa, my gut screamed trap. I even changed direction at the last minute so I could get Toby as backup."

"Why'd you go through with it then?"

"I don't know." He shook his head as if replaying that night. "I figured he'd use the assignment to discredit me if I failed or refused to do it. And like a fool, I underestimated the lengths he would go to get rid of me. So I took in backup and hoped I'd be able to turn the tables on him. I didn't count on the whole thing being bogus."

"I hope Reznik gets the gas chamber. I'd like to be the one who drops the pellet."

Eric picked up his coffee and relaxed against the back of his chair. "Believe it or not, he did me a favor. Because of him, I saw my need for God."

"Don't blame this on Reznik." He shoved his plate and tipped over his coffee. "It's those people. They hounded you when you were weak." He dabbed the spill and crushed the napkin into a tight wad.

"Nobody hounded. You know me. I'm a Templeton. Do you really think I could be manipulated into doing something I didn't want to do?"

Bob didn't bother with an answer. His mouth tightened as he flicked the wet napkin away from his plate.

"I almost died. Technically, I did. For about two minutes."

"What do you mean?"

"My heart stopped. The whole team refused to give up. They fought to bring me back. They're good people, Dad. All of them. And they were good to me. They treated me like the most important person on the planet. I felt loved, like I really mattered to someone."

Eric's words stung. This wasn't going the way he planned. He took a sip of what was left of the coffee and kept his gaze on the cup cradled in his hands.

"Their love became my lifeline. Like a drug. I wanted it. Needed it. I fell in love with Ellie, and I guess in love with everyone there."

Brock Whitfield. Hate churned inside him.

"But the thing that drew me to God wasn't their love."

Bob jolted back, ready to arm himself with ammunition.

"I was afraid." Eric shrugged his shoulders. "For the first time in my life, I felt death breathing down my neck, and it scared me. I had nightmares. My confidence was gone." Eric leaned in and met his gaze. "I knew I didn't want to die."

"So you went to Brock Whitfield, and he pressured you to turn to God."

"More like challenged me. Since I was stuck there for a while, I took him up on it. Kept me from staring at the ceiling fuming over Reznik. He gave me a Bible and told me some places to read, and then he basically left it up to me. I asked questions. Everything he answered seemed right. I didn't understand all of it, but what he explained had the ring of truth."

"And you chose to believe this God stuff to make up for the missing leg?"

Eric shook his head and set down his cup. "I chose God before I lost my leg. I'm glad. Losing my leg was the hardest thing I've ever had to go through. It devastated me."

Bob resisted the urge to roll his eyes. "You seem happy with just one leg."

Eric lowered his chin. "I'm. Not. Happy. But I can tell you this. God is real and the Bible is true."

"You can't know that."

"I do know it. God has filled my life with love and peace. Peace I can't explain. And sometimes"—Eric looked up as if he were searching for the right word—"I can almost hear God talking to me."

Bob swore under his breath. "Don't tell me you hear voices."

"No voices. Nothing audible, but I feel in my gut when He's trying to tell me something." Eric's face softened as he folded his hands and leaned closer. "Dad, haven't you noticed I'm different?"

He had him there. "I figured it was because of your girlfriend."

Eric grinned. "She's part of the reason, but I've changed because God's in my life." Eric's forefinger pounded on the table. "This life doesn't end with death. I'm sure of it. And it's up to us to choose whether we want to go to God when we die or—"

He pushed away from the table. "I'm done here." Lesson learned. He wouldn't bring it up again.

"I didn't mean to sound holier-than-thou. I'm glad you asked. I like talking about it."

"Good for you." He didn't try to hide his sarcasm.

"I do have a request though."

That's it. One more word about God and he'd—

"I want you to go to the doctor."

"The doctor? What for?"

"I knew you'd say that. Just humor me. I'd feel better if you got a checkup before I go back to Africa."

He'd agree to anything if it wasn't about God. "All right. Fine. I'll get a check-up if it'll make you happy." And quiet.

〰〰〰

Eric set up the appointment with a civilian doctor reputed to be thorough. "Day after tomorrow. 0900." Eric could almost see the wheels turning in his dad's mind. "I'm going with you."

"You don't have to."

Oh, yes, he did. "I want to. I might need to hold your hand."

He got the withering glance he expected.

"You're pushing it."

He did more than push it. On the day of the appointment, he accompanied his dad into the examination room. After a soft knock, a small-framed man from either India or Nepal entered carrying the preliminary chart. Each heavily-accented question received a terse and non-cooperative response. Eric filled in details that otherwise would have been omitted.

The doctor ordered a blood profile and a series of outpatient tests. His dad's gaze burned a hole on the side of Eric's face.

Cold, stony silence could have frosted the windows as his dad drove home. He went to his bedroom and slammed the door before Eric made it halfway up the stairs.

Later that afternoon, his dad came into the kitchen as Eric stood at the counter slicing tomatoes. "You'll be sedated for the procedure on Friday. Ben can drive both of us to the clinic."

"I'm not doing it."

"Not doing it? Why not?" One glance at his father told him everything he already knew. Red face. Narrow eyes. If the vein bulged out, he'd be in trouble.

"Look, I agreed to see a doctor. Nothing else."

Time to play hard ball. He laid the knife on the cutting board and mirrored his dad's scathing look. "You're afraid." He shook his head in mock disbelief. "I never thought I'd see Bob Templeton put his tail between his legs and run from a challenge." Cheap shot he hoped would work.

His dad charged him and grabbed the scruff of his shirt as he'd done many times before. Only this time, Eric didn't move or flinch. Even through the string of curses. Or the balled up fist barely an inch from his face.

Eric raised his chin and stared him down. He'd switched the leg out for the crutches, or his dad probably would've sent him reeling into next week.

His dad heaved out his breath in one angry backlash. "Back off."

"I can't, Dad." He kept his voice quiet and controlled. "You've got to do this."

His dad released his grip on the shirt with a vicious shove and stormed out of the room. Eric sank into the nearest chair, more shaken than he realized. He'd won the battle but at what cost? Maybe he should've backed off after all.

CHAPTER FIFTY

By the third week of September, the maple tree in the backyard had turned a vibrant red and yellow, and many of the leaves had filtered down to the ground. With no need of crutches, Eric walked out to the patio carrying his Bible and a cup of coffee. The crisp air, now more comfortable than oppressive, held the moist, moldy smell of dirt and dead leaves that always signaled the end of summer.

Lucky followed him outside and sprawled on the one spot where the sun still hit the concrete.

Dismissed from physical therapy, the only thing keeping him in the States was his unspoken commitment to ensure his dad was all right. Eric was more scared than he cared to admit. Each medical test led to other more invasive ones until the prescribed CT scan revealed a large mass on his dad's pancreas. The technician extracted tissue during the procedure to send for a biopsy. The waiting was the worst, and tomorrow the wait would be over.

What if his dad had cancer? What if it were terminal? What if his dad died without God? He rubbed his chin and cracked his knuckles before flipping open his Bible. The words on the pages seemed to run together. He leaned forward burying his face in his hands. "I can't even think straight. God help me. Give me something." The wind blew the pages from Psalms to Isaiah. He reached to flip back to his place, but one underlined verse leaped out at him. "Fear thou not, for I am with thee. Be not dismayed for I am thy God. I will strengthen thee, yea, I will help thee, yea, I will uphold thee with the right hand of My righteousness."

He closed the Bible and propped his elbows on the table, his hands folded against his mouth. The last time he felt this helpless, he cried out to God to let him keep his leg.

God said no.

He lost his leg but gained his father. What could be gained by losing his dad?

~~~~~~

A weather front came in during the night blasting in the first cold snap of the season. Eric wore long pants for the first time in months, and except for the slight limp he couldn't eliminate yet, no one would know his leg was missing.

The intermittent swipe of the wipers was the only sound as they drove to the appointment. The overcast sky mirrored the cloud hanging over them. Eric sipped coffee from his travel mug thankful for something to keep his hands from fidgeting.

Neither spoke on the walk from the parking deck to the office. No surprise, once in the waiting room, his dad grabbed a magazine and flipped it open as soon as he sat down.

When the attendant called for Mr. Templeton, his dad stood and walked with the same commanding purpose Eric had seen many times before.

Eric followed, determined to keep up. The consultation room resembled the conference room at Langley. The doctor entered almost immediately carrying a folder. Eric's gut twisted the moment the doctor sat across from them. His dad folded his hands and gave no outward sign of apprehension.

"The news isn't good, I'm afraid."

Direct and professional with no sugar coating. His dad would appreciate that at least.

"The mass on your pancreas is malignant. It has spread to your liver and also into your small intestine." The doctor's eyes softened as he took a deep breath and expelled it slowly. "We can buy you some time with extensive chemotherapy."

The man who in effect just had a death sentence pronounced on him showed no emotion.

"We can arrange for your first treatment before you leave today."

"How long do I have?"

"I can't answer that."

"Come on, Doc. Give me a ball park."

The doctor shrugged. "With treatment, possibly six months."

His dad stood. "Let's go home, son." He thanked the doctor and turned to go.

Eric unglued himself from the chair and tried to think of a question to ask before following his dad. The doctor stood before him, and Eric hesitated, waiting for some kind of reassurance.

The doctor shook his head slightly. "I'm sorry."

And that was it. Rain pelted the car as they exited the parking deck. His dad's face gave away nothing of what he was thinking or feeling. Eric knew better than to bring it up so he sat in silence and talked to God.

His dad maneuvered the car into the garage and got out. Without a word to Eric, he climbed the stairs to his bedroom. Eric hovered at the bottom and stared at his dad's closed door, a two-inch barrier as secure as Fort Knox.

He grabbed his Bible and headed to the back patio. He positioned his chair close to the house to avoid the horizontal gusts of rain.

A hollow ache lay heavy in his chest. Terminal cancer. This wasn't supposed to happen. He'd have to delay his return to Ellie. For how long? He rubbed his eyes. It shouldn't matter. Gray clouds hung so close he could almost touch them. Sheets of water formed a curtain around the patio awning and muffled Eric's words. "God, now what?"

He reached in his pocket for his phone. Noon here. Five there. He dialed the number, and the sound of the voice he hadn't heard in over six weeks worked better than a muscle relaxant.

"Eric. I'm so glad you called. Ellie told me you'd get the results today."

"Hey, Doc, are you in the dining area right now? I need to talk to you."

"No. I'm on the terrace. Tell me what you found out."

"Not good. Pancreatic cancer." His throat tightened and threatened to betray him. "You know what that means."

"Oh no. How advanced is it?"

"It's spread to his liver and intestines. The doctor said with chemo he might have six months."

"I'm so sorry. How can I help?"

"I don't know. Got any advice?"

The silence stretched into a long moment, and Eric checked to see if the call had dropped.

Finally, a heavy sigh. "Eric, you're good at reading people. Pay attention. Be sensitive to what he needs. Just knowing you're there will mean so much to him."

He took his first deep breath since they left the doctor's office and waited, hoping Doc had more to say.

"God has you there for a reason. You may be the only one who can reach him."

"That's the problem. We made an agreement I wouldn't talk about God if he wouldn't discourage my belief in God."

"Today's news changes everything." Doc's soothing tone became more urgent. "Your father must have the truth before he goes into eternity. This is your new assignment. But from God, not the government."

An assignment he didn't feel equal to. "I wish you and Ellie were here."

"For your sake, so do I, but your dad would be more open if we weren't there."

The rain had eased. Eric stood and paced, unable to keep still. "I don't know how to act around him now."

"Show him God's love and God's strength. God will give you peace and the grace to face this trial. He'll help you."

Calm crowded out the panic. "Thanks for talking to me. You said what I needed to hear."

"Call me anytime. Day or night.

"I will."

"I won't mention this to Ellie if you'd like to be the one to tell her yourself."

"No. You can tell her. I'll try to call her a little later. I love you both, Doc."

"We love you too, Eric."

Eric went to his room, closed the door and lay prone across his bed. "God, I don't understand. I'm not ready to lose my father. He's not ready to die. Oh God—" He choked on the words and spread his Bible in front of him. The pages fell open to Psalm 46. "God is our refuge and strength; a very present help in trouble." With each verse, his heart grew quieter. When he reached verse 10, "Be still and know that I am God," he stopped reading and rested his head on the pages. He drifted off into an exhausted sleep, his fingers still clutching the edges of the Bible.

The next morning Eric scrambled eggs, buttered some toast, and tried to act as if nothing had changed. His dad walked into the kitchen and poured a cup of coffee.

"Morning, Dad. Feel like eating?"

"Those eggs look good."

Eric filled two plates and took them to the table. His heart hammered, and right or wrong, he took the direct approach. "I don't know how to deal with this."

"Me either." His dad picked up a fork. "There's not a manual for this one. You'll be returning to Africa soon. There's not much either one of us can do."

"I'm not leaving you." Eric leveled his gaze at his dad.

"There's nothing you can do. Go. Get on with your life. I don't need you, and I sure don't want your sympathy."

"I'm not leaving. You may not need me, but I need you. For the first time in my life, I have a real relationship with you. I can't leave that."

His dad's eyes glistened with unshed tears, but he didn't leave the room. "Then stay. But don't you dare start patronizing me."

A small step or a giant leap? Eric wasn't sure. "Deal. As long as you tell me what you need."

"I don't know what I need," he snapped and then jammed a bite of eggs into his mouth. As he chewed, his mouth curled in a crooked smile as if to soften the harshness of his response. "I don't know what kind of time we're talking about."

"I'm in—whatever it takes."

His dad nodded.

Eric rubbed his hands together. "Let's assess the situation and get a game plan."

His dad raised his hand to stop him. "No chemo."

No treatment? Eric felt the punch to his gut but said nothing. He owed it to the man to let him call the shots. But how much time did that give him?

"What are you going to tell the director?"

"That I've settled on an early retirement. He doesn't have to know why. Not yet anyway. I'll work as long as I can."

"Are you in any pain?"

"Some." His dad shrugged. "I tire easily. Thought I was just run down. I wasn't expecting this one."

"Me either." Not quite the truth. Maybe Simon knew all along.

His dad left the table and scraped the rest of his eggs into the disposal. He turned to Eric. "Want to ride in with me?"

Not much had changed. His take-charge father dismissed the subject and focused on the immediate. Eric nodded and drank the last of his coffee. "I'll be down as soon as I brush my teeth."

CHAPTER FIFTY-ONE

Life settled into a quiet routine. Eric opted out of driving his Mustang in favor of riding each morning with his dad. Recruit training lasted until noon, and then Eric went to the gym to build back muscles long out of commission.

At the end of the first week, Eric hit the floor in the middle of the night to get relief from a leg cramp. He walked in the dark toward the hall bathroom. A light shone under his dad's door, and he hesitated only a moment before knocking softly.

"Come in."

Eric cracked the door enough to lean in. "Feel like a midnight snack?"

"Might as well." His dad closed the book he was reading and placed it on the bedside table.

In the kitchen, Eric stared at the contents in the fridge and then turned to his dad. "How about turkey and swiss?"

"Sounds good."

Eric grabbed everything in one load, thankful to be without crutches.

"Since when did you get so handy in the kitchen?"

Eric laid out the bread and talked while he worked. "Since I've been here. I've been trying to fatten you up."

His dad didn't answer. Eric took two glasses from the cabinet and poured some milk, then placed the sandwiches on paper plates and brought them to the table. He paused long enough to offer a quick and silent blessing for the food as his dad dived into his sandwich.

"Not bad." Lucky rubbed against the table leg. His dad broke off a piece of turkey and dropped it beside her. "I thought you'd lost your mind when you brought that cat to me."

Eric grinned. "I laughed most of the way to the airfield. Never thought you'd keep her." He dropped his hand beside his chair. Lucky ran to his fingers and rubbed against them. "So why did you?"

His dad shrugged. "I thought you'd be back in a day or two. When they told me you'd been—"

The room went silent. Eric kept his focus on Lucky who didn't mind at all being the center of attention. Should he wait it out or change the subject?

"She was my one connection to you. And good company. She sleeps at the end of my bed."

"You're kidding. So that's where she goes at night." He leaned over the table again. "Lucky, you are one spoiled cat." Eric cut his gaze back to his dad whose midnight confession sparked another wild idea. "I have a proposition for you."

His dad stopped chewing. "Now what?"

"Let's make up for lost time. Get to know each other. Have fun." Eric pushed his plate toward the center of the table and leaned back in his chair. "I shut you out of my life. I regret that now, and I don't want to waste any more of the time I have left with you."

His dad rubbed the back of his neck. "What do you have in mind?"

"I don't know." He scrambled for anything to say. "We could play chess or poker, or go to a ball game—whatever you feel like. And when you're feeling bad, I'll sit in your room and read or write to Ellie. I want to be with you. And if you want to be alone, I'll respect that too." Eric forced through his tightening throat to keep talking. "I want some good memories of our time together."

His dad's jaw worked long after he swallowed his last bite. He looked down and spoke quietly as if to his plate. "I can't make any promises. I don't know what's ahead."

"No worries. We'll take it one day at a time and figure it out as we go." Eric stood. Time to back off and give his dad some space. "I'm gonna take a pain pill so my leg will let me get some rest. Do you need any medicine?"

"No. I think I can sleep now." His father stood too and placed his hand on Eric's shoulder. "I'm glad you're here." Dad gave him a pat and left the room. Eric picked up his plate and the glasses and moved to the sink. Tonight's talk was a home run and felt almost as good as that homer he hit in the game against Bingham High. The ball went sailing over the back fence, and he zeroed in on his dad's face as he slung his bat. The brief nod and the look of pride in his dad's eyes carried him around those bases. He'd almost forgotten how good it felt.

God, give us time.

In his room, he picked up the phone from the charger and punched Ellie's number.

"Eric. Is everything all right?"

"Missing you."

"Oh. I can handle that." A door closed, but he couldn't figure out which one. "Talk to me while I get someplace private."

"Where are you?"

"I'm leaving the clinic and making my way to my bedroom. You sound wide awake in the middle of the night."

"Dad and I couldn't sleep. We had a midnight snack." His voice, barely above a whisper, almost betrayed him. "This is hard."

"I'm so sorry. I wish there was something I could do."

"Keep loving me."

"I mean something tangible. Something that would help."

"Baby, I don't know how long this will take. Weeks or months. No way of telling. Right now, Dad's doing all right—" What he couldn't say hovered between them.

Ellie's soft, wistful voice broke the silence. "He's the priority right now. Not me. Not us."

Words he had repeated many times to himself. He closed his eyes, aching to hold her.

"Ellie, I—"

"I know. Me too."

He had to change the subject quickly, or he wouldn't make it. "I was thinking today that you and I have never been on à real date."

Her laughter filtered through the phone. "Unless you count our trip to the terrace. You remember, when I pulled your arm out of its socket and you leaned over to kiss my cheek? Our first date, and almost our first kiss."

His mind conjured the image of her parted lips. "I remember."

"I'm the lucky girl who got you."

"We both know I'm the lucky one. Honey, I fight thinking this, but I hope I can be with you soon."

She didn't respond. He would bet money she was staring down, her feet drawing circles on the floor. After a long moment, she sighed. "I feel the same way. It's probably good you're not here. We've been slammed lately."

"Why?"

"Cholera broke out in one of the out-lying villages. Every day more people come in. The beds are at capacity."

Something in Eric froze. He'd seen cholera and its devastation. Why hadn't she told him?

"I won't get it, Eric."

Just like he didn't lose his leg. And his dad didn't have terminal cancer. "Ellie, I couldn't handle losing you."

"I couldn't handle losing you either. I'm not handling your absence very well. I'm glad I'm so busy I can hardly think straight."

"You probably need to get to work, don't you?"

"Yeah. Everybody's overworked. Nicci's even helping out. Dad's bringing in a crew to install a clean water system in the village."

"I'm not surprised."

"I'm glad we talked. Makes me feel better."

Made him miss her even more. He sighed and knew he'd have to be the one who ended the call, but he didn't want to. "Okay, Baby. Get to work. Stay safe."

He plugged his phone into the charger and clicked off the lamp beside the bed. He lay back with his arm draped across his eyes. A tear trickled past his ear and into his hair. His chest heaved in an unsteady breath.

"God, help me—"

CHAPTER FIFTY-TWO

Eric stopped by his dad's office on Friday afternoon. "I brought more boxes."

"Good. This one's already full."

"Where's Miss Mildred?"

"Sent her home."

The barbed wire was up, and the face was granite. Closed with a do not disturb sign. Eric went straight to the bookcase and stacked books in the bottom of the box. He slid the box to the side and jerked the clock off the wall. "How do you stand this thing?"

"What?" His dad looked up. "Oh, that. I never notice it."

Eric removed the batteries. "Where's the trash can?"

"Other side of the desk."

A framed photo lying on a pile of other garbage stopped Eric's hand in mid swing. He picked it up for a closer look. Tom Reznik was shaking his dad's hand and giving him a plaque for twenty years of service to the CIA. Five years ago. Eric studied the man. When had he gone rogue? And why?

His dad sat, his face drawn and pinched. The gray walls emphasized the yellow pallor of his skin. When he spoke, he seemed out of breath. "Both of our careers are over." His dad nodded toward the photo. "Tom's and mine. And as bad as this is, I'd rather be in my shoes, than in his."

Eric stared at the image, not knowing what to say.

His dad gave a sweeping gaze around the office. "I look at this box of stuff I built my life around, and right now, none of it mounts up to a hill of beans. My replacement will move into this office, and life will go on without missing a beat.

Remember this, son. Every man, no matter how important he thinks he is, is replaceable."

"You served your country for forty-six years. You can't put that kind of commitment in a box." By some miracle, he didn't choke up. "And the lessons you drilled in me of character, strength, and courage have served me well all my life." He faltered a little but had to say one more thing. "If God gives a child to Ellie and me, I want to pass on those same values. Your life mattered, Dad."

When his dad finally raised his head, tears ran unheeded down his face. He picked up the box, walked out of the office, and never looked back.

Bob Templeton opened his eyes and knew before he looked at the clock, it was two in the morning—the same as the past three nights.

Every other night he'd risen and made good use of the time when he seemed the most alert and pain-free. Tonight, every bone in his body ached, and the tossing and turning had failed to give even temporary relief.

He rose and shuffled into his bathroom. He washed down two pain pills and leaned on the sink. The stranger looking back at him had sunken cheeks with bags under eyes more yellow than white.

Terminal cancer carried with it the mandate to get his affairs in order. The will. The funeral arrangements. He checked off each item in his mind. But one task remained unfinished, and it ate at him as much as the disease.

He could take the coward's way and leave it for Eric to find after he was gone. But the code he lived his life by wouldn't let him take the cheap way out. He splashed water on his face and dried off. With a set jaw, he returned to his bedroom. No more procrastination.

His closet bore the same orderly imprint as everything else in his life. He slid a chair inside and climbed up to reach the top shelf. A brown box secured with packing tape occupied the farthest corner on the shelf.

It was heavy, and the effort to retrieve it winded him so much he had to sit in the chair he had used as a step ladder. He heaved off the chair and plopped the box onto the end of the bed next to Lucky. He straightened the rest of the cover to make a workspace.

The knife he kept in his nightstand slit through the tape. His heart hammered as if any moment the door would open, and he'd be caught trespassing on some forbidden territory. He locked the door, pulled the chair close to the bed, and folded back the cardboard flaps. All that was left of Nick's life lay before him exactly as he'd packed it.

Memories of that day flooded through his mind as if it were yesterday. Only fury had kept him functioning as he ransacked the house for Eric's clothes and furniture. He'd filled the back of his truck and grabbed this box to make one last sweep of the house. Eric's birth certificate lay in the top left drawer of Nick's desk along with other personal papers and photos. It hurt too much. He'd dumped the contents into the box. He left the black Bible sitting on top of the desk and taped the box shut. He made it to the front door before dropping the box and going back for the Bible. He cut the box open and threw it in. He'd sort through the contents after things settled down. Now, thirty-three years later, it was time to face it.

His chair creaked as he leaned over the box. Nick's Bible. Maybe going back for it was the one thing he'd done right. He placed it toward the end of the bed with barely a glance. Something to give Eric.

His neck muscles stiffened as he reached for the brown envelope containing all the photos. Some of Nick and Nick's wife whom he'd never gotten to know.

All the letters he'd written from Germany frayed as if they'd been read many times. Bundled together and secured with a large rubber band that had dried out and stuck to the sides of the envelopes.

At the bottom of the box lay the leather-bound volume that had been part of the contents of the desk drawer. He flipped through it, and Nick's familiar scrawl, half-print, half-cursive, pierced his heart as if the ghost of his brother had entered the room. He scanned the dates at the top corners of the pages searching for the day everything changed between them. It wasn't there. Relief canceled out the disappointment. After all, did he really want to know?

One more haphazard search produced the page. No wonder he missed it. Writing filled only half. His brother must have hated him after that day. He took a deep breath and forced himself to face whatever Nick had written.

> *April 9*
> *My twenty-first birthday. And all I want, all I care about is for Bobby to trust Christ. No way that'll be happening anytime soon. Not after today. He showed up as I was leaving work. Wanted to take me out for my first beer. Told him no way. Made him mad—madder than I've ever seen him. He shoved me against my car. I shoved back. Told him to come back when he sobered up. He shoved harder.*

The image of himself through his brother's eyes sickened him. Bob Templeton, Jerk First Class. A black smudge blotted out the next words. He held the book closer to the lamp and skimmed over what he couldn't make out.

*Here's what gets me. I'd made up my mind to
talk to Bobby one more time about Christ. It's
Good Friday. I've been thinking all day about
the cross and what You went through to pay
for my sins. Prayed for him all day. Now, I
think I've lost him forever. I'm begging You,
God, do whatever it takes to bring him to You.
I mean it. Even if it means taking my life. Do it.
I'd gladly give up my life, if that would bring
him to You. Break his heart, and let him turn to
You before it's too late. God, I love him so
much.*

His vision blurred. His finger grazed over the smudged
words, and he realized the only thing Nick had spilled on the
paper had been his own tears.

CHAPTER FIFTY-THREE

Eric glanced at the clock on the microwave. Should he wake his dad or let him sleep? Ten o'clock. Two hours past his usual wake-up time. What if he'd died in his sleep?

He had to know. Eric had mastered the trick of taking the stairs two at a time. He tapped on the door as he turned the knob. Locked. Scenarios seared through his mind, none with a happy ending. He rapped harder and called out. No response. His mind clicked through the quickest way to jimmy the door when rustling papers and a heavy thump made him release the breath he held.

A weak "Just a minute," and the door swung open. His dad appeared, bleary-eyed and disheveled.

"Sorry to wake you, Dad. I was getting worried."

His dad rubbed his eyes and ran his hand through his mussed hair.

"Why'd you lock your door?"

"I, -uh, don't know."

Eric looked past his dad into the still darkened room. Lucky scooted past them, ready to find her breakfast. Eric's radar went up. "You okay?"

"Overslept."

Overslept? Eric cut his eyes to the unrumpled bed.

"Couldn't sleep. Sat in the recliner and must have dozed off pretty hard. My body's paying for it now."

Eric could buy that, but it didn't explain the locked door. He wanted to tell him not to lock the door again in case he needed to get in fast, but he let it go. Locked doors had never stopped him before. "Sorry I woke you. Let me know when you're ready for breakfast."

"Will do." His dad nodded and closed the door.

Classic. He should be used to it by now. The distance separating them felt more like miles instead of a few feet. He went across the hall to talk to the only One Who could reach his father.

"God, time's running out."

Bob closed the door and retrieved the box he had stuffed back in the closet. He reached for the journal and forced himself to read as if the pain stabbing his heart would purge the guilt he'd carried all these years.

He flipped through the pages, his eyes like a computer scoping out every sentence with the name Bobby.

Called Bobby today. I miss my brother. Went to Bobby's work today. Refused to see me.

Nick's broken heart bled through the words on the pages.

Sweat slid down his face, and the closeness in the room stifled him. He leaned forward and turned to the last written page, dated December 31. The day Nick was killed.

Another year has gone by, and a new year is coming. God has been so good to me and my family.

His mouth twisted. How could he say God had been good?

Church tonight. Should be a great night of praise and testimonies of God's faithfulness through the past year. We'll tell the church tonight about the little one on the way.

I'm the most blessed man on the planet. If I died today, I'd die a happy man. Thank You for Becky, my beautiful wife. Take care of her with this pregnancy. And take care of Eric, my little man. He's such a joy to us. Put a hedge of protection around him. Shield him from harm

and help him grow to be a fine young man.
Lead him to Your truth, and make him a
warrior for You. And let this be the year Bobby
comes to You. Whatever it takes, don't let
Bobby die without Christ.

He closed the book and covered his face with his hands. It was time to man up and stop running. He owed his kid brother that much. Still clutching the journal, he opened his bedroom door and went in search of Eric.

Eric glanced up as his dad simultaneously knocked and pushed open the door.

"Got a minute?"

"Sure." He closed the Bible and put it on the bedside table.

"Did you make coffee?"

Odd question. "Yeah. You want a cup?"

"No. I mean yes. I, uh, could we talk?"

An invitation to talk. "That'd be great."

In the kitchen, his dad poured himself a cup and sat at the table. Eric grabbed the creamer from the fridge door and joined him. "You haven't eaten anything. You want some toast or something?"

"Just coffee."

Eric wrapped his hands around the warm cup and waited for his dad to make the next move.

"I need for you to teach me about God."

Eric almost spewed the sip he had just taken. Relief, joy, and panic warred with each other. Panic won. His mind went blank. If only he had an earpiece with Doc feeding him what to say.

"Okay." That was all he could think of to reply.

His dad's head dropped as he stared into his cup. "I turned my back on God the day my mother died. She believed in God, and I saw what He did to her. She suffered."

A door into his dad's life was cracking open. Eric waited, barely moving, not willing to risk it slamming shut again.

"I even prayed to God. You believe that?" His raised his voice and emphasized every word. "I begged God to spare her." His eyes glinted, and his mouth twisted. "She got worse, and then died." He threw his hands out in a downward sweep. "I was done. If that was the kind of help God supposedly gives, I didn't need it. I could take care of my kid brother with no help from God."

Raw pain etched his dad's face. Eric sipped his coffee and forced himself to remain still.

"When I came back from Germany and found Nicky was some kind of Jesus freak, I lost it. I wanted to hurt him." He balled up his hand into a fist and covered it with his other hand. "On his twenty-first birthday, I told Nick he was dead to me, that I wanted no part of a brother who was so weak he had to turn to God. I shoved him down and left. I never spoke to him again." He paused and grew quiet. "And you want to know the real kicker?"

Eric leaned forward and met his dad's gaze.

"I felt triumphant the night of the accident, like I had just proved I was right about God all along." He leaned back in his chair and pointed. "And I fought for you. Nobody was going to get Nick's kid. I was going to stick it to God and the whole world. I'd make a real man out of you. Somebody who didn't need help from anybody, especially God."

He stood and walked over to the kitchen door and stared into the backyard. "Looks like God stuck it to me. God got to you. Even used Brock Whitfield to do it," he spoke without turning around.

His dad had just unloaded years of secrets, but something didn't add up. Eric pivoted and placed his arm over the back of the chair. "I don't understand. If you feel this way, why do you want to learn about God?"

Without a word, his dad walked back to his chair and reached for something on the floor. He plopped a brown leather book in the center of the table. "Because of this."

With his forefinger, he pushed it over to Eric.

He cocked his head to his dad and reached for the book. Handwriting similar to Eric's filled the yellowed pages. "What's this?"

"Nick's."

Eric's throat tightened. Something tangible from his real father. He fingered the volume with a newfound reverence.

"I threw some papers and photos in a box. I didn't know what was in there. Until last night."

Eric closed the binder and folded his hands on top.

"I was wrong to keep the truth from you." He rubbed his forehead. "I was wrong about a lot of things."

The confident tyrant who had raised him disappeared. The shell of the man sat again as if all the strength had left his body.

Compassion took over. "You did what you thought you had to do." He placed his hand on top of his dad's. "Did you mean it? Are you ready to learn about God?"

If he had blinked, he would've missed his dad's slight nod. "But it may be too late. I shut God out of my life for a long time."

Eric steepled his hands against his lips, weighing his words. He thought back to his days at the mission hospital. What would Doc say? "It's not too late. God wants you to know the truth about Him."

His dad's mouth twisted with the same set expression he'd displayed in the doctor's office when he'd refused treatment.

"Give God a chance. God can handle your doubts." The words seemed to come from nowhere. "But can you handle His truth?"

His dad flinched. After a long moment, he muttered, "I don't know where to start."

Eric expelled the breath he'd been holding. "We'll take it one step at a time. I'll get a Bible for you."

He shook his head. "I kept Nick's. I'll use his."

Even better, especially if Nick underlined key verses like Doc did. "Great." He started to say more but stopped when his dad's shoulders hunched over the table. "Why don't you rest for a while?"

"I think I will." Without a word, he left the kitchen. His faltering gait slowed halfway up the stairs. Eric sprinted to stand beside him and hid the grimace as he wrapped his arm around his dad's gaunt frame. He didn't release his hold until they made it to the bed. "You need a pain pill?"

"Uh-huh."

Eric scrambled to the bathroom to get the medication and some water. "Here you go."

His dad's hands shook as they held the glass and some of the water spilled onto his pajama shirt. Eric took the glass. "I'll get a towel."

His dad held up his hand to stop him. He relaxed onto the bed and turned over onto his side. "Don't bother. It'll dry."

His dad was spent. Eric recognized the signs. Had experienced it himself more than once when he was recovering. He placed his hand on his dad's arm and gave it a gentle squeeze as Doc had done to him so many times at the mission hospital. He spread the cover over him. "Get some rest, Dad."

No response. Not even a nod, but one side of his dad's mouth curled up. Lucky pounced on the end of the bed and settled in the crook of his dad's bent legs. Eric gave her a quick pat and left the room.

The walls of the house seemed to be closing in on him, and he needed to get out quick. He grabbed his Bible and a jacket and headed downstairs to retrieve the journal. His Mustang roared to life, and he drove first to an electronics store for a special gift for his dad. Then he found the nearest coffee shop where he could be alone and think.

The morning rush had cleared out. He sat at a table in the back corner near a window and angled his chair so the sun streamed down on his back. The warmth loosened the tenseness in his shoulders. He took a deep breath and slowly expelled it. His dad was ready to learn about God. The challenge loomed over him and seemed as insurmountable as his early days at West Point. At least this time he had God to help him.

And Nick's journal. He thumbed through the worn pages. The dates on the top were spaced out as if only special days made it into the treasured volume. Like a homing pigeon, his eyes sought for the one date he hoped would be there.

> *January 4*
> *"1:21 A.M. Eric Nicholas Templeton entered this world. Head full of dark hair. Six pounds one ounce. Healthy lungs. Doctor placed our little man on Becky's swollen stomach and the crying stopped. I've never seen anything so moving or so beautiful. I'm a father. I can't believe it. Thank You, God, for this wonderful gift. Help me be what he needs.*

Eric shut his eyes and tried to conjure any memory from his life with Nick and Becky. The accident that took their lives, and changed his, happened four days before his second birthday. Not one spark flickered in his mind.

He closed the journal with a promise to Nick he'd make time soon to get to know him. But a bigger mandate lay before him, and in a strange way, made him feel even closer to Nick.

"Looks like it's up to me. Help me, Jesus. And if you can hear me too, Nick, help me know what to tell your brother."

For the second time since he became a believer, overwhelming love washed over him. And for the first time in his life, he wanted very much to make his real father proud.

Eric left the coffee shop and checked the time on his phone as he settled back in the convertible. Five in Angola. Perfect. His finger punched the speed dial.

"Eric! I'm so glad you called. I've missed you more than usual today."

"Hey, honey. Are you at dinner?"

"I am. Dad's here too. He said to tell you hello."

"Put it on speaker. I want you both to hear the latest."

"Okay. Go ahead, we're all ears."

"You won't believe this. This morning my dad came to my bedroom door and asked me to teach him about God."

For a moment, no response from either Doc or Ellie. Eric tried to imagine the shock on their faces. "Pretty incredible, huh?"

"Incredible?" Ellie found her voice. "It's the miracle we've been praying for."

"Dad found Nick's journal and must have stayed up half the night reading it."

Doc spoke up. "Sounds like God's doing things. This morning at our seven o'clock prayer time, we felt impressed to pray even harder for your father."

"Doc, what if I mess it up?"

Doc's chuckle preceded his words. "Say what God leads you to say. He'll do the rest. It's God's job to convince him."

Eric shifted his position on the seat and stretched his leg across the console hoping to avoid a cramp. Maybe Doc would outline the specific formula to lead his dad to Christ. "When you taught me about God, did you ever wonder if I wouldn't make the right choice?"

Another classic Doc pause. "God brought you to our little mission hospital thousands of miles from where you live. If God did that miracle, I knew He'd finish what He started. In fact, I was a little surprised you embraced the faith as quickly as you did."

"With you and Ellie praying for me, I didn't stand a chance."

Ellie laughed. "We're praying for your dad now. And for you— so it's just a matter of time."

"Speaking of time, I'm in the parking lot of the coffee shop, but I need to get home before Dad wakes up."

"We'll have a special prayer meeting on the terrace after dinner."

Homesickness gripped him as he pictured the group on the terrace. "Thanks. I'll probably have to call every day with questions."

"Call anytime, day or night. You're not alone, son."

He heard a click, and then Ellie's voice came through loud and clear. "You make me so proud."

He sat a little taller and grinned. "You make me so happy. I tell God I love you all the time."

"Yeah, He hears the same thing from me."

"That you love you?"

Her laughter triggered his. He needed to laugh. He needed to hold her and bury his face in her hair.

"Oh, you. I miss you so much."

"Me too, baby."

"You miss you?"

He chuckled. "Got me. I miss me being with you. Gotta go now, but I'll call you later."

"Call at five your time and tuck me in."

"You've got a date. Love you." He forced himself to say good-bye.

◇◇◇◇◇

The house was quiet when he entered. He placed Chinese take-out on the table and went upstairs to his dad's bedroom. It looked as if his dad hadn't moved. Eric froze at the door until the hand protruding out of the cover twitched. Eric settled into the recliner beside the bed and opened his Bible, waiting for his dad to wake.

Isaiah 41:10. "For I the Lord thy God will hold thy right hand, saying unto thee, Fear not, I will help thee."

Eric flexed his right hand over the pages. *I want You to help me.*

His dad stirred and opened his eyes. Then he stretched, almost knocking Lucky off the bed.

"You feel brave enough to tackle egg drop soup?"

"I think so." He pulled back the cover and swung his legs over the edge. "I slept better than I have in days." He rubbed his hand through his hair and yawned.

Eric stifled his own.

"You went out for Chinese?"

"Yeah." He stayed close to his dad, especially on the stairs. The pungent smell from the containers hit them as soon as they cleared the kitchen doors. "I'm one of their regulars. The lady at the register said, 'You come back. You good customer.'"

His dad gave a weak grin.

"How about an egg roll, Dad?"

"Just soup."

The one thing his dad seemed to keep down the best. When this ordeal ended, Eric doubted he'd ever eat Chinese again.

They sat at the table, and his dad reached for one of the fortune cookies. "This ought to be good." He broke it in half and pulled out the strip of paper. "Good things are in your future." He wadded it up and threw it down. "Right. Nothing but blue skies and smooth sailing."

Eric took a bite of egg roll and changed the subject. "I bought you an iPod today."

"An iPod? For crying out loud, you know I don't listen to music."

"Not music. I downloaded portions of the Bible. You can relax and listen to God's word."

His dad leaned over his bowl and sipped from his spoon. "Less effort than reading, I guess."

"You could listen and follow along in Nick's Bible. The first part is the gospel of John. My favorite book. I've read it four times already."

"Okay." His dad shrugged his shoulders as if he were resigned to another medical procedure.

"And you can ask me questions too. Can't guarantee I'll be able to answer, but I'll try." He stood and placed the leftovers in the fridge. "You look like you're feeling better." Out of nowhere, he added, "Good things are in your future."

SAVING ERIC

CHAPTER FIFTY-FOUR

Death. No longer someday, somehow. Soon. By cancer. Bob pressed his hand over his abdomen. Five days with no nausea. Maybe the doctor had it wrong.

He closed the bedroom door and took his regular position in the recliner by his bed. Headphones in place, he flipped opened Nick's Bible to the next chapter in John. Lucky competed for his attention by placing herself on top of the open book. He nudged her off to lie beside him. She rarely left his side, and truth be told, he didn't want her to.

Words from the verses he'd read yesterday seemed stuck in his mind. He turned back a page or two. Chapter 10? No. Chapter 11. His forefinger skimmed the page, and he read them again, out loud this time. "I am the resurrection and the life. He that believeth in Me, though he were dead, yet shall he live. And whosoever liveth and believeth in Me shall never die. Believest thou this?"

His heart hammered as fast as it had the day Brock Whitfield told him Eric was alive. Could this be true too?

Give God a chance. God can handle your doubts. Can you handle His truth?

He jerked the headphones from his ears and read on, searching, but not knowing for what. He read to the end of the book, through the section about the crucifixion and the resurrection. Then he flipped through the pages again, reading only what Nick had underlined.

"Jesus saith unto him, I am the way, the truth, and the life. No man cometh unto the father but by Me."

"Greater love hath no man than this: that a man lay down his life for his friends."

Friends? What chance did he have?

The last verse Nick highlighted stabbed him the most. Jesus' words, from the cross, "Father, forgive them, for they know not what they do."

He'd been wrong. So wrong. He fell to his knees by his bed. Too weak to hold up his head anymore, he rested it on his folded hands. How could he even presume to pray? Tears streamed down his cheeks to the bedspread, and he stammered out a prayer the best way he knew how. "I got nothing, God. No right to pray. Nick was right. And Mom was right. I—." He broke down and cried a long time. Tears from a lifetime ago. Tears for his mom, and for his kid brother, and for his own wasted life. "God, I've been a fool. And I love that kid in there so much. You win. I'm done running. I don't have much time. Forgive me. If it's not too late."

Eric put the cutting board on the counter and searched the drawer for his favorite knife. The smell of the simmering chicken permeated the house. Any minute now, he expected Lucky to rub against his legs pestering him for a handout. The chicken fell apart as he lifted it out of the pot to cool enough for him to shred. He bent to get celery from the drawer in the fridge and almost jumped when he straightened and saw his dad in the kitchen doorway.

"Dad." He blurted, hoping to cover how startled he was. "Dinner will be ready soon. Homemade chicken soup. Old family recipe—" He wiped his hands on a towel and picked up his phone for a closer look. "From the family of Ida May Johnson. Figured anybody named Ida May would know how to make good chicken soup."

He started chopping and glanced up. His dad met his gaze and gave him a crooked smile that slightly quivered. Eric needed no words to know what had taken place that afternoon.

A familiar prickling stung his eyes, but he didn't try to hide the tears from the man who had similar tears of his own.

His dad closed the distance between them and placed his hand on Eric's shoulder. He opened his mouth as if to speak, but shook his head and left the room. Eric stood, rooted to the spot. A miracle. A miracle only God could have pulled off had just happened.

Eric adjusted the heat under the pot and stepped outside onto the patio, eager to talk to the One who had become his life. Relief washed over him as he scanned the darkening skyline. "Thank You, Jesus." His full heart repeated the phrase as he sank on a chair and wiped his face. Losing his leg. Separation from Ellie. Nothing mattered more than the miracle of seeing his dad come to Christ. "I'll never be able to thank You enough."

This must have been how Doc and Ellie felt the day he came to Christ. They would want details, more than he had at the moment. A wall of warm, moist air hit him as he entered the kitchen. He threw chopped celery and carrots into the boiling broth and added a cup of rice, and then shredded the chicken mindlessly. He gave the soup a quick taste before settling the lid for the soup to simmer. "Not bad, Ida May."

With a lightness he hadn't felt in weeks, he climbed the stairs and knocked gently on his dad's bedroom door.

"Come in." His dad stood at the window, looking out to the dark street below.

"Soup's almost done." Eric hovered at the door, not knowing the protocol for this one.

His dad turned, and motioned for Eric to sit. "Got a minute?"

"Sure." Years of training had taught Eric to wait for his dad to make the first move. He sat in the recliner across from his dad, his eyes never leaving his face.

After a couple of failed attempts, his dad cleared his throat and spoke the words Eric was waiting to hear.

"This cancer thing. God got my attention big time, and today I quit fighting Him."

His dad's head lowered even further, and his shoulders shook with silent sobs. Eric moved to the bed and put his arm around him. The bones from his back protruded through the thin material of his shirt. His dad leaned into the embrace, and Eric wrapped his other arm around the front.

"I don't deserve forgiveness.

Eric strained to hear the words mumbled through heaving breaths.

"I don't deserve anything from God."

"None of us do, Dad." Eric kissed the top of the head drooping beside him. "That's what makes it so wonderful."

CHAPTER FIFTY-FIVE

Eric studied the chess board and contemplated his next move. His dad sat across from him, tapping his mouth with his finger. Eric took his time before he slid his bishop over, exposing it to the queen's attack. He couldn't make it look too obvious. As soon as the queen pounced, Eric countered with his knight. "Check."

His dad winced and leaned forward. Eric relaxed against the back of the chair and sipped his coffee, smug that his dad had no clue. He grinned and waited. In just three moves, his dad could checkmate and win the game.

His back pocket vibrated. He reached for his phone and pushed back from the table. "I have to take this."

His dad nodded, but his eyes never left the board. Eric stepped outside and closed the kitchen door.

"Hey, Sam. Let's have it."

"Your mom lives in Connecticut when she's in the States. Husband number three owns properties in three countries. She's currently at their villa in Spain."

Twenty-three years had passed since he last saw the woman who'd raised him. News of her whereabouts bit into him like the bitter wind whipping the leaves around the backyard. He moved back under the awning to escape the next blast. "Did you find my sisters?"

"Come on, man. We found Bin Laden. Two women are peanuts."

Eric smiled against the phone. "Point taken. What you got?"

"Terry lives in Oregon. Works with a brokerage firm. Divorced. No kids. Living with current boyfriend. Jackie's not far from Washington. Newport News. Married to a career Navy guy. They have a teenage son and an eleven year old daughter."

"Great. Download the file to my e-mail. Really appreciate it."

"No problem. How's your dad?"

Eric shifted his weight, the cold weather making his leg stiff. "Still holding his own. Killing me at chess." He stole a quick glance through the kitchen window. "Hey, man. I've got to run. I owe you one."

"You bet."

Eric re-entered the kitchen and bypassed the table in search of his dad. The familiar sound of retching came all the way from his dad's room. Eric pushed open the bathroom door. His dad half-sat, half-reclined beside the toilet, his face as white as the porcelain he hugged.

Eric wet a washcloth and handed it to him. "Couldn't stomach losing to me, huh, Dad?"

A weak grin preceded the next onslaught. It ended and his dad relaxed against the side of the tub. "Just sparing you the humiliation of defeat."

"Want some help?"

Eric grasped the outstretched hand and pulled him up. He gripped his dad's thin shoulders to steady him and guided him to the bed. "I'll get your nausea medicine."

His dad collapsed on his side and Eric lifted both his legs.

"Bring a container in case I get sick again."

Eric returned and nudged the pill between tight lips with no hue of color. "Here you go." He positioned the straw. "Sip enough to get the pill down."

His dad didn't lift his head or open his eyes. Eric wet the cloth with cool water and placed it on his dad's face.

A weak moan almost like a hum mouthed, "Thanks."

How could his dad go from fine to helpless in half an hour? Eric walked around the bed and stared anxiously at his dad's chalk-white face.

Maybe Simon had it wrong this time. *Please, God. Let it just be a setback and not the beginning of the end.*

CHAPTER FIFTY-SIX

No great surprise his dad's health deteriorated from that night on. With his Bible, phone, and laptop surrounding the recliner, Eric maintained his post by his dad's bed and rarely left his side. As his dad slept, Eric read Nick's journal from the beginning and discovered he had much more in common with his biological father than with the man lying in front of him.

His life would have been far different with Nick. He would've been a preacher's son. Eric closed his eyes. The distant memory of the dream-like vision of Nick and the woman had mostly faded from his memory, and the more he tried to conjure it back, the more it eluded him. And the girl. Who was she? The journal indicated his mother was pregnant. Could it have been a girl? A baby sister?

Eric turned to the next blank page and wrote his own precise words recording the event that happened just one week earlier.

October 22

> *Today, Bob Templeton came to Christ. It was your words, Nick, that broke his stubborn will and made him willing to listen to the truth about God. And I just wanted you to know, he'll be joining you soon.*

His dad roused from his sleep and stared at Eric as if confused. Eric leaned closer. "Can I get you anything?"

"Water."

Eric went into the bathroom and brought out a glass with a straw. "Here you go."

His dad took a long drink and breathed deeply as Eric placed the glass on the table.

Eric went back to the recliner and resisted the urge to ask how his dad was feeling. He busied himself so he wouldn't appear to be hovering.

His dad's weak voice broke the silence. "I dreamed about Nick."

"Oh yeah?"

"He was in a big grassy field feeding a horse." His dad glanced over to Eric. "Nick loved animals. Was a sucker for strays."

Eric grinned and catalogued the new piece of information.

"I remember one time he was mowing our neighbor's lawn, and he found a baby bird on the ground. Wrapped it up in a towel and brought it home. Didn't even have any feathers on it. I told him he was a fool, and the stupid thing was going to die anyway." His dad stared at the ceiling and shook his head. "Proved me wrong, all right. Fed him mashed up boiled eggs and potted meat with an eyedropper. Would you believe he actually taught the thing how to fly?"

Eric responded with appropriate surprise and willed his eyes not to betray him with tears for the man he never got to know.

"Anyway, Nick was in this field, and I was propped up at the fence watching him. He looked over at me, and—"

Seconds lapsed. Simon nudged him to keep his mouth shut.

"Nick's whole face lit up, and he said—" His dad cleared his throat. "And he said, 'Bobby, I've been waiting for you.' He came over to the fence and opened the gate." A tear slid down the side of his dad's face. "Then he grabbed me and hugged me. And it seemed so real." His voice, choked with emotion, he asked, "Do you think we'll know people in heaven?"

Eric nodded and reached for his dad's hand. "And I think Nick will be waiting for you at that gate."

CHAPTER FIFTY-SEVEN

Eric synchronized his breathing to his dad's labored breaths. He cracked open the window beside the recliner and hunched over the armrest to suck in the crisp fall air. It had been a long day. The flash of headlights in the driveway signaled help was on the way. Joy Stockman, the hospice worker whose mere presence brought peace.

He checked his phone. Must've lost track of time. Joy stepped out of her SUV and waved up at the window. He waved back and then zipped down the stairs to open the door.

"Joy, you must have read my mind." He reached for the bag in her hand and followed her into the foyer.

She turned and placed her hand on Eric's arm. "You've been on my mind all day. I juggled a few things so I could get here quicker."

"I'm glad you did. Dad's breathing has changed."

"When?"

Eric tried to recall but drew a blank. Not like him to forget a detail like that.

Her smile was kind and sympathetic as she handed him her coat and took the bag he still held. "I'll go check on him."

Eric trailed behind her, relieved to let the professional do her job. Joy took a moment to stroke Dad's forehead and then felt the flushed cheek with the back of her hand. "He has a fever."

Eric met her gaze and nodded. He rubbed the two-day stubble of his chin and only then realized he still wore the clothes he'd slept in the night before.

Joy reached for the stethoscope and listened to several places on the heaving chest.

Dad's glazed eyes seemed to look right through them. The restless thrashing, that kept Eric awake and on his feet most of the day, intensified.

"He started struggling sometime this morning. Like he couldn't breathe."

Joy lowered the earpiece of the stethoscope and captured his dad's flailing hands. She raised the sheet and examined the stick-like legs. "Take a look at this, Eric."

Blotches spangled the stark white legs giving them an almost purple hue.

"We often see this in patients whose time is near."

She replaced the sheet and straightened. Eric waited for her to say more. Her eyes told him what her words only implied. Dad was dying.

Joy pulled out a syringe and a small vial of liquid from the bag. "This sedative will help ease his restlessness. Why don't you take a break? It could be a long night."

Her matter-of-fact words gave him a plan of action and shook him out of the daze that had glued him to the spot. She busied herself around the patient and seemed oblivious to his departure. He showered and shaved mechanically, going through the motions while his mind replayed Joy's words: *whose time is near*. Near. As in soon? Tonight?

In the kitchen, he measured coffee beans but spilled more than he managed to get into the grinder. He needed to call Ellie. Not his mom or his sisters. One phone call to them left no illusions about their feelings. Good thing Dad never had to know.

Lucky danced around his legs and almost tripped him. When had he fed her last? Eric forked out the canned food into the bowl and sprinkled some dry mix on top. He placed it on the floor and caught a glimpse of the chess board that remained as they'd left it less than a week ago. How could it happen this fast?

Why was it hitting him so hard?

With two cups in hand, Eric climbed the stairs to face whatever lay ahead.

Joy looked up and smiled as he handed her one of the cups. "You make good coffee."

More than once during the past week, her kind words had calmed him. "Thank you. I've had lots of practice." He moved closer to the bed and placed his hand on his dad's heaving chest. "He's breathing easier."

"The sedative helped relax him."

"How long have you worked with Hospice?"

She backed up to sit on the straight-backed chair beside the bed.

"Please. Sit here in the recliner."

She shook her head. "You take it. I need to stay close to your dad."

Eric opted to stand. He resumed his post at the end of the bed and would stand there all night before he'd take the more comfortable chair.

"I was a surgical nurse for years but retired when my husband developed lung cancer. The hospice workers became my lifeline. Frank died last April, and I decided to switch gears and offer the same kind of help to others. It helped me deal with my grief."

"I'm sorry." Joy Stockman was a class act. Reminded him of Doc. "I'm really glad I don't have to go through this alone."

"I've noticed a Bible beside your chair. God's always here to walk through it with you too."

"I'm learning that. I became a believer about three months ago."

"Eric, that's truly wonderful. And what about your dad?"

"Yes, ma'am. But only a week ago."

Joy took a deep breath and let it out. "Thank God. Death is never easy, but what a blessing your dad knows Christ."

Eric nodded and swallowed hard, unable to get anything else out. He lifted the sheet for another peek at his dad's legs. Still blotched, the toes now blue.

Joy took a book from her bag and moved her chair closer to the bedside table for the lamp's light.

Eric picked up his Bible and eased himself down on the foot of his dad's bed. He tried to concentrate on the words and not on the rise and fall of his dad's chest.

Time dragged until a loud gasp from his dad energized them both into action.

Joy stood and pressed two fingers to the inside of his dad's wrist.

Eric rubbed his eyes and tried to shake the fog in his brain. "Looks like the sedative wore off." The clock beside the bed clicked to three fourteen. "Can you give him more?"

Joy's expression offered little hope as he applied gentle pressure to the frail shoulders to keep the thrashing body from falling off the bed. Each breath came short and shallow as if his dad had run a marathon. "It sounds like he's drowning."

Joy slipped the stethoscope back into place and listened to the lungs and heart. "He is."

Eric tightened his hold against surprising resistance.

She stood on the opposite side of the bed and helped hold the flailing patient. "It won't be long now. He's fighting it."

Of course he's fighting it. Templetons didn't lie down and die without a fight. Eric's splayed hand covered the width of his dad's chest. *Help him die, God.*

Another agonizing hour went by before the breathing changed. The thrashing stopped enough for Eric to release his hold. The breaths came slower and quieter, and his dad awoke with a lucidity that had been absent for days. For one brief moment, Dad's gaze connected with him."

"Dad." Eric gripped his dad's hand but had no words to say.

The hand he held, tightened the hold, but the eyes softened with what seemed to be love and pride. So quick and subtle, Eric wondered if he imagined it. Then his dad looked past him as if he recognized someone behind him.

Eric turned to see what had claimed his dad's focus and then gave Joy a questioning glance. "Is he rallying?"

She shook her head. "We see this a lot. I think he's getting a glimpse of the afterlife."

His dad relaxed against his pillow with his gaze locked onto the ceiling. With a slight hint of a smile, he slowly raised his hand and pointed.

Eric scanned the ceiling, hoping to catch a glimpse of what his dad saw. The breaths, now deeper and quieter, came farther and farther apart. The room became hushed and a sensation of peace filled the space around them.

Finally, Dad expelled the last breath. Eric held his own and waited. But no more breaths came.

Eric gently slid the eyelids over vacant lifeless eyes and then raised his own hand as he had seen his dad do only minutes before. "Thank You, Jesus. Tell my two fathers I love them." He sat beside the bed and only then realized Joy was no longer there.

He'd imagined this moment many times to prepare himself. Not once had he factored in the sense of calm and peace that descended on the room the moment his dad's breathing changed for the last time.

Eric took his dad's cold hand now more blue than white and spoke his good-bye. "I'm glad we got to know each other, Dad. That we grew to really love each other."

The tears surprised him. The joy far outweighed the sadness, but tears flowed anyway. He placed his hand once more on the now still chest and whispered into the stillness of the room. "If this is why I needed to lose my leg, it was worth it."

Joy came back and placed her hand on his shoulder. "I made the call. They'll be here soon."

Eric stood and put his arm around her. "Thank you for being here with me tonight."

"I was honored to share it with you. We witnessed something very special tonight."

Joy stayed with him until they wheeled his dad out of the house and into the waiting hearse.

He stood at the door as the vehicles cleared the driveway. The house was quiet. Too quiet.

He grabbed his jacket and went outside as the first streaks of light crested the horizon.

Good day for a run.

CHAPTER FIFTY-EIGHT

A cold blast of air whipped Ellie's hair across her face as she stepped out of the taxi. She captured a handful and turned to wait for her dad. Her heels sank into the moist ground beneath the brown grass, and she moved to the sidewalk. The wind sliced through the thin overcoat she wore more for style than for warmth.

She scooted to the side as two men dressed in black suits approached from across the street. Important men, no doubt. They walked with purpose and looked as if they had no patience for anything or anybody who got in their way. The aged stone building the men entered probably housed hundreds just like them.

Her dad shook his head when the driver handed back the change. "Keep it." He raised the collar of his coat and bristled over to her. "I'd forgotten how cold Washington can be."

Ellie grinned and slid her hand through the crook of his arm. "Are you referring to the weather or politics?"

He raised an eyebrow. "The weather. Almost thirty years in a hot climate has thinned my blood, and I couldn't care less about politics." He placed his gloved hand over hers. "My heart's in Africa."

"Then lead the way, Dr. Livingstone. My heart's in there with Eric."

Only partially true. Her heart was in her throat. She trailed behind her dad as they climbed the marble steps to the foyer of the funeral home. A man greeted them with a limp, fleshy handshake and directed them down a hallway to a large room where the service would soon take place.

Her dad opened one of the double doors and held it for
her. A group of uniformed men came from behind. Ellie
flattened herself against the wall and tried to take some deep
breaths. The men passed by and thanked her dad who remained
as the self-appointed doorman.

"Coming, sweetheart?"

She huddled close to the wall and willed her feet to move.
"I probably should've mentioned this before now, but big
rooms filled to capacity with big important people send me into
a panic."

Her dad left his post and took one of her hands. "Come on,
honey. We'll face it together."

Another group of imposing figures marched by them. Her
dad sidled closer to her and nodded to the group as they passed.
As the doors closed, her dad smoothed her wind-blown hair
back into place.

"As far as Eric's concerned, the most important person in
that room will be you. He needs you right now." He nudged her
chin up. "Hold your head high, and walk in there like you're a
child of the King."

She took a deep but shaky breath. "Okay, but don't you
dare leave me." Before she could lose her courage, she
followed her dad into the crowded room. Once inside, she
latched onto his arm and pulled him toward the back wall. For
once, being short had its benefits. In the crush of tall, granite-
like men, she almost felt invisible.

Her dad placed his arm around her and angled her toward
the right. "Over there."

Even with heels, she couldn't see above the men between
her and Eric. She craned her neck to get a glimpse.

"Shall we let him know we're here?" Her dad tugged at
her sleeve. Her arm stiffened of its own accord, and her dad
loosened his hold.

"Not just yet. I'd rather wait until there are fewer people around him." The line of people waiting to talk to Eric snaked around rows of chairs and extended almost to the door. It would be a long wait.

The mingling crowd parted, and the man who had dominated her thoughts and dreams for the past three months came into full view. Her breath caught. He looked good. Fully recovered and standing tall. He oozed confidence and held his own in this room full of egos as giant as the columns supporting the balcony.

Eric's world. He stood face to face with a man in full uniform. Probably a general. Eric seemed taller, and the cut of his dark suit did nothing to hide his muscular physique. He shook the man's hand and turned. His eyes found hers and locked into place. His hands dropped to his side, and his glance softened into a caress reaching across the room.

Another man stepped in front, blocking her view, but Eric sidestepped and started toward her. Her pulse quickened as he worked his way through the crowd, smiling and nodding and giving the occasional manly squeeze to a shoulder. He moved with the grace of a panther, no visible limp and no hint he'd ever been injured.

∧∧∧∧

In the middle of a conversation with one of the joint chiefs, Eric sensed Ellie nearby. He nodded and responded at all the appropriate places while his Ellie-radar scanned the room. Then he turned and caught a glimpse of blond hair. The general continued to talk, but every part of Eric strained to look again to see if it was really Ellie. How long had she been here? He pictured himself shoving back the crowds and scaling the chairs to reach her. He'd grab her. No crutches this time. He'd kiss her. He'd—

The last words of their conversation fell on deaf ears. Eric pivoted as the crowd around him started to disperse. Like a dark cloud breaking apart to reveal a brilliant full moon, Ellie stood before him, a breath-taking vision, who robbed him of his ability to move or think. He dropped his arms to his side and drank in every detail of her fitted black coat over a simple but elegant dress. He'd never seen her more beautiful. Eric threw protocol to the wind and excused himself from the general who had dominated the conversation long enough. He waved to the line of well-wishers. "Excuse me, gentlemen."

He reached her in seconds and hugged her close, this time with no crutches to get in the way. "Finally." He turned at the familiar hand on his shoulder. "Doc. Thank you for coming."

"I'm glad we made it in time."

Duty took over. He gripped Ellie's hand. "Come with me. There's someone I want you to meet."

She smiled up at him, her eyes huge and different somehow. Like something was wrong.

He bent down to look her square in the face. "Everything all right?"

The shadow disappeared. "Yes. Everything's great." Her face brightened, and she moved with him to the front. He didn't buy it, but he'd deal with it later.

Miss Mildred stood alone at the side of the room. He stood between the two most important women in his life and placed his hand on the elder woman's arm.

"Miss Mildred, this is Ellie and her dad Brock Whitfield."

"This is Mildred Ware, the saint who put up with my dad and kept him straight for the past twenty-five years."

"I'm happy to finally meet the girl who captured Eric's heart. I've heard so much about you."

The sparkle reappeared in Ellie's eyes. "It's good to meet you. I'm sorry for your loss."

Miss Mildred nodded and twisted the handkerchief in her hand. "I can't believe he's gone."

Eric put his arm around her. "Come sit with us. The service is about to begin."

Eric sat between Ellie and Miss Mildred, his eyes never leaving the flag-draped casket. The eulogy was short but meaningful. No one could question his dad's dedication, his integrity, and his drive for excellence. Eric remained solemn but dry-eyed, even at the graveside at Arlington. Even through the twenty-one gun salute and the playing of Taps. Templetons didn't break down in public. He accepted the folded flag and received final condolences as the crowd dispersed and made their way back to the vehicles.

Doc and Ellie stayed close by as he said his last good-bye. Then he reached for Ellie's hand and squeezed it. "Anybody hungry?"

Ellie cuddled close as if trying to escape the freezing wind. "I'm starving."

"Me too. Let's swap the limousine for my Mustang. We've got a lot of catching up to do."

They walked back to the waiting limousine, his fingers laced with Ellie's and his other arm wrapped around Doc. "Thank you for making this happen. It means more than I can tell you to have you here."

"Nothing could have kept us away, son."

He grinned and leaned over to kiss Ellie on the cheek. The faint scent of her perfume catapulted him back to his little room on the mission compound. "You look beautiful in that dress." The dimple did a number on his empty stomach.

"You look pretty good yourself, handsome. Look at you. Not even a limp."

She'd noticed. The hours he'd practiced to lose the limp paid off. "Don't look too close. It slips back, especially when I'm tired."

At the restaurant, as soon as they slid into a booth, Eric took off his tie and undid the top buttons of his shirt. "That feels better. You must be tired. I'd like for you to stay with me at Dad's house." No need to mention the cleaning service he'd hired. His mom and sisters never showed. "There's plenty of room."

Doc glanced at Ellie before speaking up. "We're here for you. Our luggage is still on the plane so we'll need to swing by and pick it up."

"No problem. We'll get it when we leave here."

The server left with their orders, and then Doc filled him in on news from the hospital. Ellie sat so close, their bodies seemed conjoined, but she remained quiet. Too quiet. He could hardly concentrate on anything Doc said. He wanted to be alone with her and find out what was eating her. If she still loved him—

He fidgeted, lining up the salt shaker and peppermill or folding the cloth napkin into geometric shapes. Finally, the server returned with their food.

He reached for the catsup and shook some onto his plate. "I wouldn't have made it through these past few weeks without your support."

Ellie broke her silence. "It tore my heart out to be so far from you during this ordeal." She grinned at her dad. "I was pretty useless at the clinic."

Eric breathed easier, so relieved he forgot to respond to what she said.

"I had to think up things to keep her busy to help her get through the days," Doc chimed in.

Her arm nudged against his. "When you left, nobody felt like doing anything. Even Rocco quit cracking jokes."

"Now that *is* serious. Have you heard from him since he returned to the States?"

"I called to let him know about your dad. He said he'd be praying for you."

"I've seen a lot of deaths." He stared ahead not making eye contact. "Have caused a lot of deaths. But that was the first time I witnessed a soul leaving the body and going to God." He told them details, glad for the chance to experience it again, this time with them. "And right before he breathed his last breath, Dad saw something. I don't know what, but the room felt different." His voice became husky with emotion. "There was peace. I could almost touch it."

Ellie moved even closer and placed her hand over his. "I'm glad you were with him."

His fingers curled around hers. Eric relaxed against the back of the seat, and fought back exhaustion. "Ready to head to the house?"

Ellie smiled and nodded. Doc reached for his wallet.

"Put that up, Doc. You're my guest." He prepared to do battle, but Doc met his gaze and put away his money.

<center>~~~~~</center>

Eric pulled into the driveway and cut the engine. "You don't know how good it is not to be alone tonight." He popped the trunk for their luggage and then skirted around to open Ellie's door. She took his hand and swung her legs around to step out. His breath caught, and he had a wild notion to pin her against the side of the car and kiss her senseless.

Instead, he folded the seat down for Doc who climbed out and arched his back. "It's been quite a while since I was in the back seat of a Mustang."

"Sorry. They're not built for comfort."

"I loved it. Takes me back."

"You owned a Mustang?"

"In college. A convertible very similar to this one." He ran his hand along the fender. "A real classic."

No mistaking the appreciation in his tone. He set down the luggage to give Doc a peek under the hood but caught a glimpse of Ellie chafing her arms.

Doc reached for one of the bags, but Eric brushed him away.

"I got this. Let's get Ellie inside before she freezes."

"Too late." She smiled and fell into step beside him.

He unlocked the door and snaked his hand inside to click on the foyer lights. "Go ahead." He followed them in and directed them upstairs to the bedrooms.

As they passed his dad's room, Eric set the bags down and pulled Ellie back. "Look." He cocked his head toward the bed.

"Lucky?" Ellie gasped as if she were meeting an old friend. She went over to her and stroked her back.

"Lucky never left Dad's side. Was right there by his feet when he died. Seems a little lost now." She rolled over onto her back, and Eric rubbed her belly. "Don't you, girl?"

Eric turned back to Doc. "Your room is the next one down the hall."

Doc nodded and grabbed one of the bags Eric left on the floor.

"Come on, honey. Your room's next to mine."

He dropped her bag and took her in his arms as soon as she cleared the door. "I swore to myself if I ever got you in my arms again, I'd never let you go."

She melted into his embrace. He caressed her head that lay nestled against his chest but then pulled back enough to grasp her face in his cupped hands. "But I swore something else too."

Her hands slid up his chest and clasp behind his neck. "And what would that be?"

"To protect you. From me. And right now, it's taking every ounce of my restraint to honor that oath."

Respect, gratitude, and something akin to adoration paraded across her transparent face. He placed his finger on her parted lips before she could reply. Before he could undo everything he'd just said. He grinned, not wanting to tear his eyes away from her. "Change and get comfortable."

He left her and became a quick change artist, dressing in jeans and a long-sleeved shirt. Her door still closed, he went looking for Doc.

Doc had changed into pajamas and sat on the edge of the bed, his Bible open on his lap.

"I'm going to light a fire downstairs. You want to join us?"

"I think I'll turn in a little early."

With his you're-not-fooling-me look, Eric closed the distance and sat beside Doc on the bed. He placed his arm around Doc's back and hugged him. "Can I get you anything? Bottled water?"

"No thanks. I have everything I need." Doc gave Eric's leg a quick pat.

"Okay then. I'll see you in the morning." He turned back at the door. "I'm glad you're here."

Their eyes met and then Ellie's door opened. He gave Doc a brief wave. "'Night."

"Dad's not joining us?"

Eric shook his head. "Turning in early, I suspect to give us privacy."

"Good ol' Dad."

"How do you manage to look gorgeous whether you're wearing a sexy black dress or jeans?"

"I'm trying to impress you."

"It's working."

He took her hand, and they scampered down the stairs like a couple of guilty teenagers finally getting some time alone.

"How do you manage to walk without limping?"

"I'm trying to impress you."

"I'd be impressed with you even if you had to crawl."

The old Ellie was back. The one who was fun, and flirty, and who made him feel ten feet tall. He placed her in the center of the sofa. "Sit here while I make a fire."

"Oh, you've already made a fire, Mr. Templeton."

He cocked his head and grinned back at her as he squatted in front of the fireplace.

She hugged her knees and watched him work. "I haven't sat by a fireplace since I arrived in Africa. It's cozy. And romantic."

He cut her a glance and winked. "Yep. That's the plan." The fire roared into life, and he stood with soot-covered hands. "Be right back. Can I get you anything?"

She shook her head. "Hurry back."

"Yes, ma'am. Uh-oh. Here comes Lucky." He dumped some food in her bowl and washed his hands in less than a minute and then joined her on the sofa.

She scooted over to make room. He plopped down and pulled her closer. "Come back here." He stroked her hair and grazed the side of her cheek. "I can hardly believe you're here. It's been so long."

She leaned back on his arm, and he forced himself to focus on her eyes and not her lips or the soft indentation below her neck.

"You want to hear something crazy? Today when I was talking to one of the joint chiefs, I could feel you in the room."

"Feel me?"

He nodded. "I didn't see you come in, but I knew you were there."

"You probably felt me staring at you."

"Okay." He drew his arm back and leaned forward. "I've got to ask you. You were really quiet when I first saw you. Was something wrong?"

"You don't miss much." Her gaze dropped to her folded hands on her lap.

A thousand thoughts pierced his soul. His fingers curled into a fist, but he forced his face not to show how terrified he was.

"If you must know, I was nervous and shy and, I don't know. Scared."

It took a few seconds for her words to sink in, and hope started to rise. "You're kidding. What spooked you? All the generals who act like they're important?"

"Yeah, that was part of it." She bit her lower lip. "And you."

"Me?" He searched her face. "You're serious." His gut tightened, but he had to know. "Ellie, are you having second thoughts?"

She raised her head, her eyes huge. "No. Nothing like that. It's just when I saw you up there—" She looked down.

He reached over and nudged her chin up. "What?"

She shook her head and shrugged. "To say you look different is a huge understatement. There you were. So wicked handsome in your suit. And confident and I don't know. Intimidating. I wasn't sure someone as great as you would still want someone like me."

He would've laughed, but she'd twisted her fingers into a pretzel. Silly girl. He wanted to kiss her. To take her in his arms and leave her in no doubt how much a person like him could want someone like her.

Instead, he took the ring from his pocket and placed it on her ice cold finger. "Marry me, Ellie." He brought her hand to his lips. "And I'll spend the rest of my life proving how much I want you."

She turned and flung herself into his arms. "Oh, Eric."

He squeezed her tight. "There you go, laughing and crying at the same time again."

He relaxed against the sofa and enjoyed the show. She extended her hand and examined the ring, and pressed the other one against her mouth as if in unbelief. "I was so afraid you'd get back here and change your mind."

He captured her hand and held it close to his chest. "I don't want to spend one more day without you. Whatever I do for the rest of my life, I want you by my side."

"As long as you're not on some dangerous undercover assignment, I'll follow you anywhere."

"Deal. Baby, I want to marry you as soon as we return to Africa. I don't care if our house isn't finished yet. We can sleep in my old hospital room. I don't care. I can't wait any longer to make you my wife."

She laughed. "I love my all-or-nothing guy. The good news is our house is almost complete, even furnished. I think you'll love it."

"If you're in it, I'll love it."

"Do you need to stay here for a while?"

"No, thank the Lord. A recently widowed lady I met through Hospice is going to move in and keep things up. She's even agreed to keep Lucky. So I can go back with you and your dad."

"Eric, I'm so happy. I'd like for my dad to marry us."

"He's a preacher too?"

She nodded. "Ordained."

"So how soon can we pull this off?"

"I'll call Nicci. She's been preparing for our reception for weeks."

"This Saturday?"

"Saturday." Her eyes widened. "As in three days from now?"

"You're right. I can't wait that long. How about Friday?"

She punched his chest. "Oh, you. Okay, we'll shoot for Saturday. If anybody can do it, Nicci can. She thrives under pressure."

He stood and extended his hand to her. "The fire's dying out, and we have a big day tomorrow."

He walked her back to her bedroom and kissed her good night. In four days, he wouldn't have to leave her at the door. Ever again.

"My ring is perfect. I love you so much."

He kissed the tip of her nose. "I love you too."

In bed, he lay on his back smiling into the darkness, too excited to sleep. At that moment, he was happier than a man had a right to be. Happier than he ever thought he could be. Events of the day paraded in his mind. Too bad his dad never got to know Ellie. Given the chance, she'd charm her way into his crusty heart and make him putty in her hands. He grinned and rolled over on his side.

She thinks I'm wicked handsome.

CHAPTER FIFTY-NINE

Ellie lay perfectly still with her eyes closed and tried for the hundredth time to will herself to sleep.

I'm getting married today. With dark circles under her eyes unless by some miracle sleep would come. She'd settle for a good nap.

I, Eleanor Katrina Whitfield, take thee, Eric Nicholas Templeton. Ellie grinned and wiggled her toes under the sheet. Dark circles it is then. At the familiar ping, she flipped over on her stomach and grabbed her phone from the bedside table. The blue glow from the message lit up the room.

"Awake?"

She grinned and propped up on her elbows to punch in her response. "Yeah. Too excited to sleep."

"Me too. Don't know if I can hold out 'til two."

"Me either."

"Good! B right there."

"DON'T YOU DARE!"

"'K. Miss you."

She bit her lower lip. Why not? "Terrace. Ten minutes."

"Really?"

"Bring coffee."

"'K."

Ten minutes. What was she thinking? She scrambled to the bathroom for damage control. Pajama pants and t-shirt, hair pulled up in a ponytail, teeth brushed and lip gloss applied. Good to go.

"Come on, girl." Ellie opened the door and almost stepped on the rose lying on the floor. She swooped it up and jogged barefoot down the hallway with Lady at her heels.

Eric and her dad stood at the edge of the terrace facing the newly-built house barely visible in the pre-dawn light. Eric met her halfway and placed a cup of coffee in her hand.

"Right on time." He kissed the top of her forehead.

"Thanks for my rose. How'd you manage to put the rose there and make coffee and still beat me out here?" She slammed her hand over her mouth. "I walked into it again."

His smile turned her insides to jelly. "I don't reveal my secrets, but I will confess. Nicci had already made the coffee. I don't think she slept much."

Her dad came over and gave Ellie a hug. "She's not the only one. Good morning, honey. I can't think of a better start to your wedding day. Look at the golden streaks peeking over those trees. God is outdoing Himself today."

She followed his gaze. "For once, I don't think you're exaggerating." She grinned at Eric, shamelessly flaunting her dimple before sipping her coffee.

Eric moved behind her and encased her in his arms. He leaned close and whispered so only she could hear, "You're flirting with me."

"I hoped you'd notice." The rock wall of his chest supported her. Her cheek rested against the gravelly feel of his. She covered the arms clasped loosely over her midriff with her own, and cradled the cup in her hands.

His arms tightened, hugging her even closer. His breath close to her ear sent a shiver down her spine. "Just wait 'til tonight." Eric released his hold on her but gave her a look before moving to stand by her dad who sat nearby.

Now who was flirting?

"What time did you say Rocco and his wife were arriving?" Mr. Innocent spoke.

Her dad shifted in his seat to look up at Eric. "Sometime near eleven, I think. He'll be flying in with Toby."

Ellie pulled a chair beside her dad. "I can't believe he rearranged his schedule on such short notice."

"Your mom didn't." Her dad reached for her hand and squeezed it. "Does that bother you?"

Loaded question with no easy answer. "It's better this way." She reached down to scratch between Lady's ears. "We're so different. She'd try to take charge and make a lot of last minute changes."

Eric grabbed a nearby chair and dragged it to the other side.

She looked around her dad and met Eric's gaze. "I think everything about this day will be perfect."

Golden shafts streamed through pink clouds. An almost reverent hush fell over the terrace. Eric must have felt it too.

He leaned forward with his arms propped on his thighs and looked at her dad. "Would you pray with us?"

They clasped hands, and the voice her dad used when he prayed seemed to usher them into the presence of God. Gratitude and worship filtered through his tone as he asked God's blessing on their lives. This moment, this prayer had not been scripted into the day, but somehow she couldn't help but know it was God's way of reaffirming His love and presence.

She raised her head at her dad's "Amen." Eric's cheeks were as wet as hers. They stood and embraced in a group hug before dispersing to begin the busy day.

Her fingers entwined with his as he walked her back to her room. "I'm glad you convinced me to break with the whole 'you can't see the bride before the ceremony' superstition."

"So I convinced you, huh?"

He could see right through her, just like her dad. She grinned and shook her head. "I didn't need convincing. Just an excuse."

She stopped at her door and cupped his face with her hand. "That was really special."

He nodded and moved her hand to his lips. "Later."

Eric left Ellie and with Lady keeping pace at his feet, he crossed the uneven ground of the field leading to their house. His and Ellie's. Pictures hadn't done it justice. Tan stucco. Simple and classic with plenty of room to breathe.

The front porch complete with a porch swing faced east and extended the width of the house. Double doors opened to a great room supported by well-placed columns instead of constricting walls. An island with stools connected the great room to the open-air kitchen. He stood in the center for a panoramic view. It had the feel of a garden paradise with indoor trees and plants, bold artwork and festive pillows splashed with red.

A musky scent, probably from sage-colored candles on accent tables mingled with the smell of fresh-cut wood.

Windows. So many windows, it was as if the whole house were a sun porch. He wandered into the master bedroom and sat on the edge of the bed to take in details he'd missed when Ellie gave him the grand tour. Blues and browns. The bed centered on a patterned area rug contrasting with the wood-grain of the flooring. Uncluttered. A place to love and be at peace.

He returned to the front porch. The tree that witnessed his cry to God spread its shade over the whole porch. It seemed to call him. He walked over and ran his hand along the knotty roughness of the bark. Every detail of that night replayed through his mind. "Thank you, Jesus. Thank you for this wonderful life You've given to me."

Chopper blades split the air. Eric reached for his phone and checked the time. Toby. An hour early. Time to get moving.

Ellie sat on a stool. Miriam's long graceful fingers braided the narrow strip of blue ribbon into a tiny portion of her hair.

She finished and stood back. "There."

Ellie leaned closer to the mirror and studied the intricate pattern. "I don't know how you do it."

Miriam embraced her from behind and smiled at Ellie's reflection. "It brings out the blue of your eyes."

Ellie reached up and covered the hand on her shoulder. "Thank you for everything. My hair. My dress. Will you help me put it on?"

"Of course."

Ellie stood still and stretched out her arms like a windmill as Miriam wrapped the sand-colored sarong around her. Blue embroidered beading decorated the neck, sleeves and hem. Miriam led her to the mirror hanging on the bathroom door and stood behind her. "What do you think?"

Ellie gave a little gasp. "Oh my goodness. It's—it's incredible." She slid her hands down the satiny material. Soft folds draped her body and clung in all the right places. "I can't believe it." She turned and flung her arms around Miriam's neck.

"It was my joy." Strong hands calloused from work cradled Ellie's face. "I am happy for you, child. You will have a good life."

Ellie swung back to the mirror for another look. A quiet knock interrupted her Cinderella moment.

Nicci stuck her head around the door. "It's time." Her eyes widened. "Beautiful."

Ellie nodded. "It is, isn't it?"

"I meant you."

"Oh." Ellie's hands flew to her face. "I do feel beautiful. Miriam worked her magic."

Her dad came to her door dressed in the khaki pants and white shirt she'd requested. "You look radiant." He closed the distance between them and kissed her forehead. "I told myself I wouldn't cry again today.

She took his hands and swung them in front of her. "It's all right. You won't be alone."

"Ready?"

Her heart skipped a beat. Finally here. Finally time. She nodded and slid her hand into the crook of his elbow.

~~~~~

Hospital staff and friends from surrounding villages crowded into the chapel. Eric waited at the front. The two o'clock sun shone through the image of the stained glass illuminating the risen Christ. Beside him, Toby cracked his knuckles and checked his pocket again.

"Still there?" Eric grinned.

"This ain't funny, man. I don't want to mess this up."

"Relax, Tobe. You've saved my neck more than once. I've got confidence in you."

The visiting nationals broke out into a traditional tribal wedding song. A happy, lively song blended with rich harmony and the beat of drums. Eric moved closer to the center aisle anticipating the moment Ellie would appear in the doorway.

And there she was. More glorious than when the sun made its spectacular appearance above the trees this morning. Never had her smile seemed more stunning. She stood poised at the door. Her gaze swept the room and welcomed the host of people. Then her glance connected with him and never wavered as she walked down the narrow aisle.

The crush of people remained standing as if too awed to take their seats. Doc placed her hand in Eric's and took his position at the front.

Ellie faced him, and he drank in the sight of her. Her eyes, wide, luminous, and even bluer than he remembered. Her hair, a golden mass, full of life and movement, the way he loved it. The hollow of her neck above the slight rise and fall of her chest. He clasped her trembling hands and kneaded them in a gentle caress.

His breath caught at her transparent innocence as she stood before him, and a fierce need to protect her filled his soul. He repeated his vows before God and man and promised to love her and keep her. To forsake all others and cleave only to her. And to himself he promised to spend every day making her the happiest woman on earth.

Doc pronounced them man and wife. His hands cupped her upturned face and his kiss sealed their promise. Rocco cheered first and then the room seemed to explode with clapping and laughter.

The next couple of hours went by in a blur of well-wishers, hugging, kissing and congratulating them. Eric steered Ellie over to one of the tents where Rocco and his wife stood next to the punch table.

Rocco hooked his arm across Eric's back. "Dude, you don't look like the same guy. Did you grow another leg or something? Not even a limp. You sure they didn't swap you out for a clone?"

Eric laughed. "Jess, is your husband ever serious?"

She shook her head. "He's even worse at home."

"You have my sympathies. But I have to admit, he kept me going. I don't think I would've made it without him."

"One unforgettable summer for sure." Rocco set down his cup and reached for a box under the table. "Got you and Ellie something to help bring back memories."

Eric narrowed his eyes as he took the box.

Rocco nodded him on. "Open it."

Eric ripped the paper and opened the box.

The clock. The one from his room with extra batteries taped to the back. Ellie burst out laughing. Eric grimaced and shook his head. "You shouldn't have."

Rocco howled. "I'm sure there's plenty of room for it in that fine house you built."

"Oh yeah. Plenty of drawers it'll fit into."

Rocco pushed another box into Eric's hands. "Here, pal. This one's legit."

Eric held the box while Ellie tore it open. A wall plaque that read, "As for me and my house, we will serve the Lord." Eric wrapped his arm around Ellie. "This one won't end up in a drawer."

The two men exchanged a brotherly embrace. "Thanks for coming. Means a lot to us."

"Wouldn't have missed it. Jess wanted to meet the guy I plan to name my son after."

Jess grinned and patted her stomach. "That's if we have a son. Just found out this week."

Eric punched Rocco's shoulder. "Congratulations." He reached for Ellie's hand and gave her a wink. "Maybe we won't be too far behind you."

Nicci joined them, followed by Toby who carried a container of punch for refills. Ellie pulled Nicci over to their group. "This is Nicci, the little dynamo who organized this whole reception."

Nicci smiled and extended her hand to Jess. "I had good help." She glanced at Toby who finished pouring the punch into the bowl and walked over to them. "We've kept Toby busy flying in food and supplies this past month.

Eric caught the look that passed between them. Son-of-a-gun. Toby'd been holding out on him.

Ellie went over to a group of villagers, and Eric walked over to Doc who stood next to Moses. Doc met him with a hearty embrace. "Well, son, it's official. We're family now."

"Yes, sir. Finally."

Moses placed his large hand on Eric's shoulder. "It was a beautiful ceremony. God will bless your lives." He gave Eric a brief nod and bow and then left them alone.

Eric turned to the man who had helped bring so much happiness to his life. "You've done so much for me. I can never thank you enough."

"You've made my daughter a very happy woman."

Eric glanced over to Ellie who was laughing with a group of children. She looked up and held his gaze across the crowd of people.

"Your daughter has made me a very happy man. I was wondering if it'd be all right for me to start calling you Dad."

Doc stared at him as if he hadn't heard, but then added. "I'd like that very much."

In less than a week, he'd lost the only family he'd ever known only to gain an even better one. Eric draped his arm around the man who barely reached his shoulders and planted a kiss on the top of his head. "Thanks, Dad."

Eric went to rescue Ellie who didn't try to hide her relief. As twilight approached, Nicci encouraged guests to take leftover food back to their villages. Toby and Rocco planned to stick around for the next couple of days. Eric nuzzled close to Ellie's ear. "You ready to go home?"

"I've been ready for a long time."

Eric clasped her hand and waved with his other. "Thank you all for making our day so special. We'll see you tomorrow."

They walked arm in arm to their house with Ellie leaning against the crook of Eric's shoulder. He stopped at the threshold and lifted her into his arms. His wife. His beloved. The blinds had been pulled down, and candles had been lit. A bottle of sparkling grape juice chilled in a bucket of ice. Grapes and chocolate-covered strawberries decorated the island by the kitchen. Ellie read the note aloud. "Relax and enjoy the first night of your lives together. Love, Nicci and Toby."

Eric poured the juice into goblets, and they both collapsed onto the sofa. She snuggled close to him. He propped his feet on the coffee table in his new house beside his wife. His wife. Every time he thought the words, he almost choked with emotion.

He sipped his drink. Cold and refreshing. He didn't realize how parched he was. "I'm glad they brought this stuff over. Looks like there's a budding romance brewing."

"They're cute together, aren't they?"

Eric chuckled.

"What?"

"Oh, I was just thinking about Toby's grandmother. She was a lot like Nicci back in the day. A real spit fire."

"I think Toby's just what Nicci needs."

Eric slid his arm along the back of the sofa and played with her hair. "She's good for him, too. Toby needs someone with spunk."

"And what about you?"

The crooked grin that always seemed to accentuate the dimple made him catch his breath.

"Mrs. Templeton, you're flirting with me."

She giggled and placed her glass on the table. "What'cha gonna do about it, Mr. Templeton?"

He did what he'd been wanting to do for a very long time. He clasped her face in his hands and pulled her to him. His hands caressed the soft curve of her cheek and slid down the silky skin of her neck. Her mouth, warm and pliant, welcomed his. He tightened his hold and without breaking the kiss, scooped her up and carried her to their bedroom.

Rose petals lay strewn about the floor. The covers had been turned back and the unity candle from the chapel cast a romantic glow across the room.

He'd thank Toby and Nicci later. Much later.

He placed Ellie on the bed, and she grabbed the front of his shirt pulling him down. He smiled at his little vixen. He supported himself with his hands on the bed. "I love you. You've made me a very happy man."

No longer the playful child or the wanton vixen, but a woman who touched his face and seemed to know just what he needed to hear. Her eyes, a deeper blue in candlelight, became serious. "I love you. I never knew I could open up my heart and love a man so much. I'm so proud to be your wife. To take your name. To share your life. To one day have your children. 'Whither thou goest, I will go. Whither thou lodgest, I will lodge. Thy people will be my people, and thy God, my God.'"

He lay above her, stunned at her words that gripped him to his very core. Words made more powerful by the sincerity in her voice. He could think of no way to tell what it meant to him, so he showed her. He kissed her with all the tenderness and love welling up in his heart. He gave her himself and made love to this exquisite creature who was now bone of his bones and flesh of his flesh.

She melted into his arms and caressed the scars on his body that she had helped to heal. Some still ugly, jagged and purple.

"I love your scars."

Was it possible she read his mind? "My body looks like a battlefield."

She placed her finger on his lips. "Every scar you have is like a medal of honor. And it's what brought you to me."

Any defense he might have still held onto, crumbled. She had him. All of him. Body and soul. And he loved her that night with all there was in him.

He awoke sometime in the night, her body snuggled so close, not even air came between them. He smiled at the gentle rhythm of her breathing. He shifted his position and wrapped his arm around her, pulling her into the crook of his body without waking her.

In the darkness, he thought back to the years when emptiness and loneliness had been his constant companions. It all seemed like a bad dream now. He whispered into the stillness. "I never knew such happiness existed."

She stirred a little within his arms, and his heart melted with love for her. It had been less than a week since he'd buried his father, a father he'd just begun to appreciate and love. What if he ever lost Ellie? He forced the paralyzing thought from his mind. She stirred again and her hair tickled his face. He smoothed it back and could not resist kissing the nape of her neck. "Sweet Ellie."

He smiled at her half-murmured sleepy response.

He was home. His home. With his wife lying beside him. Life would never be boring, or lonely again.

THE REDEEMED SIDE OF BROKEN

Saving Eric is a love story that demonstrates God's relentless love to mankind. The principal characters in *Saving Eric* have one unifying common denominator: They are broken people who are redeemed and transformed by God's forgiveness and grace.

The characters are fictional, but the truth is real. This author knows what it feels like to be broken and without hope. As a teenager, I was introduced to the Gospel of Jesus Christ. Like the characters in this book, I did not at first understand or embrace the concept of becoming a believer. Over a period of four months, I began to see my own need of a savior. On October 22, 1968, I accepted Jesus Christ as my Lord and Savior. It was the defining moment of my life.

I challenge you to read the Gospels: Matthew, Mark, Luke, and John. Take note of how often Jesus bypassed the self-righteous Pharisees to minister to the sick, the weary, the hungry, the outcasts of society. Jesus was a friend of sinners.

Jesus is still the friend of sinners. "Greater love hath no man than this: that a man lay down his life for his friends." John 15:13

My friend, have you embraced Jesus Christ as your Savior? He loves you. He is waiting with His arms open wide.

Contact me if you would like further help in understanding this wonderful gift of salvation. Or tell me your testimony of God's redeeming grace in your life. I'd love to hear from you. God Bless.

www.joandeneve.com

ABOUT THE AUTHOR

Joan Deneve teaches English in a Christian school and has a passion to help young people fall in love with Jesus and equip them to become all God wants them to be. Joan began her walk as a Christian when she accepted Christ as her savior two weeks before her sixteenth birthday. She graduated from Tennessee Temple Bible College in 1975.

Joan and Rene', her husband of forty-plus years, reside in Prattville, Alabama, a charming city in the Heart of Dixie. They count their son, daughter, son-in-law, and seven phenomenal grandchildren to be their greatest blessings on earth.

Joan enjoys time well-spent with family and friends, but finds equal joy in quiet moments of solitude on her back porch. There, surrounded by bluebirds and yellow butterflies, she began writing her debut novel, *Saving Eric*.

An active member of her church, Joan enjoys singing in the choir. She is a member of American Christian Fiction Writers and is currently working on the second book in the Redeemed Side of Broken Series. She enjoys chatting with fellow writers and readers.

Visit Joan on the Web:
www.JoanDeneve.com

OTHER BOOKS BY THE AUTHOR

Jerusha Agen Marji Laine
Theresa Anderson Fay Lamb
Julie Arduini Elizabeth Noyes
Joan Deneve Betty Owens

Romance is a joke.

After the love of Brent Teague's life came back into his world only to marry someone else, Brent is through with women. He might be through with being a pastor, too.

Brent was so sure that God brought Mara Adkins home to him so they could marry and live happily ever after. Six months after her wedding to another man, that theory is obviously a dud. If Brent could be so wrong about that, who's to say he's not mistaken about God calling him to pastoral ministry?

Tired of watching Brent flounder for direction, Brent's feisty older sister boots him out of Spartanburg and onto a cruise ship. Brent's old college buddy manages the ship's staff, and he's thrilled to finagle Brent into the role of chaplain for the two-week cruise.

As the ship sets sail, Brent starts to relax. Maybe a cruise wasn't such a bad idea after all. But there's just one little thing no one told him. He's not on any ordinary cruise. He's on The Love Boat.

What's a sworn bachelor to do on a Caribbean cruise full of romance and love? He'll either have to jump ship or embrace the unforgettable romantic comedy headed his way.

Available on Kindle.

Look for other books

published by

www.WriteIntegrity.com

and

Pix-N-Pens Publishing

www.PixNPens.com

Made in the USA
Columbia, SC
31 January 2022

55093928R00245